All
Good
People
Here

All Good People Here

A Novel

Ashley Flowers

with Alex Kiester

BANTAM

NEW YORK

Published in the United States by Bantam Books, an imprint of Random House, a division of Penguin Random House LLC, New York.

BANTAM BOOKS is a registered trademark and the B colophon is a trademark of Penguin Random House LLC.

LIBRARY OF CONGRESS CATALOGING-IN-PUBLICATION DATA
Names: Flowers, Ashley, author.
Title: All good people here / Ashley Flowers.
Description: First edition. | New York : Bantam, 2022
Identifiers: LCCN 2022006131 (print) | LCCN 2022006132 (ebook) |
ISBN 9780593496473 (hardcover) | ISBN 9780593496480 (ebook)
Subjects: LCGFT: Detective and mystery fiction. | Thrillers (Fiction) | Novels.
Classification: LCC PS3606.L68328 A79 2022 (print) | LCC PS3606.L68328 (ebook) |
DDC 782.02/8—dc24/eng/20220215
LC record available at https://lccn.loc.gov/2022006131

Printed in the United States of America on acid-free paper

randomhousebooks.com

9 8 7 6 5 4 3 2 1

First Edition

Book design by Caroline Cunningham

For all of my Crime Junkies

All
Good
People
Here

ONE

Krissy, 1994

The residents of Wakarusa, Indiana, could spin gossip faster than a spider spins its web. Each time one of their own did something they shouldn't—when Abby Schmuckers got caught shoplifting lipstick from the dime store; when the Becker kid dropped out of the 4-H volunteer club; when Jonah Schneider fell asleep and snored in church—the Wakarusa gossip chain would flap their jaws, chewing the tidbit over so thoroughly that by the time they'd finally spat it out again, the Truth was misshapen and unrecognizable, warped into the Story. And because the people of Wakarusa were churchgoing, law-abiding, capital-G God-fearing people, the Story was always adorned with pearls of sweetness to coat its sharp edges: *Bless her heart, but . . . . I'll be praying for them, because did you hear . . . ? Lord have mercy on their souls.*

Even before everything happened, Krissy Jacobs had understood the power of Wakarusa's rumor mill, which is why she so stringently avoided its teeth. She went to church every Sunday, she dressed her daughter in pink and her son in blue, she wore the right shoes and made sure her husband had the right ties. It wasn't because she believed any of it mattered; it was simply because she had so much to lose. This life—her family, their farm and house— wasn't what she'd wanted, wasn't even close, but it was more than she'd ever had before, and so she held on to it, hands tight.

On the day it all slipped through her fingers, Krissy got up to the sound of her alarm at 5 A.M. like she had every other morning in her life as a farmer's wife. She slid out of bed quietly so as not to disturb Billy, even though the alarm was for him too. Then she stepped out of the darkened bedroom and made her way down the old wooden staircase to the kitchen.

She spotted the writing on the wall before she even made it down the last step, her breath kicking out of her lungs. Scrawled in blood-red oversized letters read three horrific messages: FUCK YOUR FAMILY . . . THAT BITCH IS GONE . . . THIS IS WHAT YOU GET.

Krissy's heart pounded hard and painful against her ribs. Her first thought—bizarre and ill-fitting—was that the words looked so . . . *intrusive* here, on her old but pristine white walls, in the falling-apart-but-still-beautiful kitchen. Those nasty, violent words didn't belong in quaint Wakarusa, Indiana, full of good, pious people. When the town got wind of this, Krissy knew, those words would taint every member of her family for the rest of their lives.

She stood on the bottom step, shaking. Though the sun was not yet up and her mind was foggy, it was clear these words were the advent of something terrible. THAT BITCH IS GONE, Krissy read again, and this time shame colored her panic. Here something was horribly, horribly wrong, and all she'd been able to think was *What will the neighbors say?*

TWO

Margot, 2019

Margot pulled up to the curb outside her uncle Luke's house, turned off the engine, and slumped back against her seat. Through the passenger-side window, she gazed up at the squat seventies ranch-style and her body prickled with dread. The last time she'd spent the night here in Wakarusa, in the town where she grew up, was twenty years ago. She'd been eleven.

Margot's hometown was originally called Salem, but the name was changed in the 1850s to avoid confusion with the other Indiana Salem. The etymology had gotten lost to history, but conventional wisdom was that the Native American *Wakarusa* could be translated to "knee-deep in mud." Both the old name and the new struck Margot as uncanny in their appropriateness. One evoked the killing of innocent girls, the other insinuated just how hard it was to leave. Though to Margot, the mud seemed more like quicksand. The more you fought it, the more it pulled you under. For years she thought she'd escaped, and now here she was, back again.

But more than just the town, what was making Margot's heart

pound now was what version of her uncle she was going to get tonight. The real one. Or the bad one.

She took a deep breath, then grabbed her bags from the back seat and made her way up the path. On her uncle's front landing was a bulb in a wire cage illuminating the space with a flickering yellow light. The sound of moths beating their bodies against it reminded Margot of childhood summers here—long, hot days of skinned knees and calves cut up from fields of corn. She lifted a fist and knocked.

After a moment, Margot heard the *plunk* of a dead bolt, then the door creaked slowly, barely, open. Her pasted-on smile faltered.

"Uncle Luke?"

Through the dark crack of the doorway, she studied the changes in her uncle since she'd seen him last. The lines on his face seemed to have deepened in the intervening months and his dark hair was unusually mussed. One thing that hadn't changed, however, was the red bandanna around his neck, the one she'd given him for Christmas twenty-five years ago, which he still wore often.

His eyes flicked over her face. "Rebecca?"

Margot swallowed. Despite sharing only superficial similarities with her uncle's late wife—short brown hair and an average build—Margot was used to Luke calling her by the other woman's name. Still, it stung every time. "I'm Margot, remember? Your niece—Adam's daughter?" This was the part that twisted in her stomach. *Adam's daughter* didn't convey that he, Luke, was more of a dad to her than her father had ever been. *Niece* didn't capture that, besides his late wife, she was his favorite person and he hers. But it was best to start small, jog his memory, and the rest would usually follow.

"Margot . . ." Her uncle said her name as if he were trying out the syllables for the first time.

"That's my name, but usually you call me kid." Margot kept her voice bright and even.

Luke blinked once, twice, and then finally, as if someone had gone in and swiped a hand across old cobwebs, his eyes cleared. "Kid!" He swung the door open and extended his arms wide. "My god, you're here! What took you so long?"

Margot forced out a laugh as she rushed into his open arms, but her throat felt tight. She'd never get used to the fear that she'd finally lost him for good.

"Sorry 'bout that, kid," he said when they let go. "I've been forgetting things in my old age." He said it dismissively, as if forgetting your family was as innocuous as misplacing your keys, but there was a shadow of embarrassment darkening his eyes.

She waved a hand. "It's fine."

"Well, how the hell have you been? Oh, here, lemme help you with those bags."

Margot made to protest, but Luke was already piling her bags in his arms. At only fifty, his mind may have been failing him, but he seemed strong as ever. As he turned his back, she stole a sweeping glance at his small home and her stomach dropped. It was the first time she'd been here since his wife, Rebecca, died of breast cancer the previous year. She swelled with guilt for not having come sooner. Leaning towers of newspapers were scattered around the living room floor, the coffee table was littered with dirty plates and glasses, and she could see even from where she stood at the front door that there was a layer of dust coating the built-in bookcase and old TV. The kitchen off to the right was far worse. The sink and surrounding counter overflowed with teetering piles of dishes, bowls stacked onto cups, smears of food hardened over it all. Most unsettling was the collection of pill bottles stacked by the landline phone. There had to have been more than a dozen, some empty, some toppled over. One big one was filled with an assortment of pills, round white ones mixed in with others, which were long and pale green. How much of this was because of his diagnosis and how much of it was because he was a new widower, Margot didn't know.

"Jesus, you got a lot of stuff, kid," Luke said, his arms laden with bags. "It's like you think you're moving in."

Margot cut her eyes to him to see if this was a joke—she *was* moving in after all—but there was only the twinkle of teasing in his eye, not that of knowing. She laughed lightly. "You know me." Then, when he didn't move, she nodded toward the door at the end of the hall. "I was hoping I could stay in the office?"

A jolt of recognition as he nodded. "Sure, sure."

Her aunt and uncle's office had never gotten much use, as they'd both worked in South Bend, Luke as an accountant and Rebecca part-time at an art museum. In the first fifteen years of their marriage, the room had been a cheery yellow, a crib standing forever empty in the corner. Then, when Rebecca turned forty and gave up hope, she painted the walls gray. They'd bought a desk and a futon, and to Margot's knowledge the room was only ever used by her uncle, who sometimes liked to play solitaire on the computer before bed.

The sight of the room now made Margot's chest ache. It was clear her uncle had, in bursts of lucidity, begun to prepare the room for her visit, though most of the tasks appeared to have been abandoned midway. The futon was pulled out, a fitted sheet tucked over three corners. Two bare pillows laid on the floor next to it. She'd have to rummage around for a blanket and pillowcases.

"This is perfect. Thanks, Uncle Luke." She hesitated. "Well, I drove straight from the office, so I'm starving. Have you eaten?"

After Margot assessed the contents of her uncle's refrigerator—mostly condiments, mostly expired—she picked up a pizza from Wakarusa's only pizza place and they sat down at the kitchen table with glasses of tap water and their slices on paper towels instead of plates because there were no clean dishes. Margot had learned from their phone calls over the past few months that conversations were best when she was the one talking, so she spoke between bites, all the while aching for the days not that long ago when, if they were in the same room together, she and her uncle could talk for hours.

"Thanks again for letting me stay," Margot said, sneaking a look at Luke's face. What she really wanted to say was: *Do you know why I'm here? Do you remember your diagnosis? How are you coping with it all?* But every time she brought up anything related to his illness, Luke's voice turned hard. Margot recognized the emotion hidden beneath—her uncle was losing his mind at the devastatingly young age of fifty and he was terrified. So she talked around it. When she'd invited herself to move in, she'd told him she needed a change of pace and wanted to be closer to him, citing a made-up "new flexibility at work" as a seemingly good opportunity to do so.

"Of course," Luke said, his eyes on his pizza. "You know you're welcome anytime."

"And just remember I'm happy to help out, so if you need anything . . ."

Luke smiled, but it was tight. "Thanks, kid."

Margot opened her mouth to say something else, but he'd already changed the subject. "Hey, how's Adam doing? And your mom?"

Margot stifled a sigh. They'd just jumped from one sticky topic to another, and she didn't know how to navigate any of it. Until six months ago, she'd never hesitated to tell her uncle the truth— about his brother or anything else. But with his diagnosis, he seemed fragile, and from her research, she knew that fragility could lead to mood swings and outbursts. It had only happened a few times over the phone so far, but the thought of Luke losing himself scared her. "He's—"

"Still a mean drunk who refuses to get help?"

Margot burst into surprised laughter.

"C'mon, I may be losing my mind, but there's no way I could forget that," he said, and she laughed even harder.

It wasn't that she found anything funny about the fact that her father was fonder of whiskey than of both his only brother and his only daughter, but this was the Uncle Luke she missed. The one person in a town of fakes who'd always speak the truth. The person who made Margot feel understood without her having to try. The person whose sense of humor was the exact same as hers, who'd one time made her laugh so hard midsip that soda had come out her nose. Plus, the absence of her dad's affection, or her mom's, for that matter, wasn't new to Margot. Her childhood home had been one of shouted arguments punctuated by hurled glasses shattering against walls. It was why she was so close with Luke. Every day after school, she'd walk to her uncle's house rather than her own. On the weekends, she'd spend the night. She *would* have moved in with him and Rebecca—they'd offered many times—but her mom had worried about what people would say.

Similar was her reaction a few weeks ago when Margot told her mom she was moving back to Wakarusa. "What're you gonna tell people when they ask you why you're back?" her mom had said.

"What do you mean? I'm gonna tell them the truth, that I'm staying with Luke to help out."

"That's nobody's business, Margot. Anyway, your dad says it can't be that bad. Luke's his *younger* brother."

"How the hell would Dad know? When was the last time the two of them talked—2010?"

"If you're really this worried, why don't you just hire a nurse or something? You don't want to go back to that sad little town where that terrible thing happened."

Margot had pulled the phone from her ear to give the screen an incredulous look. "A nurse? With what money?"

"My lord, Margot. Sometimes you sound so crass." When she

spoke next, her voice had gone breathy as if the whole thing was beneath her. "You have a good job. I'm sure you'll figure something out."

Now, to Luke, Margot said, "And Mom's the same as ever. Delusional."

Luke snorted. "What's Bethany delusional about this time?"

"She seems to think I'm a millionaire because I write for a newspaper."

"Wait. You're not a millionaire?"

She grinned.

"How is the paper, by the way?"

Margot looked down. "It's fine, yeah." She hated keeping things from her uncle, but she couldn't stomach the idea of making him feel guilty for something he couldn't control. She couldn't tell him that her work had been suffering for six months now because her mind had been in Wakarusa with him instead of in Indianapolis with her paper. She couldn't tell him how reluctantly her editor had signed off on Margot's move to remote work. "Really," she added more brightly this time. "It's great."

But when she looked up, her uncle was giving her an odd look. His eyes darted from the slice of pizza in his hand to Margot's face, a hard line on his brow. "Rebecca?"

Margot swallowed. "It's me, Uncle Luke. Your niece, Margot."

He blinked for a moment, and then his expression cleared, a smile spreading across his face. "Kid! I'm so glad you're here."

"Yeah." She nodded. "Me too."

That night after Luke had gone to bed, Margot washed dishes until one side of the sink was empty, then she sat at the kitchen table and made a list. She needed to make a copy of Luke's house key for herself and organize his medications. She needed to clean the kitchen and living room and stock up on toilet paper and paper towels, both of which he seemed to be almost out of. She'd read somewhere that putting labels on things, like what was inside the kitchen cabinets, would help him navigate the house when memory failed him, so she wanted to do that as well. Also, with all the time it had taken to move to Wakarusa, she'd fallen about a week behind on work and needed to pump out some articles that weren't complete garbage. She added *Do your job* to the list. Then, at the bottom, she wrote a reminder to herself to call the subletter she'd found for her apartment in Indianapolis. He'd sounded unnervingly wishy-washy the last time they spoke and she needed him to move in, make his first rental payment. Otherwise she'd owe a full month's rental payment for a place where she was no longer living. Just looking at the list made Margot tired, but she'd have more time tomorrow.

But by the next day, the town was abuzz with what had happened—the news of it ripping through Wakarusa like a storm cloud—and it was hard to get anything done at all.

Margot first noticed something was off the next morning at the pharmacy. She'd left Luke a few minutes earlier nursing a cup of coffee and doing the book of crosswords she'd brought from Indianapolis because she'd read they could help keep him sharp. A bell above the shop's door announced her arrival, so even though no one was behind the counter when she walked in, she assumed the pharmacist would appear soon. She stood by the counter, running her fingers absently along the bags of cough drops on display, the indistinct sounds of a TV coming from the back.

"Excuse me?" she called when no one had showed after a minute. "Hello?" She waited. Still, there was nothing. "He-*llo*?"

Finally, she heard a movement in the back, then a man poked his head around one of the aisles. "Oh!" he said, plucking a pair of glasses hanging from a chain around his neck. He settled them on the bridge of his nose, squinted, hurried over. "Sorry 'bout that. I got caught up in the news, you know. Terrible what's happened, isn't it?" But before Margot could respond, he jerked his head back as if just now seeing her for the first time. "Not often I see an unfamiliar face in here."

Margot smiled. "I'm here to pick up some prescriptions for my uncle." She twisted her backpack around to the front, so she could pull the two orange bottles from the pocket. Earlier, she'd sifted through the mess of bottles Luke had accumulated, and to her relief, most of them were for the same drug, different month. She'd organized them all into three current prescriptions, two of which needed refills: one that seemed to be a statin, one for blood pressure, and one for blood sugar.

"Who's your uncle?" the pharmacist asked.

Margot placed the two bottles atop the counter. "Luke Davies."

The man's eyebrows shot high on his forehead. "*You're* Luke and Rebecca's niece? That must mean you're Margot."

His expression was more curiosity than friendliness, but Margot returned it with a smile nonetheless. "That's me."

"I'm so sorry about your aunt, dear. That cancer was so fast. And my goodness, I haven't seen your folks in ages. Good people, though, *good* people. How're they?"

Her smile tightened, but only a bit. She'd known this was coming from the moment she made the decision to move back. The uncertain look about Luke and Rebecca, the fawning one for her mom and dad. Her parents had been the perfect Wakarusa residents until the moment they moved away, which was ostensibly for her dad's exciting new job in Cincinnati, but was really so he could go to rehab, which not only didn't work, but turned him resentful and meaner than before.

"They're great," she said to the pharmacist. "Do you think you could help me out with these prescriptions? I've heard of a statin before, but is that for your heart or your cholesterol?"

Margot waited for what seemed like far too long for the man to fill two simple prescriptions, and when he came back, he looked flustered and anxious, frowning distractedly as he stapled her little white bag shut. And then, as she was walking out, she passed a woman on her way in, a phone pressed hard to her ear. The woman was so absorbed in her conversation she didn't seem to see Margot at all. But just before the door closed behind her, Margot heard the woman say, "I know. I told you. The Jacobses are innocent."

Margot snapped her head around to look at the woman through the glass, frowning. Maybe she just misheard her. The name was probably just at the top of Margot's mind because she was back after all this time. It was impossible to be in Wakarusa and not think about the Jacobs family. Plus, the woman's voice had sounded urgent, and the Jacobs story was two decades old. Still, Margot had the urge to go back through the door and ask the woman what she was talking about, but the idea of willfully inserting herself into this town's rumor mill stopped her. She'd just look it up on her phone.

Her Google search in the car yielded no new results, so she put it out of her mind. She had too much to think about already anyway.

The rest of the day passed in a blur of cleaning. She did dishes and scrubbed counters and collected an entire trash bag full of soda cans, used paper towels, food wrappers. When she walked into her uncle's bedroom that afternoon as he went for a walk, she clamped a hand over her nose and mouth. His bedsheets smelled sour with the accumulated scent of human, with sweat and urine. She didn't even bother washing them, just threw them out and bought fresh ones from the Walmart in the nearby town of Elkhart.

She was so distracted in fact that she'd forgotten about the incident at the pharmacy entirely until she walked into Shorty's Bar & Grill that evening to pick up dinner for her and Luke. She'd have to get her uncle off a diet of pizza and burgers eventually, but she hadn't yet made it to the grocery store, so takeout would have to do for the time being.

The restaurant was packed, tables full of people, their heads bent in animated conversation. The TV in the corner was tuned to a news station, but the collective din was drowning out whatever the two newscasters on screen were saying. Margot approached the bar, crowded with customers, and tried to catch the bartender's eye. But the woman was focused on the man across from her, her arms crossed and eyes wide, nodding along as he spoke, gesticulating wildly with his beer as he did. ". . . exactly what I thought all along!" Margot heard him say.

She waved in the bartender's direction. "'Scuse me?"

The woman behind the bar turned her head to look at her. "Hold that thought, Larry," she said to the man, then made her way over. "What can I get you, hon?" she asked Margot. She looked as if she were fifty, but Margot suspected she was probably closer to a rough forty. Her skin was like worn leather, her hair the consistency of straw.

"Hi, I'm picking up a to-go order for—"

"Holy shit!" the bartender exclaimed so suddenly Margot jumped. "A to-go order for *Margot!* You're Margot Davies." In her periphery, Margot saw a line of heads swivel in her direction. She forced her wince into a smile. The pharmacist had worked fast. It had been less than seven hours since she'd told him her name.

"Hi."

"How're your folks? Gosh, I haven't seen Adam and Bethany for ages!" The bartender's face dropped dramatically. "I miss them. Will you tell them Linda says hi?"

Margot nodded. "Sure. Yeah, course."

"Oh my god!" Linda exclaimed, then her voice dropped an octave as she said, "Is this why you're here?"

"Um." Margot shook her head. "Is what why I'm here?"

"Well, the story of course. You're a reporter, aren't you?"

"Yes . . ." Margot was so thrown by how much this stranger seemed to know about her, she was having trouble following the conversation. "What story? What's going on?"

Linda's eyebrows shot up. "You mean you don't know?" She whirled around, looking for something, and finally her gaze landed upon a TV remote beside an open jar of maraschino cherries. She grabbed it up and pointed it at the TV. On the screen, the volume bar grew.

"*. . . on a recent event that's happened in Nappanee, Indiana,*" a male newscaster was saying. The town name jolted in Margot's chest. Nappanee was a stone's throw from Wakarusa. If she got into her car now, she could be there in under fifteen minutes. *"Early this morning,"* the newscaster continued, *"five-year-old Natalie Clark was reported missing by her parents. According to her mother, Samantha Clark, the girl disappeared from a crowded local playground. Mrs. Clark had been feeding her youngest, an infant, when she looked up to check on Natalie and her son, but Natalie was nowhere to be found."*

A photo of the missing girl flashed on the screen, all teeth and wild brown hair, and suddenly everything fell into place: the anxious look on the pharmacist's face, the woman's phone call and her mention of the Jacobs family. Margot hadn't misheard her after all. And now she knew what Linda was going to say even before the woman turned to her to say it.

"It's happening again. January Jacobs. Her murderer is back."

THREE

Krissy, 1994

Krissy stared with blank incomprehension at Robby O'Neil's face. His features—small, dark eyes, ruddy cheeks, slick lips— swam in her vision. This man, whom she'd known her entire life, looked suddenly and completely unfamiliar. But more confusing than that was why Robby O'Neil was at their front door in the first place.

Only twenty minutes earlier, when Krissy had come downstairs and spotted the words on their wall, she'd woken Billy with a scream. Both he and Jace had run down the stairs at the sound. Jace's twin sister, January, had not.

Those words—*That bitch is gone*—had flashed in Krissy's mind as she and Billy frantically searched the house for their six-year-old daughter, and when they didn't find January anywhere, they'd called 911. So *the police* were supposed to be the ones knocking on their door—not their old pal from high school. Robby's presence here, at 5:30 A.M. on this torturous, bizarre morning, cast the whole ordeal into a strange, surreal light. Krissy had gone to kindergarten through high school with Robby O'Neil, had watched as he'd stumbled through current event presentations in social studies, had listened to her friend Martha gush about how dreamy he was.

By her side, Jace tucked his face into the folds of her robe and Krissy put a hand on his back. Then she took it off. Before she could work out what to say to Robby, Billy approached from behind her. "Hey, Robby," he said, leaning through the doorway to shake his hand. "Thanks for coming."

It was then, as Krissy's eyes flicked over Robby's uniform, that she realized he *was* the police. Of course, some dark part of her brain had known that—he'd been an officer in Wakarusa now for years—but it seemed like a cruel practical joke that when she called the police because her only daughter was missing, this was what she got: Robby-couldn't-even-give-a-current-events-presentation-O'Neil.

"No problem," Robby said with a look of exaggerated concern, as if he thought what he'd been called for was an overreaction but was treating it as if it wasn't because they were old friends.

It made Krissy's face burn. She'd stood beside Billy as he'd told the 911 operator that their house had been broken into, that their daughter had been taken.

"Why don't you, uh, why don't you come in?" Billy said. "Kris?" he added, giving her a look. "You wanna step back so Robby can come in?"

Krissy felt a jolt of anger toward her husband. Why was he acting so goddamn calm? Their daughter, their *January*, was gone, and here he was trying to make their guest feel welcome? But she knew deep down Billy wasn't doing it because he was calm; he was doing it because he was a people pleaser, down to his bones. She knew that, just as she was, Billy was the opposite of calm. When he'd rushed down the stairs that morning and had caught sight of the words scrawled on the wall, he'd stopped so abruptly it was as if he'd run into some invisible barrier. His face had widened with shock and horror. He'd given Krissy a searching look. Then, later, as he'd phoned the police, his whole body had shaken.

Billy led them through the entryway to the kitchen, Robby following behind, Krissy with Jace clinging to her robe bringing up the rear.

"So, you guys can't find January?" Robby said, his voice still light. It grated on Krissy's nerves.

"She was *taken*," she said. "Somebody broke in."

Robby shot a glance at her over his shoulder. He looked surprised but also confused, as if she couldn't possibly mean what she was saying. After all, nothing truly bad ever happened here in Wakarusa. His eyes flicked over Jace. "Jace okay, though?"

The question was innocent enough, but it made Krissy's breath catch. She hadn't known what to do with Jace while they waited the agonizing minutes for the police to get there. She'd considered pretending nothing was happening, tucking him back into bed, but the thought made her skin prickle with fear. Her daughter was gone, and now Krissy was terrified to let her son out of her sight. There was a buzzing energy emanating from him like a force field. What did he think was happening?

Krissy looked Robby in the eye. "Jace is fine."

They passed through the doorway into the kitchen, and Krissy could see the exact moment Robby registered the words on the wall and realized he'd underestimated the situation. Just like Billy's had, his eyes widened and his mouth went slack. Krissy ducked her head, unable to look. She already knew what she'd find if she did. She glanced at Jace and saw his eyes squeezed shut, his face half buried in her robe.

Robby cleared his throat. "I think my supervisor should know about this," he said, tugging a radio from a holster on his belt, then walking a few steps away to call it in, his voice hushed and urgent. When he turned back around, he gave Billy and Krissy the grave look she'd been waiting for. "My supervisor Barker's gonna be here soon." He swallowed hard, his Adam's apple jumping. "In the meantime, have you checked the house for January?"

Krissy wanted to scream. Did he think they were morons? But before she could answer, Billy said, "It was the first thing we did."

Robby nodded. "Okay, okay. Huh. Well, let's go ahead and do another sweep together, yeah? It's possible you missed something given your . . ." He hesitated, looking for the right word. "State."

Billy shot Krissy a glance that didn't quite meet her eye, and she shrugged. "Fine." She knew January was not in the house—it wasn't as if she and Billy had simply missed her, as if she'd been playing some overly tenacious game of hide-and-seek—but Robby was the expert here. She wasn't going to contradict him.

With Jace still glued to Krissy's side, the four of them walked slowly through the downstairs, stopping in each room so Robby could open cabinets and palm pillows, as if their six-year-old daughter could possibly fit behind one. He kept asking if anything was missing and Billy and Krissy kept telling him no. When they circled back to the kitchen, where the stairs to the second floor were, Robby stuck his hands on his hips, jutting his chin toward the steps. "Do you mind if I . . ."

"Of course," Billy said without hesitation.

Robby led the way, grabbing the banister hard with every step. Billy followed him and Krissy followed both, holding Jace's hand tightly in her own. Upstairs, Robby continued his search, opening every door and cabinet with such gusto that Krissy suspected he was acting out some brave rescue scene he'd envisioned in his mind: He'd thrust open their linen closet door to find January curled in a ball, scared and lost in her own house, he the gallant hero, she the victim of nothing that couldn't be recovered from with a little chicken soup and a warm bath, Krissy and Billy the silly, dramatic parents. She swelled with annoyance.

But when they made it to Jace's and January's rooms, across the hall from each other, Krissy's heart started to pound with such ferocity it drove all other emotions out of her. She stood between the doorways, unable to look through either. These rooms were where her babies should have been but weren't.

After Robby had finished looking under beds and flipping back blankets, they made their way downstairs again. Now, the only place left to go was the basement.

"This is where—" Billy began, gesturing to the basement door, his voice cutting out with a gulp. Krissy snapped her head to look at him. "This is where we, um, think somebody may have gotten in. There's a broken window. You'll see."

Robby nodded, gripping the brass knob to open the door wide. Billy followed him down, but Krissy hesitated. Bringing Jace around the house with them was one thing, but the thought of having him down there was too much. It didn't feel safe to have him in that basement. She led Jace by the hand to the kitchen table and perched him on one of the wooden chairs. She didn't want to leave him here either, but her heart was racing at the idea of Robby and Billy alone in that basement. She needed to see what they were seeing. Yes, she'd already been down there during her and Billy's search, but what if she'd missed something?

"Jace?" she said, hating the quiver in her own voice. She gripped his shoulders. "Mommy needs you to sit right here and not move for one minute, okay? I want you to close your eyes and count all the way to a hundred and then I'll be back."

Jace looked at her in that strangely solemn way he sometimes did, a look that made him seem much older than his six years. He nodded slowly.

"Stay here."

The bare bulb in the basement ceiling was on, illuminating the room with a dim, flickering glow. Krissy looked around at the space, which was cluttered with unlabeled boxes of stuff—Christmas decorations, clothes and toys the kids had grown out of, financial records of the farm. There was an old plaid couch and a few errant toys scattered around: a small trampoline, a plastic pole for a ring toss stacked with fat, multicolored rings. Robby was holding Jace's Etch A Sketch, idly rotating it in his hands, his eyes on the shattered glass on the floor. One of the three small, horizontal windows, the one closest to the bottom of the stairs, had been smashed.

Without Jace's warm body against hers, Krissy felt cold and crossed her arms over her chest. In some small part of her mind, she realized it was summer in Indiana and the cold couldn't possibly be real.

"Well," Robby said. "It does look like someone could've gotten in this way." He toed one of the pieces of glass and Krissy's eyes widened in surprise. Even she, stay-at-home mom that she was, knew you weren't supposed to touch pieces of a crime scene. She'd seen enough *Law & Order* episodes to know that.

"Mommy?"

The voice, so small and soft in the big space of the basement, made Krissy jump. She spun around, her heart in her throat, to find Jace, standing in the middle of the steps, staring down at her with wide eyes.

"Jesus!" Krissy clapped a hand over her chest. As ashamed as it made her to admit, her heart filled with resentment at Jace for not being his twin sister. "Jace, you scared me. What is it? I told you to stay where you were."

Her son's round eyes began to fill with tears and guilt billowed through her. "I'm scared," he said, his voice like a tinkling bell. "I'm scared of the men upstairs."

At the mention of a missing child, Robby's supervisor, Sergeant Barker, had apparently called the state police, because by the time

Billy, Robby, and Krissy—her hand clasped firmly around Jace's—had made it back up into the kitchen, their house had transformed. Every room in Krissy's periphery crawled with men in uniform, and through the kitchen window, she spotted one of them walking a wide perimeter of the house, a fat roll of yellow caution tape unfurling from his hands. Even the air had taken on a different quality, tense and crackling.

Suddenly, as if they'd simply materialized there, two people were standing directly in front of her. One was a man with hair like a private school boy's, perfectly combed with a part so neat it looked as if it'd been done with a straightedge. His button-down strained against his muscled upper arms. His eyes were a shocking blue. The second was a woman with an average build and thin, soft-looking brown hair pulled into a ponytail. The man was probably in his late forties, the woman ten or fifteen years younger. They were the only two people not wearing uniforms and despite this, or perhaps because of it, Krissy got the impression they were the ones in charge. The man emanated an air of authority so strong it was as if he put it on with his morning cologne.

"I'm Detective Max Townsend," he said, extending his hand to shake Krissy's then Billy's as they introduced themselves. "This is my partner, Detective Rhonda Lacks. We've heard your little girl, January, is missing. Is that right?"

Detective Townsend spoke at a fast, businesslike clip, and Krissy found herself gaping mutely at him. Beside her, Billy cleared his throat. "Yes, that's right," he said.

"We're awfully sorry for what you folks are going through," the detective continued. "We're from the Indiana State Police and we're gonna take things from here, all right? I wanna assure you that we're going to do everything in our power to bring your daughter home safely. Detective Lacks and I have a pretty good track record for these things." He paused, looking both her and

Billy firmly in the eye. If his intent was to reassure them, it wasn't working. "First things first. We'll need a description of what January was wearing to bed last night. Then I'd like you two to take me to her room, so you can spot anything that's missing or out of place. This will help our people know what they're looking for. All right? And while we're there, we'll want to take something of hers with us—a worn article of clothing's best—for our tracking dogs."

He flashed a solemn, bolstering smile and Krissy touched a finger to her temple. She wanted to hold on to his words, to look each one over and understand what it meant, but they just fluttered around her in an incomprehensible blur. It felt as though everything was suddenly happening too quickly, as if she was in a movie that was being fast-forwarded.

"In the meantime," Detective Townsend continued, "I think we ought to get Brother out of here. This is Officer Patricia Jones." He gestured to a uniformed officer who had also magically appeared out of nowhere, a tall woman with big everything: big hands, big breasts, even her ears were big. "She's gonna stay with Brother in one of our cars, all right? Get him out of all this."

Krissy blinked. It took her a long moment to realize that when Detective Townsend said "Brother," he was talking about Jace. "Oh," she said. "I'd prefer it if he stayed with me. This is . . . confusing for him. I don't want him to be any more scared than he already is."

Detective Townsend's understanding smile flashed on and off his face so quickly Krissy couldn't be sure if she'd really seen it or not. "I understand. But we're gonna need a lot from you and Dad right now, and I'm going to need you focused, all right? Officer Jones has three little ones of her own. Your son's going to be in very good hands."

The big woman stooped down to get her face closer to Jace's.

"Hi, Jace," she said, and Krissy wondered how she knew Jace's name. Had she told them? "My name's Patricia. What do you say to some lemonade? And I think I might know where to get some cookies too."

And then Jace was nodding and the big woman was taking his hand out of Krissy's and leading him away from her. As she watched her son's tiny body retreat, Krissy felt a fear so sudden and strong she thought she might crack in half.

"Now," Detective Townsend said. "When I walked in, I saw a nice sitting area off the front entryway. Detective Lacks?" He turned to his partner. "Why don't you head in there with Mr. and Mrs. Jacobs and I'll meet you in one moment? Then the four of us can go to January's room together."

At Detective Townsend's curt nod, Krissy understood that she and Billy had been dismissed, and when she turned to look at her husband, to follow him out of the room, she noticed that Robby was still standing behind them. In the whirlwind of the detectives' arrival, she'd completely forgotten he was there. Detective Lacks led her and Billy to the sitting area off the entryway, and as she followed, Krissy turned to look back just in time to see Detective Townsend glower at their old high school friend.

"And you, Officer O'Neil, is it?" he snapped, his crisp voice carrying loudly through the hallway. "It seems I have you to thank for breaking every crime scene protocol in the book. So I'm going to need you to tell me everything in this house you touched."

A few minutes later, Krissy led the two detectives and Billy up the stairs. But when she reached her daughter's doorway, she stopped, as if invisible hands were holding her back, preventing her from stepping over the threshold. Only when she heard Detective Townsend's firm "After you" did she force herself to cross it.

Standing in her daughter's bedroom, Krissy watched as the detectives entered and did not miss the pointed look they shared as they did.

She glanced around the room, trying to see what they did. She took in January's daybed with its lilac comforter and the white gauzy canopy. It was the exact bed Krissy had always wanted as a girl, but was so far from the realm of possibility, she'd never asked for it. Her eyes flicked to the closet bursting with tutus in purples and pinks, tiny tights unfurled and hanging from the shelves like tentacles, the row of little dance shoes, pink ballet slippers next to the black patent leather ones for tap. She glanced at the white bulletin board on the opposite wall hanging over the bookcase, crisscrossed with pink ribbons and adorned with medals, certificates, and photos of January throughout the years, most of them taken before or after dance recitals. It wasn't hard to see what the detectives saw: This was a girl who had everything.

"Try not to touch anything," Detective Townsend instructed from where he lingered in the doorway. "But look hard. Does anything catch your eye as out of place or missing?"

Krissy and Billy walked slowly around the room, but it seemed impossible to Krissy to know if anything was where it hadn't been before. Had January's tights been rolled neatly yesterday? Had that tutu in her hamper been hanging up? Had that picture frame on the dresser been upright? She glanced at Billy, who stood frozen by January's dresser, his hand on the corner as if he couldn't prop up his own weight. He was only twenty-five, but with the dark circles under his eyes and the premature lines on his forehead, Krissy thought he could've passed for ten years older.

"I don't know," Billy said wearily after a while. "I don't see anything."

Krissy shook her head. "No. Me neither."

The two detectives nodded, and as if that had been their cue, they began walking slowly around the perimeter of the room.

Their search was unlike Robby's had been, taking care not to touch anything, leaning deftly over the bed to examine the covers, squatting to look into the depths of the closet. When they converged at the bulletin board, Detective Townsend leaned toward it, his hands clasped behind his back, his nose inches from the cluttered surface.

"Quite a lot of medals for a six-year-old," he said, throwing Krissy a look over his shoulder.

"She's very dedicated. She's been in lessons practically since she could walk."

He nodded, returning his gaze to the board.

"Cute," Detective Lacks said, pointing to an old photo of January. In it, she was probably three, in her nightgown, her hands over her head in a crude approximation of fifth position. Then Detective Lacks switched her gaze to another photo Krissy couldn't see, one blocked by the detective's back. "Wow. Townsend, take a look at this one."

Detective Townsend turned, and Krissy watched as his gaze landed on whatever photo his partner was pointing to. The two of them locked eyes for the briefest of moments, and Krissy registered something in their look that rubbed her wrong—something like understanding.

Detective Townsend turned to face her and Billy. "Mind if we take this one? We're going to need a few recent photos of her."

"You can take anything you need," Krissy said, her voice tight. She felt something had shifted in the detectives' minds; she just didn't know what.

"This one will do for now, but we'll have you choose some more in a bit." He leaned over and unpinned the photo from the board. Then he turned and held up the picture so she and Billy could see.

Krissy's heart dropped. Now she knew exactly what these detectives were thinking. In the photo, January was posing before her latest dance recital. She was wearing a two-piece, nautical-themed costume, a white skirt lined with navy ribbon and silver rhinestones, and a matching top with a red bow tied at the center of her chest. On her head, a matching hat sat at a jaunty angle. Her chestnut hair was curled and sprayed, her eyes made Disney-enormous with fake eyelashes and blue eyeshadow. Her lips were bright red.

Krissy's cheeks burned and she couldn't meet Townsend's eye.

"Is this pretty recent, would you say?" he asked, and although his voice was light, Krissy could feel the mocking tone beneath it, judgment practically radiating out of him.

"That recital was a few months ago. She's six in it. So, yes."

Detective Townsend glanced at the photo pointedly. "Six, huh?" He let out a little chuckle, threw a look at Detective Lacks. "And here I would've guessed she's sixteen."

The unspoken accusation cut through Krissy like a switchblade: *bad parents*. Or perhaps, more to the point, because everyone knew moms were to blame just a little bit more than dads: *bad mom*. Her mind flashed to those bright red words scrawled messily on her kitchen wall—*This is what you get*—and in that moment, Krissy felt just how true they really were.

FOUR

Margot, 2019

The murder of January Jacobs, the event that put Margot's hometown on the map, happened in the middle of a hot July night in 1994. By all accounts, the story was a sensational one and it spread like wildfire, capturing the morbid fascination of Americans across regional, socioeconomic, and political divides. Overnight, the Jacobs family was famous. January became America's darling, and her elusive killer the country's most wanted. But the case was convoluted, and months passed without so much as an arrest. Eventually, the investigation grew cold and January's murder turned into one of the nation's greatest unsolved mysteries.

Yet while the little girl may have been just another cautionary tale or podcast episode to the rest of the world, to Margot, January was real. They'd been the same age, had grown up in houses across the street from one another. Though Margot's memories of her early childhood were sparse and faded, she could still conjure flashes of summer days in the Jacobs backyard while Luke and Rebecca worked, she and January pretending to be horses or playing tag in the cornfields. The two girls had existed together in that magical age before boundaries, their little bodies always overlapping: hands in each other's hair as they practiced their braids; sticky fingertips pressed together in a complicated shape, intoning *Here is the church, here is the steeple* . . . ; limbs intertwining as they collapsed into a heap of giggles.

When January had been taken from her home, Margot had been sleeping only hundreds of feet away, in her own house across the street. Afterward, Margot's parents told her that her friend wasn't coming back, and Luke explained that January had died. But it was only later, when an older kid at recess told Margot that January had been *murdered,* that she'd learned the truth about her friend's death. Although she must have missed January desperately, it was the fear she remembered most. Margot began to envision a faceless man standing between the two houses, playing eeny, meeny, miny, moe with her friend's bedroom window and her own. At night she'd lay in bed, squeezing her fists so tight her fingernails drew blood.

And now, with Natalie Clark's face splashed over the news, it felt as if it were happening all over again. The missing girl may not technically have been a child of Wakarusa, but with Nappanee only a few miles away, she was as good as.

The morning after Margot heard the news at Shorty's, she sat at her uncle's kitchen table, her laptop open in front of her, a cup of coffee in her hand. She should have been using the time to catch up on work emails, but instead she was looking for information about Natalie's missing person case.

As she clicked back to her search page, she heard the creak of a door from down the hallway. A moment later, her uncle appeared in sweatpants and a worn T-shirt, his dark hair wild, his eyes swollen and red. Margot closed her laptop with a gentle click.

"Morning," she said. "How're you feeling?"

Yesterday evening, Margot returned from Shorty's to find Luke standing in the living room, shaking. The moment she saw him, she dropped the to-go bag on the floor and rushed over.

"What's the matter?" she said, placing a tentative hand on his back. When he didn't flinch, she moved it in slow, smooth circles. The touch felt foreign to her—the Davies family had never been particularly physical in their affection—but she'd read in some online article that it could help him calm down when he was suffering from an episode.

Luke's face crumpled and he looked to Margot like a child, his body shaking beneath her hand, tears streaming unchecked down his cheeks. "She's gone," he said, his voice a croak. "She's gone."

"I know," Margot said. "I'm so sorry."

But that's when she heard the low murmuring from the TV, and when she looked over at it, she saw it was tuned to the news. Natalie Clark was gazing back at her, her smile wide and bright. And suddenly, Margot didn't know if her uncle was mourning the loss of his dead wife or that of the missing girl.

Now, standing in the hallway, Luke looked up sharply as if her voice had startled him, but when he saw her, he smiled softly. "Kid. Good morning."

Margot's chest loosened. She hadn't anticipated just how hard it would be to live with someone you loved who only sometimes loved you back. "I made coff—"

But before she could finish, her phone vibrated on the table, and when she glanced at it, she saw the name of her boss scrolling across the screen. "Sorry. I should take this." She stood, pressing the phone to her ear. "Hey, Adrienne. What's up?"

"Margot, hi. How's your uncle?"

Margot shot a glance at Luke, who was opening cabinets, presumably in search of a mug. She walked over and opened the right one, then retreated to the living room. "Um, yeah. Fine. Thanks."

"Good, good," her boss said, but she sounded distracted. "Listen, Margot. You've heard about the Natalie Clark case?"

"I was researching it now." *Research* was a bit of a stretch for the preliminary Google search she'd done that morning, but she wanted to sound more knowledgeable than she was. She worked on the paper's crime beat, and it was her job to stay on top of stories like that. The fact that she'd learned about Natalie's disappearance from a bartender had been a disheartening reminder of just how far she'd let her eye drift from the ball.

"Oh good. Well, let's have you write it up for tomorrow, yeah?"

Margot pinched the bridge of her nose. She knew she needed to make up for the leeway her boss had already given her these past few months, but she'd been hoping to get to the grocery store today. As it was, all she and Luke had for breakfast was stale Cheerios and almost-turned milk. "No problem."

"Great. So let's cover the basics. Police theories, any preliminary evidence. There's a press conference this evening and I looked it up. You're right there. Oh, and add some local color too. Talk to the family if you can get to them, someone we can call a close family friend if not—"

"Adrienne, hey," Margot interrupted with a little laugh. "I *have* done this before." It was an understatement. She'd been working at the paper for three years now, covering crime for almost as long.

"I know. But you need to nail this one. Okay?"

Margot's heart began to beat harder. Her performance at the paper had first begun to suffer a few months after her aunt Rebecca's death, when her grief had compounded with the dawning understanding of just how much Luke was really struggling. But it was only a few weeks ago, as she got ready for her move and put work on autopilot, that Adrienne had said something about it. "Right. I know. I will. Thanks, Adrienne."

Margot thought that would be enough, but her boss continued. "Listen. I think you should know that Edgar mentioned you to me the other day. He said he's noticed a decline in your work. Your output and quality."

Margot pulled the phone away from her ear to shout a silent *Fuck!*

Edgar was the paper's owner, whom she'd only met once at the company Christmas party three years ago, but he had a reputation for being merciless when it came to anything he deemed threatening to the paper's bottom line.

". . . told him about your circumstances," Adrienne was saying when Margot pressed the phone back to her ear, "but he wants to see improvement. Fast."

Margot took a deep breath. "I was thinking about drawing some parallels between the Natalie Clark case and the January Jacobs one," she said. "Pose the possibility of a connection." This had been percolating in her mind since the moment Linda had announced to her that January's murderer was back. Margot didn't know the details of Natalie's case, but whoever had taken and killed January was out there still, roaming free.

There was a pause on the other line and Margot assumed Adrienne was switching gears, from boss to editor. "Are there parallels?"

"Other than geography and age, I'm not sure yet. But I don't think it's too much of a stretch to explore."

"Okay . . . Of course, a serial offender is more compelling than a one-off." Margot recognized her boss's thinking-aloud voice, the one she used when she began to turn real events into thousand-word stories. "But don't force anything. We don't want another Polly Limon."

Margot winced. Polly Limon had been her first real assignment at *IndyNow* three years ago. The seven-year-old girl's story was like so many others: One fall afternoon, she'd disappeared from a mall parking lot in Dayton, Ohio. The missing persons investigation had spun its wheels until five days later when she was found dead in a ditch with signs of sexual abuse. Margot reported on the case for weeks, and although her articles never linked Polly's death to January's, in the office it was all she'd been able to talk about. Over the years, the death of her childhood friend had morphed from a source of grief and fear into one of infatuation. Slowly, the girl she'd once thought of as her friend January turned into The January Jacobs. Memories of them playing together were replaced with facts from her murder. So when Polly Limon showed up dead and the police started looking for her killer, Margot's mind jumped to the case of the girl from across the street.

"Polly was found in a *ditch*," she'd kept saying to Adrienne at the time. "Just like January." The cause of death had been different—strangulation as opposed to blunt-force trauma—but there had been damage done to her head as well. And while January hadn't sustained any sexual abuse, she also hadn't been missing as long. The police had never connected the two cases, but neither did they apprehend Polly's murderer, so Margot's theory had never been disproven. Though she knew what her boss meant. She couldn't afford to get obsessed with a side story. Not now.

"Right," she said. "I'll look into a connection this morning, but I'll head to Nappanee a few hours before the press conference for interviews."

"Good. Okay." Adrienne hesitated, then, after a moment, added, "I'm sorry, Margot. I know you've got a lot on your plate right now."

Margot forced a smile into her voice as she said, "It's fine. Really. I'll email you the story tonight."

After they hung up, she closed her eyes and took three slow, deep breaths.

Back in the kitchen, Luke was sitting at the table, a cup of coffee and his new book of crosswords in front of him.

"Jeez, kid," he said as she walked in, tapping the eraser end of his pencil against the page. "You got me hooked on these." He looked up. "Everything okay?"

She nodded. "Yeah, just work stuff. Hey . . ." She settled back into her chair across from him. "Could I ask you something? Could you tell me what you remember about January's case?"

They'd talked about it hundreds of times over the years, of course, but she still knew it was a risk asking. She didn't want to dredge up bad memories when his sickness could make him so mercurial, but at the kitchen table now, her uncle seemed clear-eyed, lucid.

"January's case?" he said with a frown. "You haven't asked about that in a long time."

"I'm covering a similar case for work," she explained. She'd learned over time that his long-term memory was far better than his day-to-day one. If he didn't remember Natalie Clark's name, she didn't want to make him feel bad or in the dark. "It's probably not connected, but I thought I'd dig around a bit."

"What d'you want to know?"

"What do you remember about Billy and Krissy from back then?" Margot knew the details of January's case like the back of her hand, so she didn't need his help there. And even though she'd grown up across the street from the Jacobses, these days they were a mystery to her. Her memories of Krissy, Billy, and Jace were vague at best, and they dropped off almost entirely after January was killed, when Margot stopped coming around.

"Well, as you know," Luke said with a shrug, "I didn't know them all that well. We didn't have playdates for you and January or anything—you'd just run over to their yard. And Krissy, Billy, and I may have all been in the same grade together in school, but— you know this place—high school was a little . . . cliquey."

She scoffed. "I can imagine."

"Even so, everyone knew Krissy because she was popular. Wild. She never really gave me the time of day. Billy was more reserved, I guess. And of course, he was a Jacobs, which . . . you know."

Margot nodded. He'd told her all this before, but even if he hadn't, she would've known what he meant. You didn't have to live across the street from them to know the reputation of the Jacobs family. Owning almost all of Wakarusa's surrounding land, they were the town's farming tycoons. Every farmer fed their livestock feed produced from the Jacobs crop. The school's gym was named the Jacobs Gymnasium after one of the men in Billy's line. He may not have been popular, but he'd been rich.

"How'd they end up getting married? Did they date in high school?"

Luke squinted. "Maybe? Maybe they dated that summer after graduation? I think I saw them around at parties and stuff. But I mean, beautiful girl and rich guy. They didn't exactly break the mold."

Margot asked him a few more questions, but there wasn't much he hadn't already told her before, and after about ten minutes, she realized she needed to move on. She'd had years to ask Luke about the Jacobs family, but she'd never spent any real time in Wakarusa as an adult. Now she needed to interview the people she hadn't spoken to before.

"Do you think Billy would be willing to talk to me?" Margot knew she needed to focus on covering Natalie Clark's case, but an interview with January's dad would be a huge get.

After all, speaking with Krissy wasn't an option; she'd taken her own life ten years earlier. There'd initially been some suspicion about her death—Was this January's murderer come back for her mom?—but it was quickly squashed by the police. It was a cookie-cutter case. Krissy had been on antidepressants for years, it happened in her own home, the gun that had been used to shoot her temple was found in her hand. She'd also left behind a note for Jace, the contents of which had been leaked to the press in the days after her body was found. Like many details of the case, Margot knew it by heart: *Jace, I'm sorry for everything. I'm going to make it right.* Meanwhile, Jace had disappeared from town at the age of seventeen and had been living in obscurity ever since. Which meant that Billy was the only family member Margot had a shot at.

"Oh," Luke said, looking slightly surprised. "Well, Billy doesn't really see many people anymore. But I think he still goes to church, and obviously he has to go to the grain elevator and the store. He may be a hard get for an interview. But"—he shrugged—"worth a shot."

Margot nodded. "Hey, I need to do some stuff for this article later. Would it be okay if I head out in a bit?"

"You don't need to babysit me, kid. I'm fine."

She bit the inside of her cheek. She felt guilty leaving him, but Adrienne's words were still ringing in her ears. "Are you gonna be okay for breakfast? I can pick up lunch and dinner, but I don't think we have much food in the house."

Luke laughed, but there was the slightest glint of frustration in his eyes, and Margot could tell she was embarrassing him. "How do you think I've been feeding myself before you got here? Anyway, I usually don't eat much in the mornings. If I start to think I'm gonna pass out, I'll walk to . . . to the grocery store for cereal."

Margot's gaze flicked over his face for a moment. She had a feeling that pause meant he'd forgotten the name of Granny's Pantry—the same grocery store he'd been going to for fifty years—but other than that blip, he seemed completely with-it. And she really needed to nail this article. "Okay. Sorry. Yeah, that sounds good."

"So, where're you headed?"

"Well, nowhere yet. I still have some work here to do first." As Adrienne had very clearly pointed out, Natalie Clark was the centerpiece of this story, so Margot needed to prepare for the press conference and interviews in Nappanee before she spent another minute thinking about January Jacobs. "But after that,

Shorty's, I think. I wanna hear what other people say about January's case. See if there's anything that sounds similar to the other one. Do you think I'll be able to get anyone to talk?"

At that, Luke let out a bark of laughter. "There's nothing people here love to do more. But . . . this town crucified the Jacobs family all those years ago and they may not exactly like the way that looks now. So people will talk, sure, but you won't be able to believe a word they say."

FIVE

Krissy, 1994

Krissy no longer felt that she was in her own home. The light inside seemed bright and sterile, the sounds of camera flashes and clipped tones unfamiliar. Even the objects didn't seem to belong to her anymore, and she almost asked permission from Detective Townsend to sit on the couch that had been in her sitting room since before she'd moved in over six years ago.

"Thanks for speaking with me, Mrs. Jacobs," Detective Townsend said when they'd settled across from each other.

After they'd finished in January's room, Detective Townsend had split Krissy and Billy up so they could do their interviews one-on-one. Billy was still up there, in January's room with Detective Lacks, while Krissy and Detective Townsend were back in the sitting room off the entryway, and she was grateful for the change of scenery. Being in her daughter's bedroom earlier, surrounded by all of January's things, had made her panicky and claustrophobic. Also, to Krissy's relief, Detective Townsend had closed the sitting room's French doors, cutting them off from the chaos beyond. All that bustling around and shouting of orders had her twitchy with nerves.

"Why don't we start with this morning," the detective contin-ued. "From the moment you woke up. Could you walk me through that?"

Krissy took a deep breath, a sudden wave of weariness penetrat-ing the constant feed of adrenaline she'd felt since she'd discovered January was gone. The day seemed to be unfurling in fits and starts; sometimes it felt as though time were sped up, other times it dragged like molasses. "Our alarm went off at five, like it always does," she began, and then talked him through the rest of the morning until the moment she and Billy had called the police—walking down the stairs, seeing the writing on the wall, shouting to Billy to come down, Jace running into her arms, searching the house for January.

Townsend was scribbling on a small notepad perched on his knee. When he finished, he looked up at her with sharp eyes. "And what about yesterday? Let's walk through that too. Particu-larly if you can think of anything odd happening in the past twenty-four hours or so."

"Um . . ." Krissy tried to remember what they'd done yesterday. When she couldn't, she tried to recall any errant detail about it—what she'd worn, the weather, what the kids had eaten for breakfast—but her mind was full with images of her daughter dead and discarded somewhere. After a moment, she dropped her face into her hands and pressed her fingers into her eye sockets.

"I know this is difficult," Townsend said, his tone coaxing. He'd softened since his lapse into rudeness upon finding the photo of January in her dance costume, but Krissy suspected that was due more to expedience than to sincerity. "Your mind's going a mil-lion miles a minute, but try to focus. Yesterday was Saturday. Can you remember what you did yesterday?"

Krissy took a breath. "Right. Yes. It was just a regular Saturday. Billy worked. The kids did chores in the morning. They do little things around the farm—feed the chickens, gather eggs. Some-times Billy lets them help with feeding the cows, stuff like that. They played in the house in the afternoon. I cooked and we had dinner. Then we just watched TV and did bedtime. With two young kids, that takes awhile."

Townsend narrowed his eyes. "All right . . . That was good, but would you mind going through it once more for me? This time in more detail? The twenty-four hours before someone goes miss-ing are crucial, and in an investigation like this, you never know what seemingly unimportant detail is gonna help solve the case."

"Oh," she said, feeling chastened. "Right. Sure." She took a deep breath and started again from the beginning, this time in much more detail.

"And after you put the kids to bed?" Townsend asked.

Krissy shrugged. "I took a bath then went to bed. Billy was downstairs watching TV. I was asleep by the time he came up."

"Hm . . ." He tapped the tip of his pen to the page, staring down at it as if trying to work out a particularly tough math prob-lem. But when he spoke again, he'd moved on. "And what about January? What is she like? It probably doesn't sound relevant, but I want to get a sense of the girl we're looking for."

"Right, no, I understand," Krissy said reflexively. "January's . . ."

But her voice caught in her throat before she could finish—saying her daughter's name out loud had finally broken the emo-tional dam inside her. She'd somehow been functioning like a normal human for the past few hours, walking one foot in front of the other, sitting where she was told, speaking in whole, ratio-nal sentences. But she'd felt like a marionette on strings, operating at someone else's command.

She inhaled a shaky breath. Her face felt wobbly with the sud-den emotion as though her features were distorting and melting with it. Through her tear-blurred vision, Krissy saw Detective

Townsend leaning toward her, a tissue in his hand. He always seemed to be doing that—appearing and producing things out of nowhere, like a two-bit magician. She wondered if it was something he'd mastered from years on the job, or if her brain was somehow blinking out, only registering time in scattered snapshots. She took the tissue and wiped her eyes.

"Sorry," she said. "What was I saying?"

"You were going to tell me about January. What she's like."

"Right. Yes. January is . . . She's got a big personality, loves to be the center of attention, in the spotlight. You saw all her dance stuff. She's in classes every Tuesday and Thursday and she loves to show us all the moves she's learned." She shrugged. "She's like I used to be. I was a dancer too."

The moment the words were out of her mouth, she wished she could put them back in. It was an odd thing to say in an interview about your missing daughter. Detective Townsend seemed to think so too, because just before he corrected his face to neutral, he'd raised his eyebrows in what looked like both surprise and disdain.

Krissy continued quickly. "January is very close with Jace too." Again, there was a hint of falseness in her voice she prayed Townsend couldn't hear. "They're twins."

He studied her for a moment before saying, "Twins, huh? That seems like it'd be a special bond."

Krissy shifted. He was looking at her so closely. "It is."

"Well, Officer Jones will be with him today. If he says something, she'll be sure to make a note of it. Sometimes siblings—even young ones—know more than parents do, and any lead we uncover at this point is a lead worth pursuing."

Krissy felt a tightness around her rib cage. She hated the idea of bringing Jace into all of this, but she supposed it was unavoidable. "Of course."

"Speaking of leads," he said. "Is there anyone in your life you'd consider an enemy? Anyone who might have a grudge against your daughter or your family?"

Krissy almost scoffed. "An enemy? No. This is Wakarusa. Everyone here's very . . . close."

"So, no one you can think of who'd write those words on your wall?"

Those words, Krissy thought with a jolt. Somehow, throughout their conversation, she'd forgotten about them. The only logical assumption you could make about them was that they had indeed been written by some sort of "enemy." Krissy took a bolstering breath—this was her opportunity to get the detective on the right track. Everything else was a distraction from those words.

"No one specific comes to mind," she said. "But it was obviously some psycho who wrote it, right? Some sociopath? I mean, those words are not the type you hear every day in this town." She racked her brain for every possible explanation. "What if it's a jealousy thing? Billy's family, well—you're not from around here—but they've always sort of been like royalty. In high school, we used to call Billy the king of Wakarusa. What if someone's jealous of that and wants to—I don't know, make us pay? The Jacobs family has always been so . . . looked-up-to in town. Billy's grandfather donated a ton of money to the town. The school gym's named after him. And he bought up most of the surrounding land, passed it on to Billy's dad when he died."

"I see," Townsend said. "And does Billy's father still own it now?"

"Oh. No. Billy's parents died in a car accident when he was seven. He lived with his grandmother until she died a few years back and he inherited everything."

He nodded, jotted something down.

"And if that's the case," Krissy continued, starting to get on a roll, "they probably want some sort of ransom."

The detective studied her face, then said, "We'll certainly look into it. We have people by the phones, though no one's attempted to make contact. And so far, we haven't found anything to indicate that someone's making demands. But like I said, we'll keep an eye out. Do you have any other theories?"

Krissy looked down at her lap and noticed her hands were knotted tightly together. "I . . . Well, what about the dancing thing? I mean, we take January to competitions. I know she's only six, but they're the real deal. There're judges, contestants from all over the state. There can be seventy-five, a hundred people in the audience. And January's good. You saw it—all those medals."

The detective leaned forward. "So you're saying you think it could be a competition thing? Someone was jealous of your daughter's success?"

"Well, or . . . what if there was someone in the audience who had no business being there? Some of those men . . ." But she couldn't finish the rest of the sentence. Between this and that photo of January in her nautical-themed costume, Krissy felt like the worst mom in the world. *This is what you get.*

"Ah," Townsend said. "I see. You think the performances could have attracted some unwanted attention?"

Krissy hitched a shoulder, unable to look him in the eye, fat tears dropping onto her pajama pants. "I don't know, but what else could explain those words? They're . . . You just don't hear that sort of talk here in Wakarusa."

"So you've said." Magician that he was, Townsend suddenly produced another tissue out of thin air. "Thank you for your thoroughness on this, Mrs. Jacobs. I can assure you we'll look into every possible lead." He slapped his hands on his knees. "Now, Detective Lacks should be wrapping up with your husband and I think it's about time we get you two out of here. Would you like to change clothes? Then she and I will drive you both to the station where we'll do fingerprints and some other logistical stuff.

Officer Jones will meet us there with your son. Hopefully a change of scenery will help shake something loose."

At the state police station in nearby South Bend, a new officer they hadn't met before walked Krissy and Billy through the fingerprinting process, then fixed them each cups of coffee and told them to sit in the uncomfortable metal chairs in the hallway until someone escorted them to wherever they were meant to go next. As they sat, Officer Jones, with the big ears and breasts, appeared through the front door, Jace's small hand swallowed up in hers. At the sight of her son, Krissy felt breathless with nerves. She wanted to tuck him away, to wrap him up and hide him. But she was only allowed a quick hug before he was swept off again for "coloring and maybe even another cookie."

Shortly after, Krissy found herself yet again in a room alone with Detective Townsend, sitting across from him at a rickety metal table. In the center sat an already whirring recorder.

"I'd like to take a few minutes," he said, "to ask about you and Billy."

"Me and Billy?" she repeated. "What does that have to do with the investigation?"

"Well, as you mentioned, whoever wrote those words on the wall could have been motivated by some sort of personal grudge."

"Oh. Right. Of course."

He gave her one of those flat smiles of his that she was beginning to hate. "So how did you two meet?"

She hitched a shoulder. "The same way everyone here meets. We've known each other our whole lives."

"I see . . . And how did you start dating?"

At that, Krissy closed her eyes, and then she was back to the summer of 1987.

That summer began with a party. It was the week after high school graduation, and Krissy's friend Dave had had the idea to throw one on the school's football field. Or not a party exactly, just some beers with friends and whatever "surprise" Dave had promised them.

Billy's arrival that night made Krissy both delighted and shocked. Although she'd invited him earlier that day when he was buying feed from the grain elevator where she worked, she didn't think in the four years they'd been in high school together that she'd ever seen him out before.

"Well, well," Krissy called across the darkened football field when his figure came into view. "If it isn't Billy Jacobs."

Around her, the others turned to look.

"Hey," Billy said once he'd reached their little group. He was a big guy, six feet probably, and muscle-bound from working his family's farm, but as he stood there with his hands shoved deep into the pockets of his Levi's, Krissy thought he looked small and uncertain, almost childlike.

"I can't believe you came," she said, wide-eyed and grinning. "I can't believe I am the siren who lured Billy Jacobs to slum it with the likes of us."

Billy dipped his head, looking bashful and fighting a smile.

"Aw, Kris," Martha said. "Look. You made him blush."

"Marth," Krissy snapped playfully. "Don't make our guest feel unwelcome." She turned back to Billy. "Here." Holding her can of Natural Light in one hand, she used the other to tug a beer from its plastic ring in a half-empty six-pack, then handed it to Billy and looped an arm around his shoulders. "Everybody," she said, turning to the circle. "You all know Billy Jacobs. Billy Jacobs, this is Martha"—she gestured to Martha with her beer—"Zoo, Noah, Caleb, and of course, this asshole is Dave." Krissy knew Billy was already familiar with her friends—they'd all known each other their entire lives—but despite this, he was still little more than a stranger to them.

"Sorry," Billy said, a little frown forming between his eyes. "Zoo?"

"Oh. We call Katy 'Zoo' because of her last name. Zook."

"Oh. But Noah's Noah?"

Krissy laughed. "We just do it when it fits. It's a nickname, Billy, don't overthink it. Anyway, what about you? What should we call you?"

Beside her, Dave squinted, making a show of studying Billy's face. "I think Jacobs is a Jacobs, don't you, Kris?" His eyes slid to hers. "Good work, by the way. You got the fucking king of Wakarusa to deface the field of Northlake High."

Dave reached over to tousle Krissy's hair, and she ducked away from his hand with a shriek, dropping the arm that had been around Billy's neck. "Deface the field?" she said, giving Dave a look.

He grinned. "Surprise."

Krissy rolled her eyes. "So clever." But she said it teasingly. What did she care about this shithole school?

"So," Caleb said, bending over to pull something out of a plastic bag. "I brought spray paint."

"Nah," Dave said. "Spray paint's no good. It washes off too easy." He reached down into another shopping bag by his feet and pulled out an industrial-sized plastic bottle. "Weed killer. That way they basically have to regrow the whole field."

Martha clapped a hand over her mouth. "Oh my god, Dave, that's fucking amazing."

Beside her, Krissy noticed Billy push his hand deeper into his pocket.

"What're you guys gonna write?" Martha asked.

Dave waggled his eyebrows. "We're not gonna write anything. We're gonna draw."

"Cock and balls," Caleb said helpfully.

Everybody laughed, and Krissy watched as Billy made himself laugh too. She had the urge to reach out and squeeze his hand, tell him everything was going to be all right.

"Dave," Caleb said. "You wanna start?"

"And rob you guys of all the fun?" Dave grinned, extending the bottle of weed killer to Caleb, but then he paused, turned. Locking eyes with Billy, he said, "What d'ya think, Jacobs, you wanna do the honors?"

"Oh." Billy laughed, clearly trying to play off his discomfort. "Nah, that's okay. Thanks, though."

Dave jerked his head back. "You sure? No pressure. You don't wanna do it, you don't wanna do it. But it is a good opportunity to give this place one last middle finger."

Billy chuckled uncomfortably again, shaking his head. "I don't think I hated it as much as you guys did."

"Really?" Dave said. His tone was steady and inquisitive, almost thoughtful. "This place that takes everything unique about you and spins it to make you seem fundamentally fucked up?" He shook his head, laughing ruefully. "Jesus, my teachers thought I was a devil worshiper all sophomore year because I listened to Nirvana. People *still* call Martha a slut because she had sex with Robby O'Neil two years ago—"

"Dave!" Martha snapped.

Dave gave her a look. "What? It's fucking true. *I* don't think you're a slut. You get to do whatever the hell you want to do. All I'm sayin' is—this town puts a label on us the day we're born. You remember the time Joseph Pinter called Kris 'white trash' when he found out her and her mom live in a trailer park? And Mr. Yacoubian was standing right there and didn't say anything? He's a teacher and he just let it happen because Joseph Pinter has a white picket fence and Kris doesn't."

Krissy felt Billy's gaze on her face and she lifted her head to meet it. He blinked a few times, then thrust out a hand to Dave. "Sure," he said. "Why not?"

Billy had just finished outlining the left ball, the rest of the group watching from the ground, when Krissy heard the two-note warning siren of a cop car.

"Oh shit," Zoo said, and suddenly they were all clambering to their feet. Martha let out a little shriek that dissolved into giggles and spread among the group. Caleb, who was hammered by this point, tried to stand, but fell backward again with a grunt.

"You guys, get outta here," Dave said, and in his voice was somehow both a laugh and a warning.

Krissy scanned the field for her Converses, which she'd kicked off earlier.

"Here, Jacobs," she heard Dave say as she grabbed her shoes and tugged one on. "Gimme that."

She looked up to watch as Dave extended his hand to Billy. Around them, Martha, Noah, Caleb, and Zoo hurriedly grabbed their things from the ground.

Billy frowned. "What're you gonna do with it?"

Dave nodded to the police car, which had just parked. "They're not even out of the car yet. I have time to finish."

Billy opened his mouth then closed it again, and Krissy suddenly understood what he'd thought was happening. He'd thought Dave—maybe her too, maybe all of them—had set him up, had wanted to watch the king of Wakarusa's fall from grace, had wanted to see his face splashed in the local paper as the perpetrator of what would no doubt be deemed a "tasteless, offensive prank."

"Oh, I get it," Dave said, clearly coming to the same realization. "You thought I was gonna let you take the fall." He clapped a hand on Billy's shoulder, gently prying the bottle of weed killer from his hand. "I may be an asshole, Jacobs, but I'm not that kind of asshole."

Krissy pulled on the heel of her other shoe, then hurried over to slip a hand into Billy's. "Billy," she said, grabbing him to follow. "C'mon. Let's go."

At her touch, he blinked, turned to face her, and tightened his grip around hers. "Let's go."

Krissy, Billy, and the others ran through the darkness, their footfalls stumbling and drunk. Every once in a while, laughter would bubble up in one of them, then spread to another, until they were all bent over with it. Krissy and Billy fell behind the group, but instead of running to catch up, Krissy tugged his arm, pulling him in a different direction. "This way," she whispered, and Billy followed obediently through the darkness. Before long, the sound of the other footsteps disappeared.

When they were alone, Krissy and Billy slowed to a walk. "Where are we?" Billy said.

"At the edge of the Dixon farm. We can hide in the cornfield."

"It's only May. It won't be tall enough."

"It will be if we lie down." She laughed softly, then added, "Such a farmer."

Her hand still firmly in his, she led them into the cornfield, then knelt into the calf-high crop and lay on her back in one of the rows. The ground felt cool through her T-shirt. Billy clumsily followed suit, and when he settled, there was nothing more between them than a single row of corn, a few inches of air. They lay there quietly, catching their breath.

"So," Billy said after a moment. "You're planning on leaving?"

Krissy turned her head to look at him. "Hm?"

"Earlier, at the grain elevator—you said you were leaving."

"Oh. Yeah." That afternoon, when he'd walked in, as she painted her nails behind the cash register, they'd made idle conversation, and she'd mentioned her plans for the end of summer.

"Why?"

"Why?" She laughed. "Why d'you think? We live in *Wakarusa, Indiana.*"

"Right." A smile flashed on and off his face. "So . . . where're you gonna go?"

"New York. Manhattan. I'm gonna be a Rockette." Just the thought of it made her feel brighter.

"What's a Rockette?"

"What's a Rockette?" she said incredulously. "Only the best dancers in New York. The Rockettes are famous. They're on TV all the time. Have you really never heard of them?"

Billy shook his head. "But you're definitely good enough. I still remember how good you danced in the eighth-grade talent show. You were amazing."

Krissy widened her eyes in surprise, then laughed. "Billy, that was *eighth grade*. These are, like, big-time dancers." But even so, the compliment felt warm in her chest. She couldn't believe he'd remembered her dancing from that long ago. "I'm a lot better than I was in eighth grade. Every penny I've ever earned I've spent on dance classes. And I don't go to that rinky-dink little studio downtown for kids. I go to one in South Bend every Tuesday and Thursday night."

"I didn't know that."

She nodded. "Yep." Then she turned her face back to the stars. "Now I just have to save up enough for a bus ride and I'm gone. Well, enough for a bus ride and an apartment and food and stuff." Her voice faded, her smile falling away. Thinking about everything it would take to get out of this place never failed to overwhelm her. But she didn't want to worry about that, not now. She turned back to Billy, propping up the side of her head with her hand. "Anyway," she continued, making her voice bright again. "I'd ask if you were leaving, but I know you're not. Everyone knows Billy Jacobs is to inherit and run the family farm." She said the last words as if she were saying *the royal throne*.

Billy smiled, but it looked soft and almost sad. "No, yeah, I'm not leaving."

Krissy's gaze flicked over his face. "Hey. Eeyore." She had the urge to reach a hand out, to smooth the line that had formed between his brows—so she did. "Don't think about that right now."

Even in the dim light of the moon, Krissy could see his cheeks flush at her touch. And suddenly, she knew that he wanted to kiss her, that he was thinking about doing it. But a few seconds passed and he didn't. "Well," he said, "what *should* I think about?"

"Think about . . ." Her eyes glanced away from his and back again. She couldn't quite tell if she wanted to kiss him, but then, what was the harm in taking both their minds off other things? What was the harm in kissing this boy in a field under the moon? "Think about this," she said, and leaned forward, the leaves of the corn crop brushing against her cheeks. Then she pressed her lips to his.

Krissy couldn't have known then everything that kiss would lead to. If she had, she never would have done it. If she had, she would have run fast in the opposite direction.

In the police station, sitting across from Detective Townsend on the day her daughter disappeared, the memory seemed surreal to Krissy, as if she and Billy had been mere characters in a scene that night, two different people entirely.

"Would you mind if we took a break?" she said. "I need to use the restroom."

Though really, she just needed a minute alone. She'd felt the collective weight of so many sets of eyes on her throughout the day, and she wanted one moment where she wasn't being watched, to relax her shoulders, to exhale.

Townsend gazed at her for an uncomfortably long moment, then, finally, he said, "Be my guest."

Krissy took her time in the bathroom, splashing cool water on her face, but it did nothing to mitigate the way the walls seemed to be closing in around her. So on her way back, when she spotted a set of double doors to the outside, she threw a furtive glance over her shoulder, then hurried toward them.

Outside, the hot July air was a welcome break from the oppressive cold of the station and she gulped it in like she'd been drowning. She slumped against the red brick wall, but just as she did, she realized she wasn't alone after all. A murmur of voices came from around the corner, and although they were talking quietly, Krissy would recognize Detective Townsend's clipped voice anywhere.

". . . think she's hiding something," he was saying, and Krissy's chest clenched. She felt instinctively that he was talking about her. "She's nervous, but it's more than that. Something's up with that family. I just can't put my finger on what it is."

"Seem like a nice Christian family to me," the second voice chimed in. Detective Lacks.

Townsend let out one breath of laughter. "Exactly. But everybody's got something. And back at the house, you should've heard her. Had about a hundred theories about who could've taken her daughter."

"So what?"

"When people start throwing out that many theories at once," Krissy heard Townsend say, "nine times out of ten, it's because they don't want us looking at something else. Like an old-fashioned pickpocket, waving a hand over here just so his target doesn't see that he's robbing him blind."

SIX

Margot, 2019

By the time Margot made it to the state police's press conference on Natalie Clark's disappearance, it had already begun. She tugged the door open, then slipped quietly through, joining the crowd of cameras and news teams positioned in the back of the room. At the front, behind a podium, stood Det. Rhonda Lacks, whom Margot recognized as one of the two original detectives on January's homicide. Separating her from Margot was a sea of press sitting in the section of chairs where Margot should have been, notepads clutched in their hands. She stole a glance at her watch and muttered a curse beneath her breath. She wasn't just late. The conference was halfway over.

She tried to create as little disturbance as possible as she sidled up between two camera guys, but her heart was still racing from sprinting through the parking lot and her whole body was prickling with heat from outside. She plucked her T-shirt with her fingers and surreptitiously blew onto her chest, but as she did, her elbow bumped the man next to her. He shot her a dirty look and she mouthed *Sorry* in return.

Five hours earlier, Margot emerged from her room at Luke's,

ready to head to Shorty's. She'd just spent an hour and a half prepping for interviews in Nappanee and had allotted two more to talk to people in Wakarusa. But when she walked out of her room, she stopped short. Something about the air was off. It was too still, too quiet.

She slid her backpack to the floor, then walked softly to Luke's bedroom in case he was taking a nap, but his door was open and dark, the attached bathroom empty. Back in the hallway, she called his name, her voice echoing loudly around the house. There was no response. "Uncle Luke!" she called again, but still there was nothing. She walked past the empty living room to the kitchen, where she felt idiotic as she turned in a slow circle and opened the pantry.

Margot's heart started to pound, but she didn't even know if her fear was justified. After all, Luke was an adult who, as he'd pointed out that morning, had survived many months by himself. Still, leaving the house without so much as a goodbye wasn't like him. She strode to the door to the garage and flung it wide, breathing in relief at the sight of her uncle's old Pontiac gathering dust. At least that meant he couldn't have made it far. She took a deep breath, trying to calm her nerves. Presumably, he was just on a walk. And yet, these past two days in Wakarusa had shown Margot just how bad things had gotten. What if he had an episode when he was out? What if he lost track of where he was or who he was and was wandering, confused and scared?

She turned on her heel and walked through the hallway to retrieve her cell from her backpack. But when she called him, it rang through to voicemail. She tried again and again, but it just rang and rang.

"Shit," she hissed, rubbing her fingers into her forehead.

She disconnected the call, grabbed her keys from her backpack, and rushed to the front door. The only thing left to do now was look for him.

But Luke wasn't at Granny's Pantry or the pharmacy or Shorty's, and no one she asked in any of those places had seen him. And when she checked the time and saw that she'd been driving around for almost an hour, she began to panic. How far could he have gotten? Did she need to get on the highway and widen her search, or was he simply somewhere she hadn't yet checked? In her car, in the lot outside the grocery store, Margot tried to think of all the places her uncle frequented, but her mind was maddeningly blank. She slammed her palms against the steering wheel. She knew Luke better than anyone in the world, and yet here she was, unable to find him in one of the smallest towns in the country.

From the seat beside her, her phone chimed with an incoming call. Margot sucked in a sharp breath and spun to grab it, her heart leaping to see the Wakarusa area code. Maybe this was Luke borrowing someone else's phone. But when she answered, she didn't recognize the voice on the other end.

"Hi," a man said. "Is this Margot Davies?"

"Yes?"

"Yeah, hi. This is Officer Finch down at the Wakarusa police station. I'm calling because we have your uncle here."

Margot squeezed her eyes shut in both relief and dread. Why was Luke at the police station? "I don't understand. What happened? What did he do?"

"Oh. He's not in trouble or anything. I, uh, found him walking around. He seemed . . . sort of out of it."

Margot sighed. "Shit."

"I was calling to see if you could pick him up. Give him a lift back home. I'd be happy to do it, but he refused to tell me his address, and, well, I think he may respond better to someone he knows."

"Yeah. No. Thank you. I'll be there in five."

The Wakarusa police station fit the town in which it served to a tee. It was small, provincial, and from the look of the faux-wood paneling on the walls and dingy green carpet of the lobby, it was clearly also stuck in the past. The receptionist jotted Margot's name down on a visitor's log, then led her through the door at the edge of the lobby. Margot followed, her heart skittering in her chest. She wished she could somehow anticipate what mood this episode had put her uncle in so she could prepare. Would he be angry, sad? What year would he be in? Would he recognize her face, or would he look at her as if she were a stranger?

"That's Officer Finch," the receptionist said, stopping in the middle of the hallway and nodding to a young man in uniform at the end. He was leaning against the back wall next to a glass door, his arms crossed over his chest, his eyes focused on something through the door beside him. "He'll take it from here." The receptionist waved to catch the officer's attention, then left Margot standing alone.

Officer Finch nodded, pushing off the wall, and strode down the hallway to meet her. "Hi, Margot," he said. "Thanks for coming."

Margot opened her mouth to ask where her uncle was, but stopped before she could. "Oh," she said instead. "It's you." It had been twenty years since she'd last seen him, but the face of the officer had just clicked in her mind. She and Pete Finch had gone to kindergarten through fifth grade together, and while their local high school was relatively big, merging students from Nappanee and Woodview with those from Wakarusa, the elementary school had served only their little town. With all of about twenty-five kids in her grade, Margot would have recognized one of her old classmates anywhere.

Pete smiled. "Been awhile. I heard you were back in town."

"Yeah. Hi."

Despite spending six years corralled in a classroom with him, Margot didn't know the adult version of Pete at all. As a kid, he'd been sporty and popular, while she, in the years after January's death and as her parents' relationship got more and more contentious, had turned inward. Where Pete had played soccer with the rest of the boys at recess, Margot had spent the forty-five minutes by herself in a tree, reading books about kids who solved mysteries. She supposed the two of them must have interacted plenty over the course of those six years, but the only real memory she could dredge up was of him helping her pick up her books one time after Bobby Dacey slapped them out of her hands.

"Good to see you," Margot said, hoping that was enough pleasantry not to appear rude. All she could think about was her uncle huddled in a police room, scared and confused. Meanwhile, if she didn't get him home fast, she was in danger of missing the press conference altogether. "Thanks for picking up my uncle. Is he—?"

"He's in that room back there," Pete said, hooking a thumb over his shoulder. "I was waiting with him, but then it seemed like maybe that was upsetting him."

"How long has he been here?"

"Half an hour maybe? It took me awhile to track down your number. He didn't seem to know it. Eventually, though, I discovered he'd had his phone in his pocket the whole time, and when I got him to pull it out, well, your number was all over it."

Margot thought about the twenty or so times she'd called Luke over the past hour and found it unsettling to discover he'd had his phone with him all along. He must have been more out of it than she'd even realized. "Yeah. I was worried." She glanced down the hallway behind him. "Can I?"

"Of course." Pete turned, and the two of them walked to the room with the glass door.

When she reached it and looked through, her chest clenched. Her uncle was standing against the far wall, but instead of facing outward, he was facing in. His head was bowed, his forehead pressed against the wall, the fingers of one hand wandering gently over its surface. The red bandanna she'd given him, which was tied around his neck, looked damp and filthy. The sight made Margot want to cry.

She took a deep breath, then placed a hand on the handle and twisted. She'd expected Luke to turn at the sound, but instead he remained where he was, unmoving as if he hadn't even heard it. She stepped into the room and walked quietly around the little table and chairs to his side.

"Uncle Luke?" she said gently.

But again, he didn't react, didn't move.

"Uncle Luke?"

Nothing.

She reached out to place a gentle hand on his shoulder and the touch must have snapped him out of whatever dream he'd been in, because he whirled around, flinging his arm out as he did. His hand connected with the side of Margot's mouth and she stepped backward, clapping a hand to her face.

Behind her, she heard the door fly open. "Margot—"

But she waved a hand over her shoulder at Pete. It had obviously been an accident, and her uncle was standing in front of her now like a scared animal, his breath coming in fast pants, his eyes on her face, wide and wild.

Slowly, Margot lowered her hand from her face. "Uncle Luke? It's me, Margot."

Luke stared into her eyes, and after a long moment, his breathing began to calm, his shoulders lowered. "Kid. I didn't do anything, I swear."

"I know."

"This guy just brought me to the station like a criminal." He gestured angrily to Pete, but his movements had lost their urgency and panic. "But I didn't do anything."

"I know," Margot said again. "I know."

He took a deep breath and, finally, it seemed all the paranoia had seeped out of him. "Can I go home now?"

"Yeah. Of course." She nodded, her throat tight. "I'm sorry I didn't check on you earlier."

He must not have registered the last part because he just nodded. "Good, good." He hesitated. "I have to go to the bathroom."

"Okay, yeah." Margot turned. "Pete, could you point us to—"

"Yep," Pete said. "At the end of this hall, to the left." He held the door for them both, pointing her uncle in the right direction.

Margot watched as Luke retreated down the hall and disappeared into the bathroom, then she turned to Pete. "I'm sorry," she said, feeling a kick of betrayal as she did. Luke couldn't help what he did or said. The chemicals in his brain were misfiring. "His sickness can make him act like a totally different person sometimes."

Pete shook his head. "Don't apologize. My grandpa had dementia. I get it."

"Was he angry the whole time? My uncle. Not your grandpa."

"No. He got agitated after a while in that room, thought I was arresting him. But when I found him, he was just upset. Like, sad I mean. He was crying."

Margot swallowed around the tightness in her throat. "Did he say what he was upset about?"

"No. He just kept saying *She's gone. She's gone.*"

"You probably know this, but his wife, my aunt, died last year. What with that and the memory stuff . . . it's been hard."

"Listen . . ." Pete said. "I don't want to overstep or anything, but things with my grandpa got pretty bad. My mom took care of him as long as she could, but it was a full-time job, and even then, it got to be too much. Have you . . ." He hesitated. "Have you thought about putting him somewhere?"

"He's twenty years younger than the youngest person in any nursing home," Margot snapped. "I'm not putting him in one."

Pete nodded, seemingly unfazed. "I get it. Maybe you could

think about a caregiver then. I obviously don't have a dog in this fight, so I'm not trying to convince you of anything, but when my grandpa started wandering out of the house was when things got pretty bad. This was the first time I've seen your uncle out like this, but it probably won't be the last."

"Right," Margot said, but she couldn't look him in the eye. "Okay. Thanks." At the end of the hallway, she saw the bathroom door open. Luke walked out, looking around. She waved to get his attention and he headed over. "By the way," she said to Pete, "where did you find him today?"

"He was on the grass outside Community First, by the cemetery."

Margot sighed. It made sense why Luke had been crying when Pete found him, then. That was the cemetery where her aunt was buried. Why hadn't she thought to look there?

Back at home, Margot kept shooting anxious glances at her watch as she ushered her uncle inside, then heated up two slices of leftover pizza. Technically, it was supposed to be his lunch, but now it was more like an early dinner. She should have already been in Nappanee, working on interviews for her article, and her boss's voice was echoing in her head. *You need to nail this one.*

"Aren't you eating?" Luke asked from where he sat at the kitchen table.

"I have to take off for a bit." Guilt gnawed at her insides. "Are you—is that okay?"

"Yeah, kid. No problem."

"Are you sure? Because I can stay if you need me."

"No, no. I'm probably gonna lie down in a bit anyway. Don't know why, but I'm feeling pretty tired."

She studied his face for a long time before nodding. "Okay. I'll be home in two hours. Tops." But he had already shifted his attention to his food and she couldn't tell whether or not he'd heard her.

At the press conference, Margot tried to focus on Detective Lacks instead of the self-loathing she felt for leaving her ailing uncle only an hour after he'd been picked up by the police.

"We think that is unlikely," the detective was saying to a reporter standing in the third row. "Five is young to run away, and according to her mother, Natalie had no possessions on her while she was playing that morning. Not to mention, she disappeared from a crowded playground, whereas children typically run away from their houses. Furthermore, Mr. and Mrs. Clark could name no reason why Natalie would be motivated to leave on her own."

"So you're saying you believe she was most likely taken against her will?"

"At this moment, we believe that is the most likely explanation." Detective Lacks nodded to another raised hand a few rows back.

A man with unruly black hair stood. "Yeah. Brian Smedley of the *Indiana Statesman*. What do you recommend to other parents in the area? What do they need to be doing to keep their kids safe?"

"This is an area that does not see much crime," Lacks said. "And so far, we have no reason to believe that this is not an isolated event. However, if parents hear their children mention any new names or the presence of a stranger, or if anyone sees any odd or suspicious behavior, please call our tip line. And as a reminder, if anyone out there thinks they know something about Natalie's disappearance, please call." She recited the number, then scanned the room. "We have time for just a few more. Let's get someone in the back . . . yes." She nodded at Margot, whose hand had shot up.

"Hi," she said. "Margot Davies with *IndyNow*. You mentioned that you believe this is an isolated event. Have you looked into a possible connection to the January Jacobs case?"

The sound of the little girl's name made all the heads in the room turn. Up at the podium, Detective Lacks blinked. "The January Jacobs case," she said after a moment, "is almost twenty-five years old. In that one, January's body was found only hours after she was reported missing. The crime scene at her home was . . . extensive. So far, Natalie's case is different in almost every way. So, no, we do not believe there to be any connection between the two."

She turned her head to move on, but Margot said, "Is there enough evidence to preclude a connection completely? After all, January's killer was never apprehended. Is it something you're willing to look into?"

Detective Lack's eyes settled back onto Margot's. "We do not believe," she said in a cool voice, "that there is any connection between the two cases."

There was a look of certainty in the detective's eyes that Margot didn't understand. How could she be so sure, when January's killer had never been caught, when he could still be out there, roaming free? It was perfectly normal for detectives to keep things from the public during an investigation, but they were always up front about it, their speech peppered with *No comment* and *We are not disclosing that at this time*. But this—this sounded more like an evasion, and it gave Margot the distinct feeling that whatever Detective Lacks was hiding had to do with January's case rather than Natalie's. So what did she know that she wasn't saying?

SEVEN

Margot, 2019

Margot was sitting on the pulled-out futon in her uncle's office and talking on the phone with a caregiver agency when another call came through. It was the morning after the press conference on Natalie Clark and Margot had stayed up well past midnight to get her story to the paper in time for publication. Now, her stomach churned from the lack of sleep.

Margot glanced at her phone's screen, and her heart began to pound. Her boss's name had never induced this level of anxiety in her before, but since their call yesterday, Adrienne's words had been echoing ominously in her head. And although she'd done her best to write a compelling story last night, Margot knew it hadn't been her best work.

"Sorry," she said to the woman at the agency who was in the middle of explaining how they could customize their caregiver's visits to fit Margot's schedule. "Something just came up. I'm gonna have to call you later." She switched calls, then pressed the phone back to her ear. "Hey, Adrienne."

"Hi. How're you?"

"Fine." But from just those few words, Margot could tell her boss wasn't calling with good news and she couldn't stomach any small talk. "What's up?"

There was a pause, then, "Margot, I'm so sorry. Edgar took a look at your piece this morning and he wasn't pleased."

Margot closed her eyes. "I know it was a bit rough."

"That's not the point. We told you to cover the Natalie Clark case and you gave us a January Jacobs anniversary piece."

"Wait. But you said a connection would be compelling."

"I also said not to get sidetracked on an embellishment. You didn't have a single quote from someone who lives in Nappanee."

Margot pinched the bridge of her nose and tried to breathe. She hadn't included a quote from any residents of Nappanee because she hadn't made it there in time to interview anyone. But she refused to use her uncle as an excuse. Plus, it didn't matter why she couldn't do her job, just that she couldn't do it.

"And on top of that," Adrienne continued, "the connection was based completely on your own personal hunch. You even have a quote from the lead detective saying there was no basis for one. It read a little accusatory, suggesting the police aren't doing their job properly."

"Well, what if they're not?" Margot snapped. "Isn't that our role as journalists to provide checks and balances?"

"Of course it is," Adrienne said, sounding tired. "But you didn't have enough evidence to prove anything—a connection between the cases or police negligence. You had fifteen hours. Your assignment was a cut-and-dried coverage piece on Natalie Clark's disappearance, not a speculative opus about a case that's twenty-five years old." She took a breath. "I'm not saying you're not good at what you do. You are. And your instincts are usually on point. But I think you're blinded by your relationship to the January Jacobs case. Not every little girl in the Midwest to go missing was taken by the person who killed her."

Margot had to take a deep breath before responding. "You're

right. I get it and . . . I'm sorry. I should've listened to what you asked of me. I'll do better next time. I promise."

"Well. Margot . . . I'm sorry. I thought you understood. There's not going to be a next time."

Margot froze. She opened her mouth, but nothing came out.

"I'm sorry," Adrienne said again. "I thought I made it clear yesterday that this piece was Edgar's test. I've fought hard for you over here, but I also know how much you have going on in your personal life right now, and I really think this is the best thing for you. Take a step away from work, focus on things with your uncle, and get back out there when you're ready."

"You think *firing* me is the best thing for me?"

"I wish I could do more. I do. You're a great reporter and you know how much I care about you, but . . . it *has* been a few months now, and the paper can't afford to pay a salary to a writer who's not producing consistent work."

A stab of humiliation cut through Margot's anger. "Right." Her throat was so tight the word was almost indiscernible.

"I'm really sorry—"

But Margot had had enough. "I should get going."

"I—" Adrienne let out a heavy sigh. "Okay, Margot. Take care."

When she hung up, Margot hurled her phone across the room, where it bounced against the carpeted floor. She grabbed her pillow, pressed it to her face, and screamed.

She couldn't believe this was happening. Ever since she was young, before high school even, Margot had known she wanted to be a reporter. Since before she could remember, she'd felt compelled to understand things, to research them, dissect them, then turn them into something comprehensible. And even though *IndyNow* didn't have the budget for the level of investigative work she wanted to do, even though they prioritized quick turnover and easily digestible stories over asking questions and digging in, it was a good paper, and until now, they'd always supported her.

But more than the loss of the career she'd worked toward her entire life, what worried her most was the loss of the paycheck. If this had happened a year ago, it would have been devastating, but survivable. She'd live off her savings and ramen until she found the next best step. But she couldn't afford not to work now—not when she was supporting her uncle as well as herself. Although his house was paid off, she was still paying her rent in Indianapolis until her subletter moved in, the date of which he had yet to confirm. Meanwhile, she didn't want to use Luke's credit card for anything until she had a better idea of his finances. So she was paying for his exorbitantly priced medications, food for them both, all their utility bills when those came in, and now, possibly an in-home caregiver whose price had given her heart palpitations when she'd heard it over the phone. What the fuck was she going to do?

A knock on the door brought her out of her thoughts.

"Kid?" Luke called. "Can I come in?"

Margot pulled her face out of the pillow. "Just a second!"

She hastily wiped the tears from her face, and as she did, she noticed a sharp stinging in both her palms. She looked down at them to find bright red indentations scattered among the little half-moon scars. Apparently, she'd been digging her nails into her skin. She dropped her hands and looked away. She hadn't done that in a long time. Taking a breath, she tucked her hair behind her ears, stood, and walked to the door.

When she opened it, she could tell immediately that something was wrong. Her uncle's face was clear and lucid, but his eyes were worried. "There's something you should see."

Margot followed him into the living room, where the TV was on and tuned to the news. Two anchors, one man, one woman, were looking into the camera.

". . . was discovered early this morning by an employee of Billy Jacobs," the man was saying. Margot's stomach lurched at the name, and she took an involuntary step closer to the screen. "Apparently, Mr. Jacobs was away at a farming equipment convention these past few days, and when he returned this morning, his employee told him there was something he needed to see, a message written on the side of the Jacobses' barn."

As he said this, the screen filled with a photograph of a scene Margot knew well. It was the view she'd had from her childhood bedroom window, the big red barn in the yard across the street. Only now, it was marred by words scrawled in black spray paint. The sight of them sent a shiver up her spine.

"Holy shit."

Margot stared at the photo on the TV, her heart thumping so hard she could feel it against her ribs. She felt paralyzed, unable to move or even think. Finally, after a long moment, she snuck a glance at her uncle. What would this do to his already fragile state of mind? The news of Natalie Clark's disappearance two days ago had unraveled him, and this was far closer to home than the little girl of Nappanee.

Margot breathed a sigh of relief when she saw him. He looked concerned—his arms crossed over his chest, his chin dipped in concentration, a hard line between his eyes—but he was very much in control.

"Hey, Uncle Luke?"

He turned his head to look at her.

"I'm gonna go to the grocery store."

To Margot's surprise, this elicited a wry grin. "The grocery story, huh? Is that what they're calling crime scenes these days?"

Despite everything that was spinning out of control around her, despite the rawness she felt from losing her job and the anxiety bubbling inside her from those ominous words on the barn, Mar-

got laughed. Her uncle's illness had a way of making her appreciate him more. Every joke, every glimpse of the man he used to be,
was a little treasure she wanted to hold in her hands. And he was
right, of course. She may have just gotten fired from her job as a
reporter, but this was a potential development in a twenty-five-
year-old murder investigation. And it had happened less than half
a mile from where they now stood. She wouldn't be able to stay
away if she tried. She had a fatalistic way of coming back to January Jacobs, again and again.

"Okay," she said, "you caught me. I'll probably swing by the
Jacobs place on my way home. But I am going to the grocery
store. For real. I want to eat three square meals that are not all
takeout for at least one day. Are you . . . are you gonna be okay
for a bit?"

There was a rare flicker of annoyance in his eyes. "I don't need
a babysitter, kid."

"Right." It was the same thing he'd told her yesterday, only
hours before Pete Finch had found him wandering outside the
cemetery. Though in this moment, she believed him. In her past
few days here, she'd begun to get a feel for his rhythms, and it
seemed he was the most lucid in the mornings. "I'll have my
phone," she said. "Call me if you need me."

She grabbed her backpack, phone, and keys from her room,
then headed for the front door. As she closed it behind her, she
threw one last glance at Luke, but his attention was back on the
TV, his face lined with worry once again.

They'd had a rare summer storm the night before; the town was
still wet, and Margot drove slowly. As she drew nearer to the road
on which she grew up, her palms began to prickle with nerves.
All her memories of the place were tainted by January's death, and

now it was a crime scene yet again. The words that had appeared on the Jacobs barn overnight echoed in her head.

As Margot turned onto the road, she was relieved to see it hadn't transformed into a media circus. There were a handful of bare-bone news crews there, but it was by no means the mob she knew it had been twenty-five years ago. No doubt all the reporters within a twenty-mile radius were in Nappanee, too preoccupied hounding Natalie Clark's family and Detective Lacks's team to detour here for a few words on a barn.

She pulled to the side of the road, parking behind a van with a large satellite affixed to its roof. Through her car window, she gazed at her childhood home, the small two-story across the street, and realized she hadn't been back in two decades. On the rare occasion she day-tripped to Wakarusa in the intervening years, she'd only ever gone to her aunt and uncle's place. After all, that house, not this one, was where she'd spent most of her childhood. Now, her eyes flicked to the little round window at the top—her old bedroom—and for the millionth time, she imagined a faceless man standing in the middle of the street, his gaze oscillating between that window and January's, then making a choice.

As she walked on the rain-slicked pavement to the Jacobs driveway, Margot tried to look past it to the barn, but the view was blocked by a line of lush green trees growing on both sides of the drive, so dense they created a wall. Billy must have planted them after January's death, because Margot didn't remember them from her childhood. A yellow line of caution tape had been pulled across the mouth of the driveway, and standing in front of it were two uniformed police officers. Though they had their backs to her, she could tell they were both men with brown hair, and like the rest of the population in Wakarusa, both were white. As she approached, she could tell the shorter of the two was clearly in the middle of telling some story, but at the sound of her footsteps, they turned.

"No media beyond this point," the short one said.

But Margot wasn't looking at him. "Hi," she said to the other officer.

Pete grinned. "We have to stop meeting like this." He turned to his partner and said, "This is Margot Davies."

The short officer looked to be a few years younger than the two of them, and he clearly didn't know or care about the older generation's gossip, because he greeted her blandly, then got distracted by something over her shoulder, and with a quick nod to them both, made his way over.

"Are you covering this now too?" Pete said.

"I was going to, but it looks like you aren't gonna let me." Her eyes darted to the caution tape drawn across the driveway entrance.

"Well, it is a crime scene, so we're treating it accordingly. But between you and me, this won't be here for long. I think my supervisor's just being extra cautious because . . . you know. This *is* the Jacobs place."

Margot raised her eyebrows. "That's all this is—extra caution?"

"As opposed to . . . ?"

"Wait. Are you saying the police don't think this barn note is connected to January's murder? They don't think the timing means it's connected to the disappearance of Natalie Clark?"

"Well, Wakarusa PD has nothing to do with the Clark girl's investigation, but the state police just issued a statement saying this message has nothing to do with it. As far as January's case goes"—he shrugged—"no. Our department is treating this as vandalism."

Those spray-painted words appeared in Margot's head, and she gave Pete a disbelieving look. "But this message—I mean, don't you think whoever wrote it was talking about Natalie? And why would it have been written here if they weren't also referring to January?"

"Well, sure, I think that's what this asshole was going for, but so far there's no reason to think it's anything but a hoax."

"A hoax? You think this is a hoax?"

"I'm just repeating our official stance. That's all."

She gave him a look.

"What?"

"I don't think this town's gonna buy it. I think you're gonna have a mob on your hands. I mean, I was at Shorty's for five minutes the other day and I know everyone here believes that whoever kidnapped Natalie Clark also killed January. I'd bet you anything they're gonna think this barn note was written by the same guy."

This time, Pete was the one who looked skeptical.

"What?" she said. "I heard them talking. Linda, the bartender, told me to my face she thinks January's killer is back. You think they're all lying?"

"No." He shook his head good-naturedly. "It's just that, well, people in this town can get caught up in January's memory. It's a compulsion, talking about it. But people here turned on the Jacobs family a long time ago for what happened to January and I think once some time passes, folks will find their way back to that."

Margot's eyes flicked over his face, the word *compulsion* settling uncomfortably in her stomach. "Interesting theory."

"You think I'm wrong?"

She shook her head. "I don't know what I think." But as she looked around at the very place she used to call home, the words on the barn flashing in her mind, the tail of yellow caution tape flapping in the wind, Margot knew one thing for sure. She did not think this was a hoax.

The moment she was back in her car, Margot pulled her phone out of her backpack pocket, opened her banking app, and logged in to her account. For a long moment, she stared at the number in her savings, trying to calculate how quickly she would go through it without a steady paycheck. Though it wasn't a completely anemic amount—she'd done her best to save over the years—with all her extra expenses and no money coming in, it wouldn't last long.

"Two weeks," she said aloud. She'd give herself two weeks to research and write this article. If this story was as big as she thought it was, her byline beneath it would be enough to get her old job back. Or, she thought, suddenly feeling excited, it could help her win a new job at a bigger paper, one that valued thoughtful work and supported its writers. Two weeks was far longer than she'd ever had at *IndyNow*, and if she couldn't get it done by then, she'd ask Linda for a waitressing gig at Shorty's until she could find something else. If she could break this story, she didn't care what she had to do after. Because in her bones, Margot knew the state police were wrong. The local police were wrong. Pete Finch was wrong. In a town eight miles away, a little girl went missing, and less than twenty-four hours after the press conference covering her case, a message appeared on the Jacobs family barn. Maybe the age of the two victims and the close proximity of their hometowns could be construed as coincidence, but the timing of this barn message could not. Someone was trying to connect January Jacobs with Natalie Clark, and Margot was going to figure out why.

She turned her key in the ignition and looked toward the Jacobs yard one last time. Though she could only see the pitched roof of the barn above the line of trees, she could see the spray-painted words clearly in her mind: *She will not be the last.*

EIGHT

Margot, 2019

When Margot walked into Shorty's later that Saturday morning, it looked almost unrecognizable as the place she'd been two nights previous. In the daylight, she could see that all its surfaces, from its dingy carpet to the faux-wood-paneled walls, seemed to be sticky with beer. Dust particles floated lazily in the air. And far from the bustling hub of action it had been the other evening, now it was completely devoid of customers. The only thing that was the same was Linda behind the bar.

"Hi, Margot," Linda said. There was an eager glint in her eye, which Margot attributed to her own newcomer status—newcomers were always potential sources of gossip in Wakarusa—but then Linda continued. "Have you heard about what was written on the Jacobs barn?"

Margot nodded. "I have."

"It's horrible, isn't it?"

"It is, yeah. Actually, that's sort of why I'm here. I was hoping to do some interviews about it. But . . ." Margot glanced around at the empty tables. Two nights ago, she'd gauged the place's vibe as the town's go-to for gossip, where people went to talk when there was news. But maybe she'd been wrong. If so, she wasn't going to waste time away from her uncle to sit alone in a restaurant. She'd swung by his house to check in after visiting the Jacobs place earlier and he'd seemed completely fine, but losing him yesterday had her rattled. If she was going to finish this story by her self-imposed two-week deadline and also manage to help Luke around the house, she needed to be smart with her time. "Where is everybody?"

"Church, honey," Linda said with a look that told Margot it was a dumb question.

"Church? But it's Saturday."

"They got some event going like they always do. Think it's a midsummer something or other. *That's* where everybody is. Or, should I say, no one's willing to show their face at a bar until the church thing is over." She glanced at her wristwatch. "But folks will be here soon. They always come here to drink after that kind of thing. In about ten minutes, you'll be lucky to get a table."

"Guess I'll have to grab one now then."

Linda swept an arm around the room. "Sit wherever you like."

Margot made her way to the far side of the restaurant and settled at a table sandwiched between a dartboard and a cardboard cutout of a Miller Lite bottle that was taller than she was. Linda finished filling a plastic caddy with napkins and maraschino cherries, then strode over. She handed Margot a sticky plastic menu, but Margot put it down in front of her without looking at it.

"I'm gonna get something to go later for me and Luke," she said. "But for now, I'll just have a cup of coffee."

"How is Luke, by the way?" Linda said. "There was so much going on the other night, I didn't get a chance to ask you."

"He's good," Margot said automatically. She wasn't sure how much people already knew about his diagnosis, but the look of curiosity in Linda's eye bordered on hunger, and Margot had the sudden, uncomfortable sensation of agreeing with her mom—it was none of their fucking business. "He's great. Anyway, Linda, I've been thinking about what you said the other night. That Natalie Clark was taken by the same person who killed January. Do you really believe that?"

"Well, of course I do. We're only big enough for one child-napper round these parts."

Margot leaned over to grab her notepad and phone from her bag. "Do you have a few minutes to talk? And would you mind if I record?"

Linda's eyebrows shot high on her forehead. Then, just as quickly, her face corrected, her back straightened, and she dipped her chin in a magnanimous gesture. "Not at all." In the briefest of moments, she'd gone from surprised at the invitation for an interview to regally accepting it, as if she'd been patiently sitting by all day just for someone to ask her.

"Thanks." Margot smiled as Linda settled in the chair across from her. "So you believe whoever killed January also took Natalie Clark. And what about this note on the Jacobs barn? Any ideas about who wrote it?"

"It's all the same guy, isn't it? He kills one little girl, takes another, and now he's trying to terrorize *us*, the whole town. It's what everybody's saying. That this is January's murderer, come back again."

"Let's talk about January's case," Margot said. "What can you tell me about the Jacobs family? What were they like back then?"

"Well, before everything happened, the Jacobses were like royalty around here. Billy and Krissy were ten years older'n me or so, so I didn't know them in school or nothing, but I knew them because everybody knew them. They owned basically the whole town, and both Krissy and Billy were so attractive, you know? Billy with his golden hair and all those muscles? And Krissy, well, she was a knockout, pure and simple." Linda made a little sound in her throat for emphasis. "They were basically the all-American family, walking around with those adorable twins. Bless Jace's heart, but the town's jewel was really January. Whenever she'd go off to one of her competitions, the dance studio would make a banner and hang it right in the town square to wish her luck. When she was found in that ditch"—Linda shook her head— "a little bit of all of us died with her."

"What was it like in the days after she was found?" Margot asked. From her experience, interviews worked best when the subject steered the conversation, so she was content to follow Linda's train of thought wherever she went.

"At first, we all rallied behind them like you wouldn't believe. I bet they had enough casseroles to last a lifetime. Their front stoop turned into a January shrine—flowers, balloons, framed pictures of her. I brought a teddy bear because I thought, you know, it'd be nice for her to have, wherever she'd gone."

Linda's eyes grew glassy. Too-early deaths did that to people. They didn't just rob children of their lives; they robbed them of their futures. Alive, they could grow up to become famous dancers or hard-hitting reporters. Dead, they turned into nothing but lost potential.

"But it wasn't long before the town turned on them," Linda went on. "And it all started when they went on TV. Krissy was— well, I'm sorry, but she was just not acting normal, not like a grieving mother. She would just stare off into space, her knuckles white on little Jace's shoulder. And then people started to talk. Krissy always wanted to be a dancer—that was no secret—and here her little girl was winning competitions at the age of six. She was more successful than Krissy had ever been or would ever be. At the rate she was going, January could've been famous. And everyone knows jealousy is a powerful motivator. So that's when people around here started to be not so nice to them."

"Sorry," Margot said, "but it kind of sounds like you think *Krissy* killed January."

"Oh!" Linda's eyebrows shot up high on her forehead. "Gosh. No. *I* don't think Krissy killed her little girl. I'm just saying what people were thinking back then. Isn't that what you asked? *I* think whoever took little Natalie Clark took January too. It's what I've always thought, that she was killed by some . . . *intruder*. Some bad man traveling through."

Margot had to fight to keep her face neutral. It was revisionist history at its most clumsy. Luke had been right the other morning. The locals had turned on the Jacobs family and now were feeling guilty.

Linda continued. "I mean, why else would there've been all that broken glass?"

Despite the jump in topic, Margot understood what Linda was talking about: the supposed way the intruder had come into the Jacobs house. When the police visited their home on the morning of January's disappearance, they'd found one of the basement windows smashed in, glass littering the floor.

"I think," Linda said, "an intruder punched in that window, came in through the basement, and grabbed January from her bed. I don't know what he's been doing in the meantime, but by the looks of it, now he's back."

Just then, the front door opened and both women turned to watch a family of four walk in. Behind them was a train of others. Linda had not been exaggerating about the after-church-event swarm. "Shoot," she said. "It's time."

Margot nodded. "Right, of course. Thank you." Linda got up and started walking toward the front, but turned when Margot called her back. "Hey, Linda, would you mind spreading the word about what I'm doing? That I'm a reporter and if anyone wants to talk, they can find me here?"

Linda grinned, and Margot could tell she'd won the waitress over. In her experience, everyone wanted the same thing: someone to listen while they talked. "Sure thing, hon," Linda said, and just before she turned back to the front, she threw Margot a wink.

Word quickly got around that the Davies girl, a reporter from Indianapolis, was in town conducting interviews about the Natalie Clark and January Jacobs cases. And just as Linda had said, all the locals seemed to believe the perpetrator of both crimes was one and the same. Subsequently, they also believed the Jacobs family was innocent. Within twenty-four hours, the sentiment of the town seemed to have done a one-eighty. But it also seemed this change of heart had been so swift that people were having a hard time keeping up. Like Linda, even as they voiced their new-found support of the Jacobses, they still managed to cast suspicion on them—or rather, on Krissy. Though both Luke and Pete had said the town had turned on the entire Jacobs family, it seemed to Margot most of their ill will now was targeted at January's mom.

"Krissy was undeniably jealous of January," one woman told Margot. "Because of her dance stuff and all the attention people lavished on her. But of course, I don't think she'd ever *murder* because of that."

"Krissy *was* jealous of January," the town's butcher agreed. "But it wasn't because of dance. She couldn't handle knowing that Billy loved January more than he loved her. So people used to suspect that had something to do with the murder. But of course, now they know better."

"Billy and Krissy got married when they were eighteen," said one woman whom Linda introduced as her best friend. "And January and Jace came along not much later. Could've been nine months, but I wouldn't be surprised if it was less. They were babies raising babies! And Krissy couldn't handle a family. So some people thought that maybe, you know, she murdered January to escape motherhood, but chickened out before she could get to Jace."

"Krissy was absolutely an unfit mother," the Sunday school teacher told her. "Just look at Jace—*always* getting in trouble. I don't think that had anything to do with poor January's death, but I do think you should know the full picture."

After she'd thanked the teacher for her time, Margot finished jotting down a few notes, headed to the bar to place her to-go order for lunch, then slipped out the door. The bright light outside was a sharp contrast to the dim interior of the restaurant, and she leaned back against the front of the building, rubbing her eyes. When she opened them again, a movement—a figure across the street—caught her gaze. It was a woman, in a white T-shirt and loose-fitting jeans, probably in her midforties with what looked to be dyed auburn hair. It hung lanky and unwashed over her shoulders. Something about the way she darted her gaze away from Margot's made the hair on Margot's arms stand up. Had she been watching her?

Before she had a chance to do anything, though, the door to Shorty's opened and Linda poked her head out. "Margot—oh sorry, hon, didn't mean to scare you," she said when Margot jumped. "Just wanted to let you know your food's ready."

"Thanks," Margot said hastily, desperate to return her gaze across the street. "I'll be in in a sec."

Linda disappeared inside, and Margot turned back to where she'd caught the woman watching her. But the woman had vanished.

NINE

Krissy, 1994

Krissy paced the small room at the police station while Detective Lacks sat by the rickety metal table and pretended not to be keeping an eye on her. In front of the detective were two un-touched Styrofoam cups of coffee, damp napkins curling around their bases, a token offering of comfort while they waited.

Half an hour earlier, Krissy had been telling the detective her most concrete theory about what had happened to January. She knew, after overhearing Lacks and Townsend outside, that she needed to narrow her focus to just one, and when she thought of the broken basement window and those unnerving words on her kitchen walls, the most obvious explanation in her mind was that it had all been done by an intruder with a personal connection to her daughter. An unstable, lecherous man who took whatever he wanted—*that's* what Krissy would think if she were a detective on the case. She put together a list of faces in her mind, cataloging all the men she'd ever been wary of at January's dance competitions: one man, who wore polo shirts buttoned to his neck and watched the performances with a wolfish look in his eyes; another guy, junkie skinny and balding, who hung around the hallways where the girls flitted between performances. Krissy wanted them arrested, interrogated with a taser.

Halfway through the interview, though, Townsend interrupted with the announcement that their team had found the dead body of a little girl, discarded in a ditch less than two miles from their home. The detective had escorted Billy to the morgue to identify the body, but Krissy knew this was a mere formality. She knew, deep in her bones, that the little girl was January. Of course it was; they lived in a town of less than two thousand people and January was the only one who was missing.

A sudden movement from beyond the window caught Krissy's attention and she watched as Detective Townsend and Billy appeared through the glass double doors of the police station. Sure enough, in the moment she saw her husband—his eyes red-rimmed, his body strangely slack—Krissy knew she'd been right.

And yet, the confirmation of it still felt like she'd been shot in the stomach. Disjointed thoughts tumbled through her brain. *Not my baby.* And *Where's Jace?* And *I need to act how they expect me to act.* Then Townsend and Billy were in the room with them and Townsend's mouth was moving, but Krissy couldn't make out what he was saying. Her body was thrumming, the edges of her vision beginning to blur and blacken. Suddenly, the two detectives were beside her, Townsend pulling out a chair, Lacks's hands on her elbows as she guided her into it. In the moment the detectives were distracted, Krissy lifted her eyes to meet her husband's and saw that Billy was gazing down at her with—what? Fear? Disgust? It crawled up her back like spiders. And then it was gone. She slumped into the chair and buried her face in her hands.

"Mrs. Jacobs, Mr. Jacobs," Krissy heard Detective Townsend say. She blinked and realized some time had passed. Billy was now sitting next to her. In front of them were two untouched cups of what looked like tea. Her body, Krissy noticed, felt a little steadier. She forced herself to look at the detective.

"We're very sorry for your loss," he continued, his gaze flicking between Krissy and Billy. Neither spoke, neither met his eye.

"With this development," he continued, his tone matter-of-fact, as if finding the dead body of their daughter in a ditch was in fact a mere "development," "as you can imagine, the investigation has shifted. We'll loop in a few more detectives from State, but Detective Lacks and I will continue to take the lead here. We're gonna do everything in our power to find whoever did this." He paused a moment, letting his words sink in. "We're going to need your full cooperation for the next few weeks or so, but for now"—he glanced at his wristwatch—"you two have had a long day. Detective Lacks will escort you both to your house to pack a bag, and then she'll take you to a hotel for the night, okay?"

Krissy frowned. As everything else had that day, this moment seemed to be happening too quickly. They'd just found January's body at the bottom of a ditch and now they were telling her to pack a bag? It seemed Billy was as lost as she was, because, rubbing one temple, he said, "I don't understand. Pack a bag?"

Townsend looked at him. "Your house is a crime scene, Mr. Jacobs. We'll expedite things as best we can, but you three won't be able to stay there until tomorrow at the earliest."

It was then, at *you three,* that Krissy remembered Jace. Fear sliced through her stomach. What would he do when they told him his twin sister was dead? "Where's Jace?"

"He's still with Officer Jones," Lacks said. "Would you guys like to see him now?"

"No." Krissy realized she must've said it too quickly, because all the heads in the room turned to her. "I don't want to tell him yet. I think it'd be better if we told him in the hotel. Away from . . ." She looked around. "All this."

Detective Lacks nodded. "Of course. You can pack a bag for him too, and I'll tell Officer Jones to meet us at the hotel. Sound good?"

In her mind, Krissy reached out and slapped the detective hard. *No, Detective Lacks,* she wanted to scream. *My daughter is dead. Nothing sounds good. Nothing will ever sound good again.*

As her mind spun with the impossibility of what was happening, Krissy had the strange sensation that the last seven years of her life had been a mere fever dream. That she'd gasp in a breath and suddenly she'd be eighteen again, back to the summer of '87, before everything had changed, before everything had gone so terribly wrong.

With Billy and Dave by her side, Krissy spent the summer after high school in a blur of shimmering nights. All June and July, they drove around in Dave's car, stole six-packs from garages, and met up with people from school to drink warm beer in abandoned barns outside town. Every once in a while, when there were no other plans, Krissy would sneak onto Billy's farm, and they'd have sex in the hayloft or skinny-dip in the pond under the stars.

But then, in August, Krissy took a test and everything changed.

"So . . ." Billy said, and Krissy could hear the nerves fluttering in his voice. "How're you feeling?" It was four days after she'd told him the news and they were sitting together on the bench by the pond, a full moon glowing above them. "Do you have any motion sickness?"

Krissy snapped her head to look at him. "You mean morning sickness."

"Right. Yeah."

She turned back to the pond and stared blankly into its dark water. "Billy, I don't know what to do."

"Do about what?"

She hesitated. The words she needed to say felt like stones in her mouth. "Money. I don't know what to do about money."

"Oh, that." He sounded relieved. "Krissy—don't worry about that. You don't have to worry about that."

She turned her head to look him full in the face. "Really?"

He hitched a shoulder. "Of course. I mean, maybe you could help out with the books or something—" She frowned. *The books?* But before she could say anything, he rushed to finish. "But you don't have to, of course." He let out a little laugh. "We're gonna be fine. You can do whatever you wanna do."

Her eyes held his, searching for that previous hint of hesitation. But he was smiling, broad and easy. She exhaled, her shoulders sagging, her head sinking into one of her hands. "Thank you," she said in a small voice. "I just . . . I've been saving all summer but I don't have enough. Not for this and for New York too."

Next to her, Billy grew still, and when he spoke again, it sounded as if he were choosing his words very carefully. "Well, Kris, the only reason we'd have money is because of the farm." Krissy blinked her eyes open, then slowly lifted her head from her hand. "I mean," he said. "I know you wanted to go to New York, but I can't leave. Not now anyway. But, Kris, I promise, if we stay here, I'll take care of you. And we'll go to New York someday. We'll stay in a fancy hotel and see the Rockettes."

"Billy," she said after a moment. "What're you talking about?"

"I— What'd you mean? I'm talking about our future. I just don't want you to get all worked up about money right now. We'll be fine. We'll be okay."

She shook her head. "Wait. Are you saying you wanna have this baby? You wanna—get married?"

Billy gave her a look. "Well . . . yeah. Kris, you—you're *pregnant.*"

And then suddenly he was digging a hand into the pocket of his Levi's and Krissy was watching, heart thumping hard in her chest. He stood from the bench, turned to face her, and knelt ceremoniously onto one knee. He lifted his hand and she saw a delicate ring pressed between his thick, calloused fingers. In the center of the gold band was one small, square diamond. Krissy had the sudden sensation of being trapped in a whirling tornado, too fast and strong for her to fight.

"Krissy Winter," Billy said, swallowing thickly. "Would you do me the honor of becoming my wife?"

In the moonlight, the diamond glinted, and Krissy stared down at it for a very long time. She knew the ring was a tether, forever binding her to this man she was just now realizing she hardly knew. But it was also a ticket to so much more. This ring could open up her world in ways she'd only ever imagined. It would mean, for the first time in her life, that she could stop worrying about money, that she could stop fighting so fucking hard for everything. It would mean, for the first time in her life, she might finally be able to exhale.

Just before she opened her mouth and said yes, Krissy made a silent promise. If Billy hadn't understood that what she'd come here tonight for was money for an abortion, she wouldn't tell him. Nor would she tell him the other thing. The cost of this marriage, she knew, would be keeping those secrets. She just hoped it would be worth it.

As Krissy followed Billy and Detective Lacks into their house, she thought back on that moment by the pond, the moment that changed everything. For seven years, she had kept that promise to herself, holding her secrets tight inside her. Now, the stakes were higher and she had so much more to hide.

She, Billy, and the detective moved through their home in a serpentine route, skirting around strangers photographing and labeling, bent over clipboards of notes and crouched by floorboards, their gloved hands efficient and meticulous. As their trio passed, each crime scene worker looked up then down, their expressions unnervingly blank, as if they'd been trained to pretend the inhabitants of the house were invisible. Krissy felt like a ghost.

They made their way into the kitchen, past those words, and up the stairs, Billy like an obedient dog at Lacks's heels. When Krissy joined them at the top of the landing, she stole a glance at her husband's face, but he avoided her eye. What was he thinking? she wondered. What was going on in his brain?

"Okay, you two," Detective Lacks said. "Let's do this quickly so we can get you out of here." She glanced around the hall and open doorways, her eyes landing on a nearby officer who was sticking orange Post-it notes around January's room. "Ah, Tommy. Could I get a hand?"

The uniformed officer, who was crouching at eye level with January's vanity, turned his face to look at them. "Sure thing, Detective." He stood and strode over.

He was probably only a few years older than Krissy, with acne scars on his cheeks, and he had the same detached look as all the others, his eye contact flat and unfeeling. Krissy was sick of all these people treating the death of her daughter like a Tuesday at the office. "Tommy," Detective Lacks said. "Why don't you escort Mr. Jacobs while he packs a bag for him and his wife. I'm gonna take Mrs. Jacobs to get some things for their son."

Billy's eyes snapped to Lacks, looking panicked. "I don't know what to pack for her," he said as if Krissy weren't standing right beside him.

Lacks reached out a hand and clapped him lightly on the shoulder. "You'll figure it out. Just try not to touch anything you don't need to touch."

This send-off clearly made Billy more nervous, but he swallowed, nodded, and followed the young officer down the hallway to their bedroom.

He, Krissy, and Detective Lacks were in and out and at the

Hillside Inn in Nappanee, overnight bags in tow, in under half an hour. At the sight of the hotel, Krissy felt a bitter laugh bubble at the base of her throat. The exterior was painted red with white wooden crossbeams, making it look like an oversized, bizarrely shaped barn; no matter how hard she tried, no matter what she did, she seemed to be doomed to the farming life.

Inside, as Detective Lacks checked them in, Krissy registered random details. Two clocks hung on the wall, one labeled Nappanee, the other inexplicably France. A terra-cotta pot on the front desk was filled with cheap pens, plastic flowers adjoined to their ends with thick tape. Next to it was a little red barn.

Lacks handed them each a plastic key card, then led them to their room on the second floor, stopping abruptly outside a door with brass numbers that read 218. Krissy could feel Billy's gaze on her, but when she turned to look at him, he averted his eyes. Why did he keep doing that?

"I made sure there was a second bed for Jace," Detective Lacks was saying.

Billy nodded. "Thank you."

"Detective Townsend and I will be in touch tomorrow, but feel free to call us if you need anything or if anything comes to mind."

Billy gave Lacks an obsequious smile and then, as if he couldn't help it, he shot Krissy another look she couldn't read: Was it fear in his eyes? Paranoia? Was there some hidden message in his expression or was he trying to find one in hers? "Thank you, Detective Lacks," he said. "We appreciate everything you've done for us."

Krissy wanted them both to just shut up. She wanted to punch, to hit, to shred something with her bare hands.

"I want to warn you two," Lacks said, "that tomorrow could be a bit . . . chaotic. The press will've gotten wind of everything by now and—"

But Krissy had had enough. Billy's gaze and Lacks's voice felt like fingernails clawing at her skin. "Detective Lacks," she interrupted in a tight voice. "My daughter died today. My house is crawling with strangers and I haven't seen my six-year-old son in hours. I can't think about whatever it is that you're saying. So can you *please just leave*?"

Detective Lacks's face remained neutral, seemingly unfazed by this outburst.

Billy, on the other hand, began to bubble with apologies. "I'm so sorry, Detective Lacks," he stammered. "My wife is upset. She doesn't mean to be rude."

Lacks gave him a perfunctory smile. "No need to apologize. You've both had a long day. Try to get some sleep. I'm afraid tomorrow's going to be just as bad." With that, she gave them a nod and turned on her heel.

It took Krissy four tries to get the key card into the slot, but finally the door swung open and she stumbled through. The moment the door clicked behind them, Billy grabbed her shoulder, his fingers digging in hard. He spun her around to face him. "Krissy, what the hell," he spat. His voice was shaking. "You shouldn't do that."

Krissy brushed his hand off and strode to the other side of the room, throwing the Power Rangers backpack she'd packed for Jace onto the bed. "Do what?" she snapped.

"You shouldn't be rude to a detective investigating the murder of our daughter."

"Jesus Christ, Billy. What? You think your fucking bowing and scraping is gonna make them like you?"

His whole body was shaking now. "All I'm saying is we don't want to give them any ammunition, any reason to look at us any closer than they already are."

Krissy jerked her head back. "Billy," she said slowly. "What're you talking about?"

Billy tugged the overnight bag off his shoulder and dropped it to the floor. He crouched down, unzipping and rifling through it furiously. "*This*"—he tugged something out—"is what I'm talking about. I found this in the hamper. Thank god I got to it before the police did."

Krissy narrowed her eyes in confusion. In his hand was a mass of baby blue—her robe, she realized suddenly, the one she'd been wearing that morning, the one she'd taken off before the police had arrived. Clutched tightly in Billy's fingers was the sleeve, and Krissy could make out something on the hem, a red slash. Not blood, but spray paint.

Her eyes jumped to Billy's, and he looked back at her with a mixture of panic and revulsion. "*What did you do?*"

TEN

Margot, 2019

The first full day of Margot's self-imposed two-week deadline was a Sunday, and for the first time in twenty years, she was going to church.

After conducting interviews at Shorty's the previous afternoon, she'd done everything she could to hit the ground running with the investigation the next day. First, she didn't have the time or money to keep getting takeout for every meal, so, as promised, she did a grocery run to Granny's Pantry, stocking up on granola, milk, coffee, frozen lasagnas, apples, peanut butter, sliced meats and cheeses for sandwiches—anything she could think of that would be easy to prepare. She also decided hiring a part-time caregiver could wait. Pete's suggestion had been innocuous enough, but googling and calling an actual agency had made Margot prickle with guilt. She and Luke didn't need help. They were good together, the two of them against the world. Plus, without the promise of a paycheck, the price of a caregiver would eat through her savings in a matter of weeks. She'd just have to juggle—helping out around the house and investigating the story at the same time.

That evening, while Luke drowsed in front of the TV and she did his laundry—clothes and bedding—she figured out her next steps in the investigation. With all the other news outlets preoccupied with Natalie Clark's case, Margot knew she wouldn't be able to touch that story, especially not now when she didn't have any current credentials to legitimize her questions. So she decided to come at the story from a different angle, to focus on January's case, and the people she wanted to talk to most were Billy, Jace, and Detective Townsend—those who'd been closest to it. The detective, she soon found out, was one year into his retirement, and the state police in South Bend gave Margot his cell number without qualm or question. Townsend himself had jumped at her request for an interview, agreeing to one the very next afternoon, which gave Margot the feeling that he didn't quite know what to do with all his free time.

The other two, however, were far more elusive. Jace was nowhere to be found online and Margot couldn't figure out how to reach Billy, whose very front yard was now a blocked-off crime scene, and who, according to Luke, had become intensely private since Krissy's death ten years ago. But then that evening, as she cooked a stir-fry for her and Luke's dinner, something her uncle had said popped into her head. *Billy doesn't really see many people anymore. But I think he still goes to church.*

So the next morning, Margot dug through the mess of clothes she had yet to unpack from her suitcase and threw together the nicest outfit she could: a gray wrap skirt, a white T-shirt she tucked into it, and a pair of leather sandals. She hooked her small gold hoops into her ears, swiped on some mascara, and called it a day. At the very least, she hoped people would be able to tell she'd made an effort.

"You look nice," Luke said when she emerged from her room. He was sitting at the kitchen table with a cup of coffee and his book of crosswords.

Margot grinned. "I'm going to church. You wanna come?"

Luke's eyes widened in surprise, then he threw his head back with laughter. After a moment, he caught his breath, wiped a finger beneath both eyes, then looked at her. "Wait. Are you serious?"

Margot laughed. "I'm also leaving early so I can buy a pie from Granny's. I'm trying to woo Billy Jacobs into talking with me."

"Ah, I see," he said, taking a sip of coffee. "You have good journalistic . . ." He hesitated, looking for the right word, then finished with "integrity," which Margot guessed was a stand-in for *instincts*. "I assume this is for work?"

Margot looked down, pretending to adjust the waist of her skirt. "Yep." She felt as if she'd lied more to Luke in the past few days than she had in her entire life, but when Pete told her at the station that he'd never found her uncle wandering the streets until two days ago, Margot realized that Luke's sudden decline was probably because of her. For months, he'd been living in solitude, without help but also without provocation. Since she'd moved in, all she talked about was the disappearance of one little girl and the murder of another.

She needed to remember he was more sensitive now, more volatile. She needed to stop talking about unsolved crimes, and she definitely did not need to tell him that she'd gotten fired. "It's for a piece I'm working on," she said. "So wish me luck."

"You don't need luck, kid," Luke said with a wink. "You got talent for days."

Margot stepped through the church's double doors and into the bright, blinding sun. The muffled sounds of the organ's closing hymns reverberated behind her as she blinked furiously, trying to get her eyes to adjust. When her vision finally cleared, she could see the retreating figure of Billy Jacobs, walking quickly down the sidewalk, his hands tucked into his suit pant pockets, his head bowed.

Margot had arrived at the church ten minutes before the service began and was surprised to see how many people she knew. She spotted almost everyone she'd spoken to at Shorty's, except Linda, who was no doubt working, plus a handful of her parents' old friends and one of her former elementary school teachers, all of whom greeted her with bright smiles and sharp, curious eyes. But Billy had arrived only moments before the service began, after she and the rest of the congregation had already settled into the pews. Afterward, the moment the organ started up, as the ladies began to sling their purses over their shoulders and catch the eyes of their friends, Margot watched as Billy stood and slipped quietly out the door. She followed.

"Mr. Jacobs!" Margot called, hurrying down the stairs to the sidewalk. But Billy just continued walking fast in the opposite direction. "Mr. Jacobs! Billy!"

Finally, he stopped, hesitated for a moment, then turned.

Margot walked quickly to catch up with him. "Hi, I'm Mar—"

"I know who you are," he said not unkindly. "You're the Davies girl."

She smiled. "That's right. I grew up across the street from you. I was friends with January." His eyes softened at his daughter's name. "I'm a reporter now," Margot continued, and it was only after she'd said it that she realized it was no longer technically true. "I'd love to talk, if you have a minute."

But at the word *reporter*, his expression had closed again. "I don't know anything about that message on my barn. I didn't even find it. One of my employees did."

"That's okay. I'm also looking into the Natalie Clark case, trying to find out if there's any connection between hers and January's."

"Natalie Clark . . ."

The name seemed to mean very little to him, but Margot knew he'd heard it, because the missing girl had been the subject of that morning's sermon. The pastor had used her disappearance as an opportunity to talk about faith during times of hardship and the mysterious nature of God's ways. Margot had paid little attention from her seat in the back, her gaze flitting around the heads of the congregation, wondering if inside any of them was the brain of a kidnapper, a killer.

"I wish I could be more help," Billy said, "but I don't know anything about Natalie Clark."

"No, I wouldn't expect you to. But if you'd be willing to talk about January's case, it could help me understand if there's anything connecting them."

Billy stuffed his hands deeper into his pockets and squinted over Margot's shoulder as if hoping to find someone to pull him away from the conversation. "Listen, Margot, I don't mean any offense, but I haven't had the best experience with reporters in the past. It's nothing personal, but I just don't think I should be talking with one."

Margot nodded. "I understand. But those reporters back then—they didn't know you or your family. They were trying to sell a story." She paused. "I knew January. I remember playing in your backyard, having snacks in your kitchen. I'm not out to spin anything, I promise. I just want to understand what happened to my friend."

Maybe it should have felt wrong using this as leverage, but everything she'd said was true. And although she knew that the weight of January's death had probably never gotten easier for Billy to carry, and that reliving it again would be painful, there were new developments in the twenty-five-year-old case. If rehashing his memories could help find his daughter's killer, didn't he have some sort of obligation to do so?

"This is an opportunity for you to set the record straight," she continued. "And if it all comes to nothing, at the very least, it could be nice to sit down and talk with someone else who knew her." She held his gaze. From the look in his eye, she could tell he was starting to give in. "Oh!" she added, unhooking one arm from her backpack, then twisting it around to her front. She dug a hand around inside, and after a moment, pulled out the box she'd bought earlier at Granny's Pantry. "And I brought apple pie."

Billy's eyes widened in surprise. He looked from the pie to Margot's face, then let out a small, stuttering laugh, as if the action was rusty from lack of practice. "Oh, all right," he said. "But not here. Let's go to the house."

The Jacobs place was no longer the bustling crime scene it had been the day before. The few members of the press who'd covered the story of the barn message had disappeared, as had Pete, his partner, and the yellow line of caution tape blocking the driveway. Margot parked along the curb, followed Billy up the front porch stairs, and then, for the first time in her life as an adult, she stepped over the threshold into the Jacobs home.

It was like walking into a memory. Margot had spent countless summer afternoons running through these rooms, and she marveled at how unchanged they all were, as if the house were a time capsule of 1994. The sitting room chairs were the same floral they'd been back then, the floors the same hardwood. As she walked through, long-forgotten details of the house began popping into her head—how the right side of the staircase creaked more than the left, how one of the whorls in the railing looked like a face, how, if you crawled beneath the dining room table and looked at its underside, you'd be able to see her and January's initials carved into the wood.

Margot followed Billy into the kitchen, and as he reheated a pot of coffee and selected plates and forks for the pie, she couldn't help envisioning the room as it had looked that July morning twenty-five years ago. *That bitch is gone* spray-painted in garish red against the white walls. Who had written that message? she wondered. Was it the same person who'd vandalized the barn?

"I'm sorry about earlier," Billy said as he sliced two pieces of the pie and placed them onto little porcelain plates. "I didn't mean to be rude, I just . . . I haven't had many friends in this town for a long time."

"I understand," Margot said, accepting a slice of pie. "Especially now, in light of what was written on your barn."

"Hm." Billy nodded thoughtfully as he placed the mugs onto the table in front of them, then settled into the chair across from her.

Margot took a sip of her coffee. "I know you said you don't know anything about it, but do you have *any* guesses about who would write something like that?"

Billy let out a breath. "To be honest, Margot, I just assumed it was done by some high school kids. In fact, the police told me earlier today that they believed it was just a stupid prank."

"Really?" She knew from Pete that this had been the police's theory, but she hadn't realized they'd made their official verdict yet.

Billy hitched a shoulder. "My friends and I used to do the same dumb stuff." His eyes glazed as he got lost in some memory, but then after a moment, they hardened. "Well, we never did anything as mean as what they wrote on the barn, but like I said, I'm not very liked in this town. Not anymore."

Margot knew it was true, but she'd also been watching earlier, as Billy had slid into the church pew at the start of the service. He'd caught a few of his fellow congregants eyeing him and had nodded by way of greeting, terse but polite, and Margot had been surprised to see the gesture reciprocated. He may not be well liked, but he wasn't the pariah Krissy had been.

"Can we talk about what your life was like back then?" she asked. "Before January died?"

"What do you want to know?"

Margot shrugged as if she hadn't prepared and thought through every question she had. "What was your family like? I knew them all too, of course, but not as well as you. Obviously. And, well, I was six." It was far from the most pressing thing she wanted to ask, but she was trying to loosen him up, get him comfortable and talking. She took a bite of the pie and then, as if it were an after-thought, said, "Oh, you don't mind if I record this, do you?"

Billy raised his eyebrows in surprise, but then shook his head. "No. No problem."

"Thanks." Margot pulled out her phone to begin recording, then said, "Why don't you start with January?"

At that, Billy's face lit up. "Well, January, she was . . . She was a firecracker, you know? Always bright and happy. Whenever I'd walk in the door, she'd bound over to me and wrap her little arms around my legs." His eyes filled with tears suddenly and he cleared his throat, brushing them away roughly with the back of his hand. "She was sort of the glue that held us together. Without her, the rest of us—we were a little lost. Because, she was always so kind, you know?"

Margot smiled. She did know. Most of her memories of the girl from across the street were blurred flashes, mere snapshots of time, but the clearest one she had was of January's kindness.

Margot could still see the image of it, trees and dappled light—on her school's playground maybe, or in someone's back-yard. In the memory, she was sitting, her knees tucked beneath her chin, her back pressed against a tree. She'd been scared for some long-forgotten reason, and suddenly, January was by her side, pressing something into Margot's palm. When she looked down, she saw that it was a quarter-size piece of ripped fabric. It was light blue, a snowflake printed in the center.

"When I'm scared," January said, "I squeeze this and it makes me brave."

So Margot tried, but it didn't work, and January told her she hadn't done it right; she needed to do it again, harder this time. Margot squeezed again, her nails digging into flesh, the fabric snowflake crumpling between her fingers, and that time, she felt it. That time, it made her brave.

It wasn't much longer after that, weeks or days, when January died and Margot had learned from that older kid at recess that her friend had been *murdered*. That night in bed, she'd grabbed the little snowflake from her bedside table and squeezed so hard her nails had drawn blood.

Now, Margot rubbed a thumb over her palm, the tiny scars like braille. "Did you notice any change in January?" she asked. "In the days or weeks leading up to her death?"

"Like what?"

"Like . . . her behavior, her moods, habits, likes, dislikes. Anything."

His expression didn't change as he thought about it. Then, after a long moment, he dragged a hand down his face. "I'm sorry. It was such a long time ago. If January did change at all before, I don't remember. In my memory, she was always bubbly. Always smiling."

"What about Jace?" Margot said. "What was he like back then?"

"Jace was . . ." Billy's eyes darted to hers then away again. "Quiet. Shy."

Margot studied him. She too remembered Jace as solemn and watchful, but there had been another side to the boy across the street, and she wondered how much Billy knew about it and how much he'd say.

Margot's most distinct memory of Jace, so unlike that of January, had happened one day during fifth-grade recess. She had been reading in her favorite spot, curled into the Y of a big oak tree, tucked away on the lowest point of their playground. It was a quiet little place where no one usually went, but that day, as she was reading, she heard the sound of a twig snapping, and when she looked up from her book, she saw Jace. After January's death four years earlier, Margot had stopped going over to their house, and whatever relationship she'd once had with him had disappeared. His eyes cast downward, he didn't seem to see her up in the tree and she didn't call out to him, didn't announce her presence at all. Instead, she watched as he walked beneath the branch she was in and crouched down to put something on the ground. When he stood up again, she saw that it was a small dead bird, a sparrow maybe or a wren. She watched, holding her breath, as Jace pressed the toe of his shoe onto the bird's breast. He pushed slowly harder and harder until finally, Margot saw its head swell and its black eye bulge.

"Jace was into arty stuff," Billy said. "He was never really interested in the farm or sports or anything. Didn't really fit in here, so he went off on his own a lot. And then, when he was older, he tended to get into a bit of trouble. Nothing too bad, just boy stuff. He was a good kid, but he had a hard time after January. Well, we all did." He hesitated. "Especially Kris. But I suppose you know about that." He shot her a glance.

"I do, yeah," Margot said. Everyone in the country knew about Krissy Jacobs's suicide. "I'm sorry. You were the one who found her, right?"

Billy swallowed, nodded tightly. "I'd been at a convention all weekend, and when I walked through the door—" He made a fist and pressed it to his lips.

"That's where you found her? By the front door?" That, Margot hadn't known, and it struck her as odd. When most people took their own lives, they went somewhere private—a bedroom, bathroom, their car.

Again, he nodded. "After January, Krissy was . . . Well, it was hell for her after that. I think after a while, it just got to be too much."

"Do you . . ." Margot hesitated. There was really no tactful way to ask what she was about to ask. "Do you think guilt could've had anything to do with it?"

Billy stared at her blankly for a long moment before her meaning sunk in. "Oh, Christ. Don't tell me. You've been talking to people in town." He shook his head, and when he spoke next, his voice was hard. "My wife did not kill our daughter. Krissy loved January. She may not have been the perfect mom, but"—he took a breath—"she loved her. She wouldn't have hurt her in a million years."

"What made her 'not perfect'?"

"What? No, I didn't mean it like that." Billy shook his head, looking suddenly skittish. "Krissy was a great mom. She was always really involved in January's dance and stuff. Really pushed her to do well. She didn't kill January. She wouldn't—*couldn't* have done that."

Margot studied his face. It seemed that his emotion surrounding January's death was real, but her questions about Krissy had gotten him flustered. And those about Jace had made him evasive, vague. Even though it had been over a decade since he'd seen either of them, it seemed to Margot that Billy Jacobs was still trying to protect his wife and son. He may have told her the truth about his family, but he certainly hadn't told her all of it.

"And believe me," he continued before she could press him. "I've thought about who could've done it every day since it happened."

"And?" Margot said. "Any ideas?"

"What I've always thought, the only thing that makes any sense, is that it was some . . . man. Some creep who'd caught sight of her at the playground or one of her recitals and— I don't know, maybe you're on to something with this story, Margot. Maybe whoever took this Natalie Clark girl took my January too."

Margot stayed another half hour or so to ask Billy about the details of his daughter's case, but everything he told her was something she'd already known. And each time she'd steered the conversation back to Jace or Krissy, he'd repeat his "good kid" and "good mom" appellations like a politician with a party line. Eventually, the two of them drank their last sips of coffee and ate their last bites of pie, and Margot thanked him for his time.

"Oh, one last thing," she said as Billy walked her to the front door. "Would you mind if I took a look at your barn?"

"Well, sure," Billy said. "The police finished this morning, so I don't think there's anything to mess up. I can walk you over if you want."

"Oh no, it's fine. It's on my way out, so I just thought I'd take a look."

"Be my guest." He hesitated, his eyes flicking over her face. "I remember you from back then, you know. I remember how the two of you were always running around together. And now, look at you, so grown up—" His eyes filled with sudden tears and he dug a knuckle into them, laughing self-consciously.

Margot smiled, welling with sympathy. Though its repercussions had happened over a very long time, that July night twenty-five years ago had robbed this man of everything: first his daughter, then his son, finally his wife. "Thanks again for your time."

Billy nodded. "Come over whenever you want."

The Jacobs barn was one of those big industrial types, separated from the house by a patchy, yellowing field. Margot made her way over, the summer sun hot on her skin. From the photo that had been on the news, she knew the message had been written on the far side, but when she rounded the corner, she deflated. The words were gone. In their place on the red wall was nothing but a faded black smear.

"Shit," she said.

She walked slowly along the barn's side, scanning the wood planks for remnants of something, anything, but there were none. She looked at the ground and, in the dirt beneath her feet, were dozens of different shoe prints. There was no way of telling which, if any, belonged to the author of the message.

She will not be the last. The words played over and over in Margot's mind, as did the circumstances surrounding them. Natalie Clark had gone missing mere days before the message appeared on January Jacobs's barn, which meant whoever wrote it was clearly tying the two girls together. The only logical conclusion therefore was that January's murderer and Natalie's kidnapper were one and the same, though the actual wording was still ambiguous. The author could have meant *January Jacobs will not be the last to be murdered* or *Natalie Clark will not be the last to be taken*—though Margot had a sneaking suspicion it was both. And either way, Wakarusa was not a safe place for little girls right now. But the biggest question in her mind was who had written the note—the killer or someone else?

Margot plucked her T-shirt with her fingers and tried to create a breeze against her skin as she walked around the corner to the two big doors, which were closed but unlocked. The inside of the barn was packed: tractors, lawn mowers, a worktable full of tools. It would take hours—days—to sift through it all. But what had she been expecting? It wasn't as if the author of the message had signed his name and the police had somehow missed it. Had this just been some mean-spirited prank by a few high schoolers? It was possible, she supposed, but she felt deep down that it wasn't the truth. She believed somebody out there was trying to tell their little town something, and Margot was worried what would happen if they didn't listen.

She was walking back to her car when she stopped short. There, tucked beneath her windshield wiper and fluttering in the breeze, was a small scrap of paper. Margot glanced around, but she didn't see anyone and her heart began to beat just a little bit faster. She made her way over and plucked the paper from the windshield. It looked to have been ripped from a notebook and the writing on it had been done by hand. Margot read the message, and despite the hundred-degree weather, a chill traveled up her spine. Once again, she looked around her for whoever had left it there, but the road was empty.

It couldn't have been Billy, she knew. He would have needed to pass her both on the way there and back. And even if she'd somehow missed him, his driveway was gravel; she would have heard his footsteps. Suddenly, Margot remembered that auburn-haired woman outside Shorty's, the one she thought had been watching her. With everything that had happened in the past few days, the moment had been scrubbed from Margot's mind. And at the time, she'd just assumed she was being paranoid anyway. Now, it seemed ominous.

Standing by her car, Margot's fists instinctively clenched as the words in her hand pulsed against her skin and pounded in her brain: *It's not safe for you here.*

ELEVEN

Margot, 2019

Margot stood by her car door, her heart thumping, the slip of paper tight between her fingertips. She looked around again for a sign of the person who'd left this on her windshield, but the road where she'd grown up was empty, the houses quiet and dark.

She took her time as she pushed her key into the door and slid into the driver's seat. If whoever had left her this note was watching, she didn't want to let on how shaken she was. But the moment she was in, she clicked the lock and squeezed her hand into a fist, allowing herself the comforting sting of nails against skin for one, two, three seconds, before forcing herself to stop.

It's not safe for you here. The meaning of the words was obvious, but Margot didn't understand the intent behind them. Was the author trying to protect her or threaten her? More to the point, who had written it? She started to mentally sift through everyone who knew about the story she was working on, but the list of names would've taken up two full pages in her notepad. She'd interviewed almost half the town by now. It was unsettling, being so exposed.

From inside her backpack, her phone vibrated and she jumped.

She unzipped the pocket, pulled it out, and glanced at the screen: Hank Brewer, her old landlord.

Margot closed her eyes as she answered. "Hi, Hank."

"Margot, hi. Is this a bad time? You sound . . . preoccupied."

She glanced at the slip of paper still in her hand. "Now's fine. What's up?"

"I'm calling about July's rent. Can you go ahead and send that over when you get a chance?"

"Oh. Um. I don't understand. Didn't . . ." She searched for the name of the subletter she'd found on Craigslist. "Didn't James pay you?"

There was a pause. "No one's paid me since I got your check for last month's rent. And I haven't heard from anybody about moving in or anything. You sure the guy you found wants it?"

Margot's shoulders slumped. "I thought he did." Calling her subletter had been on her to-do list right under make a copy of Luke's house key, neither of which she'd done. What with her botched Natalie Clark piece, then getting fired, then the barn note, they'd seemed like tasks that could wait. Apparently, she'd been wrong. "I'll call him. Can you give me a few days to figure out what's going on?"

"I'll give you till Wednesday to send the money, okay? I don't care who it comes from so long as it comes. That'll buy you some time to find a subletter for August. I know you got some . . . life stuff going on and I'm not uncompassionate, but you *did* sign a lease through October."

Oh, is that how renting an apartment works? Margot wanted to say, but chose instead, "I'll get the money to you by Wednesday."

She disconnected the call, then slammed her palms against the steering wheel. "Fuck!"

Her body radiated with anxiety. First the fucking note, now this? She looked at the clock on her dashboard. She knew she should report the note to the police, and she would, eventually.

But she was supposed to be in South Bend for her interview with former Detective Townsend in half an hour and she needed this story to be a story—one that would help her get a job—now more than ever.

Taking a deep breath, she slipped the note into the front pocket of her backpack, zipped it up, then turned her key in the ignition. On her way to South Bend, she called her subletter, James, then Luke to check in, but neither answered.

Former Det. Max Townsend's house was an old ranch-style tucked away in the suburbs of South Bend, and the moment Margot walked in, she could tell it was the home of a single man. The furniture was dark, primarily leather, with no apparent attempt at cohesion or any design scheme. The walls were bare, and the only nod toward decoration was the slew of framed photos scattered over every flat surface, all of which featured the same girl and spanned what looked to be twenty years of her life.

"Your daughter?" Margot said with a glance to the top of the TV console, where a handful of photos were on display. In one black frame, the girl looked to be about seven, blond and blue-eyed, grinning in a soccer uniform, a ball tucked beneath one arm. Next to it was one of her and Townsend, on a beach, pink-skinned and smiling.

Townsend followed Margot's gaze and smiled a complicated smile. "Jess."

"Cute," she said. "Thanks again for meeting with me."

He nodded, gestured toward the brown leather couch for her to sit. He chose the brown leather armchair, which, although it wasn't currently reclined, clearly could. Hooking an ankle over a knee, he laced his fingers over his stomach, which hadn't expanded in his retirement. In fact, he looked almost completely unchanged from the photos and footage Margot had seen from the investigation all those years ago. He was still big and broad, with astonishingly blue eyes and neat gray hair. The only major difference was that the lines on his face had deepened and expanded.

"It was no trouble." His tone was clipped, but even so, something about the look in his eye gave Margot the feeling he was grateful for the opportunity to be a detective again, even if it was just for an interview. "You said over the phone you wanted to talk about the January Jacobs case?"

Margot leaned to retrieve her phone from her backpack pocket, her fingers brushing against the note. When she sat up again, she showed him her phone. "Do you mind if I . . . ?"

He shook his head. "Not at all."

She pulled up her recording app, hit the red button, then said, "I'm also looking into the Natalie Clark case and the note that appeared on the Jacobs barn yesterday. Have you heard about those?"

"I have, though I'm not sure what the Natalie Clark case has to do with the other two."

"Well, neither do I exactly. But there are similarities between Natalie's case and January's. As I'm sure you know, Nappanee and Wakarusa are only eight miles apart, practically the same town. Natalie's five years old. January had recently turned six when she died. And the message on the barn appeared only days after Natalie was taken. I think whoever wrote it was trying to connect the two cases. So that's what I'm looking into."

"I see," Townsend said. "Well, I can help you out there. They're not connected."

She frowned. He had that same assured note in his voice that Detective Lacks had had at the press conference, and suddenly, Margot's ex-boss's words intermingled uncomfortably with Townsend's in her head. *You're blinded by your relationship to the January Jacobs case.*

"Um." She shook her head. "I'm sorry, but how can you be so

sure?" It was the same question she'd asked his former partner, but Margot knew she had a far better shot here than she'd had there. The rules that governed the police were strange ones: Any active members of the force were bound by strict policies about what they could and couldn't say about open cases, but the moment a law enforcement official retired, they were liberated from these restrictions. Townsend could tell her anything.

"First of all," he began, "the cases are vastly different. From what I've seen of the Clark girl's investigation, it's a cut-and-dried kidnapping. She's a young girl who was taken from a crowded playground. Scumbag perverts do that all the time. January's case, on the other hand, couldn't be more different. The crime scene was in her own home, the crime far more personal. That crime scene—the message on the Jacobs kitchen walls—indicates that January's murder was one of hate. And hate is up close and personal. Which suggests she was killed by someone who knew her."

A crime of hate. Margot had never thought of it like that, but she realized he had a point. A little girl's head bashed in, her body abandoned in a ditch, angry words all over her walls.

"But say January was kidnapped just like Natalie," she said. "Say she put up a fight with her kidnapper. Couldn't he have snapped out of anger? Couldn't he have gotten upset that his victim wasn't cooperating and slammed her head into something until she did? January was the closest thing to a public figure a six-year-old can be. She must've attracted plenty of attention from scumbag perverts who obsessed over her. And obsession can turn to hate like that. Especially in an unstable mind."

Townsend nodded. "That's true."

"Which means that none of what you said proves January's killer and Natalie's kidnapper are not the same. Not unequivocally. So . . . how can you be sure?"

"Because my team and I solved January Jacobs's case twenty-five years ago."

Margot blinked. That, she hadn't been expecting. She opened her mouth, then closed it again. "I'm sorry. What?"

Townsend gave her a small, wry grin. "That's right. It's why I can assure you the cases aren't connected. The person who killed January couldn't possibly have kidnapped Natalie Clark, because January's murderer is dead."

Margot sat frozen, reeling. His words echoed in her mind. *Hate is up close and personal. Killed by someone who knew her.* She thought back to Billy, so adamant and defensive that his wife had loved their daughter. She thought about all those interviews at Shorty's, everyone in town saying January had been envied by her own mother. She thought about the guilt-ridden suicide note Billy had found by his wife's body: *I'm sorry for everything.* But more than all that, there was only one person the former detective could be talking about, only one person connected to the case who was dead.

"Krissy," Margot said, the name no more than a whisper.

Townsend nodded. "Bingo."

TWELVE

Margot, 2019

Margot sat across from the detective, head spinning. *Krissy Jacobs* had killed January? Was it possible? This was by no means the first time she'd considered it, but it was one thing to hear this theory bandied about by prejudicial, uninformed people at Shorty's, another entirely to hear it from the lead detective on January's case. Margot thought back to her childhood, trying to conjure the face of Jace and January's mom. She knew what Krissy looked like from all the photos and videos she'd seen online, but she didn't think she had any organic memories of the woman from across the street. To Margot, she'd been just like any other mom, a faceless adult who appeared every now and then to tell the twins it was time for dinner or to produce an afternoon snack.

"But how . . ." Margot's voice faded and she shook her head. "How do you know? How did you solve it?"

"Krissy Jacobs's fingerprints were all over that original crime scene—literally and figuratively."

Over the years, Margot had read and reread every article that existed about January's case. She knew that during the initial investigation, the detectives had located the can of spray paint that had been used to write the message tucked away in the Jacobs barn. When they'd processed the fingerprints on the canister, most had belonged to Krissy. "But prints on a can of spray paint? And around her own kitchen? It looks bad, sure, but it's not exactly a smoking gun."

Townsend shook his head. "No. It isn't. But that's not all, not nearly. I began to suspect Krissy from the get-go. She was acting off the moment we met her. And not like grieving off or stressed off. But suspicious off. It was clear she wasn't telling us something. At first, we didn't know what it was. Sometimes people in investigations lie about stupid stuff because they think it'll get them in trouble—drugs, an affair. So, for the first few days or so, I thought she might've just been hiding an addiction to sleeping pills or a garden-variety tryst with the next-door neighbor.

"But then," Townsend continued, "we found the fingerprints, which is when I started to really look at her as a suspect. After we discovered January's body, we got cadaver dogs to search the two crime scenes and the surrounding areas to see if they could pick up a trace of decomposition, something to show us where the body had been. It was pretty clear Krissy Jacobs was our guy after that."

"How so?" Margot asked.

"The cadaver dogs hit on the trunk of her car. We searched it and forensics found fibers from the nightgown January was wearing on the night of her death." He gave Margot a meaningful look. "Krissy transported her daughter's dead body in her trunk that night."

"Jesus," she said on an exhale. Her chest felt kicked in from the revelation. Then, after a moment, she added, "But, I don't understand. Why did she do it? What's the motive?"

The former detective shook his head. "You don't need a motive to prove a murder. The evidence does it for you."

While that may have been true for solving crimes, Margot was a journalist. She dealt in stories, and characters in stories needed motives. And no matter what direction of thought she went in, Margot couldn't understand Krissy's. "Do you have a guess?"

Townsend shrugged. "Krissy Jacobs was smart. She was ambitious and attention-seeking. It was obvious within five minutes of meeting her that she was . . . *different* from most people in that town. She felt wasted in it. And I think she went crazy there. I don't know what ultimately made her snap, but I do know she was overly invested in January's dancing, jealous and controlling. And don't get me started on her relationship with Billy. They put up a good front, but there were problems there, under the surface. Honestly, I wouldn't be surprised if she did it just to hurt the guy."

He leaned forward to rest his forearms on his knees. "It's hard to understand, but people like that do exist. Most envision these kinds of crimes to be perpetrated by strangers. They see Ted Bundy, Son of Sam."

Margot thought about her younger self in the days after learning about January's murder. She saw her small body curled in the dark, squeezing her fists so tightly her nails drew blood as she imagined her friend's murderer outside her window.

"And those people are out there," Townsend said. "Don't get me wrong. But more often than not, crimes are committed by people who know the victim."

Everything he was saying made sense, and yet still something about his theory felt . . . off. Incomplete. And Margot couldn't help but feel some deep-buried prejudice in his words. It wasn't that she didn't believe women were capable of depravity, but saying Krissy was guilty because she was different? Margot thought of Wakarusa's original name—Salem, and all those women burning.

"So that's how I know Natalie Clark's kidnapper and January's killer aren't the same," Townsend said. "As for the barn message, I think the local police got it right this time. It was probably writ-

ten by some punk kids capitalizing on the town's legacy and looking to rile people up in the wake of another girl's disappearance.
People in Wakarusa"—he shook his head—"it's a rite of passage,
hearing about January's story. You told me over the phone that's
where you're from originally?"

She nodded.

"So you know that her murder is a part of that town's DNA. It's
no wonder kids fixate on it. Instead of an underpass, they tag the
Jacobs barn. Instead of genitals, they mimic those original words
on the kitchen walls."

Margot thought back to what Pete had said only yesterday. *People in this town can get caught up in January's memory. It's a compulsion,
talking about it.* It was true—that compulsion was one of the reasons she'd gotten fired. But was it possible that's all the barn message was? And then what about the message left on her car? Was
she supposed to believe that was given to her by some high
schooler too?

She leaned over and grabbed the slip of paper out of her bag,
then handed it to Townsend. "I found this on my car earlier. I assumed it's because I'm digging into the story."

Townsend held the piece of paper delicately, insubstantial looking between his thick fingers. It seemed impossible that something so small could engender as much fear as it had. "When did
you find this?"

"Half an hour before I showed up here. I went to get into my
car and found it on my windshield."

"And your car was parked outside the place you're staying?"

Margot shook her head. "It was outside the Jacobs place. I'd
been speaking with Billy."

"And you think someone gave it to you because you're looking
into January's murder."

"Well, that. Or Natalie's case or the message on the barn. Or all
three."

"Hm." Townsend gazed down at the slip of paper, his brow furrowed. After a few moments, he turned it over and studied the back as he held it up to the light. "Well," he said finally. "I'm sorry this happened to you. That must've been unnerving. But . . . thinking about it logically, a lot of reporters are covering Natalie Clark's disappearance. It doesn't make sense for someone to drive a town over to target the one member of the media who isn't paying it her full attention. And it's not as if Krissy Jacobs is walking around town handing out warnings to people getting too close to the truth. So the most plausible explanation in my mind is that it is indeed written by the same guy who wrote the message on the barn. It sounds like he's skulking around the Jacobs place and saw you as an easy target. My guess is he doesn't even know who you are or what you were doing there.

"Nevertheless," he added, handing the slip of paper back over. "You should report this to the police. It could help them apprehend whoever is terrorizing your town."

Margot took the note from him, then slipped it back into her bag, feeling oddly disappointed. While she'd obviously love to be wrong about someone following and now threatening her, she didn't think she was. But there was no point arguing about it.

"I still don't understand, though," she said after a moment. "About January's case. If all that evidence had you so certain it was Krissy, why did you never arrest her?"

Townsend let out a long sigh. Krissy Jacobs, it was clear, was the former detective's white whale. "I wanted to. I tried. But it was an extremely high-profile case and it wasn't a slam dunk, which is a bad combination, and the prosecutor didn't go for it. He maintained that the case was too convoluted, that it would take more than what I'd presented to get a jury to convict a mother for killing her own daughter." He gave her a rueful smile. "Essentially, Krissy Jacobs messed up the crime scene so much, no one could fucking understand it. And because of that, she walked free."

THIRTEEN

Margot, 2019

Margot stared at the police officer sitting across from her. "That's it?"

The officer—Officer Schneider, or was it Schmidt?—blinked up from the sheet of paper he'd been writing on. "Um . . ." His eyes shifted sideways then back again. "Yes?"

Margot had driven straight from South Bend to the Wakarusa police station to report the note she'd found on her windshield. And although she wanted to get home, although she was starting to prickle with anxiety about leaving her uncle alone for so long, the reporting process had been maddeningly brief. Officer Schneider-Schmidt—in plainclothes, he wasn't wearing a name tag—had asked her all the same questions Townsend had and jotted her answers on a notepad. When he asked if she had any theories about who could have written the message, he'd taken notes as she described the auburn-haired woman who'd been watching her outside Shorty's. And yet, afterward, when he told her that they'd do everything in their power to find the culprit, his tone had been light, almost flip.

"Listen," Margot said, trying to keep her voice pleasant. "This person"—she pointed at the note, which was now nestled in the corner of a little ziplock bag on the table between them—"I think they're threatening me because they're scared of what I'll write. I don't think this is some simple, mean-spirited vandalism. I think they don't want me telling this story. That should concern you."

Schneider-Schmidt nodded slowly. "If they don't want a reporter telling the story, though, why write the thing on the barn? One minute they're drawing attention to it, the next they're threatening people who listened? It seems a little . . . disorganized."

"I don't know." Margot threw up her palms. "Maybe they're not the same person."

He nodded again, but it was indulgent, condescending. "We are looking into the barn note, Ms. Davies. And we'll look into this too." He nodded at the piece of paper. "I can promise you that."

"And the woman I described? Are you gonna try to find her?"

Schneider-Schmidt narrowed his eyes, glanced down at his notes in front of him. "The woman with the . . . auburn hair." He hesitated. "What *is* auburn, by the way?"

Margot's eyes bulged. "It's a mix between red and brown."

"Huh. That sounds pretty. And you've only seen this woman the one time?"

She inhaled a long, deep breath. "Yes."

"I have to be honest with you, Ms. Davies. A middle-aged woman doesn't exactly fit the mold for the type of person to graffiti a barn wall. And since you've only seen her the once, it's possible she hasn't been following you. It's possible you just bumped into each other."

Margot wanted to scream. And it wasn't because she wasn't being taken seriously; it was because he was probably fucking right. In this conversation, *she* sounded like the irrational one, not Schneider-Schmidt. Was she being completely paranoid? Were all these messages just a part of some teenage boys' prank? Was the auburn-haired woman just a woman walking outside a building Margot also happened to be outside of? Worst of all, was she wasting precious time trying to use this message on the barn to connect January and Natalie when there was, in fact, nothing to connect?

She stood slowly, pressed her palms onto the table top, and forced a polite smile. "Thank you for your time."

She was on her way out of the police station's double doors when she heard her name. "What?" she snapped, spinning around.

Pete Finch, who'd been jogging toward her, stopped in his tracks, his face stricken.

"Oh," Margot said, feeling chastened. "Pete. Hi. Sorry."

"Are you okay?"

"I'm fine. It's just been a long day."

"What're you doing here?"

So, she told him.

"Oh shit," he said when she finished. "No wonder you're shaken up."

But the truth was, it wasn't just that note that had Margot feeling so irascible. It was everything. It was getting fired and getting that call from her old landlord. It was wondering how she was going to pay for an apartment she was no longer living in on top of everything else. It was seeing Natalie Clark's face on the news every time she walked past a TV and the déjà vu it gave her from when she'd reported on Polly Limon three years ago. It was the gut feeling that something was happening that no one else could see and the conflicting, terrifying dread that maybe she was actually the blind one. It was being back in this claustrophobic town and watching her uncle, her favorite person in the world, slowly lose his mind.

"I'll take a look at the report, okay?" Pete was saying when she tuned back in. "I'll try to keep an eye out for that woman."

Margot smiled weakly. "Why're you being so nice to me?"

"I mean, it *is* my job."

She raised her eyebrows. "You're more diligent than the other guy."

"Well. I guess it's also a little bit of payback."

"Payback? For what?"

He ducked his head. "Oh, come on. Don't make me say it."

"What're you talking about?"

"Third grade . . . ? Recess . . . ?"

Margot gave him a look.

"Wait. You really don't remember?"

"Remember what?"

"Well, shit. Now I wish I hadn't brought it up." Pete laughed, running a hand through his hair. "So, there was this one day during third-grade recess when I went to that part of the playground where no one really went, you know? With all the trees, and it was kind of lower than the rest?"

Margot nodded.

"I went down there because earlier, I'd been hanging out with a bunch of kids and Jordan Klein said something that cracked me up—I don't remember what it was, but I laughed so hard, I sort of peed my pants."

"Oh no."

"Yeah. Obviously, I was mortified and didn't want anyone to see, so I just put my hands over my crotch and slunk away to the nearest place I could find that wasn't swarming with kids. I couldn't go to the bathroom because I would've had to cross right past that big red jungle gym where everybody used to hang out. Anyway, I was standing on the far side of this big tree, blocking myself from view of the rest of the playground, when suddenly, you appeared."

Margot narrowed her eyes, his words dredging up the long-forgotten memory. "That's right. I remember now." As usual, she'd been reading in her favorite tree when she'd heard footsteps.

"I was trying not to let you see," he continued. "But I guess you already knew, because you grabbed my arm and dragged me over to the water fountain no one ever used and started splashing water all over both of us. Remember how water fights used to be a thing? Every once in a while, two kids would try to see who'd get the other the wettest?"

She laughed. "Yeah. So weird."

Pete smiled. "You told me that's what we'd say when people asked. Instead of being the loser who'd peed my pants, I was the cool kid who'd gotten into a water fight with a girl. I can't believe you didn't remember that. It was pretty traumatizing for me. Or almost traumatizing I should say."

Margot thought back to when she'd been scared and alone and January had sidled up next to her, pressing a fabric snowflake into her hand. *When I'm scared, I squeeze this and it makes me brave.* "I guess we just remember our own stuff."

"Well, anyway. Enough about me peeing my pants." He stuffed his hands into his pockets. "How's your uncle doing?"

"Um. Yeah, he's okay," she said, then wondered if it was true.

She'd managed to get a hold of Luke on her way back from her interview with Townsend, and thankfully, he'd seemed fine. He hadn't been able to tell her if he'd eaten lunch and he'd seemed vague about what he'd been up to that day, but he'd also been emotionally even, not angry or upset or significantly confused. And when she'd reminded him there was sliced meat and cheese in the fridge, bread by the toaster, she'd heard him start to rustle around the kitchen. Before they hung up a few minutes later, he said he may lie down for a nap. And yet, that was over an hour ago. With his condition, everything could be different now.

"I should probably be getting back to him," Margot said. "But now that I have you . . . Are you familiar with January's case?"

Pete raised his eyebrows. "Uh . . . kinda. I mean, being here, it's something you hear about all the time. But I've never, like, seen the file."

Margot glanced at her watch. She was torn between the desire to get home and check on Luke and the need to dissect what Townsend had just told her.

During the half-hour drive back to Wakarusa, she hadn't been able to stop picturing the look in the former detective's eyes as he explained why he'd never been able to arrest Krissy. Despite the nonexistent rules for law enforcement officials in retirement, despite the fact that throughout their interview he'd seemed entirely forthcoming, the way he'd looked in that moment had given Margot the unmistakable feeling that he wasn't telling her the full truth. Had she been making it up, that strange, secretive glint? She'd always prided herself on being able to read people, but her life felt as if it was starting to unravel, her confidence starting to slip. Plus, why would Townsend, a retired detective, feel the need to hide something from her?

Margot bit the inside of her cheek. It was getting late, but she had a Wakarusa police officer who felt he owed her a favor right there and a question gnawing at her mind. "Do you have a few minutes?" she said. "There's something I want to ask you."

The two of them settled onto a bench half a block from the police station and Margot proceeded to tell Pete everything she'd just learned from Townsend. It was clear from his reactions as she spoke that he'd heard all of it before.

"Well," Pete said when she finished. "He wasn't *lying* when he told you why the case never went to court, why he could never make an arrest. Not exactly. He just wasn't telling you the full truth. It's not surprising, actually. It's exactly why Wakarusa PD has a grudge against him, against the whole state police."

"A grudge against the— Why?"

"The older guys always say that the state police waltzed into town without knowing a thing about this place or its residents and made a snap judgment about what happened to January. A lot of them thought Townsend was so blinded by his belief that the killer was Krissy that he overlooked details that didn't fit his own narrative."

"What details?"

"Um . . ." Pete furrowed his brow as if trying to remember. "I guess I only know of one in particular, but the rumor around here is that there's this one piece of evidence that prevented Townsend from selling his case to the prosecutor. Because it muddied his version of the events that night and diverted the blame from Krissy."

"What piece of evidence?"

He hesitated. "Can this be off the record?"

"Of course."

"Okay. So, you have to remember Krissy and Billy's statement about that night for it to make sense. Remember how they said that they'd all slept through the night that night, Jace included?"

Margot nodded.

"Krissy had a pattern of taking sleeping pills before bed and Billy said he always slept soundly, so it was hard to really vouch for anyone but themselves, but they said something like Jace was a heavy sleeper and rarely woke in the middle of the night. And whenever he did, he always called for one of them. Well, they said he hadn't called for them that night, so he clearly hadn't woken up." Pete shook his head. "Whatever, they made a big deal about it."

"Okay . . ."

"Well, according to a report by state, they confiscated the pajamas Jace was wearing that night and took them for forensic analysis. On them, they found blood. It was concentrated and fresh and fit January's blood type. As twins, they probably had the same blood type, although it wasn't a given. But Jace didn't have any cuts and January had a lot of internal bleeding, which, when it's in your head like hers was, it can often, like, leak out of your ears and nose. And of course, there was some blood on the back of her head where she'd been hit. Anyway, the point is it was her blood on Jace's pajamas."

Margot listened, transfixed. She'd studied the case many times over the years and she hadn't heard any of this before.

"I don't know if you remember," Pete said, "but neither Krissy nor Billy had ever made any statement suggesting that January had bled before she'd gone to bed, which means that the blood had gotten onto Jace's pajamas sometime after. It means that in all likelihood, Jace was up that night and that he saw—or did—far more than he or his parents were willing to say."

That old memory of Jace filled Margot's mind, and suddenly she was ten again, sitting in an oak tree, gazing down at the boy from across the street. She watched as he pressed the toe of his shoe onto the chest of a dead bird, pushing harder and harder until its head bulged. Years later in college, Margot had taken a psychology course and had learned the vast array of effects grief can have on people. She'd remembered that dead bird then too and had thought she'd finally understood Jace's bizarre behavior. After losing his twin sister, he'd developed a preoccupation with death as an effort to comprehend what had happened to her. But now, Margot wondered if she'd been wrong. Had there been something else, something darker, growing inside him?

Pete continued. "So word around here is that Townsend brushed this evidence under the rug because it didn't help his case against Krissy. And from what you told me, it sounds like he's still unwilling to admit it." He glanced at his watch. "Hey, sorry to cut this short, but I should probably get going."

"Oh," Margot said, feeling as if she were in a fog, everything he'd just said swirling around her head in a storm cloud. "Yeah. No, absolutely."

Pete slapped his palms onto his knees, then stood. "Hope this helped."

"It did. Thank you."

He turned to leave, then turned back again. "I will take a look at that report, by the way. Try to figure out who sent you that note."

Margot, who was reaching into her bag for her phone, looked up at him and smiled. "Thanks, Pete. I appreciate it."

As he walked back to the station, she wrote out a text to Luke. *One more thing to do,* she typed, pushing away the guilt she felt as she did. *Then I'm coming home :)*

A few minutes later, she walked into Shorty's, which was already bustling with an early dinner crowd, and spotted Linda behind the bar, popping the tops off two bottles of Bud Light. Margot caught her eye as she walked over and Linda grinned.

"Hey, Margot," she said brightly, sliding the beers to two men across the bar. "You here for some more interviews?"

"Not today," Margot said. "I was hoping to talk to you, though."

Linda raised her eyebrows, clearly trying to mask her delight with a cool, casual look. "Oh yeah?"

"Yeah. Would you mind spreading the word about something for me?"

Linda grinned. "Well, sure, hon. I'm good at that. What d'you want me to tell folks this time?"

"Tell them I'm looking for Jace Jacobs."

FOURTEEN

Krissy, 1994

Krissy was shaking. The room at the Hillside Inn was closing around her, its blandly painted walls shrinking. She thought she'd been so good, thought she'd covered all her tracks, but Billy had found her out after only a few hours.

"What did you do?" he spat again.

The blue velveteen sleeve of her robe was still balled in his fist, and it looked as though he was fighting the urge to slam her head against the wall. Krissy's gaze flicked from the red spray paint on the sleeve of her robe to her husband's snarling face.

On the day they'd gotten married, seven years and an eternity ago, it was as if a switch had flipped in Billy's brain, turning him from teenage boy into husband. Suddenly he was saying he loved her because, Krissy assumed, that's what people who were married said. He expected dinner on the table at six; he stopped doing his own laundry. For Krissy, on the other hand, being a half of that whole hadn't come naturally. She burned meals. She never knew when he needed new socks or when he was running out of shampoo. She didn't call him honey or sweetie or dear. As the years passed, she simply stopped trying. And yet, as long as she went through the motions, as long as she put on a dress for church and made breakfast for the kids, Billy never seemed to notice that she wasn't really there at all.

Standing across from him now felt like the first time he'd really looked at her in years. And it was clear from the fury in his eyes that the time of his complacency was over. Krissy couldn't tell this angry man her secret. They weren't a team, nor did she trust him enough to keep it. The stakes were too high. "What exactly are you accusing me of here, Billy?"

"I—" He blinked. The look of certainty that had been hardening his features slowly began to morph into something more tentative, a deep but nebulous suspicion. "What—why is there spray paint on your sleeve?"

"Why do you think? I probably brushed up against the wall." Krissy knew that by the time the two of them had gone downstairs that morning, the spray paint would have been dry, but Billy didn't.

He gazed at her for a long moment, his eyes narrowed. Now, behind the suspicion, there was a seed of confusion. He clearly didn't know what to think. Finally, he released his grip on the robe, the soft blue sleeve crumpling to the hotel bed, then he dropped his head into his hands. "I don't understand." His muffled voice sounded like a croak. "None of this makes any sense. I—"

"I know," Krissy said. "I don't understand either. Here." She extended her hand, and when he looked up, she nodded at the robe in front of him. "Give me that."

Billy blinked, looked down. "This?" He grabbed the sleeve with soft fingers. "Why?"

"I'm gonna wash it. In case the police find it. It doesn't mean anything, but"—she took a breath—"but what if they think it does?"

The moment the bathroom door clicked shut behind her, Krissy twisted the lock into place and turned the bathtub faucet on as hot as it would go. Then, with a little bar of soap she had to unwrap from plastic, she held the sleeve of her robe beneath the scalding water and began to scrub.

Just as she was getting the color faded into an unrecognizable stain, a loud knock sounded on the hotel door. She jumped, heart hammering.

"Kris," came Billy's voice through the bathroom door. "That's Officer Jones with Jace. I'm changing. Could you—"

"Shit," Krissy hissed, yanking the tap off. She hurried to wrap her robe in a towel, stuffed it into the corner of the bathroom, then tossed another on top, so it looked like nothing more than a used pile of towels. "Coming!"

Taking a deep breath, she walked out of the bathroom to their hotel room door and swung it open to reveal Officer Jones, standing side by side and holding hands with her son. Krissy knew she should have been grateful to have Jace safe here with her, away from the watchful eyes of the police, but she wasn't. Instead, all she felt when she saw him was a deep resentment that he wasn't his sister.

Jace was hard from the moment he entered the world. While January met all the milestones babies were expected to—smiling at two months, laughing shortly after—Jace only oscillated between solemn and furious. With no need to be changed or fed or burped, he could cry for hours on end. If Billy hadn't been so helpless with the babies, perhaps Krissy could have coped better, but throughout the twins' entire infancy, her husband never missed even an hour's work at the farm or an hour's sleep. This wasn't due to malice, Krissy knew, so much as to a lack of imagination. In Billy's mind, men worked and women mothered. So, for the first year of her children's lives, she and her son were in a world of their own.

At night, while January slept peacefully in her crib, Krissy would walk through the darkened downstairs of the house, rocking a wailing Jace in her arms. *I didn't ask for this,* he seemed to say with his incessant cries. *I didn't ask to be born.* And Krissy, sleep-deprived and embittered, would think back, *Neither did I.*

Those early years passed by in a blur of loneliness. Most of Billy and Krissy's friends had left for college, and even the ones who hadn't largely disappeared from their lives. And how could Krissy blame them? They were in their early twenties, spending their nights driving to concerts in Indianapolis, drinking cheap booze, hooking up with each other in the backs of the boys' pickups. Meanwhile, Billy and Krissy had a family. Dave was the one who hung on the longest. He'd job searched in all the nearby towns and eventually landed something in Elkhart, but it was a short twenty-minute drive from Wakarusa, so instead of moving towns, he'd moved homes, out of his parents' place and into a rented two-bedroom house only a few blocks away. But even so, he didn't fit into their new life, and eventually he faded from it as well.

In a blink, the twins were walking then talking. Living with January was like living with a bright star; she was shining and happy in everything she did. Jace, on the other hand, still seemed angry at the world. He was sullen and quiet one moment, then in fitful, indignant tears the next. When the twins turned three, Krissy signed them up for lessons—dance for January, football for Jace. In ballet, January thrived, making fast friends with the other little girls and coming home after every lesson to show her mom what she'd learned. Each time Krissy took Jace to football, though, he refused to even walk onto the field. After four identical tantrums in a row, she unenrolled him.

Krissy encouraged Billy to spend time with their son, to teach him to fish, to throw a ball, even just to let him sit in his lap as he drove the tractor, but Jace never wanted to do any of that either, and eventually Billy stopped trying. Which meant that every other afternoon, Krissy would drag Jace to January's practice, where he'd sit soundless in the lobby, absorbed by nothing more than his colored pencils and a stack of paper.

But it was clear something inside Jace had been building, because on the night after January's first recital, it all boiled over.

As Krissy helped get January ready for the show, fussing over her makeup and costume, Jace had watched, white-lipped and glaring, then he'd sat still and wordless throughout the entire recital and car ride home. To anyone else, he may have looked like a particularly well-behaved kid, but his silence unnerved Krissy.

The moment they walked back inside the house, January announced, "I wanna do my recital!"

Billy laughed indulgently, but Krissy said, "Sweetie, you just did your dance."

"I wanna do it again!" January was bouncing on the balls of her little ballet-slippered feet.

"C'mon, Kris," Billy said. "Let her do it again." January squealed and ran to him, her stick arms wrapping tightly around his legs.

"Billy," Krissy snapped, inclining her head toward Jace, who was standing so still and stiff he looked like a tiny mannequin.

But Billy just shrugged. "It's one dance."

So Krissy put on January's practice CD and she and Billy sat side by side on the couch to be January's audience for the second time that night. Jace, dressed in his little button-down and khaki church pants, squished between them. When the song ended, January bowed deeply at the waist, drawing out the moment by bowing again and again in every direction.

Billy, who was holding the bouquet they'd given her at the theater earlier, plucked out one of the dethorned white roses and tossed it onto the living room floor. "Bravo!" he called. January pounced on it and pressed it to her chest. He grabbed a few more stems and handed one to Krissy and one to Jace. Krissy tossed hers onto the makeshift stage, but Jace held his tightly between his two small hands.

"Jace," Billy said. "Are you going to throw the flower to your sister?"

Jace stared down at a spot on the floor, his little chest rising and falling with quick breaths.

"Here," Krissy said lightly, reaching over him to pluck a flower from the bouquet in Billy's hands. "Why don't you keep that one and throw this one?" She handed him the second rose.

When he still didn't move, Billy said, "Jace, your sister just danced for us and she did a really good job. Do you have anything to say to her?"

By now Jace was trembling.

"That's okay," Krissy said. "If you're not feeling it right now, maybe you can say it later."

"No." Billy shook his head. "Jace, tell your sister congratulations."

Krissy shot him a look. "Billy, it's fine. They've had a long day."

"No. Jace, say 'congra—'"

But before he could finish, Jace stood. His face crumpled, turning red. "No!" He threw both his roses onto the floor and stomped on them. "I hate dance!"

"Jace," Billy bellowed, his voice hard. "We do *not* behave like that. You just earned yourself a spanking."

Krissy shot him a look. "Billy—"

But Jace was screaming over her. "I hate you!" he shouted to Billy, thrusting his tiny palms into his thighs. "I hate Mommy!" He shot around the coffee table toward his sister, who'd been watching the scene unfold with wide eyes. "And I hate January!" He shoved her so forcefully she fell backward, her hip and shoulder colliding against the hardwood with two painful-sounding cracks. She burst into tears. Jace ran out of the room.

The next night, as Krissy tucked her into bed, January turned onto her side and Krissy spotted a bruise blossoming on her shoulder. It was right on that tender spot beneath the bone, almost the size of a fist. It was then, as she stared at the dark splotch on her daughter's body, that Krissy realized she was afraid of her own son.

Now, standing across from Jace in the doorway of their hotel room, Krissy thought of everything she'd done last night to protect him, every lie she'd told Billy and the detectives to keep him safe. And she wondered, as he gazed back at her with those flat, serious eyes, if she'd made the right decision, or if protecting him had been a horrible mistake.

FIFTEEN

Margot, 2019

It was just after eleven on Monday morning and Margot was driving to the hardware store to make a copy of Luke's house key when her cell vibrated from the seat beside her. She stole a glance at the screen, and when she saw the name at the top, she grabbed it.

"Hi, Linda."

On the other end, she could hear the sounds of Shorty's, the loud murmur of an early lunch crowd, ice clinking in glasses, the TV playing in the background. "Margot?" Linda nearly shouted her name and Margot yanked the phone from her ear. "Hey, hon. You okay? You sound tired."

"I'm fine."

It was a lie, though. Margot had slept poorly the night before, tossing irritably on the futon as her mind pinged from Luke to January to Natalie Clark then back to her uncle again. She was beginning to feel that she was in over her head when it came to helping him out, unsure how to navigate the choppy waters of his condition and guilty for not being more available, more compe-tent, more . . . everything.

The previous evening, after her string of interviews that day, Margot returned to her uncle's place, eager to eat, shower, and crash, only to find she'd been locked out of the house. She rattled the doorknob a few times to be sure, nudging the door with her foot, but it wouldn't budge. She closed her eyes. Making a copy of Luke's key was on her to-do list, of course, but it had been languishing at the bottom, seemingly nonurgent beneath the other tasks like making sure he had food to eat and preventing him from falling behind on his meds.

She knocked loudly on the door, then waited, but nothing happened. The house remained quiet and dark. "Uncle Luke!" Margot called through the door. "Are you in there?"

She gazed at the closed garage door, envisioning its one and only clicker clipped on to the visor in Luke's car. Then, with a pang of panic, she realized she didn't even know if his car was in there. He rarely drove places these days, but what if he had today? What if he had an episode on the road? What if he forgot where he was going, got flustered, and had an accident? Margot shouldn't have left him as long as she had. She should have researched what to do when it came to his driving. She should have made a copy of the fucking house key. All the ways in which she'd failed her uncle began to stack one by one on top of her shoulders.

She banged her palm against the door. "Uncle Luke! It's me! Your niece, Margot."

Nothing.

"Uncle Luke! Are you there? Please open the door."

Still, nothing.

"Shit," she hissed. She pulled her phone from her backpack and called his cell, but he didn't answer. He didn't answer the house phone either. "Shit, shit, shit."

She stepped off the little concrete landing onto the ground next to it, then tromped around the bushes lining the house's exterior. When she made it to the window that looked into the kitchen, she pressed her face against the screen, cupping her hands around her eyes to peer inside, but the kitchen was dark and empty. She walked around the corner of the house, the bushes scraping against her thighs through her skirt. Along this wall was another window, but the ground had sloped down and she had to stand on her tip-toes to look through.

When she did, her shoulders sank in relief. "Thank fucking God."

There, in the living room, sitting on the couch and watching TV, was Luke.

Back at the front door, she knocked again. "Uncle Luke!" she called, trying to make her voice both loud and calm. "Can I come in? It's me, Margot."

And then, finally, there was the *thunk* of the dead bolt, the creak as the door slowly opened. In the sliver of space between the door and its frame, Luke peered out at her.

"Kid?" His gaze darted from her face to the yard and the road behind her. "Thank God you're here. Come in." The hard, wor-ried line between his eyes made Margot's heart beat faster. What was going on? He ushered her through the doorway quickly, and the moment she was inside, he clicked the door shut and twisted the dead bolt back into place. "Where's Rebecca?" he said. "I thought she was walking you home from school today."

Margot blinked, reorienting. While she always felt a sting to discover her uncle was lost in another time, what she felt most keenly now was relief. She was relieved to have him home and safe, relieved to know where exactly he was in the past. "Oh," she said. "I was fine by myself."

Luke shook his head. "No. I don't like you walking home alone. Not now. Not after what happened to January."

The name struck Margot like a slap. She swallowed, nodded.

"There are bad people in the world," her uncle said, his voice uncharacteristically hard. "Okay? You have to be careful."

And even though Margot knew he was stuck twenty-five years in the past, even though she knew none of what he was saying made sense anymore, his words still slipped up her spine like a shiver.

In the car now, she switched her phone from one ear to the other. "Yeah, I'm fine," she told Linda. "I just had a long night. What's up?"

"Mm," Linda said. "You know my cousin swears by that pill. What's it called? Ambien? Says it makes her sleep like a baby. You could try that."

"Yeah. Maybe I will. So . . . what's up, Linda?"

"Well, little miss busy bee, I think I might've found you a lead."

"To Jace? Wow. You work fast." It'd been less than twenty-four hours since she'd asked Linda for her help.

"Told you I was good." Margot could hear the smile in her voice. "I spread the word to a bunch of people yesterday, and a few minutes ago, Abby Mason—you know Abby, don't ya? Knows everything about everyone?" Before Margot could respond, Linda had already continued. "Anyways, Abby just walked in and told me that she heard from Brittany Lohman who heard it from Ryan Bailey that I said you were looking for Jace Jacobs. She said that Jace was kind of a loner, but she remembers one guy he ran around with. Name is Eli Blum."

Margot scanned her mental catalog of kids she'd gone to school with. "Doesn't ring a bell."

"Well, it wouldn't. He and his folks moved here 'bout five years after January . . ." She trailed off. "You two were ships in the night. Anyway, Eli's a bit of a . . . odd bird, if you know what I mean."

Margot did not know what she meant. In a place where anything other than mainstream Christian Americana was odd, the possibilities were endless. "Right. And did Abby have any idea where Eli is now?"

Linda chuckled. "I keep forgetting you been gone for so many years. Everybody knows Eli Blum works at Burton's on West Waterford."

Margot raised her eyebrows. She'd assumed an "odd bird" would've moved away by now, but West Waterford Street was three minutes away, tops. It was, she realized, on the way to the hardware store. She shot an anxious glance at her backpack pocket where she'd stashed Luke's house key. She didn't ever want a repeat of last night, but talking to Eli wouldn't take long. She'd just pop over to Burton's and make a copy of the key after.

"By the way," Margot said. "What's Burton's?"

"Well, the DVD rental place, of course."

"Right. Of course."

Walking into Burton's DVDs was like walking into the past. The walls were covered in old movie posters—*A Clockwork Orange, Black Snake Moan*—and the glass counter had been decorated in a collage of photos hand-cut from magazines. The guy reading a book behind the cash register—Eli, Margot assumed—looked straight out of the nineties. Around Margot's age, he had dyed black hair that hung over one eye, a silver nose ring, and he was probably the only person in this town who had tattoos.

He looked up from his book as the bell above the door chimed Margot's arrival. "Welcome."

"Thanks." Margot hesitated by the doorway. She'd been planning on asking him directly about Jace, but something stopped her—the curtness of his voice maybe, or the cool look in his eye. Perhaps it'd go over better if she eased into it. She turned toward an aisle and pretended to browse, hoping he'd initiate a conversation, but he stayed quiet. As she walked along the aisle, the images on the DVD covers changed from old black-and-whites to darkened houses and words written in blood. She grabbed one at random and brought it to the register.

The guy glanced at the DVD as she placed it on the counter. "Classic," he said.

Margot looked down at the movie, surprised to discover she'd actually seen it before. It was about a young girl who comes back from the dead over and over to torture then kill. "Tale as old as time."

As he rang her up, Margot kept waiting for the guy to say something—everyone else in this town was so curious about who she was and why she was there—but he accepted her credit card wordlessly, then handed over the DVD and receipt. "Due back by Thursday."

"Thanks." Margot slipped the movie into her backpack. "Hey, are you Eli, by chance?"

The guy looked up from the book he'd already gone back to. For a moment, he was silent, then, "Yes."

"I'm Margot Dav—"

"I know who you are."

"Oh. Right . . . Then you probably also know that I'm looking into the January Jacobs case. I know you moved to Wakarusa after it happened, but someone mentioned that you used to be friends with Jace. I was hoping to ask you about him."

Though she hadn't asked a direct question, most people would have felt compelled to respond, if for no other reason than to avoid an awkward silence. Eli, on the other hand, just stared passively back at her.

After a moment, she said, "Is that true? Were the two of you friends?"

"We were friends."

"Do you guys still talk?"

"No."

"Do you happen to know where he is?"

"No."

"Okay . . . Listen, I'm sorry I'm prying. I'm not trying to get Jace in trouble or anything. I—"

But Eli cut her off. "I don't give a shit about that. I'm not, like, hiding anything. I just haven't heard from the guy in over a decade."

"Right. Okay." Margot hesitated. She was pretty sure he was telling the truth, but she also suspected he knew more about Jace than he thought he did. She just needed to coax it out of him. "Could you tell me what he was like when you *did* know him then?"

"I honestly didn't know him that well. We mainly just . . . smoked weed together."

"That's way more than anyone else in this town did with him. You probably remember more than you think. Please. I'm not using this for an article or anything. I'm just trying to find him."

Eli eyed her for a moment, and then, finally, he sighed. "What do you wanna know?"

Margot gave him a grateful smile. "Did he ever talk about the future? What he wanted to be, where he wanted to live?"

"Not that I remember."

"Okay . . . What *did* he talk about?"

"I don't know. He was pretty quiet."

Margot forced her face to remain neutral. "What was he like? Personality, likes, dislikes, that kinda thing." She was getting further away from what she actually needed, but at this point, she just wanted to get Eli talking.

"Um . . . He liked art, painting and shit. He hated his family."

"Really?" Margot raised her eyebrows. "How d'you know?"

"Because he'd say things like *I hate my fucking family.* And, you know"—Eli shrugged—"I'd read between the lines."

"Huh. Was his sister included in that?"

"January?" For the first time, Eli looked surprised by the question. "I don't know. He didn't ever really talk about her." His eyes roved around the store and it seemed he was trying to remember whether or not that was true. "Yeah, no. He couldn't have hated her. He used to bring flowers to her grave every year."

Margot blinked. "Jace brought flowers to January's grave?" She'd heard him clearly enough, but she was having trouble wrapping her head around it. It didn't jibe with the boy she remembered or the grown-up version of him she'd created in her head. "Every year, when?"

"In high school."

"No, I mean, what time of year? Do you remember? Was it the same time every year?"

"Oh. Maybe. I don't know. I just remember this one time when we were smoking. It was like midnight or something, and suddenly he said he had to go. And he never had a curfew, or at least not one he ever cared about, so I asked where he was going and he told me he was bringing flowers to his sister's grave. Said he did it every year. I remember because he'd never really talked about her before and he got all weird when he did."

"Weird how?"

Eli hitched a shoulder. "I don't know. It was like he thought he'd slipped up or something. Said something he shouldn't have."

"This was in the middle of the night?"

He nodded. "And I'm pretty sure it was during summer because"—he shot a glance at the ceiling—"yeah, I remember I was working at Granny's Pantry at the time. It was my summer job during high school. God, I fucking hated that job."

Just then, the bell above the door chimed and in walked another customer.

"Welcome," Eli said, then looked at the new arrival. "Oh. Hey, Trevor."

"Dude," Trevor said. "What the fuck was up with that fight scene at the end?"

And then, the two guys were talking, and Margot knew it would be near impossible to steer the conversation back to Jace, but she didn't care. Her mind was whirring.

If Jace used to visit January's grave the same time every year, he most likely did it in accordance with some significant date. And the only meaningful date connected to January during summer that Margot could think of was July 23, the day she died. So Jace had visited his sister's grave every year on the anniversary of her death. Now the only question was: Did he still? Margot checked the date on her phone as she headed out the door: July 19.

As she made her way to her car, a flash of movement caught the corner of her eye and she snapped her head up to see a figure across the street. When she realized who it was, Margot's heart began to pound. It was the same woman she'd seen outside Shorty's, the one with dyed auburn hair. Officer Schneider-Schmidt had almost convinced Margot that she'd turned some random, innocuous stranger into a nefarious stalker, but now it seemed she'd been right after all. This woman was following her. Across the street from each other, they locked eyes, and the woman turned, ducking behind the building she'd been standing in front of.

Margot took off across the street at a run. But she hadn't checked the road before sprinting across it and she turned just in time to see a black SUV slamming on its brakes. She stopped, the car less than a foot from her. Her body crackled with adrenaline, the screech of brakes echoing in her ears.

"Sorry!" she shouted to the driver, a woman with a hand clapped against her chest and breathing hard. Then, shooting a glance both ways this time, Margot ran toward the building where she'd seen the woman disappear. But when she rounded the corner, all she saw was an empty street.

SIXTEEN

Margot, 2019

On her way to the church cemetery, Margot thrummed with nerves. Why was this woman following her? Was she the same person who'd left that note on her windshield? What the hell did she want?

It's not safe for you here.

Margot darted her eyes yet again to the rearview mirror, but it seemed the auburn-haired woman had paused her pursuit for the moment. That, or she'd just gotten better at hiding.

Margot flicked her blinker, and the moment she turned onto Union Street, the church came into view. Without the swarm of congregants in front of it, it somehow seemed smaller than it had yesterday before the Sunday service. The grass around it was brittle and yellow. On a marquee sign in the yard, plastic letters spelled out the message: EVEN THOUGH I WALK THROUGH THE VALLEY OF THE SHADOW OF DEATH, I WILL FEAR NO EVIL, FOR YOU ARE WITH ME. PSALM 23:4.

Margot pulled to the curb in front of the little white building and got out of the car, glancing around for any sign of the auburn-haired woman tailing her. Though the street was quiet and empty,

Margot still got the unsettling feeling of eyes on the back of her neck. She pushed the thought away, then strode quickly to the gate in the white picket fence surrounding the graves, undid the latch, and slipped through.

Like the church, the cemetery was small, with no more than a hundred graves or so. Margot made her way through the recent ones, their headstones still smooth and gleaming in the fading evening light. As she stepped past a particularly big stone, another came into view behind it and Margot stopped short. There, engraved in the marbled granite, was her aunt's name: REBECCA HELEN DAVIES, MAY 2, 1969–OCTOBER 7, 2018. But before Margot could even register the grief swelling inside her, she noticed the headstone next to it and her breath caught in her throat. Engraved on a matching stone was Luke's name, his birth date etched beneath, his death date a clean blank space. She turned away.

She'd only taken two steps toward the older graves when one caught her eye. The headstone was larger than most of the others with a white cherubic angel sitting at the top. The base was surrounded by offerings, spilling out onto the graves on either side. There were bouquets of flowers wrapped in plastic, daisies dyed unnatural blues and greens. There were grinning teddy bears clutching stuffed hearts and little plastic candles, their ever-present flames flickering weakly.

Margot made her way over to read the inscription, although she didn't need to. She already knew to whom the grave belonged. Sure enough, when she stepped in front of it, the engraving read: JANUARY MARIE JACOBS, APRIL 18, 1988–JULY 23, 1994. Margot stared at the death date. She'd spent that summer of '94 with the very girl whose body she was now standing on top of. They'd played pretend and ran through cornfields and braided each other's hair. Now, that time felt so far away. In the two and a half decades since, Margot had lived so much life; she'd grown into a different person entirely. Had she been afforded that life because some man had picked January's window instead of hers? Did she have all those years because January had not? The gratitude she felt at the thought made her burn with shame.

Suddenly, a twig snapped behind her. She spun around, half expecting to see the woman with the auburn hair, but instead, standing twenty feet away at the edge of the cemetery was a man.

"Hi there," he said. He looked to be in his sixties, with thinning hair and long limbs.

She cleared her throat. "Hi."

"What brings you to our neck of the woods?" His voice was steady, calm.

"To Wakarusa?"

"To our cemetery."

Margot blinked. He was wearing cargo shorts and Velcro sandals, his arms full of stuffed animals. Her heartbeat slowed. If he was there to follow or threaten her, he wasn't exactly dressing the part. "Just visiting. Do you work here? At the church?" She didn't recognize him from yesterday's sermon, so she knew he wasn't the pastor.

He smiled. "More like a full-time volunteer. I sort mail, help organize bingo. That sort of thing . . . Are you here to visit January?" He inclined his head to the stone behind her. "She's gotten a lot of love this past week."

"Because of the message on the barn?" Those words flashed through Margot's brain. *She will not be the last.*

"Maybe. But what with that Natalie Clark case, it didn't make much of a splash on the news." He stepped through the little gate as he continued. "No, I think it's because the anniversary's coming up. Of her death. The twenty-fifth year. The same happened for year five and ten and so on, people sending things. Although there's less each time." He walked over and bent down to deposit his armful of stuffed animals, taking his time arranging them.

"Who are all those from?" Margot asked, watching as he

swapped a teddy bear for a pink dolphin. Her gaze flicked over all the bouquets of flowers, wondering if any of them were from Jace.

He shrugged. "People across the country."

"Do you always take care of the cemetery?"

The man stood, wiping his hands on his shorts. "Well, there's usually not much to do. But I mow occasionally, water the flowers that are growing on some of the graves, that sort of thing."

"What about January's grave? Other than every five years, do you get any regular visitors or deliveries?"

The man shook his head. "No visitors, 'cept the odd tourist. And no deliveries, 'cept those." He nodded toward the bric-a-brac surrounding the headstone, then stuffed his hands into his shorts pockets. "Though there is the ghost that visits every year."

Margot snapped her head to look at him.

"Yep," he said with a little chuckle. "Every year, around this time, a bouquet of flowers appears overnight on the grave. I never see who delivers it, so I call them 'the ghost.'"

Margot's heart pounded. An annual flower delivery in the dead of night? That was Jace; it fit Eli's anecdote to a tee. But what did the tradition mean to Jace, she wondered. Eli clearly thought his old friend had done it out of love, but Margot knew there were more possible explanations than that.

"Have the flowers come this year?" she asked. "The ones from . . . 'the ghost'?"

"Sure have." The man shot a glance toward the headstone. "Those ones there."

Margot followed his line of sight, but there was so much surrounding the stone she couldn't tell which bouquet he was looking at. She bent down, touched a hand to a plastic-wrapped bouquet of lilies. "These?"

"The ones to the right."

To the right was a glass vase, its flowers buried beneath the lilies and a leaning teddy bear. "Do you mind if I——?" Margot looked to the man, who shrugged. She gently moved the other objects to the side to reveal a dense bouquet of white roses, their petals already yellowing with death. "Do they ever come with a note?"

The man shook his head.

"And do you remember when they came this year? What day?"

"Well, now, lemme think." He sucked his teeth. "I should remember because they showed up a bit earlier than usual and before all the rest of the stuff did. Oh, I remember! They were wet when I found them, so they must've showed up the night of the storm. You remember the storm from a few days back?"

"Of course." The summer had been hot and dry, so the recent storm stuck in Margot's mind. Though what day it had passed through their little town, she couldn't remember. She stared at the roses for another long moment, then stood. "Well, thanks for talking with me. I appreciate your help."

"Sure thing. Not every day someone takes an interest in this little plot of land." He inclined his head. "You have a good day now." He was across the grassy knoll and almost at the church's back door when he turned to look at Margot over his shoulder. "And, hey," he called, "you ever find out who the ghost is, you let me know, okay? I've been wondering 'bout them for years." With that, he turned and disappeared into the little white building.

Margot spun back around, knelt at January's grave, and gently lifted the vase of roses from the ground, the slew of stuffed animals surrounding it falling away. On her knees, she inspected the vase and flowers, looking for anything that could indicate where they'd come from. But there was no note, no ribbon, nothing. Then, just before she was about to give up, something caught her eye. On the clear glass bottom, she spotted something white and opaque: a little oval sticker that read "Kay's Blooms."

Margot hastily returned the vase to its spot, then pulled her phone from her backpack. She typed the name of the shop into her internet tab and scanned the results quickly, praying Kay's Blooms wasn't a franchise. After a moment, she breathed a sigh of relief. It turned out there was one and only one city in which the shop was located—which meant that Margot had finally found Jace. He was in Chicago.

She was driving back to Luke's place a few minutes later when she slammed on her brakes. Back at the cemetery, she hadn't thought anything of the fact that the flowers had arrived the night of the storm. She'd only been associating their arrival with the anniversary of January's death. But now, she realized what night the storm had happened. She remembered because she'd visited the Jacobs place the morning after and the pavement had been slick on the drive over. If Jace had delivered the flowers to January's grave that night, it meant that he'd been in Wakarusa only forty-eight hours after Natalie Clark had disappeared from a playground fifteen minutes away. It also meant that he had been here the night someone had spray-painted the Jacobs family barn.

SEVENTEEN

Margot, 2019

"Hey, Luke?" Margot said. "I'm thinking about leaving town for a few days."

It had been several hours since Margot had returned from the cemetery and she and her uncle were in the kitchen. He was at the table, she at the counter, making them sandwiches for an early dinner. The last thing Margot wanted right now was to leave her uncle alone, but she'd thought through every other option, and if she wanted this article to be a success, if she wanted to be able to continue to afford to help him, she needed to follow the story where it led her. And right now, it was leading her to Jace.

"Where're you going?" Luke asked.

"Chicago." Margot squeezed out a Z of mustard onto two slices of bread. "For work. Would that . . . be okay with you?" She finished the sandwiches, then cut them both into halves and carried the plates over to the table.

"Of course. Thanks for the—the . . ." He paused, and she knew he was searching for the word *sandwich*. "Thanks for the food."

Margot walked to the sink to get them glasses of water, her chest tight. "No problem. Anyway, I'll probably be gone for a few days, so I was thinking of asking someone to come here." She kept her voice deliberately light, her eyes focused on the tap. "Just in the afternoons. To give you a hand with stuff."

When she'd returned from the cemetery earlier, Margot had looked up the caregiver agency she'd found a few days previous and she'd prickled with guilt as she entered the number into her phone. She hadn't arranged anything with the woman on the other end of the line, just inquired about whether they had a caregiver with availability to come by for the next few days while she was gone—they did. His name was Mateo, and apparently he was very good at his job. Margot knew this would be a hard sell to Luke, and the truth was that for most of the time, he was fine. He was forgetful and occasionally irritable and misplaced things, but he could still pour a bowl of granola for himself in the morning, and he could still put himself to bed in the evening. But it was one thing to leave him alone for a few hours while she did interviews and errands. It was another thing entirely to leave him overnight.

Margot stole a glance at her uncle, but from where she stood at the sink, all she could see was his back. "Uncle Luke?" She walked over and set the glasses of water onto the table. "Did you hear me? I thought I'd ask someone to come over in the afternoons. To give you a hand."

She slid onto her chair, and when she caught sight of his face, she nearly contracted with guilt. He looked humiliated, furious. After a moment, he turned to look at her, and Margot had to force herself to hold his gaze.

"You mean you want to hire a babysitter."

"Uncle Luke—"

But he had already stood and was walking toward the refrigerator. He tugged open the door, then pulled out a beer.

"I'm sorry." Her cheeks burned. "But, Uncle Luke, you're sick. It's not your fault, but you are. And it would make me feel more comfortable leaving if I knew you had someone to check in on you. Not babysit you. Just come over for a few hours and make sure everything's okay. That's all."

"Look, kid," Luke said, closing the refrigerator door too hard. He opened the drawer next to it, looked around in it for a moment, then closed it roughly and moved on to the next. "I'm happy to have you here. And I get that you wanna help out because I'm not as sharp as I used to be. I'm not blind—I know you didn't come to Wakarusa for a 'change of pace.' And I appreciate everything you've been doing. Really. I do."

He examined the contents of that drawer, then, not finding what he was looking for, moved on to the cabinet above where he kept the drinking glasses. Margot realized with a sinking sensation that he was looking for a bottle opener for the beer. He was on the wrong side of the kitchen.

"But this is still my house," he continued. "And I'm not going to have some stranger coming in here every day to wash my goddamn underwear." He slammed the cabinet door, then opened the next and slammed that one too. "I'm fifty years old. So, please quit infanti—infanti—"

Margot stood and opened the drawer where her uncle had kept a bottle opener for the past thirty years. A great well of emotion surged inside her chest. She felt pity that her uncle, who'd always had a big vocabulary and sharp wit, couldn't remember the word *infantilize,* and she felt ashamed for doing that very thing to him in the very moment he was asking her not to. She felt a deep sadness that this unmerciful disease was robbing her uncle of his autonomy, when that was the most important thing he'd ever taught her. And on top of everything, she felt an anger, raw and raging, at the injustice of it all.

"Please just quit infanti—" he tried again as he looked in yet another wrong drawer, but his mouth caught on the word. "Goddammit! Why can't I find this fucking—"

"Here," Margot said, holding out the bottle opener.

Luke froze. He stood like that, staring down at the opener in her hand, then he hurled his bottle of beer across the kitchen, where it exploded against the wall.

Margot flinched. Then she stood very still, her eyes downcast, her heart hammering in her chest. For the first time in her life, Luke had reminded her of her father.

The two of them stood across from each other like that for a long, wordless moment. Beer frothed and foamed on the floor, shards of glass glittered among it. Luke's breath was coming in ragged gulps.

"Shit," he said finally, his shoulders slumping. "I'm sorry, kid. I don't know why I did that."

Margot shook her head. "It's okay. It's fine."

From his back pocket, Luke pulled the red bandanna she'd given him for Christmas all those years ago and rubbed it over his face, suddenly looking twenty years older. "No, it's not. I'm sorry. I shouldn't have done that. It's this"—he pounded the heel of his hand against his forehead—"this fucking thing."

"I know," she said, because she did. The disease was like a tapeworm in his brain, eating away at everything that made him who he was. "It's okay."

Luke dropped his hand to his side and his face fell. "I really am sorry, kid."

"I know."

He heaved a tired sigh, then put his hand on her head, squeezed twice in quick succession. "You deserve much better than the likes of me."

"Don't I know it," she said with a small, wry grin. Luke let out an exhalation of laughter, and that was when Margot knew her uncle—the real one—was back.

The two of them cleaned up the beer and glass, then grabbed two fresh bottles from the fridge, which they drank as they ate their sandwiches. Alcohol probably wasn't a good idea, but Margot felt they both deserved it. After they finished eating, she cleaned up, then retreated to her room, where, sitting on the edge of her futon, she tracked down the number for Pete.

"Hello?" he answered.

"Pete, hi. This is Margot Davies."

"Oh, Margot, hey." He sounded pleasantly surprised. "How'd you get my number?"

"I called the station and Deb at reception gave it to me. Didn't take much convincing, actually."

Pete laughed. "Ah, yeah, Deb's not exactly a steel trap. What's up?"

"I'm calling for a favor." Margot squished up her face. Asking for help did not come easily to her.

"Okay . . . What is it?"

"I'm leaving town for a few days and I was wondering . . . Do you think you could swing by my uncle's house a couple of times? Just, like, once a day to check on him? I'm sorry to ask, but I suggested a part-time caregiver and it didn't exactly go over well and I don't know what else to do."

"Oh. Sure," he said. "No problem."

Margot let out a breath she hadn't realized she'd been holding. "Really?"

"Yeah, of course. Like I said, I went through this with my grandpa and it's tough. I get it." The kindness in his voice made Margot's throat tighten. "Anyway," he said. "I'm on patrol for the next few days, so it'll be easy to stop by. Just give me the address."

"Thank you," she said after she'd told him the street name and number. "That's . . . thank you. And if it's possible . . . could you sort of try to be, like, subtle about what you're doing there? Maybe say you're looking for me or something? I don't want him to . . ."

"Hey," he said before she could think of how to finish. "I get it. No problem."

She closed her eyes. "Thank you, Pete. I owe you."

"You're good. Anyway, where're you headed?"

"Chicago. I'm pretty sure that's where Jace went. I'm gonna try to track him down for an interview."

There was a brief silence, then, "Wow. Okay . . . Are you sure you wanna do that?"

She let out a small breath of laughter. "I'll be fine, Pete. This isn't the first time I've interviewed someone about a crime."

"No, I know. But it's more than that. I remember Jace from school. He was . . . not a good guy."

Margot thought back to her conversation with Eli. He'd painted a picture of Jace as a regularly angsty teenager, one who stayed out late, smoked weed, and probably did a bunch of other stupid stuff teenagers did. It was no more than she'd done herself. "We can't all be perfect, Pete."

"No, Margot, you don't get it. You left when we were—what? Eight?"

"Eleven."

"Eleven. Okay. So before any of us really grew up. You didn't see what Jace was like. He was fucked up."

Margot frowned. "Fucked up how?"

"Like, he got busted in seventh grade for starting a fire in one of the bathroom trash cans. I don't think he was trying to burn down the school or anything, but it got out of control and we all had to evacuate. He got into a lot of trouble for it."

"What?"

"Yeah. And in ninth grade, he beat up Trey Wagner so bad the guy had to go to the hospital."

She closed her eyes, thinking about how Billy had described his son in the years after January's death. What had he said? That Jace *tended to get into a bit of trouble. Nothing too bad, just boy stuff.* She'd gotten the feeling he'd been protecting Jace when he'd said this, but the discrepancy between a bit of trouble and putting a kid in the hospital was a pretty big gulf. "Jesus."

"And that evidence I told you about? January's blood on his pajamas? A lot of the older guys here think that means he killed his sister." By this point, Margot had assumed some of the Wakarusa PD must harbor that theory, but hearing it spoken aloud still unsettled her. "I have no idea what happened that night," Pete said. "But if they're right and Jace, at the age of six, did kill someone, accident or not, think about what he could be capable of now."

"Yeah. Okay." Margot pinched the bridge of her nose. "Listen, I should go. Thanks again for checking on my uncle."

She hung up, feeling unnerved. It wasn't so much that Pete had painted such a violent portrait of Jace, but rather that she'd had no idea about it. There seemed to be endless versions of the boy from across the street. Along with that memory of the dead bird, Margot could also pull up vague, fuzzy recollections from before January's death of the three of them—she, Jace, and January—running around in the fields behind their home, playing hide-and-seek around the farm. In those memories, Jace had been a regular kid, just a boy. And then to everyone Margot had interviewed at Shorty's, he was a troublemaker, the product of bad mothering, but not inherently *bad*. To Eli, he'd been nothing but an outcast.

Margot realized, as she packed her suitcase, that Pete's warning had backfired. Rather than deterring her from finding Jace, it had only made her need to understand him stronger than ever. Because she didn't know what his role was in all of this. All she knew was that he was a missing piece of the puzzle and she couldn't see the greater picture until she understood where he fit in.

The next morning, she filled a to-go cup with coffee, threw her bag into the car, and said goodbye to her uncle, pushing away the guilt building inside her as she did. Then she headed out for the two-hour drive in the early morning light, news radio murmuring softly in the background, her mind whirling with thoughts of Jace. She was so preoccupied, in fact, that as she merged onto

US-20, she almost missed the sound of Natalie Clark's name through her speakers.

When she realized what the announcer had said, Margot gasped and reached over to spin the volume knob all the way to the right.

"The five-year-old-girl's body was found early this morning," the voice blared, "in the woods nearby the playground where she disappeared, and she was pronounced dead on the scene. While the police have not yet received the results from the autopsy, they believe that she was most likely sexually abused and that the cause of death was blunt force trauma to the back of her head."

The announcer continued her report, but Margot was no longer listening. All her brain could do was conjure up images of the young girl, dead. In them, Natalie Clark was lying on the earthen floor, killed the exact same way January had been, her eyes still wide with fear, her head bashed in.

EIGHTEEN

Krissy, 1994

It was midafternoon on the day after January was murdered when Detectives Lacks and Townsend escorted Krissy, Billy, and Jace from the Hillside Inn back to their house. It had, apparently, been fully inspected, documented, and cleared out—ready to be inhabited once again. In the back of the unmarked police car, Jace sat between his parents, and Krissy spent the ride pressed against the window, simultaneously trying to avoid his touch and trying to appear as if she weren't.

When they turned the corner onto their street, Krissy's breath caught in her throat. Both sides of the road were lined with media vans, news channel logos printed on their sides in bold fonts. Krissy read the logos, feeling dizzier with each one. Some she'd never heard of—WRTV, WNDU, Channel 4 News—but there were some anyone would recognize—CBS, ABC. At the start of the long driveway to their house was a wall of media: overweight men with sagging waistbands, enormous cameras perched on shoulders; their on-air counterparts, thin, sleek women with hard eyes and perfect hair, holding microphones and smoothing their blouses with flat palms. They looked like beetles, scuttling around each other, their equipment black and glinting.

Townsend directed the car into the horde, inching forward in sickening lurches, laying on the horn—an annoyed Moses parting the Red Sea. Krissy watched in horror as the swarm of reporters circled the car, swallowing it like a single organism. By the time Townsend shifted into park, they were surrounded once again. From her seat in shotgun, Lacks turned to face them, her gaze flicking between Krissy and Billy. "One of you should hold Jace's hand. And get ready to run."

Before Krissy could do anything, before she could take a breath or arrange any particular look on her face, the two detectives were out of the car and swinging open the back doors, and the cacophony beyond slammed into them like a wave. Jace slid his little hand into her own and Krissy forced herself not to shake him off. And then they were out of the car and the three of them were following the detectives as they darted through a tunnel of reporters, blinded by flashes.

"We're sorry about January!" so many voices called in manic, detached tones that belied the sentiment of the words. Far from sorry, they seemed downright gleeful. "What was she like?" "Tell us about her!" "What happened two nights ago?" "Who do you think murdered your daughter?"

Townsend led them up the stairs of the porch, ushered them inside, and slammed the door shut behind them. Instantly, the swell of voices in the yard turned muffled and faint. Krissy dropped Jace's hand.

"What the fuck was that?" Billy spat, a trembling finger pointed at the front door.

"Billy," Krissy snapped, dipping her head toward Jace. She bent down in front of her son, her hands clasped around his wrists, her eyes on the collar of his shirt because she couldn't look him in the eye. "Jace, can you go to your room and play for a bit?" She didn't actually care about Billy's language; she just wanted to get her son as far from the detectives as she could.

"But . . ." Jace said. "What do I do?"

"Why don't you color with your colored pencils? Or play with your Lite Brite. Whatever you want."

Lacks cleared her throat. "If you need to arrange someone to watch him——"

"No," Krissy said. She didn't want some stranger hovering and asking questions. "He'll be fine. He's okay being alone for a while."

She turned back to Jace, holding out the Power Rangers backpack she'd packed the day before. He took it and dutifully slipped his little arms through the straps.

After he'd disappeared through the doorway, Lacks turned to Billy. "Mr. Jacobs," she said. "I did try to warn you last night. I'm afraid this will be a big story. When we did the press conference yesterday——"

"You—what? Why'd you do a press conference?"

The detectives shared a look they didn't try to hide. "Well," Lacks said slowly. "This is a homicide investigation. It's standard practice."

Krissy rubbed her temples. They should have been expecting it, she now realized, but they'd been so insulated at the police station and in the hotel; the TV had been tuned all day to Cartoon Network for Jace. And even if they had been ready, being swarmed by all those reporters was far more unnerving than she ever could have imagined.

"Look," Lacks said. "We get it. The press can be a bit much. But getting the word out can garner a lot more tips and information from the public. At the end of the day, we all just wanna catch the bad g——"

The sound of the doorbell cut her off.

Lacks smiled patiently, clasping her hands behind her back.

When neither Krissy nor Billy made a move to answer it, she said, "Do one of you two wanna get that?"

"Oh." Krissy nodded her head. She felt like a child around the detectives, needing their permission to do anything. "Sure."

At the door was a huddle of women Krissy knew well—the moms of the little girls in January's dance class. They'd all gone to her high school, but had graduated five to ten years before she had. The Birds, she called them, because of how they always dressed in bright colors and flapped around the studio importantly, passing along bits of gossip like juicy worms. Standing on her front porch, the Birds looked at her, pity on their faces, a Tupperware container in each set of hands.

"Oh, Krissy," the Bird at the front said. Tracey Miller. "We're just so sorry." The last word got caught in Tracey's throat.

Krissy felt something harden inside her—all these women, their daughters alive and well, come to get off on how benevolent and sad Krissy's story made them feel. She would gladly murder any one of their daughters right now to have hers back for one more day.

"We just can't believe it," Tracey said. "We just—*can't*. And my god, all those *cameras*?" She shot a glance behind her at the swarm of media at the end of the drive. "Absolutely no respect for what you folks are going through."

The Birds shook their heads with a collective clucking sound, and then the one beside Tracey, Sharon Meyer, spoke up. "We know nothing we can do can ease your pain, but we wanted to bring you guys some food. At least take that off your plate for a while." She extended an orange Tupperware bowl with a mismatched red lid. On it, she'd taped a card printed with the image of a cross and an airborne dove. Cursive letters spelled out: *Blessed are those who mourn, for they will be comforted.*

Krissy envisioned herself smacking the Tupperware out of

Sharon Meyer's hands, imagined it landing with a thud on the front porch, burping out entrails of macaroni salad. "That's very kind. Thank you."

The Birds smiled, nodded, didn't move. Krissy realized with a jolt that they were expecting to be let in. She opened the door wide. "I'll show you to the kitchen."

She felt like a reluctant tour guide with the line of Birds marching behind her, their heads swiveling toward Billy and the two detectives. Billy darted his eyes between the floor and the women uncomfortably. Lacks and Townsend watched it all, looking completely at ease.

The moment Krissy turned the corner into the kitchen, she stopped short. The detectives had assured her their house would be returned to normal, but it seemed the spray-painted words had been too much of a hassle. They'd been halfheartedly scrubbed at, so that her white walls were a gory pink. She could just barely make out the word *bitch* above the coffeemaker. She turned around to stop the women from seeing, but it was too late. They were staring, eyes round as silver dollars.

They censored themselves quickly, pressing their lips in pert little smiles, turning their gazes blank and friendly, but Krissy knew the damage had been done. If the town hadn't already known of the spray-painted messages, they would soon—and that handful of words would set her and her family apart for the rest of their lives.

Tracey led the fridge-stocking initiative, which she turned into a full production, moving juice boxes and cartons of milk around with overblown authority, snapping at Peggy Shoemaker that they had to "put the big ones in first," when Peggy tried to put her Frito pie in before Rachel Kauffman's tuna casserole.

After what felt like a lifetime, Krissy ushered them back outside with a tight, plastered-on smile. As they filed out, each Bird gripped her hand in their own and promised to pray. When she finally shut the door behind them, she let out a breath, closed her eyes, and rested her head against the door.

When she opened her eyes again, she realized she was alone. The detectives and Billy had disappeared. From down the hall, she heard Billy's voice, and he must've been talking on the phone because it was the only one she could hear. After a moment of muffled conversation, she heard a click as the receiver was put back in its cradle, then footsteps in the hall.

"Where did the detectives go?" Krissy asked when he appeared in the doorway.

"They left. For now, at least. Said they'd be in touch tomorrow."

She sighed. It had been two days of grief and interrogation and it already seemed like it'd been a lifetime. She felt the exhaustion in her bones. "Who was on the phone?"

Billy cleared his throat. "A TV producer. From *Headline with Sandy Watters*."

"*Headline with Sandy Watters*?" Along with *20/20* and *60 Minutes*, *Headline with Sandy Watters* was one of the biggest investigative shows on TV.

He nodded. "They want us to do an interview."

"Jesus . . ."

"I think we should do it."

Krissy snapped her head up. "You—*what*? Are you insane?"

"That producer, she said our case is already getting twisted in the news. That they're skewering us on *Lisa and Bob in the Morning*."

"Billy—"

"She said if worse comes to worst, if one of us is . . . *arrested*, she doesn't think we could get a fair trial anywhere in the country right now. Because of, like . . . biases and stuff. Like, the jury would've seen how we're being represented and wouldn't wanna be fair. She says we need to take control of the narrative—"

Krissy rolled her eyes. "Billy, of course she's gonna say that. It's her job."

"No, Kris." His voice was unusually firm. "Just listen. She said she bets there are a dozen news teams outside our house right now, which there are, and that the public is gonna expect us to say *something* to one of them, to make some sort of statement. And she said Sandy would be the best person to help us shape what we actually want to say."

Krissy, who'd been rubbing the bridge of her nose, dropped her hand. "This isn't a good idea, Billy. We don't know what the police are thinking right now and we don't know what some TV host could ask—"

But Billy interrupted. "She said if we don't do something, if we don't make some sort of appearance, it's gonna look like we have something to hide. And we can't look like we have anything to hide right now."

Krissy snapped her eyes to his. "We *don't* have anything to hide."

Billy held her gaze for a long moment and she could tell he didn't believe her. "Exactly," he said finally. "That's exactly why we should go on this show."

The *Headline with Sandy Watters* studio in New York City was bigger in real life than it looked on TV. Whenever Krissy watched the show, Sandy and her guest always looked cozy, tucked into leather chairs, flowers on the coffee table between them. But as she, Billy, and Jace walked into the room where they would film the interview, Krissy could see that it wasn't a room at all, but a set with three fake walls. Where the fourth would have been was a slew of enormous cameras on rolling stands, men in headsets guiding them around. The place buzzed with energy and self-importance.

Their entrance was a whirlwind of introductions—to the producer, who gave them the rundown of what to expect; to the sound guy, who affixed little microphones to their collars; to the makeup woman, who patted their foreheads with a brush; and, finally, to Sandy Watters herself. Unlike her studio, Sandy looked smaller in person. Her iconic red hair was, as usual, hairsprayed into an immovable wisp around her head. Her skirt suit was baby blue, her earrings pearls. In her midforties, she was the perfect balance of down-to-earth enough to be relatable and professional enough to be taken seriously.

After they'd all shaken hands, the four of them were arranged on the furniture, Jace between Krissy and Billy on the couch, Sandy across from them in an armchair. Sandy gave her introduction to the camera, in which she recapped the brutal murder of January in neat bullet points, then announced her very special guests.

"Welcome, Jacobs family," she said in her honey voice as she turned to them. "Thank you for being here with me tonight."

Krissy nodded tightly. Before they started rolling, Sandy told them not to be nervous because they weren't live, but Krissy didn't think she'd ever been this nervous in her life. She had not wanted to do this with Jace, but Billy had argued that he would make them look like the wholesome family they were supposed to be. Krissy couldn't insist without telling him the truth, so eventually, she'd given in, though only after telling Sandy's team there were to be no questions targeted at Jace. The next thing she knew, she was booking the three of them flights to New York at the end of the week and a hotel by the airport, praying that a twenty-four-hour trip in the middle of a long investigation would inflict less damage than sticking around and doing nothing.

When their plane had begun its descent, Krissy had gazed through the little oval window, down at the city of possibility and light, aching with regret. For so long she'd dreamed of coming here, of escaping Wakarusa and her dead-end marriage, dreamed of a big, dazzling life. How different the circumstances of this trip were. How different her life had turned out, so far from how it was supposed to be.

"This story," Sandy continued, leaning forward slightly, "January's story—is such a tragedy. Every parent's worst nightmare. But on top of that, it's also a confounding one. From everything we've seen on the news up to this point, the investigation looks like a bit of a mess. So, tonight, I invite you to tell your version. To set the record straight."

Sandy's first few questions were, Krissy knew, intended to be softballs to get her and Billy talking: *What was January like? What has the town's reaction been? Can you walk through that awful morning when you discovered she was gone?* That last one Krissy had answered so many times for the police she could probably recite the words in her sleep.

"Now," Sandy said after they finished. "I think most of America, myself included, is interested in January's dancing." Krissy felt Billy shift beside her. "By now we've all seen the photos. And those costumes seem so . . . grown-up."

Krissy's cheeks burned, but she'd been expecting this and she'd rehearsed her answer. "The pictures in the media are of the most extreme costumes she ever wore. Most of them were just your run-of-the-mill children's costumes—bumblebees, ladybugs, that sort of thing."

"And one of them was of a sexy sailor."

Krissy blinked. "January loved to dance. And she took it very seriously. The costumes were a part of that world."

Sandy shifted her narrowed gaze to Billy then back again. "But are the two of you at all concerned that your daughter's dancing and those costumes are a part of the reason she's now dead? That it attracted the attention of some sort of predator?"

Krissy bit the inside of her cheek and heard Billy swallow beside her. She knew they shouldn't have come on this fucking show. No matter how many times she'd rehearsed answers in front of their bathroom mirror, she couldn't have prepared for this. No matter what they said, they were admitting guilt. They'd either dressed their daughter up as a human lure or they didn't believe it was a stranger who'd killed her, which would direct the attention of Sandy—and the rest of the country—onto them.

"Looking back," Krissy began after the silence had grown unbearable, "I wish we'd chosen different costumes."

Sandy sat, seemingly content to let that linger in the air for a long moment before continuing. "Speaking of theories, let's shift to the ongoing police investigation, in which you both have been questioned. I think most of America, myself included, don't quite know what to think about you two." Her sharp gaze flicked between Krissy and Billy. "On the one hand, you seem like regular, nice people. You own a farm, you're a part of a close-knit community. You go to church every Sunday. On the other hand, the police have said you're cooperating *to an extent,* and both of your fingerprints are on the can of spray paint used to write those horrific words on your kitchen walls."

There was a ringing silence as Krissy sat frozen in her seat. How had she known? Detective Townsend had sprung this on Krissy in an interview less than forty-eight hours ago, and she was just as shocked by it now as she had been then. Had *Townsend* leaked it to the show's producer? Were the police trying to set them up? The thought sent a chill of fury up her spine.

Before she could say anything, though, Billy cleared his throat. "I bought the spray paint for a project I was doing on the farm. I was touching up the paint on the barn doors."

"Hm." Sandy shifted her narrowed gaze from his face to Krissy's. "And what about you?"

"I went in the barn the other week," she said, her voice feeble, "to look for some WD-40 for a noisy hinge. I was rummaging around and I moved it." This wasn't true, of course, but it was what she'd told Townsend when he'd asked.

"Hm," Sandy said again, then turned to Jace.

Krissy's heart stopped. She'd insisted Sandy not question him. That was the one condition she'd given.

"I'd like to hear from you, Jace," Sandy said in a voice both kind and firm. "Can you tell us what happened that night from your point of view?"

Krissy swelled with fear, adrenaline coursing through her bloodstream so fast it hurt. She opened her mouth, then closed it. What could she do? Jace was shrinking into her body and she had the urge to jump away from him. A sudden movement caught her attention from the corner of her eye and she glanced over to see the producer who'd briefed them earlier miming to the guy behind one of the rolling cameras. By the hand gesture she was making, it looked as though she wanted the cameraman to zoom in on Krissy and Jace. *Fuck.* Krissy hadn't been thinking. Far too late, she wrapped a stiff arm around her son.

It was then that Jace finally spoke up, his words coming out in a flat, solemn voice. "I don't like to talk about it."

"Why is that?" Sandy asked, all patience and understanding.

"I just don't."

"I understand that this is probably scary and it's sad to talk about your sister when she's gone, but sometimes talking about it can help."

Jace hesitated. Krissy wanted to scratch Sandy across the face. The sound of her own heartbeat hammered in her ears.

"I don't like to talk about it," Jace finally said, "because I don't wanna get in trouble."

That night, as she, Billy, and Jace slept in their shitty hotel room near the Newark airport, Krissy awoke with a start. She thought something had touched her neck—cold, soft fingertips. She swiped her hand at it, but there was nothing there. Blinking into the darkness, she saw a figure standing by her bed, and when her eyes adjusted, she realized it was Jace.

She inhaled sharply. "Jace? What're you doing?"

But he just stood there. If she couldn't feel his breath on her face, she might've thought he wasn't there at all—just a figment of her imagination, a specter come to haunt. "Jace?"

"I'm sorry about January, Mommy."

The words sliced into her, her chest and stomach contracting with their force. In the five days since January had died, Krissy had done so well at keeping the memory of that night buried deep in the recess of her mind. But now, in the darkness and in the wake of her son's apology, it all came flooding back.

The first thing Krissy remembered was the sound of a crash.

Hours earlier, as she'd gotten ready for bed, she had taken a sleeping pill—just as she had almost every night for the past four years. Before marriage and motherhood, she never used to have trouble sleeping. At night, she'd fall into the unencumbered rest of a teenager, and in the morning, she'd wake full of energy and possibility. But then, in a blink, she was a wife to a man she hardly knew and a nineteen-year-old mom with two infants. Suddenly, the sheer act of existing felt like a burden she wasn't capable of carrying on her own. Loneliness, like teeth through her chest, was her constant companion. Wine helped dull the edges, but pills, she discovered, were best: Valium to get her through the days and sleeping pills for the nights. Maybe, after all these years, she'd grown inured to the little white pill, or maybe the sound of the crash was so out of the ordinary, but whatever the reason, in the early hours of that morning, Krissy woke from her medicated fog.

She sat up in bed, heart beating fast. The farmhouse sometimes seemed alive, creaking and groaning in the night, but the crash had been different. She glanced over at Billy's back, but he was silent and unmoving.

Quietly, she slipped out of bed, tiptoed into the bathroom, and tugged her robe over her pajamas. She padded down the hallway toward the stairs, stopping outside the twins' rooms. The crash had sounded far away, from somewhere in the depths of the house, but she'd feel better knowing her children were safe and sleeping. And yet, when she poked her head through the doorway to January's room, the bed looked empty. Krissy blinked, trying to clear the lingering sleep from her mind. January's nightlight was one of those revolving ones, slowly projecting shapes onto a paper box around it, horses and flowers and rabbits retracing their steps night after night. The images danced around the room, distorted and flickering, making it hard to see. Krissy stepped closer to the bed, but January was still not in it. Nor was she under it or inside her closet or in the hallway bathroom. When Krissy discovered that Jace was also missing from his room, she began to panic.

She hurried down the stairs, the old wood creaking beneath her feet, shadows gathering and shifting around her. When she stepped into the kitchen, something unusual caught her eye: The basement door was open, the blackness beyond a yawning mouth. She thought briefly of retrieving one of Billy's guns from the case in the sitting room, but that was so far away. Plus, if the kids were down there, she didn't want them to see their mom materialize out of the darkness, a shotgun in her hands.

At the top of the basement stairs, Krissy felt unease like a cold fingertip crawling up her spine. Something felt . . . wrong down there. She forced herself to breathe, then peered into the stairwell, but the three horizontal windows at the bottom were black with night. She took a few slow, tentative steps into the depths of the old house. As she did, the moon came out from behind the clouds, and suddenly, the room was illuminated. That's when she saw it.

There, lying at the bottom of the stairs, was January.

The breath kicked from Krissy's lungs. Her daughter's eyes were closed, her body straight and unmoving. Her white nightgown was incandescent in the moonlight, her chestnut hair pooling around the nape of her neck. But her face looked all wrong. The skin was puffy and ashen, her lips strangely stiff. Gazing down at her, Krissy could feel the truth like a stone in her stomach: Her darling daughter was dead.

And crouching over her lifeless body was Jace.

As Krissy stared at the horrific tableau beneath her, her mind felt scrubbed except for one word: *No.* She heard a sound—a soft, guttural moan—and realized it had come from her own mouth.

Jace must've heard it too, because he straightened and slowly turned his head over his shoulder, his impassive gaze pinning her like a butterfly to a corkboard. He stared at her quietly for a moment before opening his mouth, and his words, spoken in his small little-boy voice, were a blade across Krissy's stomach, slicing into skin, intestine, womb.

"Can we play tomorrow, Mommy? Just you and me?"

NINETEEN

Margot, 2019

In her hotel room, Margot slid the chain lock into place. She was fairly sure the woman with the auburn hair hadn't followed her all the way to Chicago, but the words that had been written on the Jacobs barn and those of the note left on her windshield still filled her brain. *She will not be the last. It's not safe for you here.* Especially now, after the news of Natalie Clark's body being found, Margot took comfort in being locked safely inside her room. She knew she wasn't in the same danger as Natalie or January had been, but she'd clearly attracted the attention of someone, and she wasn't sure what they wanted or how far they'd go to get it.

Margot grabbed her laptop and settled onto the bed, her back against the pillows, the cheap bedspread rough against her legs. Since she'd begun digging into January's case days ago, she'd spent countless hours trying to find Jace online to no avail. Once she'd discovered he'd gone to Chicago, she'd been able to narrow that search, but still, it had been fruitless. Which was why the first thing she did, once she'd made it to the city and checked into a hotel, was visit the courthouse to request all the legal documents containing Jace's name. It wasn't a sure thing, but it could yield results Google couldn't.

And sure enough, it did. The first set of documents she received from the clerk at the courthouse, at only two pages long, was made up of one report—an arrest of Jace Jacobs for battery and assault back in 2007—which was proof, at the very least, that Jace had been in Chicago, but little else. But then, as she read over the pages again, more slowly this time, she saw it. On the second page, in a section she'd previously skimmed over, was a line titled "Known Aliases." Typed beneath was the name Jay Winter. As she stared down at it, finally all those futile searches made sense. Jace had changed his name.

So Margot ordered all the documents containing the name Jay Winter, and this time, the stack of papers that came back was thick. Flipping through them, she could see they covered two years' worth of crimes, everything from public intoxication to disturbing the peace. And there, on page three, was a mugshot. Standing in front of a white concrete wall, dark hair in disarray, green eyes unfocused, Jace Jacobs stared back at her, his mouth twisted in a strange smile.

On her hotel bed, Margot tapped her fingertips impatiently against the keyboard as she waited for it to come to life. Since leaving Wakarusa, a part of her mind had been perpetually on her uncle, and although she'd told herself that coming to Chicago was the right thing to do for the story and her career, and therefore the best way to help him, guilt gnawed at her. She just wanted to find Jace, talk to him, and get back home as soon as she could. Luckily, with his new name, tracking him down should be easy. These days, it was almost impossible to disappear without a trace.

Margot started with social media, but every one—Facebook, Instagram, Twitter, LinkedIn—came up dry. There were a few Jay Winters in the world, but not the one she was looking for. She switched to a broader search, googling *Jay Winter* plus *Chicago,* and still there was nothing. Not a photo, not a place of employment, not a single person who knew him. Jace, it turned out, had done the thing right.

Margot slumped back into the pillows, glancing at the time on her laptop. It was already midafternoon and she was nowhere closer to Jace than she'd been three hours ago. Where could she go from here, when she had nothing more to go on? Almost everything she knew about Jace was from a twenty-five-year-old investigation. Other than that, she knew his crime record and what he looked like a decade ago. She knew that he had a tendency toward violence, smoked weed in high school, and brought flowers to January's grave every year. But the last one was the only road she could explore, and she already had. From the courthouse, Margot had driven straight to Kay's Blooms, the florist shop where Jace had bought that bouquet of white roses. But the woman behind the counter had just shaken her head blankly at Jace's mugshot. She was a part-time employee, she'd explained. The owner, who worked most days, was out of town.

Margot squeezed her eyes shut, trying to dredge up any scrap of information she'd left unexplored, but all she could remember was Pete's warning about him. *He was not a good guy.* She dragged her hands down her face, letting out a frustrated groan.

But then, something Eli had said popped into her head. *He liked art, painting and shit.* It had been a throwaway remark, but it hadn't been the first time Margot had heard something like it about Jace. What had Billy told her? That Jace was into *arty stuff?* An idea, flimsy and vague, formed in Margot's mind.

She sat up, adjusted her laptop, and typed in the search bar: *art* plus *Chicago.* The first few results to pop up were the Art Institute of Chicago, the Museum of Contemporary Art, and a few lists of the highest-rated art galleries in the city. Margot scrolled through their sites and social media accounts, searching for any hint of Jace's presence, but she didn't have much hope. Those weren't the type of places where you worked when you were trying to disappear. She spent more time on the websites of the smaller galleries, but after an hour, she'd still found nothing, so she switched her search word from *art* to *paint*.

"Huh," she said aloud as the new results popped up. The first was for a place called Bottle & Brush, and she could tell immediately from the photos what the business was. In Indianapolis, they had a similar place called Syrah's Studio, a franchise of painting studios for nonpainters. Bridal parties went there to drink wine and finish their own Monet in an hour and a half. The instructors were all recent art grads looking to make extra cash, their turnaround quick and uneventful. It was the kind of place you could work with art and remain anonymous, the kind of place that might attract someone like Jace.

Margot clicked on the first of the two locations, then navigated to its photos. Most featured a classroom full of people, either posing with their finished paintings or sitting in front of easels, brushes in one hand, glasses of wine in the other. She scanned the faces of who she assumed were the instructors, the ones in paint-splattered smocks at the front of the room. Most seemed to be Jace's age, late twenties or early thirties. There was a brunette girl, her hair piled artfully on her head and tied with a bandanna. There was a Black guy with dreads, and a white guy with thick-framed glasses. But she didn't see Jace. Then she clicked to the second-to-last photo and stopped.

In the picture, the class was scattered about the room, making final touches to their canvases or mingling as they drank the last of their wine. In the back, standing next to an industrial-looking sink, Margot spotted a guy in an apron with a fistful of paintbrushes. From the way he seemed to be slipping quietly past a group, she guessed he was some sort of assistant. He was turned slightly, so she couldn't see his face, but his hair was the same shade of brown as Jace's in his mugshot. It was longer in this photo, past his chin and tucked behind his ears. She zoomed in, and his face blurred, but she could make out the shape of it, the coloring.

Margot's heart beat fast. She hastily slid her laptop off her legs, then strode to her backpack, tugging out the pages she'd gotten at the courthouse. She clambered back onto the bed, her feet tucked beneath her, and held up Jace's mugshot next to the blurred image of the guy on the screen. Her eyes flicked back and forth, studying the faces. Yes, Jace in the mugshot looked younger, and yes, his hair had been shorter then, but Margot was almost positive they were one and the same.

A few hours later, Margot peered through the glass door of Bottle & Brush. The long right-hand wall was filled with amateur paintings: grinning llamas in flower crowns, endless *Starry Nights*, still lifes of potted plants and olive-adorned martinis. The place was dark and empty.

Margot knew from their website that they had a Paint Your Dog! class tonight at seven. She'd gotten there a little after five, in hopes of catching the employees before the participants arrived, but it seemed she was too early. She knocked loudly on the door, then cupped her hands to the glass and peered through. Nothing. She waited, knocked again. In the far back was a door, an employee-only room, but it remained closed.

"Shit," she said, turning to leave. She'd just have to wait in her car until people started to arrive. It was frustrating to spend hours on a lead she didn't even know would pan out, but it was the only lead she had.

As she was stepping off the curb, she heard the sound of a door swinging open behind her. "Can I help you?"

Margot's chest fluttered with hope. The business wasn't big; surely all the employees would know each other. If Jace worked there, whoever was at the door now would know. She turned around, her mouth open to explain, but then she froze. Standing in front of her—brown hair, bright green eyes, and sharp features— was the male version of January Jacobs.

When he self-consciously tucked his hair behind his ears, Margot realized she'd been staring. "Yeah, hi." Her voice sounded breathless. "Um . . ."

He cocked his head. "Are you interested in a class? We're not open now and our class tonight is sold out, but I could give you a calendar."

"Oh, thank you, but actually . . ." Her head was swimming. At the sight of him, vague memories of their childhood flooded her mind, images of running around in his backyard, playing hide- and-seek on the elementary school playground. "I'm actually here to see you."

"Excuse me?"

She hesitated. "You're Jace Jacobs, aren't you?"

Panic darted across his face and he began to turn away.

"Wait! My name's Margot Davies. I used to live across the street from you. I was friends with January."

Jace hesitated, slowly turning back around. His eyes were wary. "Margot?"

She gave him a tentative smile. "Do you remember me?"

"I do, actually."

This surprised her. He and January were branded on her brain because of the tragedy surrounding them, but she assumed she'd faded from his memory long ago.

"How did you find me?"

She lifted a shoulder. "It wasn't easy."

"And . . . why are you here?"

"Do you know what happened at your family's farm last Saturday? The message written on the barn?" She studied his face, looking for some sign that she'd caught him out.

His jaw tensed and his eyes went flat as if he'd slammed a window shut. Suddenly, she could see his face from the mugshot. "Are you a reporter or something?"

"I just wanna talk."

He let out a sharp bark of laughter. "Un-fucking-believable."

"Jace, please—"

"I go by Jay now," he snapped. "Or didn't your research tell you that?"

"Jay. I'm just trying to understand if there's a connection between that barn note and what happened to your sister. I just want to hear your version of what happened that night."

"It was nice seeing you again, Margot," he said as he turned to leave.

But Margot couldn't let him. Not now when she was so close. She wanted a story, yes—she wanted to be a real, credentialed journalist again—but this was so much more than that. This was about understanding what had happened to her friend that night across the street from her bedroom window. This was about unraveling the thread that connected January to Natalie Clark. This was about making sure no more little girls got taken, then showed up a day later, their bodies cold with death. Margot made a fist, brushing her fingertips against her palm's scattering of half-moon scars.

"Have you heard about Natalie Clark?"

Jace stopped, glanced over his shoulder. "What?"

"Natalie Clark," she repeated, studying his face for any hint that the name meant something to him, but his expression remained neutral, almost blank. Was he acting or did he really not know anything about the little girl? To Margot, Natalie's name was almost as familiar as January's now, but that wasn't normal. Most people didn't pay half as much attention to the news as she did.

"She was from Nappanee," she continued. "Five years old. She was taken from a playground a few days ago and police found her this morning, dead. She was murdered just like January."

Jace stared at her. Had he had something to do with the death of his sister? With the death of Natalie? So many conflicting images of him swirled in Margot's mind: Jace playing tag in the Jacobs backyard, Jace pushing his shoe into that dead bird, Jace beating up another kid, Jace putting flowers on his sister's grave. Margot had no idea what to think about the man in front of her. All she knew was that she needed him to talk.

"Jace—Jay, what happened to your sister, it's happening again. And I'm trying to figure out who's behind it before any other girls show up dead."

If he was innocent, or if he wanted to *look* innocent, refusing to talk to her now would look bad. Margot knew it and she knew he knew it too.

Jace stood still like that for a long moment, then finally he sighed and turned to face her. "I can't talk now. I have to get the studio ready."

"Okay."

"What about after? Around ten-thirty?"

She nodded. "Do you have a place in mind? A restaurant or a bar or something?"

He glanced down the sidewalk in one direction then the other. "No. I don't want to talk in public. You can come to my place."

Margot hadn't made up her mind about Jace yet, and she didn't love the idea of going to his apartment alone at night in the middle of a city she didn't know. But she'd text Pete the details. And anyway, it wouldn't be her first time to sit across from a potentially dangerous man for a story. She smiled up at him. "Just give me your address."

TWENTY

Margot, 2019

Margot knocked on Jace's apartment door and waited. Her throat felt tight with anticipation, though whether that was because she felt she was on the brink of understanding January's story or because she was nervous to be alone with Jace, she wasn't sure.

When the door swung open, Margot tried not to stare, but it felt surreal to be standing in front of the boy from across the street after all these years. And Jace's face was so like January's. Though, unlike his sister, there was that unsettling blankness in his expression that he'd had earlier, the same one he got after he'd guessed she was a reporter.

"Hi," he said. "Come in."

When Margot passed through the doorway, she was hit with a smell—earthy and a bit floral. On the coffee table, she spotted a stick of incense slowly turning to ash alongside a lighter, a small glass pipe, and a paperback copy of *The Bonfire of the Vanities*.

"You want a drink or something?" he said. His cadence was slow and flat, almost as if he was taking the time to weigh out every word, as if he'd had a lifetime of holding things in. Perhaps he did.

"That'd be great, thanks. I'll have whatever you have."

He turned toward the small, outdated kitchen, then turned back. "You can sit if you want." He nodded to the couch.

Margot sat, and as he rummaged in the refrigerator, she gazed around. Homes gave away a lot about their inhabitants, and from his—the old, mismatched furniture; the bare, beige walls; the red and orange tapestry hanging over the window as a makeshift curtain—she guessed he lived paycheck to paycheck, spending whatever was leftover on weed.

"Here ya go." Jace reentered the room with two bottles of beer. He popped the tops off both with an opener, then handed one to Margot.

"Thanks again for agreeing to meet with me," she said as he settled into the armchair across from her. "Do you mind if I—" She pulled her phone out of her bag to record.

He stared at it for a moment, then said, "I don't wanna be recorded. I'll talk to you, but that's it."

"Okay." She slipped her phone back into her bag. "No problem." In any other scenario, she probably would have pushed. Quoting an anonymous source was far less powerful than quoting a named one, especially when that source was Jace Jacobs. But his tone had been resolute and his face stony. "I know after everything you've been through, you're probably not a big fan of the media."

"I said two sentences on TV at the age of six and people still call me 'the spawn of Satan' online. I didn't change my name for nothing."

Margot blinked. "Right." She'd seen the interview the Jacobs family had done with Sandy Watters all those years ago. *I don't like to talk about it,* Jace had said, his little-kid voice flat and solemn. *I don't wanna get in trouble.* "Can I ask you then . . . why you're talking with me?"

Jace looked down. "I didn't know about that Natalie girl. I don't give a shit about your story, but if it helps catch whoever killed her, then . . ."

His words faded and Margot's mind raced with the implications of them. Did he think January had been killed by an intruder? Some strange man who was back at it? Or was he simply pretending to think that? She studied his face, but it was unreadable.

Earlier, in her hotel room, Margot had prepared her questions methodically, planning to ease Jace into talking like she had with Billy. But he was too good at hiding behind that mask. She needed to crack through it.

"I saw the flowers you put on January's grave," she said. Jace jerked his chin back, clearly surprised. "They were pretty. You do that every year, don't you?"

Jace hesitated, then nodded.

"Why?"

"Why do you think?"

She shook her head, her eye contact steady and unassuming. "I don't know."

He stared back at her for a long moment. Then, slowly, his hard exterior began to melt away. "I do it because . . . I feel bad, I guess. I wasn't a good brother to her when she was alive."

Margot waited for him to continue, and when he didn't, she said, "How so?"

"Honestly? I was jealous of her, because she, well, she . . . *sparkled*. And I was never like that." He gave her a wry look. "If you can imagine." Again, Margot waited in silence, and this time, after a moment, he continued. "Everybody loved her so much, ya know? My parents—they didn't even pretend to love me as much as they loved her."

Margot's gaze flitted over his face, as everything she'd learned about him ricocheted through her mind. The fire in the school bathroom, the dead bird, sending that boy to the hospital, the laundry list of crimes typed out on that thick stack of paper. Was it possible he'd done all of it because his parents hadn't loved him? Well, she thought, of course it was. Wasn't that why anyone did anything destructive? From feeling unloved? The only reason Margot was even mildly well adjusted was because of Luke.

"Can you tell me what happened that night?" she said, her voice gentle. She didn't want to break the spell that had been cast in the wake of his vulnerability. "In 1994?"

Jace took a sip of beer, then placed it on the coffee table with a clink of glass against glass. "I woke up in the middle of the night . . ."

Anticipation buzzed in Margot's veins. This was, to her knowledge, the first time he'd ever recounted this publicly. During the investigation, he and his parents had repeated the same line over and over again—the three of them had slept through the night.

"I don't know if something woke me or if I just woke up naturally, but I got up and went into January's room. I *was* jealous of her like I said, but we were also close, you know? We were twins." He looked at Margot and she nodded. "Every once in a while," he continued, "one of us would wake up and climb into the other's bed. Like if we had a nightmare or something. So I went into her room, but she was gone and I got scared."

"Scared? Like that something had happened to her?"

Jace shook his head. "No. Just little-kid scared. She should've been there and she wasn't. I remember I snuck into my parents' room, but she wasn't there either, so I walked downstairs to try to find her."

"Wait. You went to your parents' room that night? Were either of them there? Do you remember?"

"Yeah. They were sleeping."

"Your dad *and* your mom?"

He gave her a sort of confused look. Then after a moment, he said, "Oh, because you think my mom killed January." He said it lightly, as if he were inured to the idea. "Well, she didn't. She and my dad *were* sleeping that night. I saw them."

Margot struggled to keep her expression even. Until now, she hadn't been sure whether or not he was lying, whether or not he was responsible for January's death, but if he was, he'd just squandered the most effective cover story he had at his disposal. When the entire world believed Krissy had killed her daughter, it would've been all too easy for him to let her take the fall, especially now that she was dead and couldn't defend herself. In Margot's mind, Jace exonerating Krissy was almost as good as Jace exonerating himself.

"Anyway," he said. "I went downstairs, and when I got to the kitchen, I saw that the basement door was open. The basement door was never open." He took a deep breath. "I walked to the top of the stairs, the ones that led into the basement, and when I looked down them, I saw her. She wasn't moving."

Margot's eyes widened. Jace had found his sister's dead body that night? *Inside* the house? She had always assumed January had been killed somewhere along the way to the ditch.

"I was six," Jace said. "I had no idea what was going on. At first, I thought she was just sleeping. And I wanted her to get up, because we weren't supposed to be in the basement. But I was scared to go down there. So I walked to the kitchen table where I'd left my Etch A Sketch from earlier." He glanced at Margot. "Do you remember those? Etch A Sketches?"

"Of course."

"Right. So, anyway, I grabbed it and threw it down the stairs. Stupid, I know, but I was trying to wake her up. And it was loud, the Etch A Sketch. God, I remember that sound so clearly. The basement steps were concrete, and with everything else quiet, it was as loud as a gunshot. Still, January didn't move.

"That's when I went down the stairs. I remember how peaceful she looked. Like, I still thought she was just sleeping. Her face was . . . serene, and there was a little scrap of her baby blanket in her hand. Dad gave us both blankets when we were born, and January loved hers. Mom had washed it so many times by then, all that was left was a little square. Anyway, I tried shaking her arm and I remember that it felt weird, like too soft and too hard at the same time? I don't know how to explain it." He seemed to get lost in the memory, his eyes glazing over as he stared at a spot on the coffee table.

After a long moment, when he still hadn't continued, Margot used the opportunity to ask the question that had been nagging her since he'd started. "Do you really remember all this that clearly?"

He shrugged, looking suddenly very tired. "Yes and no. I've told this story to myself every day for twenty-five years, but I'm not sure if my brain remembers it all because it was so traumatic or if it just filled in the gaps. Some things are completely clear about that night. The sound of the Etch A Sketch for one, and seeing January at the bottom of the stairs. But it's not all one long memory. It's more like splotches of one."

Margot nodded. "And what do you remember next?"

"I was bent over her, checking if she was asleep, when I saw blood coming from her nose. I assumed she'd gotten a bloody nose and was lying down to stop it from bleeding. That's what our mom always had us do, like, tilt our heads back. And I remember leaning over to touch it. I don't actually know why I did this, but I remember it, because when I saw it on my finger, I freaked. I just wanted it off. I've never been good with blood. Or maybe I've never been good with it since. I don't know."

He took a sip of beer, and for the first time in her life, Margot could finally see all the strange pieces of evidence falling into place. She assumed he was about to tell her that he wiped the blood on his pajama pants.

"I wiped it off on my pajamas," he said. "And that's when I heard something behind me. I turned to see my mom standing at the top of the stairs and—this part I remember so clearly. The look on her face was—I can't even describe it. It was terrible, sort of a mixture of horror and rage. So I—" His voice cut out.

"So you . . . ?"

He shook his head. "Nothing. I just. I felt bad for her. I remember wanting to make her feel better, but I didn't know how. Do you mind if I smoke?"

He said the last so abruptly that for a moment, Margot didn't understand what he'd asked. "Oh, no, course not."

He grabbed the pipe from the table, lit the bowl, and took a hit. "Want some?" he asked, smoke curling from his mouth.

She shook her head. It wouldn't be the worst thing for her to relax, but she wanted a clear head and she was already drinking. "So what happened after that?"

He let out a hollow cough. "What happened after that is . . . nothing really. The next thing I remember is it being morning. For years, I believed January had been taken by whoever wrote those words on the kitchen wall—because that's what my parents told me happened. I later learned that wasn't true."

He went on to tell Margot that a decade earlier, he'd written to his mom and they'd struck up a correspondence about that night. "She told me that when she found me standing over January's dead body, she assumed I'd killed her. Pretty fucked up, huh?" He laughed bitterly. "It must've looked pretty bad, though, me standing there, January's blood on my clothes. But I guess my mom loved me more than I realized, because she decided to protect me.

"She staged the scene as a break-in, to divert the police from finding out 'what I'd done.'" He said the last part with air quotes.

"She found a hammer in the barn to smash in the basement window from the outside, to make it look like that's where the intruder came in. And when she was putting the hammer back, she found the spray paint and got an idea. She knew writing that message was risky, knew it was complicating the scene, but that's exactly what she thought she had to do. So she wrote all that shit on the wall, put the spray paint back in the barn, and then . . ."

His voice faded and he took a sip of beer. "She moved January's body. She put her into the trunk, drove to that ditch, and dumped her there. Which is why all the evidence pointed to her. The entire country thinks my mom is a murderer because of me."

Margot reeled with the impact of Jace's story. It was incredible, unbelievable, and yet it explained everything. Everything except who the actual killer was.

"What about your dad?" she asked. During her interview with Billy, she'd suspected he'd been holding something back about Krissy and about Jace too. Had he known about his wife's suspicions of their son? Had he known what she'd done to protect him? "What did he know? Did he help your mom that night?"

Jace shook his head. "According to her, he slept through the whole thing, but that's all she really said about it. I can't imagine he didn't suspect something, though—of me or her, I'm not sure. After that night, we all just sort of fell apart . . . And before you ask, I don't like my dad, and he wasn't a good dad, but he's not a murderer. Like I said, he loved January. More than he loved me. The media made us all look insane, but we were just a family. We might not have been happy, but we were normal."

They sat in silence for a moment, and then Margot said, "So, what d'you think happened? If you didn't kill January and neither did your mom or dad, who did?"

He leaned forward to grab the pipe from the table and took another hit. "I've always guessed that it was someone else.

Some . . . man with an infatuation. I mean, the police said the side door was unlocked when they got there, which—it was Wakarusa, 1994. Everyone slept with their door unlocked. Someone could've just walked right in. That's the irony: The story my mom wanted everyone to believe was what actually happened, but she fucked everything up so much that night we'll never know who really did it."

And if that were true—that a stranger had broken into the Jacobs house that night—that same someone could have written those words on the barn a few days ago, could've taken Natalie Clark from the playground in Nappanee, could've left that note on Margot's car.

"Have you told any of this to the police?"

He let out a short, humorless laugh. "I told Detective Townsend. A few months after my mom died, I showed him everything she'd sent me."

"What happened?"

Jace shrugged. "Not much. He clearly didn't believe what she'd written was true. Said the letters didn't reveal anything concrete other than that she'd fucked up the crime scene. Said there was no way to even confirm the handwriting was hers now that she was dead. I've never had much credibility when it comes to the cops, but it pissed me off and, well, things sort of fell apart for me for a while after that."

Margot's mind flashed to that long list of crimes. "Can you remember anyone from your childhood who showed a special interest in January? Anyone who was at her recitals or practices who shouldn't have been? Anyone you saw around in odd places?"

"No. And believe me—I've thought about it. I don't remember a strange man ever lurking around."

"What about a woman?"

He raised his eyebrows. "A woman?"

She nodded, an image of the auburn-haired woman in her mind. None of what Jace had said about that night had begun to explain her.

"Uh . . . Not that I can remember."

"What about someone January talked about? Was there anyone she mentioned a lot back then?"

"Jesus, I don't know. She talked about the other girls in her dance class. She talked about her dance teachers, Miss Morgan or Miss Megan or something. I think there was a Miss April, maybe. I don't know. Oh, she had an imaginary friend," he said with a breath of sarcastic laughter. "Are you interested in him? *He* went to her recitals and played with her at the park. She called him Elephant something because she said he had big ears." He smiled at the memory, and when he spoke again, his voice had softened with nostalgia. "She made up a funny last name for him too. God, what was it? Elephant . . . Elephant . . ." He snapped twice slowly. "Oh! Elephant Wallace!"

For a moment, as he laughed, Jace looked happy, light. But then he seemed to remember what had gotten him talking about January's invisible friend in the first place and his smile dropped. He looked weary once again.

"Listen, Margot, I wish I could help you more. But the truth is up until a few years ago, I hated myself so much I couldn't think straight. I know now that it's called survivor's guilt, but when I was actually in it, all I could think was *It should've been me.* I was six, seven, eight years old, and I actually wished I had died instead of her.

"And then, for a long time, I tried burying all of it. I tried drinking and drugs and nothing, *nothing* made it go away. I've been arrested, I've lied, I've cheated. I mean, I'm better now—well, not totally, but whatever. What I'm saying is that night ruined my fucking life. Of course, I've thought about who it could've been. I think about it every day. And I *don't know.*"

Margot nodded, stayed quiet. She burned with shame for putting him through all of this again. And also, somewhere deep beneath that, something was nagging at her brain. Something he'd said had triggered something inside her, but what it was, she couldn't quite put her finger on.

"Sorry," Jace said after a moment. "I don't mean to be . . . What happened that night took everything from me. It robbed me of my sister, my childhood—no one was allowed to be friends with me after that. And then when I finally told my mom the truth—the first person I'd ever told—it robbed me of her too."

Margot shook her head. "Wait. What d'you mean?"

"The day she got my last letter was the day she killed herself. Her suicide was her way of apologizing for getting everything wrong. She'd still be alive today if I hadn't told her the truth." ·

The words of Krissy's leaked suicide note filled Margot's mind—*Jace, I'm sorry for everything. I'm going to make it right*—and another piece of the puzzle clicked into place. Krissy took her own life not out of guilt for killing her daughter, but out of guilt for getting it all wrong, for suspecting her own son of murder.

"And I let her slip between my fingers. In every letter she wrote, she asked to meet up, but I never would. I wouldn't even give her my address, had her send her replies to a PO box. I was so fucking angry. Now . . ." Jace's voice faded and he shook his head. "I hope you find this guy, Margot, whoever he is. I hope you find him and I hope he burns in hell."

Throughout the rest of the night, Margot continued to feel that strange sensation of something nagging at her mind. But what it was or what Jace had said that triggered it, she couldn't put her finger on. It felt just out of reach, like an old memory buried beneath layers of junk. It tugged at her brain as she brushed her teeth and as she slipped under the covers of her hotel bed.

Her subconscious had clearly worked at it all night, though, because when she woke the next morning, she realized it was January's imaginary friend, Elephant Wallace, who meant something to her. The name, the big ears—it all felt familiar. But how could it? Had January mentioned him to Margot? Had Margot been introduced to the invisible stranger all those years ago? Had she, Elephant, and January all sat down to tea together once upon a time? Somehow, she didn't think so. And yet, what other explanation could there be?

It continued to bother her as she threw her things into her backpack and checked out at the front desk. And then, finally, it hit her, smacking into her consciousness with the force of a semi-truck. She was on the highway when it happened, halfway home, and she nearly swerved into the next lane.

Jace had gotten it wrong. Elephant Wallace wasn't imaginary, nor was his name Elephant. Margot knew because she knew who he was; she even knew where he lived and what he looked like—big ears and all. Three years ago, she'd interviewed him in conjunction with the Polly Limon case. Elliott Wallace had been one of the suspects.

TWENTY-ONE

Krissy, 1994

The interview with Sandy Watters backfired. Far from rehabilitating the Jacobses' image, it served as ammunition with which the American people used to declare their guilt. Billy had sweat too much, people said. Jace was a creepy kid who looked like he knew something he wasn't saying. And Krissy was an unfit mother. The media had picked apart the footage of her begrudgingly wrapping her arm around Jace so many times that the three-second clip was famous. *Lisa and Bob in the Morning* had shown snapshots of Krissy's face as she'd done it, her eyes hard, her jaw set. "I'm not saying that's the face of a killer," Lisa said. "But it does certainly seem to be the face of someone who's hiding something." Krissy hadn't needed any more fodder for her resentment toward Billy, but he'd certainly given it to her by coercing her onto *Headline with Sandy Watters*. Overnight, casseroles stopped showing up on their doorstep; letters of sympathy stopped arriving in the mail. When Krissy went to the grocery store, people who used to call themselves her friends would cut their eyes away from hers coldly.

The detectives, on the other hand, were as persistent as ever.

Townsend in particular seemed suspicious of Krissy, his cold blue gaze always watching. Once, he and Lacks asked her to come to the station to talk, where they dropped the bomb that their cadaver dogs had hit upon her trunk, detecting the scent of decomposition. When forensics searched it later, they found fibers from the nightgown January had been wearing on the night of her death.

Krissy could feel herself sweating through her shirt as she told the detectives that she often put the kids' things in the trunk, especially January's stuff for dance. It got funky in the heat, which could possibly explain the scent. As for the fibers, like she'd just said, her daughter's clothes were in the trunk all the time. "I keep telling you," she added in a shaky voice. "I had nothing to do with January's death. Who you should be talking to is all those men who lurked around her competitions." Since that first day of the investigation, Krissy had never veered from her story. It was an intruder, a stranger, a bad man.

In the days following the interview, Krissy waited like a tightly wound spring for Detectives Townsend and Lacks to knock on their door with a warrant for her arrest. But they never did. The days turned to weeks, and eventually the urgency with which the detectives spoke about the case fizzled into something closer to resignation. Townsend stopped looking at her as if she were an animal he was trying to catch and began looking at her as if she were one that had gotten away. Months went by without any new developments, and then, in a blink, the world was in a new century and the case had gone cold.

For Krissy, the years passed in a blur of Valium and sleeping pills. She continued to dress in the right clothes for church and put on makeup when she left the house, but her mind was perpetually blank, numbness her only relief from the grief of losing her daughter and the torture of living with the boy who'd killed her and a man who'd never been what she'd needed.

And then, in 2004, ten years after losing January, something happened that made the days tolerable again. For the first time in her life, Krissy fell in love.

It all started on a Thursday afternoon in autumn. Krissy had spent the day running errands as usual, mindlessly checking off the menial tasks that made up her life, and when she pulled up to the farmhouse around five, she found she couldn't get out of the car. She sat, blank and unmoving, as the minutes ticked by. The idea of unbuckling her seatbelt, opening her door, and walking into the home she shared with Jace and Billy struck her as physically impossible. Without thinking about what she was doing or where she was going, she turned the key in the ignition and backed out of the driveway.

Half an hour later, Krissy found herself in South Bend, pulling into the parking lot of the first bar she found. When she walked through the front door, for the first time in a long time, she didn't feel the heat on her face as everyone turned their eyes to her, didn't hear the familiar murmur of whispers in her wake. The place was a dive, with dim lighting and a jukebox on the far wall. The only real attempt at decoration was the ceiling, which was covered with toothpicks, their ends wrapped in colorful plastic. Krissy loved it.

She slid into one of the booths, the red plastic sticky against her jeans, ordered a pinot grigio from the waitress, and basked in the unfamiliar relief of being unrecognized. Though the feeling didn't last long—she was on her second glass of wine when she heard her name.

"Krissy?" a voice said from beside her. "Krissy Jacobs?"

Heart dropping, Krissy looked up. She just wanted one night free from the judgmental, probing gaze of others, one night where she could breathe. She assumed being recognized in South Bend meant whoever this was had seen her on the news, and strangers could be even worse than people in Wakarusa. But when she saw the face in front her, Krissy was surprised to see it didn't belong to a stranger after all. "Oh," she said. "Hi."

"Jodie." The woman touched her hand to her chest. "From Northlake High? My last name's Palmer now, but I was Jodie Dienner back then."

"No, yeah. I remember you."

Jodie opened her mouth to say something and Krissy steeled herself for the inevitable. *You look so good,* people had told her in the months following that infamous TV interview, their tones bright and full of condemnation. *If I'd been through what you did, I'd never be able to get out of bed again, let alone put makeup on.* Or when she'd turn her back, she'd hear them whisper, *I can't believe she's got the nerve to show her face.*

But when Jodie spoke, all she said was, "My god, you look exactly the same."

Krissy searched Jodie's face, but it looked guileless and open. "You don't," she said. "You look . . . amazing." Krissy remembered Jodie as a wallflower. She'd always been tall and thin, but the way she'd carried herself, with a slight slump of her shoulders, had made people look right over her. She'd had dishwater blond hair that had hung limply around her face and she'd never worn any makeup or clothes that could ever be construed as trying to attract attention. The woman standing in front of Krissy now looked transformed. She was wearing a cream silk button-down tucked into form-fitting blue jeans, and though her face was still bare save for a swipe of mascara, with her hair tucked behind her ears, she no longer seemed to be hiding from the world. "I didn't mean you looked bad in high school," Krissy rushed to say. "Sorry."

But Jodie just laughed. "No, no. I know what you meant." She opened her mouth, then closed it. "Hey, would you mind . . ." She nodded at the empty seat across from Krissy.

"Oh, no. Please." It made Krissy anxious to accept company,

but she'd learned long ago that being widely perceived as a child killer meant her manners had to be impeccable.

Jodie placed the beer she'd been holding onto the table, then slid into the seat. "So, are you in South Bend these days?"

"No. I just had some errands up here. We're still in Wakarusa."

Jodie raised her eyebrows. "Really? Wow. I just assumed with everything that happened . . ." Again, Krissy waited for some snide remark, but it never came.

"We thought about moving," she said with a shrug. "But Wakarusa's home." She forced a smile to go with the well-worn lie. The truth was she'd begged Billy to let them leave. Moving hadn't appealed to her as much as divorce, but she hadn't known how to survive on her own. She'd never held a single job, save her summer position at the grain elevator all those years ago. And she hadn't known what she'd do with Jace if she and Billy split. She hadn't been able to stomach the idea of leaving her son, nor had she wanted to live alone with him. So, she'd asked to move instead. She craved a life in the city, somewhere big and anonymous, but Billy had refused. That was exactly what they'd do if they were guilty, he'd said. If they were innocent—which they were—they'd stay in Wakarusa, heads held high.

Jodie's eyes flicked over Krissy's face, but she just smiled softly. "Hey, you know what I was thinking about recently? Do you remember that one time in sixth grade when Dusty Stephens ran for class treasurer and he made that speech in the cafeteria and the whole time his sweatshirt was on backwards?" She and Krissy both started grinning at the memory. "Like, do you think he knew? Was it on purpose? What was the point?" Jodie laughed and Krissy couldn't help but join in. Soon they were both shaking with it.

For the rest of that drink and for the rest of another, the two women reminisced about their shared past, and Krissy felt lighter than she had in years.

"Do you have to go?" she asked at one point when Jodie stole a glance at her watch. Her voice was casual as she said it, but the idea of ending the night now was a wrench in her stomach. It had been a very long time since she'd felt this good. "Don't let me keep you."

"Sorry, but I probably should. I need to throw something together for dinner. My husband should be home by now, but he's worthless without me there to hold his hand." She rolled her eyes, laughing.

Krissy smiled, but it felt tight. "Of course, no problem."

"But maybe . . ." Jodie hesitated. "Maybe we could do this again sometime?"

There was the slightest hint of nerves in her voice, and Krissy's heart sank. Her old acquaintance may have been kinder than most, but Jodie clearly still thought she was sitting across from a killer. "Thanks. But you probably don't wanna go around town with a murderer." She'd tried to sound flip, but her eyes prickled.

Jodie gave her a long look. "I don't think you killed your daughter, Krissy."

Tears fell so suddenly down Krissy's cheeks it was as if she'd been slapped. Jodie's words felt like sunlight on her skin after a long, dark winter. "Okay then," she said, brushing her fingers beneath her eyes. "I'll give you my number."

The two women got drinks again the next week and then coffee two days after that, and soon they were meeting up almost every other day. Through all their conversations, Krissy learned that Jodie had also spent her high school years burning to escape Wakarusa. Upon graduation, she'd moved to South Bend for the fall semester at Notre Dame and never left. There, she'd studied Spanish and art history—*so practical, huh?*—and met her husband. They'd gotten married a few years out of college, and while Jodie had dreamed of a career in the arts, she'd gotten pregnant with her firstborn shortly thereafter. Her second kid had come only a year later, and by the time she'd had her third, she was a full-time mom and her brain was too crammed with feeding and sleeping schedules to fit anything else. Over the years, Jodie and her husband had drifted further and further apart until she felt like they were friendly co-workers with only sometimes overlapping shifts. *I still love him,* she told Krissy once. *But I haven't been in love in a long time.* Jodie's story was all too familiar to Krissy, and it made her ache for her new friend. What small tragedies their lives had turned out to be.

There was something open and unassuming about Jodie that allowed Krissy to relax around her in a way she hadn't with anyone in a very long time. The band of tightness around her chest loosened when she was with her. Her shoulders and jaw unclenched. For years, she'd pasted on tight smiles, forced cordiality, endured backhanded compliments. But with Jodie, she laughed. Sometimes, she even forgot.

Krissy was in the kitchen one morning about three months after their first run-in in South Bend when her phone chimed with a text from Jodie. *The kids are at sleepovers this Saturday, so I'm treating myself to a staycation! Want to get dinner at the hotel that night? Maybe face masks in the room after?*

By this point, Krissy had developed a near Pavlovian response of excitement to seeing Jodie's name on her phone, and she felt herself biting back a smile as she typed her response. *Duh! I'll bring the masks and wine.*

For the rest of the week, every time she thought about their plans, Krissy got a little jolt of excitement, and when the night came, as they ate in the hotel's restaurant, the air felt electric. For the past few months, Krissy had felt something building between them, though what it was exactly she didn't know. The last time she'd felt something similar had been that summer after senior year—not with Billy, but with Dave. Her friendship with Jodie felt like a fluttering, a giddiness, a literal spark. But every time her brain went in that direction, it ground to a halt. She wasn't gay. So perhaps this was simply what it felt like to have a real friend. Perhaps she'd been starved of companionship for so long she couldn't tell the difference between that and romance.

That night at dinner, they split a bottle of wine, and afterward, giggling and tipsy, they took the elevator to Jodie's floor. When the doors dinged open, Jodie walked out, but Krissy, who'd just noticed a button on her blouse had come undone, stopped.

"Oh no," she said, laughing. "Has it been like this all night?" She looked up, fumbling with the button, to see Jodie, her fingers pressed to her lips. When they locked eyes, Jodie snorted out a laugh. "Oh my god," Krissy said through her giggles. "It has!"

Jodie lifted her hand. "I didn't notice it, I swear." But then she burst into another fit of laughter that morphed into a shriek as the elevator doors began to close. "The doors!" She threw out an arm, grabbed Krissy by the hand, and tugged her over the threshold.

They walked to Jodie's room, then tumbled into it, breathless with laughter, their fingers still intertwined. The heavy door swung shut behind them and they fell against it, shaking. Eventually, the laughter slowed and they caught their breath, smiles lingering on their lips. The moment came when it would have felt natural to let go of each other's hands, but neither did, and soon the moment passed, and then another and another.

"Um." Jodie turned toward Krissy, her shoulder still pressed into the door, her eyes downcast. "Would you mind if I just tried—" Her voice cut out and suddenly she was leaning forward, pressing her lips against the spot between Krissy's jaw and ear.

Krissy's breath came out of her in a fast rush. Her body melted; her mind swirled. "Have you, uh . . ." Her voice was hoarse and breathless. "Have you done this before? With a woman, I mean?"

Jodie pulled her head back to look her in the eyes. She nodded. "Have you?"

Krissy swallowed, shook her head.

"Are you . . . Do you want to?" Jodie's eyes flicked over Krissy's face, lingering on her lips.

But Krissy couldn't speak. She just nodded, and suddenly Jodie's mouth was on hers and Krissy no longer cared that she wasn't gay or that she didn't have a label for what she felt for this woman. That spark between them had ignited a flame, and now she simply surrendered.

The next time they saw each other, at lunch in South Bend a few days later, Jodie invited Krissy over afterward and they were kissing the moment the front door shut behind them. To Krissy, their connection felt both magnetic and safe, and when Jodie told her that she loved her a month later, Krissy didn't hesitate before saying that she loved her back.

Although she initially worried Billy would discover her secret, it turned out to be relatively easy to hide an affair from him, as long as it was a gay one. She simply told him the truth—that she'd reconnected with Jodie Palmer from school and they'd struck up a friendship. As long as she was home when he woke in the morning, and as long as there was food in the fridge, he didn't seem to suspect a thing. Meanwhile, Jace had grown into a volatile teenager, sometimes sullen, sometimes angry, always in trouble. Krissy, who often wondered if she'd done the right thing all those years ago by protecting him, had long since learned that the best way to deal with him was the path of least resistance. It seemed if she didn't ask questions about his life, he didn't ask about hers. She and Jodie knew, however, that not everyone would be so blind, so they made sure to enter and exit hotel rooms separately. They only touched each other behind closed doors.

The years passed and their affair soon grew into something solid. Although they didn't live together, it was Jodie, not Billy, with whom Krissy now shared her life. The only thing she didn't share was her secrets.

But then, in 2009, something happened that changed everything.

It was a Saturday morning and Billy was working the farm while Krissy did laundry and cleaned. She'd just retrieved the mail, tossed the little stack onto the kitchen table, and was turning to the stairs to switch the sheets from the washer to the dryer, when an envelope caught her eye. The return address was a PO box. In the center, her name was scrawled in neat, slanted letters. Her heart thumped hard in her chest. She hadn't seen Jace's handwriting in years.

Four years earlier, when Jace was seventeen, he walked down the stairs and told her he was dropping out of school and moving out. To where, he didn't say. He was packed by lunchtime, and as Krissy watched his old hatchback retreat down the driveway, her knees almost buckled with relief. She didn't know how to be a mother to this strange ghost-like creature, the boy who killed his sister. Unexpectedly, though, another emotion that felt oddly like regret bloomed in her chest. She didn't know how she could've done better, but she felt she'd somehow done something wrong.

Now, Krissy stood in the kitchen, staring at her son's handwriting on the envelope for a long moment. Then, with a trembling hand, she reached down and plucked it from its spot in the stack. The letter inside was handwritten in blue ink.

Mom,

When I left a few years ago, I didn't think I'd ever want to talk to you or Dad again. But I'm going through a program now and I'm supposed to make amends. Though if I'm being honest, I don't really think I need your forgiveness. There's no way everything I did to you could even begin to balance our scales. Yeah, I know I messed up, but I was the kid. You were the adult. You should've done better.

I know losing January was hard for you—she was your daughter—but it was hard for me too, and I never understood why her death meant I had to lose my mom. And please don't act like you don't know what I mean: For eleven years, you never even looked me in the eye. Do I really have to tell you how unfair that is? *I* was alive. But the only thing you ever cared about was January.

I knew you loved her more than me long before she died. All those dance lessons for her, while you stuffed me into a corner. And after she died, it was like I ceased to exist. Dad was just as bad, don't get me wrong. But he'd never understood me because I wasn't like him. You were different. We had a chance and you threw it away. And there's nothing that feels shittier than not being loved by your own mom.

I know I've gone and fucked up the "making amends" step with this letter, but I don't really care. I haven't been good in my life, but I think you need my forgiveness much more than I need yours.

J

The letter fluttered from Krissy's hand, landing on the table, open as a wound. She'd thought about this day for years, the day her son might break his silence. Now it had come and she had no idea how to respond. She didn't know what he was referring to when he said he'd "messed up." Was he talking about all the times he'd gotten in trouble—the weed, the school bathroom fire, when he'd punched another boy so many times he'd put him in the hospital because the boy said his family were all murderers? Or had his "mess up" been killing his own sister? Maybe he was right, Krissy thought. Maybe she did need his forgiveness, but what she knew without a shadow of a doubt was that he also needed hers.

Slowly, she folded the letter and tucked it into the back pocket of her jeans. All day, as she moved through her chores in a daze, her hand kept touching the fabric of her jeans as if her son's letter was a living, pulsing thing. Then, late that night, after Billy had gone to bed, Krissy sat at the kitchen table, pen in hand, and began to write.

Dear Jace,

Thank you for the letter. It was hard to read, but I'm glad you sent it. I will always be your mom, and unlike what you seem to believe, I will always love you.

How could you ever believe otherwise when everything I did that night—*everything*—I did for you? To protect you. I thought you were going to be taken away from me and thrown into some juvenile institution, or if not that, I thought you'd be labeled a murderer for the rest of your life and I couldn't bear that. It was the worst thing I've ever done, and I would do it again. For you.

I admit that afterward I didn't know how to be your mom anymore. Every time I looked at you, I thought of what you'd done to January and it broke my heart. I did shut down, but not just because I'd lost my daughter. Because I'd lost my son too. And yet, throughout all those years, I never stopped loving you. So please don't say I didn't when my life is a testament to the love I have for you. I've made many mistakes, and for those I'm sorry, but not loving you was never one of them.

Could I call you sometime, or maybe we could even meet up? I'd love to see you. At the very least, please write back.

Love,
Mom

Krissy slid her letter into the post office drop box in town the next morning and began checking their mailbox obsessively in the days that followed. She felt so desperate to know what he'd say that it was a physical thing, as real and biting as hunger. And yet nothing could have prepared her for what he did eventually write back the following week, just a few scribbled lines that turned her world upside down.

Mom, your letter made no sense to me. What did you do for me that night? Why did you think people would believe I was a murderer? I don't know what you think happened to January, but I'm not the one who killed her.

TWENTY-TWO

Margot, 2019

Margot made it home from Chicago in record time. From the moment Elliott Wallace's name had popped into her head, she'd driven fifteen miles over the speed limit all the way back to Wakarusa. Because this was it: Elliott Wallace was the connection she'd been looking for. As a suspect in Polly Limon's case, *he* was the link between her and January and now Natalie Clark. *He* was the faceless stranger Margot had envisioned her entire life, the man who'd strolled down her childhood street and slipped into the house across from hers.

Margot burst through her uncle's front door to find Luke at the kitchen table, nursing a cup of coffee and working on a crossword. Despite her buzzing, propulsive need to track Wallace down, the sight made her stop short in relief.

"Uncle Luke," she said, mortified to feel a stinging in her eyes. She'd only been gone one night, and Pete had texted the previous afternoon to tell her he'd stopped by and all was well, but still, her whole body slackened at the sight of him. "How are you? Are you okay?"

"I think the question is . . ." Luke said with a wry grin over his cup of coffee. "Are you?"

Margot laughed. No doubt she looked as frantic as she felt. The name Elliott Wallace was thumping in her brain like a drumbeat. "I'm good. I just have some work to do. I know I just got home, but . . ." She shook her head. "Are you sure you're okay?"

"Kid, you're acting a little nuts. Why don't you go do whatever it is you gotta do."

She let out another small laugh. "Okay." She took a few steps toward the hallway, then turned and walked into the kitchen instead, put a hand on her uncle's shoulder, and kissed his temple. "It's good to be back."

In her room, Margot flung herself onto the floor, grabbed her laptop from her bag, and pulled it open. She drummed her fingers against its edge impatiently as it booted up. The moment it did, she opened her storage in the cloud. As she scrolled through her long collection of folders, looking for the one labeled Polly Limon, she tried to remember the details of the little girl's case.

Polly had been seven at the time she'd disappeared from a mall parking lot in Dayton, Ohio, three years ago. According to the police report made by Polly's mother, on that fall afternoon, the two of them had been walking back to their car after a shopping trip. Polly had run ahead, but when Mrs. Limon had made it to their car, her daughter hadn't been there. She'd reported Polly missing within the hour and the official search had lasted five days until the girl's body had been found in a ditch less than a mile from where she'd been taken. The police reported signs of sexual abuse and injuries to her head, though the cause of death was technically strangulation.

Unlike both January's and Natalie's cases, the search for Polly and the subsequent search for her killer hadn't garnered much attention from the public. Right around the time she was reported missing, Margot remembered, there'd been a mass shooting at a middle school in Columbus, and the faces of those seven gunshot victims were the only thing on the news, local and national. It was why Margot had been able to get so close to the case in the first place, because all the other reporters had been seventy miles away.

During the weeks she'd spent covering the story, she hadn't been able to get the similarities between Polly's case and January's out of her head. They'd been more or less the same age, they'd both been found in a ditch, they'd both sustained trauma to the head. Dayton wasn't extremely close to Wakarusa, but it was under a four-hour drive away. Neither of their killers had ever been found.

Sitting on the floor of her uncle's old office, Margot finally located the folder. She double-clicked it open and scrolled through a series of subfolders all the way to the very bottom, where she found the one labeled Elliott Wallace.

The contents of the folder were sparse—one document of notes and a recording of Margot's interview with him. Although she was disappointed, she wasn't surprised. The Elliott Wallace lead had been a quick dead end, both in the police's investigation and in her own. The detectives had been alerted to Elliott Wallace as a possible person of interest by a local woman, a parent of another girl in Polly's young equestrian program. According to the woman, he had a history of lurking around the stables during the children's practice. The police had interviewed Wallace multiple times, but lacking any direct evidence linking him to the murder, they eventually let him go.

Margot clicked first on the document of notes, which turned out to be little more than the basics of who Elliott Wallace was, or, at least, who he'd been three years ago. At the time of Polly's murder, Wallace had been forty-eight. Originally from Indianapolis, he'd been living in Dayton, working as a security guard for a gated community. His parents were dead and his only remaining family was an older sister living in Indianapolis, with whom Wallace rarely spoke.

Beneath this basic fact sheet, Margot had included a photo of Wallace she'd found on the internet. In it, he had dirty blond hair, parted and combed on the side, a sharp jaw, and smiling brown eyes. But his most prominent feature was his ears. Disproportionately large, they stuck out from his head at an angle, making him look a little like an elephant. Despite them, he was, by all standards, attractive, and the image gave her a jolt of recognition. She remembered sitting across from him in his living room. He'd been tall and slender, with long fingers he interlaced over his lap and long legs he crossed at the knee. He'd seemed completely at ease during their interview and unfailingly polite.

As she gazed at him now, heat crawled up her chest and neck. She felt, deep inside her, that this was the man who'd killed all those girls, that she was staring at the face of a murderer.

She clicked out of the file, selected the recording, and hit play. Within moments, the sound of her own voice filled the room.

"So how long have you lived in Dayton?" Margot heard herself ask.

"Oh, let's see," a second voice said. Elliott Wallace had a smooth, almost musical, cadence. He clicked his tongue thoughtfully. "Not long. A year maybe. Actually, I suppose it'd be closer to two at this point. Moved here from Indianapolis."

"And are you married? Any children?"

"Neither, sadly. I would've liked to get married, I think, but the right woman never came along. I date occasionally, but it becomes more challenging the older you get. You get sort of stuck in your own ways, I suppose." He chuckled. "At least I have."

Margot closed her eyes to focus on Wallace's words. She remembered thinking at the time how collected he was, how poised. Here she'd been questioning him in relation to the homicide of a little girl, and yet he'd managed to stay calm and cooperative. But

now, Margot heard a performative lilt to his words she hadn't recognized sitting across from him. Was she being biased because of
everything she knew now or had she been blind then?

"And you were questioned recently by the police," her voice
continued on the recording. "About the murder of Polly Limon."

"That's right." Wallace's voice turned suddenly solemn.

"Why did they think you were involved?"

"Oh." Wallace heaved a sigh. "Because in the past, I've visited
the stables where the girl practiced and competed. Honestly, I
don't blame the mother who gave the detectives my name. I realize I'm a single, adult man, and in this day and age, it's a sad reality
that the optics of that . . . aren't good. Unfortunately, I didn't
consider that when I went. If I could turn back time, I wouldn't
have gone at all, not now that I know I made this woman feel
uncomfortable. But the truth is I'm a fan of the sport. And of
horses in general. I often visit the stables when no one's there at
all."

"And when you were at the stables," Margot heard herself say,
"did you ever talk to Polly Limon?"

"I didn't even know who she was until I saw her name on the
news. Her face looked vaguely familiar, but I'm not sure I would've
placed where I knew it from if they hadn't mentioned her equestrian stuff." Wallace sighed. "It's terrible what happened to her. As
I've said, I don't have children, but I imagine there's nothing
worse than losing one of your own."

"Can you tell me what you were doing on the night of Tuesday,
May third?" she asked. Though present-day Margot didn't remember the significance of the date, she assumed it was the night before Polly's body had been found.

"I can. Typically, I wouldn't remember my whereabouts so
readily, but, as the police just asked me the same thing, it's top of
mind." There was the slightest chill in his voice as he said this, a
subtle but clear signal of his indignation at being asked. "I worked

till about six that evening, then I went home and fixed myself some dinner. Just a simple pasta recipe, nothing special. Afterward, I went to Barnes & Noble, where I bought a copy of *The Heart of Darkness*—I'm working through the classics. And then I came home, where I was for the rest of the evening."

"So, you don't have an alibi for that night?"

"Well, one of the booksellers can vouch that I was at the store. I'm sure she remembers me because I couldn't find *The Heart of Darkness,* and as she walked me over to the section, we struck up a friendly argument about the virtues of reading the classics. She was, I remember, more of a fan of fantasy novels." There was a slight pause, and Margot envisioned him giving her a smile. "As this bookseller no doubt told the police, I was at the store for quite a while reading. Till eight-thirty, perhaps. Maybe later. I can't remember. Then I came home, read a bit more, and went to bed. So other than the bookseller, I do not have an alibi." His voice turned just slightly bitter as he added, "Which is a shame. I would very much like *not* to be embroiled in a homicide investigation."

Leaning back against the futon now, eyes closed, Margot shook her head. Even his alibi seemed calculated to her. It was flimsy enough to make it seem offhand, solid enough to ensure he was telling the truth, and still left the rest of his night wide open.

"What about January Jacobs? Did you know *her*?"

Margot's eyes flung open. She hadn't remembered asking him that. She remembered she'd told Adrienne about her theory connecting the two cases, but she hadn't recalled actually broaching the question to Wallace. Sitting there now, she felt almost giddy with gratefulness to her younger self.

"January Jacobs?" Wallace repeated, sounding genuinely surprised.

"That's right."

"Well, I mean, I know *of* her of course. Doesn't everybody?"

"Did you ever meet her?"

Wallace scoffed. "Uh . . . no." But despite the indignation in his tone, he also sounded flustered. "I'm sorry, but what are you getting at here?"

"Have you ever been to Wakarusa?" Margot asked.

"Waka . . ." His voice faded. "I don't know. Maybe. I'm not sure."

"You're not sure if you've been to Wakarusa, Indiana?"

"I'm forty-eight years old. I've traveled a lot in my life, so it's possible that I have. But to be perfectly honest, no, I'm not sure. Now, unfortunately, I have to get going. I have an appointment I have to get to in half an hour." He took a breath, and when he spoke next, he sounded calmer, more collected. "Thanks for taking the time to report on this crime, Margot, and best of luck with your article. I hope this bastard gets caught. And soon. Anyone who could kill an innocent little girl like that, in my opinion, should be hung from the neck."

There was some rustling, then a muffled murmur of voices as the microphone was moved. Then the recording clicked off.

Margot sat, her back against the futon, a chill running up her spine. Wallace's answers about Polly had been polished to the point they sounded rehearsed. He'd admitted to visiting the stables where she practiced and he'd had a flimsy alibi for the night of her death. And when Margot had questioned him about January, he'd suddenly gotten rattled and ended the interview, but not before admitting that he'd traveled a lot in his life. He may not have remembered everywhere he'd been, but she had at least a few ideas: Wakarusa, Dayton, and Nappanee, the hometowns of January Jacobs, Polly Limon, and Natalie Clark.

She hadn't known it then, but now Margot felt it with a certainty that went all the way into her teeth: three years ago, she'd shaken hands with, sat across from, and listened to the lies of a killer.

Her mind raced. She didn't want to screw up this story with hasty research or reporting on it too soon, which meant she had a lot to do. Because right now, all she had was circumstantial evidence linking Elliott Wallace to two out of three cases. She could place him in Dayton, Ohio, at the time of Polly Limon's death, and he'd admitted on tape to visiting the stables where she used to ride. Other than that, Margot had the word of Jace Jacobs, who'd refused to go on record, connecting Wallace to January as—of all things—an imaginary friend. While that was enough for her to be sure she was on to something, it obviously wasn't enough to skewer him. And Margot wanted to do just that: slice him up and serve him to the police on a silver platter.

But before she could do anything, she heard an enormous crash just beyond her door. And then, the shouting began.

TWENTY-THREE

Margot, 2019

Margot threw open her bedroom door and raced out into the hallway.

"Motherfucker!" Luke's voice bellowed throughout the house.

She followed the sound into the kitchen, where she stopped dead in her tracks, her eyes widening in shock, and everything about the case was blotted from her mind. The only thing she could register was the sight of the kitchen before her. How long had she been holed up in her room? She couldn't have been in there for more than an hour, but the kitchen looked completely unrecognizable since she'd passed through it earlier.

One of the kitchen chairs was toppled over—the source of the crash, Margot guessed—and every single drawer and cabinet was wide open and empty, the counters covered in their contents. A pile of oven mitts and pot holders sat atop a tall stack of plates. Beside that was a collection of every utensil her uncle had—steak knives, butter knives, forks, soup spoons, serving spoons, ladles. Random objects from the junk drawer—a digital Yahtzee, a bouquet of pencils, an old hairbrush, a pair of rusty scissors—had been relocated to the inside of all his cups. It seemed impossible that the mounds and mounds of stuff had at one time fit into the kitchen at all. At the center of everything, with his back to her, was Luke.

"Uncle Luke?" Margot said tentatively.

Luke spun around furiously, his eyes wide and wild. In his hands was a jar of pickles. "I can't find it!" he spat.

She lifted her palms gently. "Okay. Okay. What is it you can't find?"

"Well, what do you think? The goddamn mustard!" He slammed the jar of pickles onto the overflowing countertop, nudging a giant bag of Fritos and a plastic spray bottle of all-purpose cleaner out of the way. He picked up a stack of plastic place mats, looked beneath them, then put them back again.

Margot quickly scanned the contents of the countertops for the mustard, but she didn't see it anywhere. "Let me see if I can help, okay?" Her throat felt thick and her heart was pounding.

"I don't see why you'd be able to find it when I can't." He spun around, his eyes roving to the other side of the kitchen, then locking on to the oven. He strode over and opened it, bending down to check inside.

"You're probably right. But I can at least help you look." As Luke closed then opened the empty kitchen cabinets behind her, Margot strode quietly to the refrigerator. But the mustard wasn't inside it. Everything but one carton of milk had been removed. And oddly enough, there on the middle shelf was Luke's wireless home phone. Margot surreptitiously took it out and placed it onto a stack of paper plates.

She checked the freezer next, and just when she spotted the mustard nestled behind a carton of ice cream, Luke walked to the opposite side of the little freezer door and banged it shut. But Margot had been in its way and the sharp corner of the plastic shelf slammed against her cheek, hard.

Pain, cold and searing, sliced into her. Margot gasped, clapping a hand against it.

Luke stepped around the freezer door, which, after banging against her, had swung back open. "Rebecca?" He stared at Margot, his brow furrowed, his body still.

Margot's breath came in ragged gulps as the pain sharpened and concentrated. She felt as if she'd been sliced by a knife and her cheek felt slick beneath her fingers. When she pulled her hand away, it was bright with blood.

"Rebecca?" Luke said again. This time there was a tremble in his voice. "Are you—"

Before he could finish, there was a knock at the front door.

"Fuck," Margot said through clenched teeth. She scanned the kitchen for the paper towels and found a roll stuck between the toaster and blender. She tore off a square and pressed it to her throbbing face.

Another knock came at the front door, harder and louder this time.

"Coming!" Margot shouted as she mopped up her bloody cheek, threw the balled-up paper towel into the trash, and strode to the door. As she reached to open it, whoever was on the other side knocked again. "Jesus Christ," she hissed, swinging the door wide. *"What?"*

Standing in the doorway, blinking in alarm, was Pete.

"Oh." Margot's face grew hot. "It's you. What're you doing here?"

"Uh." He raised his eyebrows. "I could ask you the same thing."

"What?" Then it dawned on her. "Oh shit. You're here to check on Luke. I'm sorry. I forgot to text. I'm back from Chicago."

Pete nodded. "I see that. You're also bleeding."

Margot touched her fingers to her cut. "It's fine."

Pete glanced over her shoulder into the house. "Why don't I come in for a bit? I'm not on patrol today, so I have a few minutes."

"This isn't a good time, Pete."

"Yeah." He gave her a look. "I sorta got that."

Without waiting for a response, Pete pushed past her into the entryway. When he saw the kitchen, his expression widened in surprise, but he corrected it quickly as Luke walked over.

"Hi," Pete said brightly. "I'm Pete Finch." He extended his hand to shake and Luke took it gently in his. Margot could tell by the vacant way her uncle smiled at him that he didn't recognize Pete from his visit yesterday. "I'm friends with Margot."

"Nice to meet you," Luke said, his voice sounding unusually small. Then he looked at Margot. "Kid? You're bleeding. What happened?"

Margot shook her head. "Nothing. I'm fine."

Beside her, Pete shot a glance toward the disastrous kitchen. "So." He clapped his hands. "You guys doing some cleaning? You need a hand?"

For the next two hours, Margot, Pete, and Luke put the kitchen back together. Most of it fell to Margot, though, as she was the only one who knew or could remember where anything was supposed to go. Throughout the afternoon, the three of them held steady, idle conversation, most of which was Pete telling them long, meandering stories of office minutiae. Margot knew he was doing it for her benefit, keeping her uncle preoccupied while she cleaned. During it all, she couldn't tell if she was more embarrassed or grateful—embarrassed that she'd been so preoccupied with the case she hadn't known her uncle was spinning out of control just outside her door; grateful for the kindness of this almost-stranger.

By the time they were done, it was a little after five and they were all hungry, so Margot ordered a pizza. Though she set the table for three, when Luke saw this, he said, "Why don't you two catch up? I'll watch TV while I eat." But Margot could tell as he took his two slices into the living room that really, he just needed a break. He looked tired to his bones. These episodes, she was learning, did that.

Margot watched her uncle as he sank onto the couch, turned on the TV, and took a bite of pizza, his eyes peeled to the screen. When she turned her attention back to the kitchen again, she saw Pete grabbing two beers from the refrigerator.

"Beer?" he said.

"Absolutely. The bottle opener's in that drawer there."

Pete popped the tops off, handed her a bottle, then slumped into the chair opposite her.

She took a long sip. "He's getting worse."

Pete's eyes flicked over her face, landing on her swollen cheek. "He do that?"

Margot had washed the cut and put a Band-Aid on earlier, but it still throbbed. She shook her head. "It was an accident."

"Is there anything I can do?"

She gave him a look. "Really? After everything you've done this afternoon?"

"I told you. I've been through this. It's . . . tough."

She studied his face a moment. "Actually. There is something." She hesitated. "Could you track down an Elliott Wallace for me?"

"Who's that?"

So Margot told him everything and Pete listened, a look of disbelief frozen on his face.

"Holy shit," he said when she finished. He dropped his eyes to the tabletop, where they roved, unseeing, eventually landing on the half-eaten slice of pizza in his hand. He frowned at it as if he was surprised to see it there, then dropped it onto his paper plate and brushed his hands against each other.

"I know," Margot said. "This is something. I can feel it."

"Yeah . . . Yeah, I think you're right. Jesus Christ."

"So, do you think you could help me track him down? Elliott Wallace? I remember he was living in Dayton when we met, but

I can't remember where and I have no idea if he's still there." She knew the location of his old neighborhood was probably buried somewhere deep in her mind, but his house had been in a cookie cutter suburb, in a city she'd never been to before. Plus, it had been three years. He could've moved.

Pete scratched his jaw. "It can be a long process tracking someone down like that. It can take weeks just to hear back from the places I'd need to reach out to. That is, if I do it aboveboard."

Margot hesitated. "And if you do it *not* aboveboard?"

Pete let out a breath of laughter. "Yeah, that wouldn't take as long, but I guess I'm wondering . . . well, are you sure this is what you want to be doing right now?"

Margot cocked her head. "What d'you mean?"

"I just mean with—" He jutted his chin toward the living room behind her, where Luke was watching TV with the volume on loud. "You have a lot going on."

"Well . . . sure. But I still have to do my job." She hadn't told Pete she'd gotten fired and she wasn't about to now. While he may have been willing to bend the rules for a journalist with a solid lead, he probably wouldn't if he knew she had no publication to back her up. Not to mention the mortification she'd feel if she told him. And she didn't need that. Not on top of everything else.

"I know," he said. "But couldn't you work on a different story or something? One that doesn't have you chasing people all over the Midwest."

"I'm doing the best I can with him, Pete." Margot had tried to keep her voice neutral, but it still came out hard.

"I know. I do. But leaving him overnight when he's like this can be dangerous."

Heat flared over her chest like a rash. "Are you kidding me?"

"Hey, listen. I'm not trying to tell you how to take care of your family, but—"

"No, I get it," she snapped, standing so quickly her chair almost fell over behind her. "You think I should be in the home, rather than out in the workforce."

"I . . ." Pete held up his hands. "Whoa. Margot, that's not what I'm saying."

"Isn't it, though?"

From the table next to her, her phone chimed with an incoming notification. Instinctively, she grabbed it from the tabletop and glanced at the screen. "Fuck!" It was a Venmo request from her old landlord, Hank, for the amount of twelve hundred dollars, July's rent. Margot had called her subletter multiple times over the past few days, but it seemed he'd disappeared. Now she had no choice but to pay.

"Everything okay?" Pete asked hesitantly.

Margot put her phone back onto the table a bit too hard. "Everything's great. I just have to pay rent for a place I'm no longer living, but yeah, maybe I should just stop working and stay home with my uncle instead." She felt idiotic and fraudulent to be defending a job she no longer actually had, but her face was throbbing, she was overwhelmed with Luke, and she felt inches away from the biggest story of her life—if she could just find the time to piece it together.

"I'm sorry," Pete said, standing up. "I didn't mean to—"

"It's fine. Really. But I think I should clean the kitchen now."

"I . . ." He sighed. "Sure. Okay."

After Pete left, Margot put the leftover pizza in the fridge, cleaned the kitchen—again—and sent Hank his money. Then she grabbed her laptop from her room and settled onto the couch with Luke.

He gave her a vague, vacant smile, then turned his face back to the TV. Margot's chest ached. She knew why Pete's suggestion had hit her so hard, and it wasn't because of any sexist undertones. It was because his condemnation was exactly what she said to herself in her worst moments. She worked too much. She wasn't there for her family. After all, here she was, in the wake of one of Luke's worst episodes yet, and all she could think about was January's case. Maybe Pete was right. Maybe she should just get a waitressing job and hire a part-time caregiver until she could find something more lucrative and less time-consuming. And yet. And yet.

Elliott Wallace's name echoed in her mind like a taunt. She'd sat across from him, had listened to his words and looked in his eyes, and he'd fooled her. The whole time he'd been acting concerned about Polly Limon's murder and he'd gotten away with it. He'd gotten away with January's murder, and now he was getting away with Natalie's too. And Margot was the only one who knew he was guilty. She knew it inside her as certainly as she knew she loved her uncle, as certainly as she knew she was meant to be a reporter. The knowledge had heft and density. It was solid as bone.

On the living room couch, Margot rested her laptop on her thighs and turned it on. If Pete wouldn't help her, she'd have to nail this fucker herself. But where did she start? She glanced absently at the show Luke was watching—some animal documentary on big cats—as she tried to remember everything Jace had told her about January's "imaginary friend." He'd said that Elephant Wallace had played with January on the playground, hadn't he? That Wallace had gone to her recitals?

An idea hit Margot and she pulled up a Google tab. She typed the words *January Jacobs* plus *dance* into the search bar, then selected the Images filter. Ordinarily, to find photos for a case like this, she'd have to go to the girl's dance studio or contact her parents. But January's case was so famous Margot knew every photo attached to it had been splashed on the internet since the moment the internet was invented. Sure enough, the results materialized within seconds, spitting out thousands upon thousands of images.

The first fifteen photos or so were all the same one, the most famous of the case: January in a nautical-themed costume, her
chestnut hair teased, her lips bright red.

After that were dozens of similar shots: January in dance costumes, posing alone, her lipsticked lips smiling. Scattered among
them were photos from the case: Billy, Krissy, and Jace at press
conferences, on Sandy Watters's couch, outside their home. In all
of them, they looked solemn and scared. Margot scrolled.

The first photo she clicked on was twelve pages deep in the
results. It was a wide shot of one of January's performances, capturing the entire stage and some of the audience. Margot zoomed
in, examining the heads of the audience members, but up close,
they turned into no more than fuzzy blurs. She clicked back to
the results page.

Margot wasn't sure how much time had passed when she finally
found something, and it was only when Luke snapped his head to
look at her that she realized she'd audibly gasped.

"Rebecca?" he said. "Are you okay?"

Margot nodded. "Fine. I'm fine. Sorry." She flashed him a weak
smile, then turned quickly back to the photo on her laptop.

It had been taken in what was no doubt one of the auditoriums
where January's dance recitals were staged. January was in center
frame, an enormous bouquet of white roses in her arms. Behind
her was a mass of people—other little girls in costumes, moms
and dads, sisters and brothers, aunts and uncles. And there, in the
far-right corner, miniscule and blurry, but still recognizable, was
Elliott Wallace. He was standing alone with his unblinking gaze
focused on the back of January's head.

Margot had found him.

She stared, heart pounding. She could hardly believe it. After
being told she was wrong so many times—by her ex-boss, by Detective Lacks, by Detective Townsend—Margot had been vindi-
cated.

But then, as she stared at the face of the man she was so sure was a killer, something else caught her eye—a familiar red smudge at the edge of the photo.

"No." The word came out of her as a whisper.

It wasn't possible. It didn't make any sense. Luke had always said he didn't know Billy or Krissy. And he certainly hadn't known January, so he would've had no reason to go to her dance recitals. But then why, in this photo that had clearly been taken after one of January's performances, was Margot staring at him now? Though half his face had been cut off by the frame, she could see his image clearly. He was far closer than Elliott Wallace, and she could see his ear, his jaw, and the giveaway: his favorite red bandanna wrapped around his neck, the very one Margot had given him for Christmas all those years ago.

Blood rushed in her ears. Margot turned to look at Luke and her breath caught in her throat. He was staring at her, his face as blank and solemn as Jace's.

"By the way," he said. "Have you seen Margot recently?"

Margot swallowed. "Why do you ask?"

He narrowed his eyes almost suspiciously at her, then turned back to the TV. "I'm worried about her. She's been asking a lot about January. I'm afraid she'll find out what really happened."

TWENTY-FOUR

Margot, 2019

argot sat frozen on the couch, her breath trapped in her throat, palms prickling. She stared at her uncle's profile as he stared at the TV. He was only a few feet away, and yet the distance between them felt like an uncrossable gulf.

Throughout her entire life, Luke had taught Margot to be honest and real. In a town of people who cared far more about appearances than truth, her unguarded and uncontrived uncle had been her salvation. Luke had never hidden who he was—or at least that was what she'd always thought. Apparently she'd been wrong. Apparently, like everyone else in this town, he also wore a mask. After years of maintaining that he didn't know January or the Jacobs family, here he was in a photograph taken at the girl's recital.

Margot glanced from her uncle in the photo to her uncle on the couch. "Uncle Luke?"

But her voice sounded weak, and he must not have heard, because he kept his eyes on the TV. She cleared her throat. "Luke?"

He turned his head, eyebrows raised, and Margot could tell by the vague look in his eye that he still didn't recognize her. Who was she to him now? she wondered. Was she his late wife or was she a stranger?

"What are you worried about Margot finding out?" she asked.

Luke frowned. "What?"

"You just said you're worried about Margot because she's been asking about January. You said you're scared 'she'll find out what really happened.' What did you mean?" She felt traitorous using his condition to mine for information, but then again, he'd betrayed her first.

Luke's frown deepened.

"Luke?" she said after a moment. "What were you talking about? What 'really happened'?"

"Hm?" He blinked hard, shaking his head as if trying to clear away cobwebs. "What're you talking about?"

Just then, a loud roar came from the TV and they both looked over at it. On the screen, a lion was tearing into some disemboweled animal, its muzzle and mane covered in blood.

"Man, I love this show," Luke said. "Don't you?"

But Margot couldn't speak. Her mind was swirling with conflicting versions of her uncle: Luke at January's recital, Luke telling Margot he didn't know the Jacobses, Luke worried she might *find out what really happened*. With a trembling hand, she clicked her laptop shut and tucked it under her arm. She needed to get away from him. When she stood, she realized her body was shaking.

"Be right back," she said, but Luke either didn't hear or didn't care. He continued to watch the TV as Margot walked out of the room.

The moment her bedroom door shut behind her, she locked it, then fell back against it and slid to the floor. What the hell was happening? A minute ago, she'd connected Elliott Wallace to Polly Limon and January, thinking she'd solved the case, and now—*what?* What exactly did she think her uncle had done? Just because Luke had gone to January's recitals, her rational brain interjected, didn't mean he'd killed her. But then why lie about it for all these years?

Margot felt as if everything she knew, her entire world, had just been flipped upside down. She grabbed her phone from her back pocket in a knee-jerk instinct to call someone, but after a moment of staring at the screen, she slammed it to the floor, pressing it into the carpet. It was Luke she called in moments like this.

She sat there, her back against the door, her eyes roving blankly around the little office-turned–guest room. After a moment her gaze caught on Luke's old desk. As a child, that desk had been the only thing in her aunt and uncle's house that Margot hadn't been allowed to touch. According to Luke, his work stuff was in there and he didn't want it getting disorganized. But now that she thought of it, she couldn't actually remember him ever using it.

She stood, double-checked that the door was locked, then strode quickly to the desk, sinking into the faux leather chair on the opposite side. On the desk's surface was a computer with a connected keyboard, a glass vase of pens, pencils, and highlighters, and a cheap-looking desk lamp with a flexible neck. Margot pressed the power button on the desktop and began quietly opening desk drawers as she waited for it to boot up. In the shallow tray centered beneath the desk, among a smattering of loose paper clips, sticky notes, and thumbtacks, she spotted a small gold key.

Just as Margot went to pick it up, the computer came to life with a loud chime and she sat up straight, craning her neck to listen for any movement from the other room. What would he do, she wondered, if he caught her snooping around his desk? Yesterday, the question would have made Margot laugh. Now, it made her scared.

She turned her attention to the screen, in the center of which was a box to enter a password. She chewed the inside of her cheek as she thought. Luke had been an accountant, a numbers person, but he also had a sentimental side. She typed in the digits of her aunt's birthday, but the little box shook in disapproval, so she tried the digits of his, with the same disappointing result. She deleted the numbers, then slowly typed in her own birthday. When she hit enter, the computer chimed happily and her uncle's desktop came into view. Margot's chest tightened. For the next hour or so, she searched every file and folder she could find. But the minutes ticked by and she discovered nothing. She decided to move on and check the rest of the desk drawers, but just as she was about to pull another open, she heard it—a thud from somewhere beyond her door.

Margot jerked upright, her hand frozen midair, her eyes on the door to the office. The noise had sounded like a footstep maybe, or a stumble. She stayed still, listening, but she didn't hear anything else. Quietly, she slid off the chair and walked to the door, holding her breath as she pressed her ear against it. But all she could hear were the sounds of the TV. She was just being paranoid.

Back at her uncle's desk, Margot continued going through the drawers, but the contents of each subsequent one were more banal than the last. There were records and receipts for all the work Luke had ever done on his car, down to every last oil change. And there was the same for the house—roof repairs and fixes for burst pipes. Among it all was a random assortment of loose papers—an old grocery list, a jury summons from 1999, a stack of letters Margot had sent him after her move from Wakarusa, written in her messy, preadolescent hand.

Finally, Margot made it to the last drawer, the tall one on the bottom right. But when she went to open it, it was stuck. She tugged it again, but it wouldn't budge. Then she saw the little gold keyhole at the top and remembered the key. She hurriedly opened that first drawer again and plucked the key from inside.

Heart beating fast, Margot tried it in the drawer, where it

twisted easily. But when she pulled it open, her stomach dropped. She didn't know what she was expecting to find, but inside was nothing more than a filing system. And as she flicked through the folders, her disappointment grew; they were the financial records of Luke's clients. It made sense, she supposed, to lock them away. She sank back into the enormous chair. She should have been relieved. She didn't *want* her uncle to be harboring some guilty secret—of course she didn't. But she wanted the truth, an explanation to why he'd been in that photo at January's recital, and these financial documents weren't it.

But then she noticed something she hadn't earlier. There seemed to be a discrepancy between the depth of the drawer from the outside and the depth of the files within—a space of about three to four inches. She lurched upright and yanked the drawer all the way open. Then, forcing herself to move carefully, she removed the wire frame that held the files and pressed her hand against the wooden bottom of the drawer. She felt along the entire surface until, in one of the corners, she felt a slight give, then a pop. Her heart leapt into her throat. The wood panel was a false bottom.

But just before she could remove it, she heard another noise. It was the same thud as before, an errant footstep or an elbow against a wall, but this time it sounded as if it had come from outside.

She rushed over to the window and peered through the blinds. It must have been later than she realized because it was dark out now, the only source of light one weak bulb. Margot scanned every inch of her uncle's small backyard, but no one was there. She craned her neck to listen, but heard nothing except the muffled sounds from the TV. Was it possible that Luke had been the source of the noise, that he was the one wandering around?

She walked to her bedroom door, creaked it open quietly, and slipped through. Tiptoeing down the hall, she paused outside the entrance to the living room and leaned her head around the corner. But Luke hadn't moved. He sat on the couch, facing the TV. On the screen now, the female lions were hunting, circling their prey methodically. Margot glanced around the rest of the room and the connected kitchen, but nothing looked out of the ordinary, nothing amiss. And the only sound she could hear was the voice of the documentary's narrator as he explained that the wildebeest had no chance against the surrounding pride. Margot turned and headed back to her room.

Locking the door behind her, she heaved a sigh. She felt absurd. There was nothing sinister going on in the house. Her uncle wasn't on to her being on to him. And, for that matter, maybe there was nothing even for her to be on to him about. Maybe there was a completely innocuous reason for why he'd been at January's recital that night. It was Elliott Wallace she needed to focus on right now, not her uncle. But then Luke's words flashed in her mind. *She's been asking a lot about January. I'm afraid she'll find out what really happened.* Margot rubbed her hands down her face. Her brain felt scrambled.

Back at her uncle's desk, she sank into the chair, then leaned forward to remove the false bottom of the drawer. Maybe she should be focusing her efforts on Wallace, but first, she needed to check this off the list. Luke had gone through some lengths to keep whatever was in this drawer hidden. Margot placed the wooden panel on the carpeted floor by her feet then turned her attention to the contents beneath, her breath catching in her throat.

For a moment, she couldn't move. All she could do was stare, her heartbeat fast and hard. Then, with a trembling hand, she reached down, pulled out the stack of folded papers, and set them gingerly in her lap.

Tears pricked her eyes as she flipped through the cheaply made programs. Each one had the same clip art on the cover: a tutued ballerina, her arms in a graceful circle over her head. Above was an arch of words: *Alicia's Dance Academy presents* . . . and below the dancer was the title of each particular show: *Spring Review '94, Autumn Spotlight '93*. Inside each was January's name.

Margot squeezed her eyes shut. Her uncle, her favorite person in the world, was a liar—and maybe also something far worse. What explanation could he have for going to the recitals of a little girl he claimed he never knew? And why, for over twenty-five years, had he kept the programs hidden and locked away?

Thud.

This time when Margot heard the noise, there was no mistaking. Someone was outside the house. She stuffed the programs back into the drawer, replaced the false bottom and the wire rack, then slammed it shut, locked it, and threw the key back where she'd found it. She strode quickly to the door, her hands in fists by her sides.

Margot slipped quietly out the door, tiptoed to the edge of the living room, and peered around the corner, half expecting Luke to be gone, but there he was, sitting at the far end of the couch, his body trained to the TV. Margot studied him for a moment. Was it just her imagination or was he breathing too fast? But the noise had come from outside—at least, she thought it had—and it didn't seem possible that he'd left and come back in without her hearing.

Margot walked to the front door and threw it open. But beyond the dim glow of the porch light, there was only blackness. She stood there, waiting for her eyes to adjust, the *tap, tap, tapping* of moths beating their bodies against the bulb overhead. Margot peered out into the night, but there was nothing to see. She listened for another sound, but the night was quiet. Adrenaline slowed in her veins.

Then, as she was turning to go back inside, something drew her attention down: a folded piece of paper beneath her shoe. Even though some of the letters had been obscured by her foot, it was clear that her name had been scrolled on its front. Margot bent down slowly, picking it up with a shaky hand. She shot one more glance around her, then opened it.

This note had been written in the exact same hand as the one that had been left on her car, but while the first could have been construed as a warning—*It's not safe for you here*—this was an order. And at only two words, its message was loud and clear: *GET OUT.*

TWENTY-FIVE

Krissy, 2009

It was late Saturday night, Billy had long since gone to sleep, and Krissy sat at the kitchen table with an overfull glass of white wine. Jace's last letter trembled in her hand, his words staring up at her: *I don't know what you think happened to January, but I'm not the one who killed her.*

That one line had her mind in chaos, as if it had wriggled into her brain and unspooled everything she knew. She took a long sip of wine and, for what felt like the millionth time over the course of her life, she relived that terrible night in her mind: the basement door open, a yawning blackness beyond. Jace, standing over the dead body of January, her own body going cold. And the bizarre, unfeeling words that had crawled up her spine: "Can we play tomorrow, Mommy? Just you and me?"

The memory felt solid, a thread woven into her DNA. How could Jace not remember? Was he lying? But why? She already knew the truth and had protected him. Had he blotted it all out? He'd been only six at the time, his brain still mushy with youth. Yet surely it was impossible not to remember killing your own sister. No matter what your age, that had to leave its mark on you, an indelible scar on your soul.

The mere possibility that Jace hadn't killed January felt like someone had upended her life, flooding her with both relief and shame. On the one hand, it would mean her son wasn't a monster; on the other, it would mean she'd alienated him for no reason at all.

Krissy needed to understand. She took a deep breath, picked up a pen, and on a blank sheet of paper wrote down every detail of what she remembered from that night, everything she'd done. Then she asked Jace to do the same. She mailed it early the next morning, and when she received his response the following week, she didn't even wait to get back to the house to read it. She tore it open there at the mailbox, reading over the pages with a hammering heart. When she got to the end, it was clear: either Jace was lying, or for fifteen years, she'd been wrong about everything.

Back inside the kitchen, Krissy grabbed the phone from its cradle on the wall and, with shaking fingers, dialed Jodie's number. Billy was spending the weekend at a farming equipment convention in Indianapolis, so it didn't matter where she talked or what she said.

"Whoa, hey," Jodie said when she heard Krissy's trembling greeting. "What's going on? What's the matter?"

"Can I come over? Now?" Krissy glanced at the clock on the kitchen wall. It was a Friday and she and Jodie had made plans for later that evening. Jodie's husband and two boys were at some overnight soccer retreat and her daughter was going to a slumber party. With Billy out of town too, it was one of those rare occasions where they had an empty house and a full night to themselves. But Krissy wasn't supposed to go over until six and it was only four.

"The boys have already left," Jodie said, "but Amelia's still here.

Let me call the mom who's hosting and see if I can drop her off early, okay? I'll call you back in a minute."

The moment Jodie called her back and told her to come over, Krissy grabbed her overnight bag and hopped into her car. Half an hour later, she was standing on Jodie's doorstep.

"Hey. Come in," Jodie said, opening the door wide and ushering her inside, where they exchanged a perfunctory hug and kiss. "What's up?"

"I just got a letter from Jace."

"Ah." Jodie nodded. Though Krissy had never told her just how afraid she was of her own son, Jodie was the one who'd held Krissy's hand during the worst of his teenage years, the one who listened while she talked, the one whose shoulder Krissy had cried on each time Jace got in trouble.

"I think it's time . . ." Krissy darted her eyes to the floor. When she looked up again, she took a deep breath, then said, "Can I tell you what really happened that night? The night January died?"

"Oh, Kris. Of course."

Jodie opened a new bottle of wine and they settled into the living room with their glasses, Krissy on the couch, Jodie sitting on the rug in front of the coffee table. Then, for the first time in her life, Krissy told the truth about that night fifteen years ago. Jodie listened, eyes wide, as Krissy explained everything, from waking at the sound of that crash and discovering Jace standing over January's body, to staging her house to look like it had been broken into.

"Jesus," Jodie said when she'd finished. Her voice sounded sad and unnerved, but it was devoid of judgment, and Krissy swelled with gratitude. Deep down, she'd known Jodie wasn't going to look at her any differently after hearing the story, but the confirmation of that came as a relief. "I'm so sorry."

Krissy took a sip of wine, nodded. She had expected reliving that night to cripple her with grief and anger like it always did, but something about the act of actually sharing it with Jodie had been cleansing. It felt as if a band had been wrapped tightly around her chest since 1994, and now, for the first time, it was beginning to loosen.

"Does Billy know?" Jodie asked.

"He found spray paint on the sleeve of my robe that morning, but I told him I brushed up against the wall. I'm not sure if he totally believed me, but if he's suspected anything since, of me or of Jace, he's never said. You're the first person I've ever told the truth." She shook her head, thinking. "And now, with this letter from Jace, I . . . I think I may have been wrong about everything. He said he didn't kill her and—I don't know—I think I believe him. He has no reason to lie to me. Not after everything I did to protect him."

"That's true."

"Jesus. What if I fucked everything up? What if I'm the reason the police never found her killer? What if instead of protecting Jace, I was actually letting some . . . *psycho* get away with murder?" She slammed a hand against the couch's armrest. "God! Fuck!" Her chest heaved with frustrated breath. Then, after a moment, she said, "And that's not all."

Jodie looked up.

Telling her the truth suddenly felt like a compulsion to Krissy, like some religious rite with the power to cleanse and make her whole again. She closed her eyes and took a deep breath. "Billy isn't the twins' father."

Jodie blinked. *"What?"*

"Do you remember that summer after high school, when everyone was having all those parties?"

She shook her head. "I moved here right after graduation."

"Oh, that's right. Well, that summer, me and Billy and Dave got really close. The three of us would hang out a lot together, but every once in a while, when Billy wasn't around, Dave and I would sometimes end up sleeping together. I honestly didn't think anything of it. I mean, I knew Billy was into me, but I didn't think we were serious or anything, and it only happened a handful of times. But then I got pregnant. I went to Billy to ask for money for an abortion, because I didn't think Dave would have any, and that's when Billy proposed."

"Wow . . . And you're sure it was Dave and not Billy who got you pregnant?"

Krissy nodded. "I got my period after Billy, before Dave. He was the only one it could've been. And even if I hadn't been sure before the twins were born, I would've known after. There's always been something about them that's . . . not like Billy."

"They look like him too. Dave, I mean." Jodie's eyes were fixed but unfocused as if she were conjuring up images of all three of them in her mind. "I don't think I would've ever put it together if you hadn't told me, but they do."

"That's exactly why I was so scared. It's why we're not friends with Dave anymore. I pushed him away because I was scared of people finding out the truth." Krissy dropped her head into her hand. She could still remember the look on Dave's face as she did it, the hurt expression as understanding dawned.

It was late one Sunday morning, five months after the twins had been born, and their little family of four had just returned home from church. Krissy had been up the whole previous night rocking a wailing Jace while Billy had slept, and she had not wanted to go that morning, but Billy had convinced her.

"Do you think people didn't notice the twins were born eight months after we got married?" he'd said. "We can't afford any more mistakes."

With those words, Krissy had felt something inside her shift.

He was right, she'd realized. The town may have already guessed that the twins had been conceived out of wedlock, but no one seemed to suspect that Billy was not their biological father. Not yet. And she needed to keep it that way, needed to make sure she didn't give people any reason to talk. She'd slid out of bed, show-ered, and dressed the twins in their Sunday best.

When they stepped onto their gravel drive after the service two hours later, Dave was sitting on their front porch stairs. Although it was only eleven in the morning, a bottle of beer dangled from his fingers, the rest of the six-pack between his feet.

"Kris!" he called when he saw them, a grin spreading on his face. "Jacobs!" He clapped a hand onto a knee and stood as they approached. "Been awhile." At the sight of him, panic flared in Krissy's chest. It felt dangerous just to have him near her babies. Their faces were starting to change and clarify, and every time she looked at them these days, she saw Dave—in the wave of their hair, in their tiny cleft chins, neither of which she or Billy had. She wasn't sure other people would see the similarity, but if Dave was right there, constantly by their side, the chances were that much higher that they would.

Beside Krissy, Billy brightened. "Dave!" he called, walking fast down the drive. He left Krissy, who was pushing the twins in a double stroller, behind.

"Jesus, man," Billy said when he reached the porch, pulling their friend into a hug. "Where the hell have you been?"

Dave shrugged. "Around. It's you guys who've been MIA." His gaze flicked to Krissy's face. He'd called a few times over the past few months, asking to come over and visit the twins, but each time he did, she told him they were busy. Billy was swamped at the farm; she was swamped with the kids. It wasn't a lie, just not the full truth, and from the look in Dave's eyes, Krissy guessed he already knew that. She just hoped he thought it was because of guilt, for sleeping with him. "Don't worry, though," he said with a wink as he glanced down into the stroller. "Can't stay mad when there's these two little Jay-cubs around."

He bent to place his half-drunk beer on the porch then strode the few steps over, lighting up at the sight of the twins lying side by side. January was asleep, her little pink dress bunched at the waist, her face cherubic and peaceful. Beside her, Jace was glaring.

"Hey, buddy." Dave offered Jace one hooked index finger, which he ignored. "They're just the two best things in the world, aren't they?"

Krissy smiled, but her throat felt tight with nerves. Her eyes darted between Billy and Dave, so sure her husband would finally see the truth, but he merely chuckled. "You might not say that if you had to live with them."

Dave grinned, glanced at Krissy. "Can I hold him? I thought I could come in, stay awhile. I brought enough beer for all of us."

Billy opened his mouth, but Krissy got there first. "It's time for their nap. Sorry. And I'm crazy behind on everything. I need to clean up and then get going on dinner." She turned to Billy, put a hand on his shoulder. "And I was gonna ask if you could finally fix the sink? Our water bill must be through the roof as is."

Billy blinked. She saw a flicker of confusion beneath his frustration, but she was counting on his sense of propriety to keep him from arguing, or at least from arguing in front of someone else. Sure enough, he pasted on a smile and said, "Okay." He turned to Dave. "Sorry, man. Maybe another time."

Dave grinned his familiar, easy grin. "No problem." But when he slid his eyes over to Krissy's, she could see the spark of bitterness as understanding dawned. He'd finally gotten the message—he needed to stay away. Her stomach twisted with guilt and she darted her eyes from his.

"Keep the beer," Dave said to Billy with a clap on his shoulder.

"You may need it more than I do." And with that, he turned and walked away.

"I think he and Billy may have seen each other a few more times after that," Krissy said to Jodie. "And we saw him in town obviously, but that was basically it." She took a sip of wine and something suddenly occurred to her. "I think I need to tell him."

Across from her, Jodie gave her a look. "Tell who—*Dave*? That he's the twins' father?"

"Yes."

"Why?"

"Jo, I've held on to this secret for more than twenty years and I'm only just now beginning to understand the damage that's done."

"But"—Jodie shook her head—"Kris, what do you think telling him is going to achieve?"

Krissy ran a jittery hand through her hair. "I don't know. It's just . . ." She was having a hard time explaining, even to herself, this sudden need to purge all the lies she'd held inside her for so long. "If Jace and I had told each other the truth sooner, if I'd only known his side of things, there's a chance that—" She huffed out a breath. "I guess I just think Dave deserves to know. Plus, Jace is growing up, and after all this time of practically being strangers to each other, he's reached out. This is my opportunity to make things right, to make up for everything I messed up. I can help him have a relationship with his dad. His *real* dad."

Jodie studied her face. "Are you gonna tell Billy too?"

"No. There's no point telling him something that will only bring him pain. But Dave . . . he has a right to know."

Jodie was staring at her with an anxious look on her face. "I don't like it," she said, gnawing slightly on her lower lip. "I don't think you should tell him."

"Why not?"

"I mean, I know you and Dave were close. But that was years ago. You don't know him anymore."

"What does that have to do with anything?"

"Kris, look at it from his point of view. You were friends with this guy. You slept with him. And then you excommunicated him from your life with no explanation, cut him off from his best friend. I understand why you did it, but how do you think he's going to feel when you tell him you've been lying to him for two decades? You're acting like he's going to be happy to find out twenty years too late that he has a son and a daughter he never even got to know. But what if he's not? What if he's pissed?"

Krissy stared back at her partner, the woman she loved more deeply than she'd ever loved anyone, outside her own children. She knew Jodie was just trying to protect her, but Krissy had already made up her mind. She was going to tell Dave the truth.

TWENTY-SIX

Margot, 2019

Margot stood on her uncle's front stoop, the piece of paper trembling in her hand, all the messages from this case tumbling through her mind. *That bitch is gone. She will not be the last. GET OUT.*

The smart thing to do with this note, she knew, would be to drive it over to the police station right now. One note on her car may have been a prank, but a second left on her uncle's front porch? They'd have to take her seriously. And yet.

Margot glanced over her shoulder through the open doorway to her uncle still sitting on the couch. As she did, she thought she saw his eyes slide from her to the TV. Had he been watching her? Or had that been her imagination?

Surely *he* couldn't be the one sending these notes, could he? For starters, the handwriting didn't really look like his, although, as she glanced down at the words, it was hard to tell. They were in all capitals and looked as though they'd been hastily scrawled. And it was impossible the first note had come from him. It had been left on her windshield outside the Jacobs place, where Luke hadn't even known she'd been going. But then, Margot realized with a little jolt, he *had* known she was going to be there. She'd told him before she'd left for church that she was going to approach Billy for an interview.

Margot thought about that stack of programs from January's recitals, thought about the words he'd said to her only an hour earlier: *what really happened* to January.

Standing on the front stoop in the hot July night, Margot folded the note in half and then tucked it into her back pocket. Until she figured out what the hell was going on with her uncle, she wouldn't go to the police.

"Uncle Luke?" she said after she'd closed and locked the front door.

He looked up from the TV.

"It's past eleven. Let's go to bed."

Margot closed up for the night as he got ready, then she went into his room to make sure he'd brushed his teeth and changed clothes.

Back in her room, after she'd bid him a terse good night, Margot leaned against the door and squeezed her hands into fists. She dug her nails into her palms until they stung, then she kept pushing. There had to be an explanation for all this. There had to be some reasonable alternative to the story her brain was churning out. Her uncle was a good man. He wasn't like Elliott Wallace. He would never, could never, hurt anyone, let alone a six-year-old girl. And yet, for the first time since she'd been there, that night she locked her bedroom door.

The next morning as Margot was making coffee, Luke padded into the kitchen, looking as if he'd aged a decade overnight. She felt the same. His episodes, this case, those notes—everything was taking its toll.

"Morning, kid."

"Morning." She flashed him a tight smile. "How'd you sleep?"

What she wanted to ask him was what he knew about January, but she couldn't force the words from her mouth. It was clear he was lucid this morning, as he was most mornings, but what would an accusation from her do to that precarious state? Worse, what would it do to *them*?

A vibration from her back pocket made her jump. She pulled out her phone and glanced at the screen: Pete. Margot hesitated. She didn't want to talk to him. She was still annoyed about how easily he'd found her underbelly and slipped in the knife. She declined the call.

She was grabbing two mugs for their coffee when her phone vibrated again. Again, it was Pete. This time she answered.

"I thought you might be avoiding me," he said.

She let out something between a sigh and a laugh. "My phone was just in the other room." She poured coffee into one of the mugs and handed it to her uncle, who settled down with it at the kitchen table.

"Right." There was something in his tone that told Margot he wasn't quite over yesterday either. "Well. How're you?"

"Yeah, I'm fine. You?"

"Fine. Look, I'm calling because I found Elliott Wallace's sister." At the name, Margot's heart lurched. After she'd all but kicked him out yesterday, she didn't think there was a chance Pete was still planning on helping her. She angled herself away from Luke, who'd begun to work on his book of crosswords. "He's been harder to track down," Pete said. "But I'll keep trying. In the meantime, I thought you might like her address. Her name's Annabelle Wallace and she lives in Indianapolis."

"Oh my gosh, Pete. I owe you one. Seriously."

"No problem."

He recited the address and Margot jotted it down on a paper towel. "Thank you. And listen. About last night——"

"Don't worry about it. I shouldn't have told you how to live your life."

"Oh. Okay. Well, sorry. And thanks again."

They said goodbye and Margot was about to hang up when something occurred to her. "Pete! Wait." She threw a glance at Luke, but he seemed completely absorbed in his crossword. Still, she stepped out of the kitchen and walked quickly to her room, shutting the door behind her. "Has anybody at the station found anything about who could've left that note on my car?"

"As a matter of fact, yeah. One of the guys brought in a few kids yesterday. Three boys in the upcoming senior class. They didn't get a confession or anything, but they have a history of shit like that. The officer told them that if anything like that happened again, they were gonna really crack down. Why?" he asked, sounding suddenly alarmed. "You didn't get another one, did you?"

"No," she said a little too quickly. "I was just wondering."

"Okay, good. And speaking of, I haven't come across that woman you described either. I'm hoping that was nothing after all, but obviously if you see her again, make sure to report it."

"Right. Thanks again, Pete."

When she hung up, instead of heading back to the kitchen for coffee, she got changed. She wanted to head out for Indianapolis as soon as possible. She preferred leaving Luke in the mornings when he was most lucid and independent, but more than that, her need to solve this case now felt dire. Proving Elliott Wallace's guilt wasn't just about securing a breaking-news story or about understanding what had happened across the street all those years ago. Nor was it even about bringing Wallace to justice. Now, what she wanted most was simply to ensure her uncle had nothing to do with January's death—to ensure he was still the man she knew, still the man she loved.

Back in the kitchen, she put up her mug and poured her coffee into a to-go cup. "I'm gonna be gone for a bit," she said to Luke. "I'll be back by this afternoon." She tried to smile, but it felt tight, and without meeting his eye, she hurried out of the house.

Three hours later, Margot was knocking on Annabelle Wallace's front door. Elliott's sister's house, a two-story red brick in a suburb of Indianapolis, was about twice the size of the one where Elliott had lived when Margot interviewed him three years ago. While Annabelle's home wasn't by any means new, it looked well kept with a manicured lawn and neat landscaping.

Margot only had to wait a few moments after knocking before the door swung open, revealing a woman in her late forties, wearing fitted jeans and a white blouse. Margot could tell at once that this woman was Annabelle Wallace. She had the same big brown eyes as Elliott and the same dirty blond hair. But more than that, Margot recognized the woman by her ears. Abnormally large, they stuck out from her head at the same sharp angle her brother's did.

She gave Margot a polite, perfunctory smile. "Can I help you?"

Margot returned the smile much more warmly. "Hi. I'm Margot Davies. Are you Annabelle?"

"I am."

"It's nice to meet you. I'm sorry to show up like this unannounced, but I'm actually trying to find your brother, Elliott."

"What's he done this time?" Margot opened her mouth to respond, but then Annabelle held up a hand. "No, never mind. I don't care. And I'm sorry, but I can't help you. I haven't spoken to Elliott in years."

"Oh, I see." Margot flicked her eyes to the ground as she pretended to think this over. When she looked up again, she squished her face into what she hoped looked like guilelessness. "In that case, would *you* be willing to talk? Just for a few minutes. I'm a reporter. Learning a little bit about your brother might help me find him."

It was a gamble using this as leverage. From her experience, the proclamation that she was a journalist either piqued people's curiosity or made them put up their defenses. To her great relief, it seemed Annabelle was one of the former.

"A reporter? What story are you working on? And what does my brother have to do with it?"

"Well, I'm a crime reporter and I'm covering a few different cases at the moment. Have you heard of Polly Limon?"

Margot watched Annabelle's face closely as she said this, searching for any sign of recognition, but the woman just stared back at her blankly. "Who?"

"She's a girl from Dayton, Ohio. I'm also writing about January Jacobs."

At first, Annabelle looked surprised to hear the little girl's name, then confused, then, slowly, her expression morphed to fury. "Excuse me, but are you insinuating that my brother is—that my brother had something to do with that girl's death? Because if you are, you're way off base."

Margot kept her face even, but inside she was dancing. Finally, the woman had given her the perfect ammunition. When she spoke next, her voice was thick with sympathy. "New evidence has been found regarding January's case. Someone came forward saying that your brother attended January's dance recitals, that he went to the playground where she played, which suggests he could have been connected to her death." It wasn't technically a lie, although the one and only person who knew of this evidence and suspected Wallace of anything was her. And possibly Pete, if he believed her hunch. "It doesn't mean he's guilty of anything, but that doesn't matter. This could turn into a witch hunt. *That's* what I'm trying to stop from happening."

Annabelle studied Margot with a furrowed brow for a long moment. Then she glanced at her wristwatch, a dainty silver thing. Finally, she sighed. "I have a dentist's appointment in an hour."

"I'll keep it short," Margot said. "I promise."

She followed Annabelle through the entryway and into the living room, which was both nice and outdated. A deep green rug softened the hardwood floors, and the couch where Annabelle gestured her to sit was upholstered in an old-fashioned floral print that matched the heavy window drapes. Sitting atop the mantel across from Margot was a collection of photos in silver and gold frames. In the biggest, a family of five, all in pastel blue, sat atop the dunes of a beach, their blond hair shining in the sun.

"Thank you for talking with me," Margot said as Annabelle settled into one of the armchairs across from her. "I know you don't have much time, so let's dive in. You seem pretty certain that your brother had nothing to do with January's death. How can you be so sure?"

Annabelle crossed her legs, taking what seemed to be a fortifying breath. "Elliott's just"—she shook her head—"not like that. He wouldn't do something like that."

Margot kept her expression blank, but she knew Annabelle's words carried no weight. No one was objective about their own family. "In that case, what *is* your brother like?"

Annabelle narrowed her eyes. "You said you believe he's innocent, right? That's what you're trying to prove?"

Margot nodded. She didn't like lying to interview subjects, but there was no way Annabelle would talk if she knew what Margot actually thought about her brother.

"Right. Okay. Well, Elliott's . . . I don't know. How do you summarize an entire person?"

"What was he like growing up?" This, Margot had always believed, was a good point of entry when getting someone to divulge about their family. It was innocuous enough to get people talking while also having the potential to be deeply revealing.

"Well . . ." Annabelle's gaze shifted to the coffee table and slid unfocused as she remembered. "As a kid, Elliott was always very particular about things. I could never go into his room, for example, and I could never touch any of his toys—not that he had many to begin with." She glanced up. "Our mother was a stay-at-home mom and our father was a high school chemistry teacher. We weren't poor, but we certainly weren't rich. I think Elliott always felt like our parents should have done better. He was always talking about a bigger, better life."

"Were the two of you close?"

She shook her head. "No, not really. He's four years older than me, and I was never interesting or smart enough for him, which he made very clear. He was always talking about books and films, art and culture. I cared about getting good grades and cheerleading. Then I went to college and met Bob. Meanwhile, Elliott had already dropped out of college and was doing . . . well, honestly, I don't know what. But, you know, we still spoke over the phone every once in a while, and I always invited him to our Christmas. He never came, except for one time. He stayed over for a few nights and I thought everything was fine, until after he left and I discovered my diamond earrings were missing and Bob's wallet was empty."

"Wow. Is that why the two of you lost touch?"

"That was more like the straw that broke the camel's back. Ever since I married Bob thirty years ago, Elliott's used us like a bank. He wouldn't call for months on end, and when he did, he'd pretend it was to catch up. But then, inevitably, he'd work into the conversation how broke he was and how he needed money for this or that. Bob always told me I was too soft, that I gave in too easy, but—" She hitched a shoulder.

"Last I knew, Elliott was a security guard," Margot said. "With a steady job and no children or spouse to support, he couldn't have been in too much financial trouble, could he?"

Annabelle raised her eyebrows. "A security guard?" She let out one high-pitched *ha.* "Maybe for a while, I suppose. But that's Elliott. He's great at getting jobs, not so great at keeping them."

"Why do you think that is?"

"People tend to like Elliott when they meet him. He can be very . . . charismatic. And when he pays attention to you, it's like you're the only thing on earth. He's passionate too, always working on some project. But he gets bored. Itchy. As a kid, he'd always get some grand idea and get all excited about it, then he'd work nonstop for a week, maybe two, but eventually, he'd burn out and move on to something else.

"Jobwise, I can imagine he's great at interviews, but the whole working every day nine to five? That would get old to Elliott very quickly. He had the same thing with places. After he dropped out of college, he was always moving. For a few months, he lived in North Dakota, then Illinois, then Nebraska. It was impossible to keep track of him."

As Margot began to better understand Elliott Wallace, she seethed at the thought that the flippant way he treated jobs and places was the same way he treated little girls—obsessive and infatuated one moment, then disposing of them the next.

"Where's the last place you remember him living?" she asked.

"Hm." Annabelle looked to the ceiling. "He was in Wisconsin, I think, when we last spoke. I can't remember which city. But that was six years ago now. I can guarantee you he's not there anymore."

Margot nodded. That much she knew too. "And you have no idea where he could be now?"

Annabelle made a sound that was halfway between a laugh and a scoff. "Honestly, he could be anywhere." She shot a glance at her wristwatch. "Anyway, I'm sorry to cut this short, but I really should get going. I hope that was helpful, because he doesn't deserve to get dragged over the coals. My brother may not be perfect and he can be an easy scapegoat for people because he's different, but he's not a killer. I promise you that."

Margot could tell from the look in her eye that Annabelle believed what she was saying. Margot, on the other hand, was more convinced of Wallace's guilt now than ever. After all, charisma and intelligence were two hallmarks of serial killers, and Wallace had both in spades. Her mind flashed momentarily to Luke, her smart, charming uncle, but pushed the thought aside. Instead, she cast around for something else to ask this woman, anything that could lead her to the man she believed was a killer.

"Just one last thing. You said Elliott was always getting money out of you. Did you ever send it to a PO box or anything?"

She shook her head. "No. If he was close or passing through, he'd stop by and I'd give him cash. But usually I'd just wire it straight to his account."

"Hm. And what kinds of things did he say he needed the money for?" Margot was grasping at straws now, but money could leave a trace. If Wallace had borrowed it to pay for a property or something, at least she'd have somewhere to start.

"Oh." Annabelle waved a hand. "Many things. Once, he had a medical bill he couldn't pay off. Once, he said he wanted to buy my kids Christmas gifts—which he did, actually. I always tried to say no when he asked, but usually, I just gave in. It was easier that way. Hell, I'm still paying for his storage unit after all these years. Which is exactly why my husband says I'm too soft on him. I'd stop paying, but I don't know what Elliott has in there and I don't want it to just get thrown out. Like I said, he didn't even like me touching his stuff as a kid—if I got rid of whatever he has in there, he'd probably go ballistic. And anyway, he's family."

"Where is his storage unit?"

"Oh, it's in this little place you've never heard of. Waterford

Mills. I think he likes to have some sort of a home base. You know, because he moves around so much."

"Right." Margot smiled evenly, but inside she was jumping, because she *had* heard of Waterford Mills. It was a little town no more than ten miles away from Wakarusa. And if there was a storage unit facility there, Margot would bet all the money she had left in the bank that it was the only one.

"Anyway," Annabelle said, "I'm late for my appointment as is, so I have to get going. But let me give you my phone number. In case something comes up. Like I said, I may not be close to my brother, but he doesn't deserve this. If you're trying to help him, I'll help you in any way I can."

Margot nodded weakly. The truth was she felt bad for Annabelle. The woman was blindly defending a depraved man because the alternative—entertaining the idea that her own brother was a murderer—was too awful to bear.

There was a twinge of discomfort in Margot's stomach as she recalled all the times in the past twelve hours that she'd assured herself her uncle was a good person. But that wasn't the same thing. She believed Wallace was guilty because the evidence had led her to him, not because his guilt meant her uncle's innocence. Still, as she stood and thanked Annabelle one last time, the thought that zipped through her mind with a ferocity she hadn't expected was *Better your family than mine.*

As it turned out, Margot was right about Waterford Mills; the little town had only one storage unit, and she made a detour on her way back to Wakarusa to scope it out. Like the town in which it was located, the facility was small, with no more than a hundred units or so. Margot drove around the perimeter marked by a tall chain-link fence and pulled up to the front gate, which was closed with a thick chain and a padlock. Attached to the gate was a sign that read: WATERFORD MILLS STORAGE UNIT, with a phone number beneath. Margot put her car in park, pulled out her phone, and dialed.

"Yep," a gruff voice answered after a few rings.

"Um, hi. Is this—"

"Waterford Mills Storage Unit? Yep."

"Great. My name's Margot Wallace. I'm the niece of one of your renters, Elliott Wallace. Um, I'm actually calling because my uncle passed away a few weeks ago and I'm helping my family organize all his things."

It was a lie that could easily be disproven if the man on the phone called Annabelle to confirm or just did a quick Google search of Elliott and discovered he wasn't in fact dead, but Margot knew that people usually believed what you told them. And even if he did call her bluff, she'd be no worse off now than she was a minute ago.

"I know he's renting a storage unit at your place," she said, "but I don't know the number of the unit. Would you mind looking that up for me?"

Margot wouldn't push her luck by asking to be let in, but with the correct name of the renter and a plausible story, she doubted the man would see the harm in sharing the unit number, especially in a small town like this. Sure enough, the gruff voice said, "Yeah, all right. What'd you say his name was?"

"Elliott Wallace."

A few moments later, the man came back on the line and told her the number of Wallace's unit. She jotted it into her phone, thanked him for his time, then hung up and immediately called Pete.

"Margot?" he said. "Hey. What's up?" By his tone, she could tell their mutual halfhearted apologies had smoothed things over as far as he was concerned, for which she was grateful.

"I found a lead to Wallace," she said without preamble. "We

need to tell state to get a search warrant for a storage unit in Waterford Mills."

"Whoa, whoa, whoa. Slow down. What're you talking about?"

Margot forced herself to take a deep breath, then explained what Annabelle had told her about her brother's unit. "It has years' worth of Wallace's stuff," she said when she finished. "What if he stored away something incriminating? It makes sense. Serial killers like to hold on to trophies of their kills, but Wallace is too transient to keep everything with him through every move. What if he stored them away?"

"Okay . . . But wait, Margot. The only thing you have on this guy is that he was a person of interest in Polly Limon's case. No detective in the world is gonna bother a judge for a search warrant because of that."

"That's not true. I also have—"

"Oh right," he interrupted. "You also have the twenty-five-year-old memory of a pothead saying that January had an imaginary friend with the name *Elephant* Wallace."

Margot huffed out a breath. "Wallace was at January's dance recital. I have a picture proving it. That's not a coincidence. He's connected to *two* dead girls."

"I know. And I agree with you. All I'm saying is that no one's gonna approve a search warrant based off what you have. I'm sorry."

Margot closed her eyes. "He's the answer to this case, Pete. I know it."

"Okay then. Keep digging. I'll do what I can over here. Listen, I gotta go, but I'll let you know if I find anything."

After they hung up, Margot slammed her phone onto the seat next to her and let out a frustrated groan that turned into a scream. She grabbed her steering wheel and rattled it hard. She felt so sure Wallace was the answer to this case—but how the hell was she supposed to prove it?

She let go of the steering wheel, giving it one last smack of her hands, then slumped back into her seat. She sat like that for a long moment, her breath steadying, her heartbeat slowing. Then, finally, she sat up and twisted the key in the ignition. By the time she got home, it was dusk, the overcast sky a gunmetal gray. Yet again, Margot had left her uncle alone for too long. Yet again, her stomach twisted with guilt. Although she was used to the feeling by now, it hadn't lost its sting.

She parked in the driveway, then walked through the brittle grass to Luke's front stoop, but when she tried to twist the doorknob, it stuck beneath her hand. And that was when she remembered she still hadn't made a copy of his house key. She'd gotten close—she'd driven halfway to the hardware store the other morning—but she'd been interrupted by Linda's call with her lead to Jace and had gotten distracted. And then, the next few days had unspooled such a flurry of revelations that making a copy of the key had simply fallen out of her head.

Margot rattled the knob again, but again it didn't budge. She knocked, waited. Nothing happened. "Shit," she hissed beneath her breath. "Uncle Luke! It's me, Margot!"

She listened, but the house was still and quiet.

"Fuck." She knocked again, harder now. "Uncle Luke! Can you let me in?"

She stopped to listen, and this time, she heard the sound of footsteps approaching. Margot let out a breath of relief, but when the door swung open a few moments later, it caught in her throat. Adrenaline coursed so quickly through her body it felt like electricity running through her veins. Her vision spotted and she swayed.

Standing in front of her was Luke, her beloved uncle, her favorite person in the world. And in his hands was an enormous hunting rifle, aimed at Margot's face.

TWENTY-SEVEN

Krissy, 2009

With a trembling hand, Krissy opened the front door of her house, rushed inside, and clicked it shut behind her. She had the feeling of being followed, hunted, but she knew it was only the truth that was hounding her now.

Despite Jodie's protestations, Krissy had met with Dave, but now that she had, she wasn't so sure it had been a good idea. If everything Jace had told her in his letter had flipped Krissy's world upside-down, Dave had exploded it wide open. She now understood just how much damage she'd done by keeping her secrets for all those years, understood how much pain and anger she'd inflicted.

She wanted—*needed*—to make it right.

She dumped her purse by the door and hurried to the kitchen, where they kept a pad of paper and pens. Krissy wished she could call Jace, but he'd still refused to give her his number, so she yanked out a chair and sat at the kitchen table to write to him instead. And yet, as she brought the pen to the page, she realized she didn't know how to start, didn't know what to say. For fifteen years, she'd ostracized her own son for a murder he didn't commit. How could she say sorry for that in a letter? And beyond an apology, there was what she now had to explain, what she needed to tell him. It was all too much.

She inhaled a shaky breath and scribbled a short note instead:

Jace,

I'm sorry for everything. I'm going to make it right.

I just learned something about your father. He isn't who you think he is.

I'm writing my number again below so you can call me— let's meet up and I'll explain everything.

I love you,
Mom

After she scrawled her cell number, she stood hastily and rummaged around their junk drawer in search of an envelope and stamp, but she couldn't find any.

"Fuck!" she spat, slamming the drawer closed.

She strode to the table, grabbed the letter, and walked quickly back to the front door. She'd drive to Jodie's and send it from there. She wanted to see her partner anyway, to talk through everything with her, to have someone help her decide what to do next. She slipped the letter into her purse where it stuck out like a white flag of surrender, and her chest wrenched at the sight of Jace's name.

In fact, her chest was so tight she felt as though she were on the verge of a heart attack, but quickly recognized it for what it was. She was no stranger to the creeping hands of panic that could crawl up her neck and constrict her breathing. She needed her pills. She'd just get her pills and then she'd be gone.

Upstairs, she yanked open the bathroom cabinet and grabbed

two bottles, one of Valium, one of sleeping pills. Jodie didn't like it when Krissy relied too heavily on her medication, but she'd just have to deal with it today. Her hands were so unsteady it took her four tries to get past the child lock of the antianxiety meds, and when she did, she dumped two of the little white tablets into her palm, popped them into her mouth, and swallowed them with a handful of water from the sink.

As the tap ran, something made her start and she hastily turned it off. She thought she'd heard something—the click of a handle, the creak of a hinge. She stood still, her heart hammering as she craned her neck to listen. She stayed motionless for one, two, three long beats, but she didn't hear anything else. The house was silent.

She met her own gaze in the mirror's reflection and saw the toll her meeting with Dave had taken. Her face looked raw and pale, her eyes red from crying. And now, on top of all that, she was being paranoid. She splashed cold water on her face, patted it dry with a washcloth, then gripped the edges of the sink with white knuckles, forcing herself to steady her breath. And then, just as she was turning to leave, she heard it: another sound from deep in the house—footsteps.

Krissy froze, her eyes flicking to her bedside clock through the open doorway. The red numbers glowed 11:13 A.M., which meant that the person in her house couldn't be Billy. He wasn't due home from the convention for another hour at least. She didn't move as she listened. She didn't even breathe. But the old farmhouse had gone silent. Was she hearing things?

She went down the stairs fast. Hearing things or not, she wanted out of that house. At the door, she grabbed up her purse, dumped the pill bottles inside, and slung it over her shoulder, but when she reached inside for her keys, they weren't in her purse's side pocket. She stilled, frowning. She could have sworn she'd put them in

there earlier. She rummaged around the bottom of her bag frantically, but still, she couldn't find them, and that was when she
heard a familiar voice behind her.

"Looking for these?"

A chill slid up Krissy's spine. She spun around, her chest contracting with fear. "H-hi." She'd been shooting for pleasantly surprised, but the word came out as a nervous stammer.

The man's face, which had once looked so familiar to her, now
looked like that of a stranger—anger was contorting it into something unrecognizable. Her eyes darted away from his, to her keys
in his hand, then finally to the sitting room beyond, from where
he'd clearly just emerged. In some dark part of her brain, Krissy
registered that the sitting room was where they kept their guns,
the one's they'd had on display, unlocked, for years.

Krissy tried to smile, but it felt weak and wobbly. "What are
you doing here?"

The man crossed the two steps that separated them and reached
a hand behind him into the waistband of his pants. Krissy whirled
around to open the door, but it was too late. From the corner of
her eye, she saw a flash of a gun, felt the cold as it touched her
temple. "You shouldn't have lied to me," he said, and then there
was nothing but blinding white.

TWENTY-EIGHT

Margot, 2019

Staring down the barrel of her uncle's rifle, Margot was seized by panic. It felt as if a firecracker had erupted in her chest and was shooting sparks throughout her bloodstream. The edges of her vision blurred and blackened and she couldn't seem to get her lungs to take a breath.

"What do you want?" Luke snarled through gritted teeth.

"U–Uncle Luke?" Margot's voice was weak and trembling. "Please. Put the gun down. It's me. Margot. Your niece." The only trouble was she had no idea if he was aiming a gun at her head now because he didn't recognize her or because he did.

The terrifying possibility loomed in her mind that he'd somehow found her out, that she'd uncovered one too many of the things he'd been trying to hide. She knew without a shadow of a doubt that her uncle loved her, and yet, after everything she'd learned about him in the past twenty-four hours, she realized that she didn't really know him at all. He'd kept his secrets from her for over two decades. She had no idea how far he'd go now in order to protect them.

"What are you doing here?" Luke snapped again. "What do you want?"

He hadn't lowered the gun, not even an inch, and the look in his eyes sent a fresh shiver of panic through Margot. She wished for all the world that she hadn't decided to dig into January's case. She wished she knew nothing at all about her uncle's connection to the little girl from across the street, wished she could unsee the photo of his face at her dance recital and the stack of programs locked away in his desk. If she'd simply come to Wakarusa and focused on helping her uncle instead of chasing answers to the twenty-five-year-old murder case, maybe she wouldn't be here right now, on the wrong side of Luke's gun.

Margot swallowed. "U–Uncle Luke?"

Luke hitched the rifle higher onto his shoulder. Her uncle had never really been a hunter, but everybody in their hometown owned a gun, and Margot knew the basics of how his worked from a few long-ago days of target practice. He had a single-action rifle, which meant if he wanted to kill her, he wouldn't have to cock the hammer or do anything else. With one simple pull of the trigger, she'd be gone.

She forced herself to take a deep breath. "Uncle Luke." This time her voice came out more clearly, more steadily. "It's me, Margot. Your niece."

Something flickered in Luke's eyes—a flash of confusion, as if she'd said something that didn't quite add up.

"I used to spend every afternoon at your house," she said. "I'd do my homework at your kitchen table. You'd make me cheese quesadillas as a snack."

Luke's brow slowly furrowed and she recognized the faintest trace of recollection in his eyes, as if she'd reminded him of a long-buried memory.

"I, um, I gave you a stupid red bandanna for Christmas one

year when I was, like, five. And you've worn it ever since. And . . ." Margot wracked her mind for something, anything, that could jog his memory. "We'd order pizza and play Battleship on Friday nights. You showed me how to stand up for myself and you taught me every SAT word I know."

Luke was still pointing the gun at her, so she continued.

"You encouraged me to follow my dream and become a reporter. You taught me to be honest, to always tell the truth."

The irony of this last one twinged in her chest, but it seemed to be working. His anger was slowly morphing into something else.

"My name's Margot," she said for what felt like the millionth time. "But usually you call me kid."

And then, finally, the look of confusion on her uncle's face cleared, as if a light had gone on in his head and he could finally see. "Kid?"

His grip on the rifle slackened, and when he looked down at it, it was as if he was seeing it for the first time. Panic flashed in his eyes and he fumbled, the gun slipping from his hands.

Margot lunged toward it, one foot through the doorway, the other still on the stoop, and seized the rifle from him before it clattered to the ground. She immediately aimed the muzzle toward the ground then stepped into the house. Luke instinctively backed away.

She hadn't unloaded her uncle's gun since she was probably fifteen years old when he'd taken her to hit Coke cans in an empty field, but she remembered how to do it. She emptied the chamber, then the magazine, stuffed the bullets into her pocket, then laid the gun down on the floor, tucked beneath the back of an armchair.

When she turned back to her uncle, her chest contracted. His gaze was fixed on the open doorway as if he could still see Margot's terrified face through the scope of his gun. Tears were streaming down his cheeks. His hands were shaking. She walked tentatively toward him and he turned his head to look at her.

"I'm sorry, kid," he said through his tears. "I'm so sorry. I don't know what's happening to me."

The sight of her uncle undone like this made Margot want to cry, but she swallowed it down. She wouldn't let him see how much he'd scared her, didn't want to cause him any more pain. She placed a gentle hand on his back, and to her surprise, Luke let himself be guided into her arms. He was almost a foot taller than she was, so his head didn't reach her shoulder, but he sobbed into her nonetheless, his body trembling.

"Shh," she said, rubbing a hand over his back. "It's okay."

It felt strange to be the one comforting her uncle, who'd always done that for her. And it felt even stranger to be hugging the man whom she still had lingering suspicions about. Because although she felt deep in her gut that Elliott Wallace had killed January and Polly and possibly Natalie Clark, that didn't explain why Luke had gone to January's recitals or kept her dance programs or lied about it all.

It was the same complicated feeling Annabelle Wallace must have had this afternoon. Despite everything her brother had done to her over the years, despite the fact that she knew he was being accused of murder, Annabelle had defended him because he was family. If it turned out Margot was wrong and Luke was a killer after all, she would hate him. She'd excommunicate him from her life, and whenever she'd think of him, she'd be filled with rage. And still, he'd be her uncle. Underneath all that anger and hate, she knew she could never quite stop loving him.

The two of them stood like that—Luke bent over, Margot getting achy beneath his weight—for a long time. And then, eventually, his crying slowed, then stopped.

"Why don't we have an early night, okay?" she said. "Why don't you go get ready for bed."

She hated treating him like a child and knew he hated it too, but he seemed too wrung out to care. He simply straightened, nodded, and wiped his nose with the back of his wrist like a little kid. Then she walked him to his bedroom and waited outside as he brushed his teeth and took a shower. She had the urge to tuck him into bed, but stood by the door instead as he slipped beneath the covers. She waited till he got settled to turn off the light, and as she was closing his bedroom door, she could already hear his breathing lengthen with sleep.

She clicked the door shut behind her, then strode to the front door, outside, and all the way to the curb. The moment she felt there was enough space between her and her uncle's house, she let go—all the resolve and strength that had gotten her through the last half hour finally crumbled.

She contracted, as if she'd been kicked in the gut, and buried her face in her trembling hands. She'd held back her tears for so long. She hadn't cried that first day when Luke looked at her and saw someone else. She hadn't cried when she'd gotten fired or when she received either of those threatening notes. She hadn't cried when she'd seen her uncle in that photo at January's show. But now, all those accumulated tears poured out of her. Her breath started coming in jerky, gasping gulps.

Vaguely, through the sound of her own sobs, Margot heard the hum of a car's engine off in the distance. After a moment, she realized it was getting louder. She didn't want anyone to see her like this—even in the blackness of night, Wakarusa was so small that whoever was driving by would no doubt recognize her—so she turned her back to the road and wiped the tears from her eyes. She was so preoccupied, so upset, she hardly realized when the car came to a stop only feet away, hardly heard the sound of a car door opening.

Suddenly there was someone behind her, a hand clapped over her mouth, an arm flung around her front, and then Margot's

TWENTY-NINE

Margot, 2019

Margot tumbled face-first into the bucket seat of an SUV, one of the armrests jamming painfully into her stomach, knocking the wind out of her. The door slammed behind her and she spun around to open it, but when she yanked on the handle, it clicked futilely. Her eyes darted around for the unlock button, but to her horror, there was none. She lunged to the other side of the car, but that door was locked too. And then, her kidnapper, in a navy hoodie, was opening the driver's-side door. In a flash, he was behind the steering wheel and already twisting the key in the ignition.

"What the fu—?" Margot shouted, but her last word was cut off as the car lurched forward and she was slammed against the back of the driver's seat. She was momentarily disoriented, but recovered quickly and began clambering over the front console. She didn't have a plan other than simply to claw at whatever her hands landed on—her kidnapper's arms, shoulders, face—anything to prevent him from taking her wherever they were headed now.

But before she could reach anything, the man threw out an elbow, connecting with Margot's mouth. Her head snapped back and pain seared through her face. "Motherfucker!" she shouted, clapping a hand over her mouth. On her tongue was the taste of blood. Her lip throbbed.

"Sorry," her kidnapper said, and that's when Margot realized that he was not in fact a he. Her kidnapper was a woman.

The woman made a sudden turn of the steering wheel and Margot was thrown to the right. She tumbled onto the other side of the car, darting out her hands to soften the fall. As she did, she caught sight of the woman's profile, and to her complete lack of surprise, Margot recognized her as the auburn-haired woman she'd first seen outside Shorty's, a few days and a lifetime ago.

"It's you," she said, and her bleeding lip stung from the movement.

"Yes. Now calm down."

Margot's eyes bulged as she climbed onto the bucket seat behind her. "You've stalked me, you've locked me into a speeding car, you just elbowed me in the face, and now you're telling me to fucking *calm down*?"

"Just wait," the woman snapped. "Give me one more minute and I promise I'll answer all your questions."

Margot frowned. This woman was planning on talking? Or was that just a ploy so Margot wouldn't attack her again? Margot's gaze flitted around the car, her mind racing. She could try to overpower the woman again, but just as the idea flitted into her mind, Margot realized how little damage had been done to her. The woman hadn't chloroformed her or bound her wrists or knocked her out. She hadn't even blindfolded her. For a kidnapper, she was a pretty nonthreatening one.

Before Margot could make sense of this or decide what to do, the woman spun the steering wheel and the paved road turned to dirt, rocks crunching loudly beneath the tires. Margot shot a glance out the window and saw that the road they'd turned down separated a cornfield on one side from a little patch of woods on the other. The only light was that from the stars and moon. After a moment, the car slowed, then stopped. The woman pressed a button on her armrest and all the four doors clicked loudly. She turned to face Margot.

"There. The doors are unlocked. I'm not holding you prisoner. I just want to talk."

Margot grabbed the handle, pushed, and the door clicked open. She sat there, staring at the little sliver of night between the door and its frame for a few seconds before closing it again. Then she turned to the woman in the driver's seat. "If you just wanted to talk, why the hell did you kidnap me?"

"I'm sorry. I was trying to protect you. I need you to write your story and I can help you with it, but you're not safe here. Plus . . . to be honest, I didn't think you'd come with me otherwise. I know you've seen me following you."

Margot shook her head. "What are you trying to protect me from?"

The woman chewed her bottom lip.

"Jesus Christ. You say you're protecting me because I'm in danger, and now you won't even tell me what that danger is?"

The woman held up her hands. "I'll tell you. I will. But you haven't listened to any of my warnings yet, so I don't think you're going to just start now. Not until you understand some things first. You need to understand who I am and how I know what I know. Otherwise, I don't think you'll believe me."

Margot hadn't needed confirmation to know that this woman was the one who'd sent her those threatening notes, those *warnings,* but now she had it. Seething with anger and frustration, she stared at the woman's face. This woman had terrorized her for days, and suddenly she wanted Margot to calmly hear her out? And yet, her door was still unlocked. Her only injury was a throbbing lip. And now that Margot's panic was starting to ebb, curiosity was filling its place. "Okay then . . . Who are you?"

"My name's Jodie Palmer. I was . . . friends with Krissy Jacobs before she died."

Margot narrowed her eyes. Something about the way the woman said this made her suspect it wasn't entirely true. "Listen, Jodie? You're the one who just threw me into the back seat of a car. You're the one who wants to talk. So why don't you start telling me the truth?"

Jodie hesitated. "If I do . . . this can't be part of your story."

"Okay. Off the record then."

"No, not just that. This can't get out at all. In any way."

Margot studied Jodie's face. She looked both fierce and a little bit scared. Margot nodded. "You have my word."

"Good." Jodie inhaled a shaky breath. "Krissy Jacobs and I were in a relationship."

"Wait. What?" Out of everything the woman could have said, this was the last thing Margot would have guessed.

"We were together for five years."

Jodie went on to tell Margot the details: how she and Krissy had grown up together in Wakarusa, how they'd reconnected years later at a bar in South Bend, how they'd been together until Krissy's untimely death. "She didn't kill January," Jodie said when she'd finished. "Krissy and I told each other everything, and the night of January's death destroyed her. She loved her daughter. She *never* would have killed her. The reason the police suspected her—"

Margot held up her hand. "I already know what Krissy did that night. I know she didn't kill January."

"You do?"

"Jace told me. About their letters—everything. But what I don't understand is if you just wanted to tell me Krissy is innocent, why stalk me? Why not just approach me?"

"I couldn't."

"Why?"

"Well . . . first of all, I didn't know if I even wanted to. I knew everybody in this town would tell you that Krissy killed January, and I needed to see if you'd believe them or if you'd dig deeper. Then I saw that press conference on TV, the one about Natalie Clark, and I heard you ask that question—you know, why the police weren't looking into connections between Natalie's case and January's. I wanted to reach out to you then, but, well, to be honest, I didn't trust you. Not yet anyway. And I couldn't go to the police, because . . ." She shook her head. "I'm still with my husband. We have three kids. I knew if I went to the police, the whole town would know everything in a matter of days."

"What does Natalie Clark have to do with you and Krissy?" Then, something hit her. "Wait a second. The morning after the press conference, that message appeared on the Jacobs barn. Did *you* write it?"

Jodie hesitated, her brow furrowed.

"You did, didn't you?"

"I was trying to help. January's murderer is still out there. Which means that whoever he is could've taken Natalie. No one was even entertaining that idea, except for you. And no one was taking you seriously. I thought it would help you and the police make the connection. Although," she added bitterly, "*they* were still so convinced of Krissy's guilt they couldn't recognize a clue when it was spray-painted in two-foot-tall letters."

Beneath Margot's whirling confusion, she also felt a tiny grain of vindication. She'd been right. The author of those words on the barn had been trying to connect January's death to Natalie Clark's. It may have been convoluted and misleading, but it had kept Margot on that path. Yet so much of what Jodie was saying still didn't make any sense. "You said you couldn't approach me because you didn't *trust* me? Why? I'm an out-of-town reporter. I was the only one asking all the questions you apparently wanted to get asked, the only one you thought was on the right track."

Jodie looked down, hesitating. "I didn't trust you because . . . I knew who you were."

"You knew who I—what? What does that mean?"

"It's the same reason I've been trying to protect you. I want you to write your story, to help catch whoever killed January and Natalie. I want you to clear Krissy's name. But to do that, you need to stay alive. And that's no guarantee right now." She cut her eyes to Margot's, holding her gaze. "Not when you're living with your uncle."

Margot stilled. "My uncle? What does he have to do with this?"

"He has everything to do with it. That's why it took me so long to trust you—because of your last name." Jodie paused, and when she spoke next, her voice was soft, sympathetic. "Luke Davies is a murderer, Margot. You're living with a killer."

THIRTY

Margot, 2019

In the wake of Jodie's accusation, Margot felt paralyzed. Even though the suspicion had been hovering at the edge of her mind ever since she'd seen her uncle's face in that photo, hearing it articulated out loud and by a perfect stranger sliced through her like a cleaver.

Luke Davies is a murderer. You're living with a killer.

No, Margot wanted to say. *No, you're wrong.*

Luke had given her a home, a refuge from her parents. He loved her more than anybody else did and she him. *He's not a killer. He's my uncle,* she wanted to say. *Elliott Wallace is the killer.* But the words wouldn't come. She just stared, head bowed and mind spinning, at a spot on the car's floor.

"I'm sorry," Jodie said after a moment. "But it's true. He killed Kris—"

Her voice broke and Margot's head snapped up. She'd been sure that Jodie had been going to finish that sentence with January's name. Margot opened her mouth, closed it again, then shook her head. "What?"

"Your uncle killed Krissy."

"No," she scoffed. "Krissy Jacobs killed herself. My uncle hardly even knew her." Margot knew this because Luke had told her so, every time she'd asked him about January's case. "Why on earth would he kill her?"

"Your uncle knew Krissy very well. He was the father of her children."

Margot froze as Jodie's words penetrated her consciousness and slowly sank in. Was this woman delusional? Unstable? Was she simply lying? And yet, even as those suspicions bloomed in Margot's mind, there was another part that couldn't dismiss Jodie's claim so easily. "Can you just . . . start from the beginning?"

"Yes. Of course." Jodie took a deep breath and then she began. "Krissy, Billy, me, and your uncle all grew up here together. I think he goes by his first name now—Luke—but the only thing we ever called him was Dave."

The nickname, Jodie explained, was an abbreviation of his last name, which they apparently sometimes did—"Zoo for Katy Zook, for example." Then she went on to tell Margot everything she'd learned from Krissy ten years earlier: During the summer after their senior year, Luke, Krissy, and Billy became close friends. Krissy got pregnant with the twins and Billy proposed, but it was Luke, not Billy, who was the father. In order to protect her secret from Billy and the rest of the town, Krissy had pushed Luke away. And then one day, twenty-one years later, when she received a letter from Jace, she decided to tell Luke the truth. Twenty-four hours later, Krissy was dead.

"So, you see?" Jodie said. "She told your uncle the truth, but in his eyes, it was too late. Jace was grown and gone, and January was dead. Krissy not only lied to him for more than twenty years, she also robbed him of his only chance at being a father." Margot's mind flashed to the nursery in her uncle's house, the one that had been forever empty. "And he lost it," Jodie said. "I warned her he would, but she trusted him."

Margot realized suddenly that she was touching her cheek, absently prodding the sensitive spot just below where the freezer door had sliced through her skin. She dropped her hand into her lap.

"But the gun found in Krissy's hand," she said. "It belonged to her—them, the Jacobses. They kept it in a case in the living room."

Jodie nodded. "Like I said, Dave—Luke—knew them. Before the kids were born, he used to go over to their place all the time. He would've known where the gun case was, and he also would've known it was never locked."

Margot shook her head. "No. No, Luke wouldn't have done that."

"I know it's hard to believe, but—"

"No," she said again, and this time her voice was hard. "That's not it. Or yes, it is. But that's not *just* it. Luke wouldn't have killed Krissy when she told him he was the twins' father, because that's not when he found out that he was. He already knew."

Margot had realized this the moment Jodie had told her Krissy's secret. Because it was then that everything she'd discovered about her uncle in the past twenty-four hours suddenly made sense. It explained why Luke went to January's dance recitals, why he kept a copy of every one of her programs. If Jace had done an activity, Luke would have gone to his events too. Her uncle didn't have some perverted infatuation with January. He loved her—and Jace—as a father.

This even explained why Luke had lied to Margot about not knowing the Jacobs family. He was keeping Krissy's secret too, not to avoid gossip, not to prevent Billy from getting hurt, but to protect his wife and niece: Rebecca, who'd tried for years to get pregnant; Margot, who was young and already felt unloved by her own parents. What it would've done to her to learn that the little boy and girl across the street were actually the children of the man she considered her own father, she didn't know.

Relief flooded through her. Of course, her uncle had known

he was the twins' father. It must've been obvious. Even though Krissy was also having sex with Billy at the time, if she'd slept with Luke that summer and nine months later gave birth, Luke would've known it was a fifty-fifty shot that the twins were his. And now that Margot thought of it, she could even see the resemblance. It was vague—Krissy's features were far more pronounced—but there was a slight dimple in Jace's and January's chins that reminded Margot of her uncle, a certain curl to their chestnut-colored hair.

Margot explained all of this to Jodie, who listened with a line between her brows and an unfocused look in her eye.

"Okay . . ." she said after Margot had finished. "But even so, Krissy told your uncle the truth, and within hours, she was dead. That's not a coincidence. *Even if* he'd already guessed he was the twins' father, we don't know how that conversation between him and Krissy went. She lied to him for over twenty years. It's the only logical explanation there is."

But the accusation held no weight for Margot now. She was convinced Luke hadn't killed Krissy for hiding the truth because he'd already known the truth. Nor had he killed January; he'd loved her.

I'm worried about her, Luke had said to Margot the previous evening. *She's been asking a lot about January. I'm afraid she'll find out what really happened.* Far from some ominous indication of guilt, Margot now realized that her uncle had just been trying to protect her younger self. For a long time, she had been told, by all the adults in her life, that January's death was an accident. Luke had been worried how six-year-old Margot would handle learning that her closest friend had actually been murdered. Just as he'd done his entire life, her uncle had been looking out for her. For the first time in twenty-four hours, Margot felt her shoulders relax.

"Margot!"

She looked at Jodie, her eyebrows raised in question.

"Did you hear me? I said it's the only explanation."

"Jodie . . . I know you believe what you're saying is true, but it's all based on one coincidence. It's just a guess. You don't have any evidence, right? You don't have any proof."

"I don't need proof. I know Krissy and she didn't kill herself."

Margot didn't respond. After all, what could she say to that? Then something occurred to her. "Wait a second. Did you write that message on the Jacobs barn to somehow frame my uncle for January's death? Because you think he killed Krissy?" It wouldn't have made much sense if she had—the barn message didn't point to Luke—but Jodie was desperate, and desperation made people do illogical things all the time.

"What?" Jodie shook her head. "No. I told you. I was trying to help you connect January's death to Natalie Clark. I'm not lying about that."

Margot looked into Jodie's eyes, and after a moment decided she believed her. "So . . . you believe January's killer is still out there? That he's some stranger?"

Jodie nodded. "It's what Krissy thought. After Jace explained what had happened that night, Krissy started to believe the story she'd tried to fake was actually right all along. But in trying to protect Jace, she messed up the crime scene so much no one could ever prove it."

Margot sat still for a long moment. The man Jodie was describing, of course, was Elliott Wallace. Other than perhaps Pete, it seemed this woman was the only person in the country who would believe Margot's theory about Wallace being behind January's death. And Jodie had been close to Krissy, knew more about the Jacobs family than almost anyone. On top of that, she was motivated to catch the man who'd ruined her partner's life.

A decision slowly formed in Margot's mind. Maybe it was stupid to trust this woman, stupid to ask for her help. While Jodie believed January's killer was still out there, she also thought that Margot's uncle was a murderer. For a lot of reasons, Pete would have made a far better ally, and yet Jodie was the one who'd proven she didn't mind breaking the rules. And what Margot needed help with required just that.

"I think I can clear Krissy's name," Margot said. "Because I know who killed January. And Natalie Clark. And this little girl from Ohio named Polly Limon. His name's Elliott Wallace. And I think I know how to find him."

THIRTY-ONE

Margot, 2019

Two hours later, Margot and Jodie pulled up to the curb outside the storage unit in Waterford Mills. It was just after midnight, and there was nothing but one old streetlight to cut through the darkness. Margot gazed out the car window at the little facility, then turned to Jodie in the front seat.

"You sure you're okay doing this?"

Earlier, from the back seat of Jodie's car, Margot had told the woman everything she knew about Elliott Wallace, from her interview with him three years ago, to scoping out the storage facility.

"I want to break into his unit," she'd said. "He moves around a lot, so it makes sense for him to keep things there that he doesn't want getting lost. Plus, if he was protecting himself from a potential search warrant, he'd want to keep anything incriminating somewhere that's harder to connect to him. The only problem is I don't know how to get past the locks. They're combination locks with these thick, like, U-shaped metal bolts."

Jodie had closed her eyes, hesitating as she made some decision.

Then, finally, she opened them again and said, "We have bolt cutters in our garage. It's amazing the things they can cut through."

So they'd driven to Jodie's home in South Bend and Jodie had slipped quietly through the front door, returning a few minutes later with an enormous pair of bolt cutters in one hand, two baseball caps in the other.

"For the cameras," Jodie had said, handing Margot a hat.

"Good idea."

After that, Margot had found the nearest twenty-four-hour drugstore on her phone and asked Jodie to swing by. She'd worn the baseball cap inside and had come back a few minutes later with two small flashlights and a box of latex gloves. "For prints," she'd said when Jodie had thrown the box a questioning look.

"Good idea."

There was no guarantee, of course, that if they made it into Wallace's unit, they'd find anything at all. And even if they *did*, breaking and entering was illegal, which meant that Margot would only be able to report their findings to the police as an anonymous tip. But she felt, in more ways than one, that time was running out. Her uncle was getting worse and she wanted to put all this behind her so she could focus on his health. She wanted to create a schedule with Luke and stick to it, provide him with a stable environment. She wanted to get a steady job again, with regular hours and benefits. She wanted enough money to be able to afford a caregiver long term. On top of all that, she wanted to bring justice to Elliott Wallace for everything he'd done. And she wasn't going to wait around while the police cut through red tape and gave Wallace enough time to slip away—or worse, enough time to kidnap and kill another little girl.

In the car, outside the storage unit, Margot turned to see Jodie studying the baseball cap in her hands. "Jodie?"

Throughout their drive to Waterford Mills, Jodie had seemed stoic, resolute. But now, the reality of what they were about to do was clearly hitting her. She was taking deep breaths through her nose and letting them out slowly through her mouth.

Jodie glanced over at Margot. "What if you just call the manager back tomorrow? He gave you the unit number. He might let you in."

"He's not gonna let some stranger into a random unit. My ID doesn't even have the same name I told him over the phone."

"Okay . . . But I still think if we just went to the police—"

"I already did. We don't have enough evidence to get a search warrant. This is the only way."

Jodie frowned.

"Listen," Margot said. "You don't have to do this. You can wait in the car if you want. I just—I at least need a ride home." It was true; she didn't absolutely need an accomplice to break into the unit. But if Jodie went with her, she could help keep an eye out for cameras. More important, once they got inside, having another person to go through Wallace's stuff would split the search time in half.

"Fuck," Jodie breathed. "Okay. Let's do it."

"You sure?"

Jodie nodded. "If everything you said is true, this man killed three girls. He ruined Krissy's life. If we can prove it . . ." Her voice faded and she finished the thought by putting the baseball cap on her head.

Margot gave her a thin smile. "Thank you."

Still wearing her own hat, she stuffed the flashlights and two pairs of latex gloves into her jeans pocket, grabbed the bolt cutters from the back seat, and got out of the car, closing her door quietly behind her. Jodie followed suit, joining Margot on the other side, and the two of them made their way over to the chain-link fence.

For perhaps the first time in her life, Margot found herself grateful for the provinciality of the Midwest small town—the Waterford Mills storage unit was far from state of the art. Though the fence was eight or nine feet high, there was no barbed wire at the top, so it was scalable, and while she had spotted a security camera affixed to the corner of a nearby unit, she had her doubts about whether or not it actually worked. Still, she felt hot with nerves. If she got caught, she'd not only lose her lead to Wallace but would be facing criminal charges. Everything she'd worked so hard for would slip through her fingers.

Margot gazed through the fence at Wallace's unit. "That's his." She gestured to it with her chin. "Seventy-four. Third from the right."

Jodie nodded tightly.

"I'll climb over first," Margot said, bending down to press the two flashlights through one of the metal diamonds. "Then you can toss the bolt cutters over and follow."

Jodie glanced at the top of the fence. "I hope I can make it."

"You will." Jodie may have been on the cusp of fifty, but she was in the kind of shape that hinted at regular jogging and Pilates.

Jodie threw her a look. "You are considerably younger than me, Margot."

"You'll be fine."

Margot glanced around one last time for any sign of someone, but there was nothing but empty fields. The night was still and quiet. She took a deep breath, then grabbed high on the fence, dug a toe into it, and hoisted herself up.

The fence wobbled violently beneath her weight, but Margot held on, and after a moment, it grew still. She reached a hand up to grab another hold. The metal dug into her skin painfully, and holding herself up with nothing but her fingers and the toes of her shoes was much harder than she'd expected, but after five minutes or so, she reached the top, swung her leg over, and headed down again. Finally, she jumped onto the patchy grass, grateful to be back on solid ground.

She bent to grab the flashlights and stuffed them back into her pocket, but just as she did, she heard the sound of an approaching car. Through the fence, she caught Jodie's gaze, and the woman's eyes widened with panic. Margot's heart thumped as she listened, her feet frozen in place. Then, she realized the sound of the car was growing fainter. She waited until it faded and let out a breath.

"Okay," she said. "Throw over the cutters."

"Jesus Christ," Jodie muttered, shaking her head before she heaved the tool over and began to climb the fence too. It took her longer than it had Margot, but eventually she made it. Jodie caught her breath as Margot retrieved the cutters and the two of them walked, fast but quiet, toward unit seventy-four.

"All right," Margot said in a low voice when they came to a stop outside the unit's massive door. She glanced around them, careful to keep her head down in case she was wrong about the cameras. "Can you keep an eye out?"

As she'd seen from scoping out the facility hours earlier, the door of Wallace's unit was, like all the rest, locked with a padlock. As she stared down at it, it seemed impossible a mere tool could break through its thick metal loop, but it was the only chance she had.

She fitted the bolt cutters around the metal and squeezed the handle fast and tight. Margot pressed as hard as she could, but the metal was thick and the blades wouldn't penetrate. She continued to squeeze, harder and harder, until her arms began to tremble. Finally, when she couldn't do it any longer, she gave up and pulled the cutters away. She felt as if the blades hadn't even scraped the surface of the metal loop, but when she examined it, her breath coming in heavy gasps, she spotted two very small dents on either side.

"Shit," she said. "I think it might be working."

She tried again.

"Here," Jodie said when Margot released the cutters. "Let's take turns."

Margot handed them over and Jodie fixed their jaws around the metal loop, pushing the handles together so hard her arms shook. When she eventually gave up, Margot could see the dents were getting deeper. They alternated like that, making more and more progress each time, until finally, during Margot's fifth attempt, as she was squeezing the handles, the metal loop split apart and the lock clattered to the ground.

She caught Jodie's eye, and a broad smile slowly spread across the woman's face.

"We did it," Jodie said.

Margot let out one wry laugh. "Now let's just hope it was worth it."

Just then, the sound of another car's engine revved in the distance.

"Shit," Margot hissed. "Get inside. Quick."

She hastily undid the latch and tugged the metal door open. The hinges creaked noisily and Margot winced, listening as the sound of the car grew louder. When the space was just wide enough to fit through, they hurried inside and Margot tugged the door shut behind them, ensconcing them in blackness so dark she couldn't see her own body. The two of them stood, unmoving, listening to the car in the distance, the sound of their too-fast breathing loud in Margot's ears. Finally, the noise from the car's engine faded into the night. Margot exhaled. She was being paranoid. No one was watching the cameras' footage live. No one knew they were here.

She tugged the flashlights from her back pocket and clicked them on, illuminating the storage unit in front of them. Finally, they could see. She handed one of the flashlights to Jodie, and the two of them gazed out over the space.

Margot didn't know what she'd been expecting exactly, but she felt disappointed at the banality of Wallace's things. There was a wooden dresser, an old-looking couch, a lamp, and stacks upon stacks of unlabeled cardboard boxes. Sifting through it all would take hours.

"Let's split up," she said with a glance at Jodie. "I'll start over here."

"I'll start with those." Jodie nodded toward a collection of boxes on the far side of the unit.

"Oh," Margot added. "I almost forgot." She pulled the latex gloves out of her pocket and handed a pair to Jodie. They both tugged them on, then headed in opposite directions.

Margot stopped in front of one of the smaller cardboard boxes at the foot of the old plaid couch. Holding her flashlight with one hand, she opened the cardboard flaps with the other, revealing a collection of old books. The sight of them reminded her of her interview with Wallace three years ago, when he said he'd been working his way through the classics. Margot picked up one of the paperbacks on top, a weathered copy of *Moby-Dick,* and flipped through the pages with her thumb.

She sifted through the rest of the books quickly, looking for anything that might have been tucked into them, but found nothing even slightly incriminating other than a well-worn copy of *Lolita* that turned her stomach, but would be useless as proof of anything.

"You find anything?" Jodie called quietly from the other side of the unit.

"No. Just books. You?"

"Nothing. Clothes."

The two of them moved through Wallace's stuff like this for about two hours, freezing every now and then at some far-off sound. Each time, they would lock eyes across the unit and stand motionless, waiting. Margot would squeeze her hands into fists by her sides, her heart in her throat, envisioning the door flinging open to reveal the gruff-voiced manager or the police or Elliott Wallace himself, but no one ever came.

And then, just as Margot was starting to think all of this was for nothing, she opened the last cardboard box and her eyes widened.

"Holy shit," she breathed, staring down into the box's contents. For a long moment, she felt paralyzed. Then she blinked, cleared her throat. But even so, when she called across the unit, her voice was little more than a croak. "Jodie! Come here."

"Did you find something?" Margot heard the woman clamber to her feet and hurry over, stepping carefully through the maze of objects. "What is i—" But as Jodie sidled up next to Margot and looked into the box, her question turned into a gasp. She clapped a hand over her mouth so her next words were muffled and weak. *"Oh my god."*

THIRTY-TWO

Margot, 2019

Margot and Jodie stood side by side, gazing down into the enormous cardboard box between them, both frozen and silent until finally, Margot forced her lungs to take a breath.

"Look at the names."

"Yeah." By the choked whisper of her voice, Margot could tell Jodie was crying.

In the box was a neat collection of matching plastic containers, probably four or five layers deep, each one about the size of a shoebox with a white lid and a name written in black. The top four read: Natalie, Hannah, Mia, Polly.

"Oh my god," Jodie said. "It's him."

Margot nodded, her eyes not moving from the stack of containers in front of her. She wasn't sure what was in them yet, but just the sight of those girls' names written so cavalierly, so possessively, made her feel sick and sad and full of rage all at once. She swallowed. "Can you hold your light up? I need to take a picture."

After she snapped a photo, Margot reached into the cardboard box with a shaking hand and grabbed the container labeled Natalie, grateful for the latex gloves. Margot didn't want her fingerprints anywhere near this. She placed the Natalie box atop the others, then pried open the lid. When she saw what was inside, her eyes stung with tears.

It wasn't fair, to have a girl's life reduced to the contents of this little box, this random assortment of things. There was a hairbrush with long brown hair still tangled in its tines alongside a purple water bottle covered in glittery butterfly stickers, NAT scrawled across it in a child's hand. Beneath these was a smattering of butterfly hairclips, and tucked to one side was a neat stack of photos.

The first picture, Margot saw when she lifted them out, was of Natalie Clark, her face familiar from her headshot on the news. In it, she was in purple leggings and a white T-shirt, swinging from a set of playground monkey bars, her legs midpump, her little face screwed up in concentration. Margot's chest ached. When she flipped it over, though, her sadness morphed into rage. The words *Natalie Clark, age five, 2019* had been written in the same neat letters as the names on the box lids. Elliott Wallace fancied himself a collector—of both classic novels and little girls.

"What a fucking bastard," Jodie said.

"Yeah." It was the only thing Margot could think to say.

She flipped to the next photo, which had clearly been taken at the same playground. In this one, Natalie was wearing jean shorts and a neon green shirt. She was going down a slide. On the back again, was her name, age, and date.

Margot went through the rest of the photos, one by one, the images blurring together. It was clear Wallace had taken his time stalking the young girl, sneaking photos and surreptitiously collecting things from the ground where she'd left them. The fastidious way he'd done it all sent a shiver up Margot's spine.

When she finished going through the little stack, she replaced the photos, snapped a picture on her phone of the box's contents, then replaced the lid.

"There have to be a dozen boxes here," Jodie said. "A dozen girls."

Margot nodded.

"Do you . . . do you think they're all dead?"

"I don't know. I hope not."

With Jodie holding her flashlight, Margot sifted carefully through the rest of the white-lidded boxes. As she did, the two of them realized the boxes were stacked in chronological order, the dates on the photos descending. And the further she went back in time, the fewer objects and photos there were. It seemed Wallace had evolved over the years, getting more patient and more meticulous with every subsequent victim.

Margot took a photo of everything in each new box, while Jodie did a Google search of its corresponding name on her phone. The girls, they quickly learned, had been located all over the Midwest. Sally Andrews had been from North Dakota, Mia Webster from Illinois, Hannah Gilbert from Nebraska—all places Annabelle Wallace said Elliott had lived.

"You don't need to look this one up," Margot told Jodie when they got to Polly's box. "Her name's Polly Limon. She's from Ohio. He killed her."

According to Jodie's searches, just like Polly and Natalie, most of the little girls had been reported missing, then found a few days later, dead. All of them had died by strangulation or blunt force trauma to the head. All had signs of sexual abuse.

Some of the Google searches, however, didn't produce unsettling news stories and heartbreaking obituaries, but rather regular results for regular, alive girls. Leah Henderson, originally from Wisconsin, was currently a sophomore at a local community college. Becca Walsh, from South Dakota, was in her high school's marching band. Apparently, Wallace hadn't succeeded with every girl.

By the time they made it to the second-to-last box, they'd discovered that seven of the fourteen boxes belonged to girls who'd been murdered. The rest had survived.

Margot reached down to grab the box labeled Lucy, but that wasn't the one she was interested in. She wanted to see the name on the one underneath it—even though she already knew what it was going to say.

Sure enough, when she removed Lucy's box, the name January was staring back at her. As Margot gazed down at the name of the girl from across the street, the girl who'd once upon a time been her closest friend, the girl she now knew had been her cousin, she realized her cheeks were wet. After all these years of wondering, of obsessing, of searching the face of every man she passed, finally she'd found the one she'd been looking for. And finally, she had the evidence to prove what he'd done.

THIRTY-THREE

Margot, 2019

Margot woke the next morning to the sound of her phone ringing. She flipped over on the futon and reached a hand to the little side table, patting around blindly. When her fingers landed on the cool plastic of her phone case, she grabbed it and squinted one eye at the screen. It was Adrienne.

Margot tried to sound awake when she answered, but her exhaustion must have been obvious, because her ex-boss's first words were, "Oh, sorry. Did I wake you?"

"No." She cleared her throat. "Just tired."

There was a smile in Adrienne's voice as she said, "I bet."

The previous night, after Margot and Jodie had documented the entirety of Elliott Wallace's perverse collection, they snuck out of the unit, climbed back over the fence, and headed to Wakarusa. As Jodie drove, Margot looked up the number for the Indiana State Police's line for anonymous tips and told them everything— the location of the storage facility in Waterford Mills, Wallace's unit number, and the incriminating evidence they'd found inside.

Jodie dropped her off at Luke's, and Margot spent the rest of the early morning writing an exposé on Elliott Wallace, connecting him to eight girls across the Midwest who'd been kidnapped and killed within the span of twenty-five years. At around six that morning, Margot sent her draft off to Adrienne then collapsed into bed.

"When I finished your story," Adrienne said, "I looked Wallace up. I'm sure you already know, but the police just made an arrest."

"Oh. I didn't actually. That's good."

A warm feeling of rightness spread through Margot at the news. She knew the evidence from his storage unit would be enough for any prosecutor anywhere to confidently put Wallace in front of a jury. It would take time, but he would go to jail for what he'd done, and every little girl across the Midwest would be just a little bit safer.

"And your article," Adrienne continued. "I mean, Margot, I know you must know, but it's fantastic." There was an apologetic undertone to Adrienne's voice that showed she realized the awkwardness of the situation. Here she'd fired Margot only days earlier for trying to pursue this very story, and now she clearly wanted to run it.

"Thanks."

"Really. Your work here is—well, it's the best I've ever seen from you. You systematically convince the reader of Wallace's guilt, without ever actually saying the words. And the structure, the way you start with Natalie Clark, work your way back and open it up to the rest of the girls, then end with that speculation about January. It's—it's just really great reporting."

"Thanks."

Adrienne hesitated. "Right. Well, I suppose this is the moment when I apologize."

"It would be nice," Margot said, but her voice was teasing. She was still upset about being fired, of course, but over the past few days since, she'd come to realize that perhaps Adrienne had kept her around longer than she'd actually deserved. And Margot had to admit, if she hadn't been fired, she wouldn't have had time to investigate January's story. She wouldn't have found Wallace.

"Well, I am sorry," Adrienne said. "Really. You're a great reporter and I wish I'd fought harder for you. But lucky for me, you fought hard for yourself. I'm assuming that's why you sent your piece to me and not some other paper? Because you want us to run it?"

"And I want my old job back."

The idea had been percolating in the back of Margot's mind throughout the four hours it had taken to write her article. Despite her ego being bruised, she believed *IndyNow* was the best publication for the story. Wallace was from Indianapolis and *IndyNow* was the biggest, most respected paper in the city, probably the best across the state. And while she'd fantasized about taking her story and her résumé to somewhere like the *Times,* she realized that she wanted to stay in Wakarusa with her uncle, wanted to work at a paper that served her community. Plus, recent events excluded, she liked working with Adrienne. She was a good editor. She made Margot better.

"I'd be thrilled to have you back," Adrienne said.

"And I want a raise." Margot told her the amount she'd come up with, one that would help cover her uncle's bills as well as her own.

"I think we can arrange that."

"And I want to work from here, from Wakarusa, and have more time and more autonomy over my stories. I'd like to cover Wallace's arrest and trial. Take my time, do it well."

"Working remotely won't be a problem. And I'll talk to Edgar about the other one, but I think he'll go for it. You've proven what you can do when you have the time to do it."

"Okay. Well . . . good." Margot closed her eyes, her heartbeat steadying. Though she'd come out swinging, she'd been terrified to ask for what she wanted. "Let me know what Edgar says. And in the meantime, I'm going to try to get a few more quotes for tomorrow's piece."

Margot had included quotes from her interviews with Anna-belle and Elliott Wallace, but she wanted to reach out to Townsend, Jace, and Billy too, to give them an opportunity to address the latest developments.

"That sounds great," Adrienne said. "And I'll send over some notes too. That is," she added a bit awkwardly, "if you'd like. It's in really good shape as is, but we have the time and we want this one to go viral."

Margot smiled. "I'd love your notes."

After they hung up, Margot tugged on a pair of sweatpants and padded out of her room. From the hallway, she spotted Luke in his regular morning spot at the kitchen table, nursing a cup of coffee, a crossword puzzle in front of him. The sight of him made her stop short, her throat unexpectedly tightening. After days of feeling estranged from him, Margot finally had her uncle back. And although he'd told lies and kept secrets like everyone else in this town, she now understood why he had. He may not have been perfect, but he was good.

That she'd ever doubted it, that she actually at one point sus-pected him of *murder,* made Margot seethe with guilt. Of course her uncle hadn't killed anyone. January had been Elliott Wallace's first victim, and although Jodie might not believe it, Krissy had taken her own life, just as everyone had always thought. Margot, for one, didn't find this sad fact all that surprising. Krissy had lost a daughter, then a husband and a son. Even though they hadn't all been killed, Elliott Wallace had robbed Krissy of her entire family, and the pain of that had grown too much to bear.

As Margot looked at Luke, a million questions ricocheted through her mind. She wanted to ask him when he realized he was the father of Jace and January, wanted to ask him what it had been like watching them grow from afar. She had so many things she wanted to tell him too, about Elliott Wallace and what had happened to January. And perhaps they'd talk about all this one day, but for now, she just wanted to sit across from him and drink a cup of coffee.

"Morning, kid," Luke said when she walked into the kitchen.

"Morning."

"You slept late. You feeling okay?"

She smiled. "Yeah, just had a thing for work."

"How'd it go?"

"Good. Really good." She walked over to the coffee maker. "Hey, Uncle Luke, do you wanna do something tonight? Just, like, hang out or something?"

He smiled. "That'd be great."

"Okay. Cool." She poured herself a coffee and took a sip.

"Hey, kid?"

Margot looked up.

"I'm really glad you're here."

Her throat tightened. "Yeah. Me too."

Margot spent the rest of the day editing and getting more quotes. She knew that by the time the papers came out tomorrow morning, everyone across Indiana would have some sort of blurb on Wallace's arrest. But no one would have anything near as extensive as she did, and by the time her piece was finished, she felt prouder of it than she had of anything she'd ever written before. She sent off the final to Adrienne around six that evening, then she printed off a copy, stuck it into her back pocket, and with a quick goodbye to Luke, promising she'd be home soon with a pizza in hand, she slipped out into the waning light of the day.

Five minutes later, Margot had walked to the Jacobs place and was knocking on Billy's door.

For Margot, finding Elliott Wallace had given her a sense of closure about January's case, a sense of peace. But for Billy, she knew, the news of Wallace was vastly more complicated. While it gave him the answers he'd no doubt long been seeking, it also inflicted the fresh pain of knowing his only daughter had been stalked in her own town and snatched from her own home by a very depraved man. When Margot told him the news on the phone earlier, Billy had broken down, and she wanted to give him the gift of reading the details early and in private.

After a moment, she heard footsteps approach, then the front door creaked open. In the sliver between the door and its frame, Margot saw Billy's blue eyes peering out. When he registered her face, he opened the door wide, smiling broadly.

"Margot."

She smiled back. "Hi, Billy. Sorry to bother you. I just walked over because I wanted to give you this." She grabbed the printed copy of her article from her pocket and held it out. "It's the story running in tomorrow's paper."

"Oh." His face wobbled and he pressed his lips together tightly as he accepted the pages.

"Thank you for speaking with me the other day," Margot said, giving him a moment to collect himself. "And for your quote."

She wasn't going to point out that he'd whitewashed the truth about his family during that first interview, because he'd been try-ing to protect Krissy, who'd been trying to protect Jace. And al-though the two of them may have unwittingly damaged an investigation that could have led the police to Wallace all those years ago, Margot understood all too well the instinct to protect your family.

Billy looked up from the pages, his eyes blinking furiously. "No." He shook his head. "Thank you. For everything."

She nodded. The moment felt both monumental and like nothing at all.

"Would you, um"—he cleared his throat—"would you like a

cup of coffee? I know it's almost dinnertime, but . . ." He shrugged, looking a bit awkward.

"Coffee would be great."

Margot stepped over the threshold into the old familiar house, following Billy through the hallway of family photos. As a reporter, she'd always believed that understanding the truth was one of the most important things in the world, but as her eyes flicked over the images of his children, whom he'd not fathered, and his wife, who'd loved another, Margot wondered if sometimes believing a lie was better. There was no point in Billy learning the truth about his family. It would only tear him apart.

They walked into the kitchen, where he already had a pot of coffee on. He pulled an old ceramic mug from a shelf and filled it with coffee then topped off his own. "Milk or sugar?"

"Milk, please."

They settled at the kitchen table together, and Margot couldn't help her gaze drifting to the white walls where those terrible words had been written all those years ago. It was ironic, knowing they'd been written out of love rather than hate.

Across from her, Billy cleared his throat. "I can't believe you figured it out. After all this time. You were just the little girl from across the street. I was here and I couldn't even see." His face flared with sudden emotion. "I should've seen."

Margot studied him. Although she'd slept a total of four hours over the past thirty-six, Billy looked more exhausted than she felt. "You know . . ." she said, keeping her voice gentle. "Wallace kept his distance when he was stalking those girls. Especially with January. It was his first time to do it and he was cautious."

The plastic box with January's name had been the sparsest of them all. Wallace had saved a few of her dance programs—the parallel to Luke had sent a chill up Margot's spine—but other than that, he'd collected nothing that had belonged to her. And the stack of photos in her container had been thin. While he'd probably had two dozen of Natalie Clark, he'd only had five of January, all of which had been taken from afar. Although he'd made enough contact with January that she told Jace his name, it was clear to Margot that, when he was stalking her, he hadn't yet worked out how to be the predator he'd evolved into. It was why January's murder was unlike those of the other seven.

Margot had gone over it a hundred times, piecing together what must have happened that night, and what she'd come up with was that Wallace had walked through the unlocked door, planning to simply walk back out with January in tow. But something had gone wrong along the way. Perhaps, as Krissy had always purported, January had fought back or cried out, and Wallace had panicked. He'd either bashed her head in, most likely with a weapon he'd brought with him, then left her body at the bottom of the basement stairs, or they'd scuffled in the kitchen and he'd thrown her down there, where she'd cracked her head on the concrete floor.

It was why January was his only victim not to have sustained sexual abuse before her death. And that made Wallace change his MO. After January, he started taking girls from playgrounds and parking lots, where it was easier to abandon the plan if it didn't work.

"I think," Margot said, "especially in January's case, it would've been hard to notice anything was wrong until it was." She may have been overinflating this—after all, Wallace had made contact with January, probably multiple times—but she felt sorry for the man sitting across from her. He'd had everything taken away from him and she wanted to give some of it back, to erase some of the guilt he'd lived with for the past twenty-five years.

"Do you have kids, Margot?" he asked.

She shook her head.

"Well. When you do, you'll understand. Your job as their parent is to protect them and . . . I failed. I failed." A broken sob hiccupped out of him. He made a fist with one hand, clasping the other around it, and pressed them both to his lips, as if to push the emotion back in.

"I can't imagine how hard this must be. I'm sorry to dredge it all up again."

Billy shook his head. "I don't have much left in the world, but you gave me answers and you brought this asshole to justice *and* you cleared Krissy's name. I'm very grateful."

Margot's throat tightened. She was gratified to have caught Wallace and solved the mystery of January's death, but there was still so much she wanted to know about everything else. She wanted to ask Billy if he'd ever looked at his twins and seen the face of another man. She wanted to ask if he'd ever felt his love for Krissy go unreciprocated, either during that summer when she'd been sleeping with Luke, or years later when she'd gotten to-gether with Jodie. But of course, she couldn't ask any of this. So, instead, she said, "And *I'm* grateful for this coffee. I haven't slept in days."

Billy chuckled.

"Anyway, I should probably get going. I'm picking up dinner for me and my uncle." She paused. "You could stop by sometime if you'd like. I know the two of you were friends a long time ago." It seemed a shame to waste that friendship, especially now when Billy had no one else in the world and Luke was fading from it.

But when she said it, something dark flashed in Billy's eyes. "Maybe," he said with a tight smile. "Anyway, thanks for coming by, Margot." She searched his face, but any sign of that darkness had vanished, leaving Margot to wonder if she'd even really seen it in the first place.

They retraced their steps through the house, the old floorboards creaking beneath their feet, and as they passed through the hall-way of photos, a candid of January caught Margot's eye. In it, January looked five or six, perhaps only months from her death.

She was perched on the tire swing Margot recognized from the Jacobs backyard, her eyes squinched with laughter, her little mouth wide. But what caught Margot's attention was something in her hand: squeezed between her fingers and the rope was a scrap of fabric—light blue with white snowflakes.

Margot's mind flashed to that memory from so long ago, when she'd been scared and crouched against a tree. January had sidled up to her and pressed a snowflake into her hand, the edges of the light-blue fabric jagged as if it had been ripped. *When I'm scared,* January had said, *I squeeze this and it makes me brave.* As Margot looked at the photo, she balled her hand into a fist, her fingertips grazing the half-moon scars on her palm.

Billy, who'd reached the front door, turned to face her.

"What is this?" she asked, pointing to the photo.

He squinted. "Oh, the thing in her hand? That's her baby blanket. Or, what was left of it. I used to give it to her whenever she got scared and told her if she squeezed it, it would make her brave. I think I told her it had some magic that made it powerful." He chuckled, his gaze softening with the memory. "It was our thing, just between the two of us."

Margot smiled, but something, some memory, was pushing at the edge of her mind. And then Jace's words hit her: *I remember how peaceful she looked,* he'd said of January, dead, at the bottom of the basement stairs. *Like she was just sleeping. And there was a little scrap of her baby blanket in her hand.*

"Just like the night she died," Margot said, the words slipping thoughtlessly from her mouth.

The moment they did, she realized her mistake.

January had died from blunt force trauma to the head; it would've been impossible for her to have held on to her baby blanket through whatever had killed her—which meant that someone had put it into her hand after she died, before Jace and Krissy had found her.

Margot froze, her heart pounding.

A suspicion bloomed inside her, coalescing into something hard and solid. Her mind raced as all the pieces of January's murder began clicking into place. She was the only little girl who hadn't been sexually abused. She was the only one who'd been killed in her own home. Margot had assumed all of this meant that Elliott Wallace had simply evolved as a murderer, but what if January had been one of the girls he'd stalked but never killed? Someone had tucked her baby blanket into her hand after she'd died, before Jace had found her—that wasn't some perverted act of a pedophile, but an act of love.

Margot thought about that dark look that had just passed over Billy's face at her mention of Luke. It had been so fleeting she thought perhaps she'd fabricated it, but she hadn't. That look, she realized now, had been one of hatred. Billy loathed her uncle. And Margot had a good guess why—he knew about Luke's affair with Krissy, knew Luke was the father of the twins.

Had she been wrong about everything? Had she, as so many people had accused her, been so convinced January's case was connected to Natalie's and Polly's that she'd overlooked the stark differences between them?

Could it have been Billy, not Elliott Wallace, who'd killed January all those years ago? But—*why*?

Though the why didn't matter right now. She'd just revealed she knew something she wasn't supposed to. Had Billy heard? Did he understand?

Her brain raced with thoughts of self-preservation. *Put on an act. Don't let him see what you suspect. Get out.* She forced a smile onto her face as she turned from the photo to Billy, who was standing by the open doorway, hand on the knob.

"Cute," Margot said, taking a step forward.

But Billy was looking at her with a strange look on his face. "What'd you just say?"

Margot took another step toward the open door, only a couple of feet away. She'd walk calmly through it, and once she got out of his sight, she'd run straight to the police station. "Oh, I just said she looks cute." Margot smiled, but her voice was tight. "Thanks again for the coffee."

But just before she reached the door, Billy closed it and sighed. "That's not what you said."

Margot mustered a confused little laugh. "Uh. I'm sorry, but I really should get going."

He shook his head, not quite meeting her eye. His face had fallen. Margot stared at his enormous shoulders, his thick forearms—muscles hardened from decades of work on a farm. She willed him to just open the door. "I think you know what you said. And I . . ." He hesitated, running one hand through his hair, the other still firm on the doorknob. "And I think you know what it means. I can see that you do."

Margot shook her head. "I'm sorry. I don't know what you're talking about."

"I loved her, you know." His face crumpled. "It was an accident."

Everything in Margot sank. The door was closed and he had confessed. He wasn't going to let her walk away now.

As if to confirm it, he said, "I'm sorry. But I can't let you leave." Then he twisted the dead bolt into place.

Panic coursed through Margot's body. She stood, shaking, mind racing. She needed to get out of there. But how? Billy was blocking the front door. She could make a run for the door in the kitchen, but he was too close for her to do that now. If she tried, he'd outrun her, overpower her. She took the smallest step backward. She needed time to increase the distance between them, then she'd run.

"Really," she said, her voice weak. "I don't know what you're talking about."

"You can stop acting. It's obvious from the way you're looking at me that you know. It's the same look Krissy had when she found out."

Margot froze. Despite her almost blinding fear, she felt momentarily sidetracked. Krissy had found Billy out too? Krissy, who'd been shot in the head with one of Billy's guns. Krissy, who'd been found by Billy, not somewhere private but in their entryway. *I know Krissy,* Jodie had said, *and she didn't kill herself.* "Did you"—Margot swallowed—"did you kill her too?"

"I had to," Billy said. "She found out what I'd done and I could tell she wasn't gonna let it go. She was gonna tell Jace—I saw a letter in her purse saying so."

Margot was inching backward when what he'd said snagged in her mind. A letter? In none of the letters Jace received from Krissy had she implicated Billy. And the last thing she'd ever written to her son was— "Her suicide note. But that was just an apology to Jace. It didn't say anything about you."

"The top part was an apology. But there was more. She told him she'd found something out about me."

Margot's eyes darted around the hallway as she worked out what must have happened. On the day she died, when Krissy met up with Luke to tell him he was the twins' father, Luke must have told her something about January's death. What it was, Margot couldn't imagine, but it had clearly led Krissy to the truth about her husband. She'd written it in a letter to Jace, and when Billy discovered it, he'd torn off the incriminating bottom half and left the top to look like a suicide note.

"I obviously couldn't have her telling anyone what I'd done," Billy said. "And I—"

But Margot had heard enough. She didn't know what exactly he had done to January, but he'd shot his own wife for knowing less. Margot needed to get out of there. Heart pounding hard in her chest, she took one more step backward, then spun around and ran. As she did, Billy lunged after her, his footsteps fast and heavy. Margot rushed into the kitchen toward the back door, but when she wrapped her hand around the doorknob, it rattled futilely.

"No," she breathed as she fumbled with the lock, the sound of Billy's footsteps fast behind her. Her body felt electric with the need to flee, but the lock didn't seem to be working properly. Then, finally, she managed to twist it and fling the door open. But just as she did, an enormous hand reached over her head and slammed it shut.

Billy crashed his body into hers and Margot flew sideways, clattering hard against the kitchen floor. Her shoulder and head lit up with pain. She tried to clamber to her feet, but Billy got to her too fast. He reached out, grabbing her by her hair. Tears sprung to her eyes.

Then he was dragging her and she was kicking, punching, slapping his arms, but his grip was too strong and too soon he stopped in front of a closed door. Billy swung it open and the house's basement gaped before them like a wide, screaming mouth. And suddenly, although most of her mind was on struggling and clawing and shouting, some dark part of her brain flashed to January all those years ago—dead at the bottom of these very stairs, killed by this very man.

Margot thought of Krissy, of Natalie, of Polly, of all the girls in Elliott Wallace's box and all the girls across the world who'd been trapped alone in rooms with men just like him and others just like Billy, men who, in one way or another, threw girls away. To so many, those girls were nameless and faceless, numbers on a sad and growing list. There was nothing she wouldn't do, Margot thought, as Billy dragged her closer to the basement doorway, to keep him from turning her into one—just another forgotten girl added to another list.

EPILOGUE

Billy, 1994

It had all started with a phone call.

Or perhaps, it had all started years earlier, back in the summer of '87 when he'd first started hanging out with Krissy Winter and Luke Davies, but when Billy looked back over the course of his life, it was the phone call he would undo.

The line rang twice before Dave picked up. "Jacobs?" he said after Billy told him who it was. "What's up? Everything okay?"

Billy pulled the receiver from his ear to give it a baffled look. Normally, whenever Dave heard it was Billy on the line, he'd make up some excuse and hang up. But something was different about Dave's voice tonight. It sounded thick, wet.

"Everything's fine. Just watching TV." Billy hesitated. After so long without talking to his friend, he felt rusty doing it. "I started thinking about that night, the one on the football field, with the weed killer." He laughed. "Remember that?"

"How could I forget? God, we were such idiots back then."

"Yeah," Billy agreed, although that wasn't actually how he felt. He loved Krissy and the kids—of course he did—but marriage and fatherhood weren't exactly how he'd imagined them. For him, that summer was the best time of his life. "Well, anyway, just thought I'd give you a call. It's been awhile."

"Yeah."

Billy's gaze roamed around the kitchen where he stood next to the landline. Maybe it had been a mistake reaching out to Dave, maybe he should just hang up now before it got any more awkward. But just before he could, Dave said, "Hey, you wanna go for a drive? Like old times? I got a six-pack I could use a hand with."

Again, Billy gave the receiver a look of disbelief. Not only was this an unusual invitation—he and Dave hadn't hung out in years—it was already almost midnight. But he didn't care. Krissy and the kids had long since gone to bed, and he deserved to have a little fun. A smile spread slowly over his face. "That sounds great."

Ten minutes later, he and Dave were driving outside town past cornfields that sprawled for miles. The streetlamps were few and far between, and the only other light was that from the thin sliver of moon. Dave was unusually quiet. Whenever Billy tried for conversation—"Remember our teacher Mr. Yacoubian? God, I hated him." Or, "Remember that party in the cornfield when Robby O'Neil got into a fight with Caleb Shroyer?"—Dave would just nod vaguely in response.

But then as he turned onto a dirt road that separated a cornfield from a patch of woods, Dave said, "How're the kids doing?"

Billy took a sip of his beer. "Yeah, they're good." But Dave had shifted the car into park and was angling his body to him, clearly waiting for him to go on. "Uh," Billy continued. "January's dancing is going good. She's always running around the house doing moves."

Dave smiled, but his eyes were far off and sad. "I hear about her sometimes from Margot. They seem to be getting close."

"Who?"

"My niece. Margot." He paused. "She lives across the street from you, dude."

"Right, right." Adam Davies from across the street was so different from his old friend, sometimes Billy forgot they were actually related, but he knew Dave's niece. She and January were always running around the farm together. "I need another beer," he said, bending down to pull a can from the ring. "You want one?"

"Sure. Why not." But there was a slight edge in his voice. Dave accepted the beer from Billy and cracked it open. "What about Jace?"

"Huh?"

"How's Jace doing?" He articulated Billy's son's name clearly as if Billy might not recognize it.

"Uh, yeah, he's fine. Both the kids are fine." He took a long sip of beer, staring out his side window at the cornfield beyond. In the night, the crop looked black. He didn't want to talk about his son, whom he didn't understand. He didn't even want to talk about January. He just wanted to drink and joke with his friend like old times. "But what about you, huh? You up to anything fun these days?"

For a moment, Dave stayed silent. Then Billy heard a choked sound from the driver's seat and he snapped his head around to look, eyes widening. Dave, whom Billy had never once seen cry, was pressing a fist against his mouth, eyes closed tight. His chest was heaving, little sobs hiccuping from his throat.

"Whoa, dude," Billy said. "You okay?"

But Dave couldn't speak. He kept his eyes squeezed shut, his fist pressed to his mouth. Then, finally, his breathing slowed and he opened his eyes, which were thankfully still dry. Looking straight ahead, he said, "Rebecca had a miscarriage."

Billy swallowed. He had no idea what to say to that. The word *miscarriage* sent a shiver of discomfort through his body. He couldn't believe Dave had just revealed something so private. "Wow, man. I, uh, I'm sorry."

"It happened, like, a few hours ago. She wasn't far along, but . . ." He shook his head. "It was bad."

Billy frowned as Dave's words slowly sunk in. Rebecca's miscarriage had happened that night? Billy had assumed a few days had passed at least, but now it all made sense. That was why Dave had talked to Billy over the phone. That was why he'd suggested a drive—not because he wanted to see Billy, but because he needed a fucking shoulder to cry on. And yet, for the past six years, every time Billy had needed a friend, Dave hadn't been there. It would've been nice to go for a drive that one night after he and Krissy had taken January to the hospital with a fever of 103. It would've been nice to grab a beer with his friend after Jace had thrown a fit because he didn't want to ride in the tractor with him. But through it all, Dave was nowhere to be found. Billy felt all the sympathy he'd had harden in his chest.

He took a sip of beer. "Wow. That sucks."

Beside him, Dave froze. Slowly, he lifted his head. "*That sucks? My wife has a miscarriage and you say that sucks?*"

Billy felt indignation spread through him like a flame. He was the one with the right to be mad, not Dave. "Kids are hard, man. Maybe it's a blessing in disguise—give you guys some time to get ready."

Dave sat motionless, his eyes fixed on Billy's. Then, to Billy's surprise, he threw his head back and laughed. But it wasn't the same laugh he'd had in high school, full of mirth and mischievousness. This one was hard, bitter. "Wow. You are unbelievable, Jacobs. I knew you could be an idiot sometimes, but I didn't know you were such an asshole." He shook his head. "*A blessing in disguise?* You're the luckiest guy in the entire fucking world and you don't even *care*."

"Right," Billy snapped. He had a job where the work never

stopped. He had a wife who was restless and discontent, and a son who seemed to hate him. January was his only real bright spot, but he could already see glimpses of the teenager she'd become. In a few years, she'd stop running to him when he walked through the door. "I'm the luckiest guy in the whole wide world."

"God," Dave scoffed. "You have no fucking idea, do you?"

Billy stilled. "What're you talking about?"

Dave gazed at him for a moment, then shook his head. "Forget it."

"No. What'd you mean?"

"I said forget it."

But a dark, nebulous suspicion was blooming at the back of Billy's mind. "No." His voice was hard. "Tell me what you fucking meant."

"It's nothing, Billy." Dave turned to the steering wheel and twisted his key in the ignition. "Let's just call it a night."

"Dave, if you know something about my family, I have a right to fucking know. Okay?"

Dave heaved a sigh. "Maybe you're right. Maybe it's time." He closed his eyes for a long moment. When he opened them again, he turned to Billy. "Did you ever notice how Krissy pushed me away after the twins were born? Did you ever stop to think about why?" He looked to Billy for a reaction, but Billy stayed quiet. "The twins," Dave said. "Have you ever noticed how the twins look like me?"

Five minutes later, Billy wordlessly got out of Dave's car and slammed the door behind him. He didn't move as the sound of tires on gravel faded then disappeared. He stood in front of his home, staring up at the dark window of the bedroom where, for seven years, he'd slept next to Krissy—his lying, cheating wife. Rage radiated through his body.

He thought back to that night so long ago now, when he'd gotten down on one knee and held out his grandmother's ring. He'd been so full of hope then, a soon-to-be father and the future husband of Krissy fucking Winter. But now he understood that her acceptance of his proposal was a lie. He'd thought she loved him, but in reality, she'd been sleeping with his best friend. He'd thought she loved him, but she'd only ever used him.

.Billy walked slowly up the porch steps and through the front door, his hands flexing by his sides. Inside, he gazed around at the dark and quiet house, at the hallway lined with family photos, all of which were lies. Their entire home was a lie, their entire life. All because of her—that bitch, slut, whore.

Billy made his way into the kitchen, then froze. He'd heard something. Footsteps, soft and distant. He looked around, his gaze snagging on the basement door. It was open, swung out into the kitchen, which was odd. They never kept the basement door open. Then he heard it again: footsteps coming from deep within the house followed by the high-pitched creak of the dryer door. A fresh wave of fury erupted through him. Krissy. Apparently, his whore wife wasn't asleep after all, and a sudden fantasy began to swirl in Billy's mind.

What if Krissy took a tumble down the basement stairs? What if she cracked her head open against the cold concrete floor? What if she bled out down there, moaning in pain, but with no one to hear her because he and the kids were sound asleep two flights up? She was probably so doped up on her sleeping pills and wine that no one would second-guess her misplacing a step in the dark.

He closed his eyes, basking in the fantasy. All he'd have to do was slide up against the kitchen wall, hide behind the open basement door, wait for her to walk up the stairs, and then slam the door into her face. And Billy would be able to listen to her body cartwheel down the steps, would be able to crouch over her as she died and watch the look in her eyes as she realized what he'd done and why. *You shouldn't have lied to me,* he'd say. *You shouldn't have used me. You shouldn't have been such a whore.*

In the dark of the kitchen, Billy shook the image from his mind. He couldn't do that. It was absurd. And really, did he actually want Krissy to die? Or did he just want to teach her a lesson, to scare her? Once she was good and afraid, he thought, she'd never cheat on him again. Maybe she'd even stop bitching about their life. Maybe she'd actually be grateful to him—for their life, their house, their money she used to buy all her clothes and pills and wine. Maybe she'd actually put a little effort into cooking dinner, or wear some makeup, or kiss him on the lips when he came home at night.

Billy heard another creak of the dryer door, and then, without quite telling his legs to do it, he was walking quietly across the floor and slipping into the space between the wall and the open basement door. He listened as his wife's footsteps began to ascend the stairs. And then, she was there, at the top, stepping onto the landing.

Billy held an image of Krissy in his mind—she was sorry, she was begging forgiveness, she was promising to be a better wife—and he wrapped his fingers around the doorknob and swung it hard. There was a loud *thunk,* like a hammer against wood, as the door collided with her. He heard her tumble down the stairs, landing with a *crack* at the bottom. The silence afterward was deafening.

Billy stood in the darkness, his hand still on the doorknob, paralyzed. He couldn't believe he'd done it. Panic began to bubble in his stomach. He opened the door and stepped gingerly around it. But something was wrong. The body at the bottom of the stairs was too small. He blinked down at it, his brain working in slow motion. Krissy didn't wear that nightgown. Her hair wasn't that light. When he finally understood, he contracted. His stomach lurched. It was January. It was his baby girl.

"No."

Panic blurred his vision as he made his way down the stairs to her. He tried to move fast but he felt as if he were underwater, the air around him viscous. January's body looked all wrong—her limbs bent at sharp angles, her face slack. He reached out a hand and softly touched her cheek.

"January?" His voice was tentative.

She didn't move.

"January?"

Still nothing.

"No," he breathed, clapping a hand over his mouth. Bile rose in his throat. "No, no, no."

Shaking, he reached down and scooped her body into his arms, cradling her like a baby. "January, wake up. I'm sorry. Daddy made a mistake. I'm sorry."

But her body remained limp, her face expressionless. If it weren't for the extreme angle of her neck, she could have been sleeping. "January." Now his voice was a harsh command. "Wake up!" His arms tightened around her, shaking her body, trying to get her to open her eyes.

And then, he saw it—the flutter of her eyelids. His heart soared in his chest. He let out a sob. She was alive. She was alive, she was alive, she was alive. In his arms, his daughter let out a little moan, turning her head slightly in his arms.

"Good girl," Billy said, his voice trembling. "Good girl."

He shot a look up the basement stairs. He needed to get to the phone in the kitchen to call an ambulance, but he didn't know if he should move her body. Would that make it worse? He looked into January's face. By now, she'd blinked her eyes open and was gazing up at him, looking confused. "D–Daddy?"

"Shh, baby. Don't talk. I'm gonna leave you here for one second, okay? You're gonna be okay. I'm gonna get you help." Moving more carefully than he ever had, Billy placed her body down, straightening out her arms and legs.

He stood to leave, but then, just as he was turning to race up the stairs, January's little voice said, "You hurt me, Daddy."

Billy froze. An iciness flowed from his head through his body. She knew. She knew what he'd done. He stood, unmoving, for a long time, and then, finally, he turned and knelt down.

"No, no, January. I didn't," he said slowly. "Don't say that."

January started to whimper, looking scared. "You did."

"I *didn't*. So don't say that."

Her eyes widened in fear. "Where's Mommy?"

"Shh," Billy hissed. "Be quiet."

But she was crying now, her voice getting louder. "I want Mommy!"

Billy grabbed the sides of January's face, his fingers white. "Shut up."

She began to scream, "Mom——" but Billy clapped a hand over her mouth.

As he did, her head turned ever so slightly, and in his daughter's face, Billy suddenly saw the shape of Krissy's eyes, the angle of Dave's chin, and Billy remembered that January wasn't his daughter after all—not really. And then, his mind was a blank. He heard himself saying, as if from a great distance, "Shut up, shut up, shut up." He watched, detached, as his hands tightened around January's head, his thumbs closing her eyes and pressing them shut so she couldn't see him anymore, so he couldn't see Krissy. And then he looked away as he lifted her head and slammed it against the floor. It only took once for her to stop moving.

Billy crouched, motionless, over her body, his breath coming in ragged gulps. From somewhere very far away, from underwater or through layers of glass, he heard someone crying, and then, vaguely, he registered tears on his cheeks, growing sticky on his jaw.

"Oh God."

What had he done? He gazed down at January and his stomach twisted. What had he done to his darling girl? Then, ever so slowly, he stood as a new question formed in his mind: What was he supposed to do now?

He gazed around at the blackness of the underground room, feeling as if he were standing in the mouth of a monster. He did not want to leave January down there in its jaws, but it was beginning to dawn on him that he had no choice. He couldn't call an ambulance now. He couldn't call the police. It was too suspicious— him finding January in the middle of the night, moments after she'd died. He needed to put distance between her body and himself. He needed January's death to look like an accident. When he and Krissy woke the next morning and found January dead at the bottom of these stairs, the only logical assumption would be that she had sleepwalked and fallen to her death. It would be horrible and believable.

He didn't look at her as he turned to the stairs. He took one step, then another, and that was when he saw it: the little scrap of baby blanket on the basement stairs. So that was why January had been down there that night. She never slept without her baby blanket, but Krissy had put it in the wash earlier. He remembered because January had made a big deal about it at dinner. She must've woken in the middle of the night and gone to get it.

Quietly, Billy stepped up the stairs to retrieve it, then returned to January's side. He couldn't just leave her like that, cold and alone. He'd given the blanket to her the day she was born. He always told her it would make her brave if she just squeezed it tight enough. It was their thing together—their little secret. He leaned over to tuck the scrap of snowflake-patterned fabric into one limp hand. He knew it was stupid and worthless, knew she wouldn't need it wherever she was now. But—who knew?—maybe, just maybe, it could bring her some peace.

Billy turned from January to climb the stairs, his mind already spinning with what the next day would bring, preparing himself for the performance of a lifetime.

Acknowledgments

oremost, thank you Alex Kiester and Jenny Chen, who helped me write and edit this novel. They spent many long hours dedicated to bringing my vision to life, and without them this book would not have been a reality. And a special thanks to my literary agent, Meredith Miller from UTA, who helped make my dream of becoming an author a reality.

We also could not have made this book feel so authentic without those who contributed their expertise on subject matter: My best friend, Brit Prawat, who grew up in Wakarusa and helped me make the town feel real. My colleague Delia D'Ambra, who helped shape Margot's role as a journalist. My friend Steve Dubois, who gave his expertise as a law enforcement veteran, and Brooke Henion, who has worked as an advocate and counselor for human trafficking victims.

I'd also like to thank my husband, Erik Hudak, who has supported and encouraged me through every step of this process. There were times when the days were long as I worked to complete this book while running my company and hosting multiple shows (all while pregnant), but he was my rock and made it possible for me to follow my dreams.

And finally, I'd like to thank my parents. My mother, Lisa, is the one who fostered a love for mysteries from a young age, and my father, David, is the one who taught me how to tell a good story.

ABOUT THE AUTHOR

ASHLEY FLOWERS is the founder and chief executive officer of audiochuck, the award-winning independent media and podcast production company known for its standout content and storytelling across different genres, such as true crime, fiction, and comedy, among others. She also hosts and produces several audiochuck shows, including the top-rated podcast *Crime Junkie*. In addition to her work with audiochuck, Flowers has collaborated with Parcast to launch and host several podcasts, including *International Infamy, Very Presidential,* and *Supernatural with Ashley Flowers,* which debuted at number one on the podcast charts. Flowers was born and raised in Indiana, where she continues to live with her husband, daughter, and their beloved dog, Chuck.

ashleyflowers.com
Instagram: @ashleyflowers
Twitter: @Ash_Flowers